HIDDEN PICTURES

HIDDEN PICTURES

A NOVEL

JOHANNA FLYNN

Palatine Press

Cover designed by Amy St. Onge

Johanna Flynn

Visit my website at www.JohannaFlynn.com

Printed in the United States of America

First Printing: August 2019

Palatine Press

ISBN-978-1-949844-04-7

For Frank Brink, Seamus, Connor and especially, Jim

PROLOGUE
1987

Watching his employees go had been an act of surrender. His new rival had snapped them up, and he knew he could not run the family business alone. He stood before the entrance to his store, Carlson's Hardware, and thought how insignificant all those times had seemed, when he or his father or grandfather had paused in that spot in the bright morning sun. How insignificant inserting the brass key and turning his wrist had been, feeling the deadbolt slide, shoving the door open and stepping inside.

He knew of only two momentous occasions. The first was the day in 1892 when his grandfather had inserted the key for the first time. Old photos and newspaper articles in the museum depicted him in a morning coat and top hat before a crowd of Forester residents, a fledgling community that was just minutes by train to Chicago.

This was the second momentous occasion.

He wondered what kind of boss he had been. A fair one, he hoped. He wondered what kind of boss they reported to now. He'd soon find out. As some kind of cosmic booby prize, Superior Hardware had hired him as well, his role to convert Forester do-it-yourselfers to their loyal customers. He was thankful the cosmos had at least spared his wife and mother from witnessing this.

Dressed in stained overalls, Gordon walked to the heart of the store, the fluorescent lights dim in the unheated space. Discarded placards bellowed "Going Out of Business" and "Everything Must Go."

He skimmed his palm across the dusty surface of an empty display case. Above him, a rusted hairline fracture snaked across the painted tin ceiling, the result of a broken pipe he'd fixed a few years back.

Gordon turned his back on the bare interior, made his way outside, and shut the door. He twisted his wrist to lock the store and removed the key. Carlson's Hardware was officially closed.

The limestone building now belonged to the bank. In a few minutes, he would hand the keys to the property manager. The substantial key ring that held them had worn a number of holes in his pockets over the years and, most assuredly, those of his father and grandfather.

His house key had occupied a place on that ring for so long, removing it was tough. Gordon knew that when he returned home, inserting the lone key in the lock and twisting his wrist would not be insignificant.

CHAPTER 1
BREAKFAST, 1996

Olivia Dimato, get in the car this minute." Patricia Wrenowski's voice ricocheted off the houses lining the street.

The girl ignored the vehicle and kept walking, focused on her pink and gray Moon Boots, focused on getting to the school bus stop. Recalling the day before—her former friend, Brian, doubled over, his face contorted in pain—she attempted to increase the distance between herself and the van, the path slippery in the late winter slush.

The outraged driver yelled, "Olivia!"

She looked for refuge at the house on her right. Lace curtains in the windows hung motionless, dark. Nobody home, so she set her sights on another, her boots lifting and falling, lifting and falling. Olivia didn't dare check where Patricia was, but she could hear the slursh of chemically induced road muck.

"Stop right there," Patricia's voice barked.

Now desperate, she reached the driveway at the side of Gordon Carlson's house. She barely knew him, but her parents said he was an eccentric, sweet old man.

"Olivia!" Patricia shouted. "I told you to get in the car, and I mean it."

She made a choice, turned her back to the van, raced along the front walk, shot up Gordon's steps, and fell onto the veranda, the wood hard against her belly.

"Do you hear me, Olivia? Come here! I want to talk to you!" Patricia pulled into Gordon's driveway.

The girl scrambled across the porch. Ringing the bell and pounding the door with her mittened hand, she prayed for Gordon to please be awake and answer.

Olivia whipped around and saw Brian's profile in the front passenger seat. Her clenched mitten raised to pound again, she swiveled back, her fist connecting with the soft pile of a frayed bathrobe.

"You won't get away with this. Your mother will hear from me, so don't think this is the end of it!" Patricia gunned the engine in reverse, backed out of the driveway, knocked over a garbage can, and sped away.

"I'm sorry," Olivia stuttered. A tall man with stubble on his chin filled the doorway. She took in his quizzical stare. "I didn't know what else to do. She was chasing me."

"All right, then come in. I was about to make some breakfast." His tone was hesitant, edged with irritation.

"Oh. Well. Okay, sure." She would now miss the bus, but she was more afraid of that lunatic woman and her bullying son. She stepped into the foyer, dripping gritty slush onto a worn area rug, while Gordon shambled toward the kitchen.

Around her the piles of boots and shoes huddled by the coat tree, smothered by a mound of jackets, hats, and scarves. To her right, piles of paper, books, and magazines staggered up the stairs. Olivia wrinkled her nose, removed her backpack, coat and boots, making her own pile, her neon hat and scarf on top like a dollop of raspberry sherbet.

She followed the sound of kitchen cupboards being opened and shut, passed closed pocket doors, and stopped in the kitchen's entrance, the faint odor of cabbage and garlic still circling from the previous evening. Like all the Victorian houses in Forester, the kitchen was small by modern standards, similar to hers, except for missing the rich cherry cabinets and granite countertops.

Along the wall, a brown stove kept company with a matching fridge, minus the door handle. The cupboards had been painted many times, but not recently, spatters of caramelized grease filling the cracked surfaces like some old masterpiece in the Art Institute. This was a house no one ever visited.

Gordon pried the fridge door open with the tips of his fingers. "You live across from Patricia, right?" He pulled out a quart of milk, set it on the counter, and fished out an egg carton. "That her son in the car?"

Olivia nodded.

"Hell of a way to start the day, being chased by a banshee. What got her hair in a frazzle?" He used the finger-prying technique to open a drawer and select a fork.

"Not sure." She watched him work, curious about this man no one ever saw.

"Must've been something. She runs this block with a whip," he said, breaking eggs into a bowl.

"Yeah. Guess so." Her lungs burned from running.

Gordon seemed more interested in the eggs than her. He added milk and began beating. "You know her boy, right? What's his name?"

"Brian Wrenowski."

"Have a seat." He handed her plates and jerked his head toward a built-in breakfast nook.

Olivia sidled toward it and slid onto a bench. The cold linoleum seeped through her socks, and she shivered, longing for her coat.

"We're both freshmen at Forester High." She thought of her mother's admonitions to be polite and not just answer in monosyllables.

"That so? My mom taught Patricia at Oak Elementary. As a girl, she was very quiet. Hard to believe, isn't it?" Gordon pulled a skillet from the drain board and moved toward the gas stove. "Somewhere along the line, she changed."

Olivia swung her feet under the table, still indecisive about leaving or staying. The crisis was over, so she could go. But her mom's rules about being polite told her it would be rude. The smell of bacon wafted her way. Before she could make up her mind, Gordon placed an oven mitt on the table and balanced the skillet on it.

"Why was she yelling at you? Help yourself." He eased onto the bench across from her.

She busied herself with spooning eggs onto her plate. Patricia was right to be angry. Yeah, but Brian was such a jerk. As she thought about what had happened, it just slipped out. "I kicked Brian."

"Kicked him." Gordon nodded. "He probably deserved it."

"Not according to his mom." Maybe this old man would take her side. For sure, Mom and Dad wouldn't. She took a taste. "That's why she was chasing me."

"And according to you?" Gordon's lips closed over a forkful of eggs.

Olivia took a breath. "He won't leave me alone cuz I won a computer programming contest, and he thought he should have. First, it was teasing, calling me names. Mom said to ignore it. I did. He started giving me a bad time in the cafeteria at lunch. I still ignored him. Then he got caught throwing spit wads at me and had detention."

"He got what he deserved." Gordon rose, grabbed two glasses, and put them on the table. "So why did you kick him?"

He turned his back to her and reached in the fridge.

"Because he trashed my locker. I saw my Boyz II Men poster sticking out of his backpack, so I know it was him that did it." Gordon splashed some orange juice in each glass.

"He called me a 'ho.' So I kicked him."

Olivia took a gulp of orange juice. It tasted fizzy, old. She swallowed. "In the balls. Patricia got there just after I did it." She watched Gordon chewing a slice of bacon, waiting for a reaction.

"Want some toast?"

"No, thank you." She wanted salt and pepper, but this man had given her refuge, so she thought better of asking. She didn't want that either. She wanted to kick Brian again, maybe harder. She swung her legs at the sudden thought.

"I'm not ignoring you, Olivia. I'm thinking about it, giving it careful consideration." The furrows between his eyebrows deepened.

Okay, here it comes, she thought. *The lecture. You should have just ignored him. Eventually, Brian will go away. Now all you've hurt is yourself.*

Outrage at having to deal with yet another righteous adult hardened around her chest, along with an awful tension in her shoulders that told her she should not have lashed out so violently.

"He called you a 'hoe,' and that was it. That was what did it. You hauled off and kicked him." Gordon wiped his mouth with a napkin.

"Yeah," she said.

"I may be a little behind the times here. But a hoe is what I use in my garden."

"No, not that," Olivia said. "You know, a 'ho'." Her voice dropped. "A whore."

"Tell me about the poster."

"You never heard of Boyz II Men?"

"Probably. But this was your poster," Gordon said.

"I'd taped it inside my locker door. He took it."

"You liked this poster. It was your property."

"Yeah." She said.

"He must have figured out your combination to get in. He must have been watching to know when you wouldn't be around."

Olivia quit kicking her feet, sat very still, concentrating on her hands folded on the table. She nodded.

"He broke into your locker, took something you like. Something that means a lot to you."

"It's the raddest concert I ever went to. I'd wanted to see them like, forever. My dad took me. He said, 'Do you think you should get a poster for your locker?' I stood in line for hours. Everyone was soooo jealous."

"And on top of it, Brian calls you a 'ho'? I'd be pretty insulted too."

"It's worse than that. He ripped it!"

Olivia met his eyes, which were looking straight at her, not at something else, but at her, like she was important to him.

"Did you get it back?" Gordon asked.

She shook her head.

"Do you know what happened to it?"

She shrugged, her words riding out as she exhaled. "I think the principal's got it. It's trashed anyway."

"So what are you going to do now?" Gordon gathered plates and utensils, ferrying them to the sink.

"Don't know. Guess I'll go home. Cuz of this stupid stranger danger, I can't walk to school and I've missed the bus. Mom says I have to be dying before she'll call me in sick. I'll probably get grounded too."

"Stranger danger?"

"Yeah, it's all over the radio."

She walked to the door, balancing on the rug as she pulled clothing from her pile, her jacket cool with a wet slick from her slide across the porch, her mittens soggy clumps around her fingers. As she slung the backpack over her shoulder, she stepped outside, feeling as indecisive as the overcast sky.

Above were the gray, tumbled clouds of late winter, bringing a light stirring that promised spring, but Olivia knew it was a lie. The arctic weather would continue for more weeks than she had patience.

Footprints marched in the other direction, and she could see the slushy swooshes where she had slipped and caught her balance, reminding her of the fear she felt when she made them, not only of Patricia but also that no one was on her side.

She blinked.

That weird old man had actually listened to her.

Once inside her own house, she scuffled to the fridge, where on the door was a magnet stating *Holy Cow, are you eating again?* A cartoon cow, black and white, with the saying in little kid letters was her dad's idea of a joke. Mom had objected sparking an argument. Olivia had insisted it remain on the fridge. She could tell when her mom was pissed off at her dad because her mom kept glancing at it.

She shoved around the fridge's contents and grabbed a carton of milk. Just as she reached for a glass, the phone rang. She froze, perked her ears. Patricia had said it wasn't the end of it. For sure the woman had called the police. At the third ring, she backed toward the vestibule door, her glass of milk sloshing, and held her breath. With the fourth ring, the answering machine clicked while the message played, then another click followed by a beep.

"Hello, Mrs. Dimato. This is Forester High School. Could you please call the office as soon as you receive this message? I'll also try you at your work number. Your daughter did not arrive at school today and we want to be sure she's safe. Thank you." Beep.

Punching buttons, she soon had her mother's extension and prepared to confess.

"This is Donna."

"Mom?"

"Olivia? Where are you?"

"Home."

"Are you okay?"

"Yeah, I missed the bus."

"Missed the bus? How did that happen? Wasn't Patricia going to give you a ride?"

"No. She chased me in the van, and I missed the bus. I went to Gordon Carlson's house."

"Chased you in the van? Why on earth would she do that? I hope you did not disturb that sweet man."

"She's mad at me and she was yelling at me to get in the van. And no, I didn't bother Gordon. He invited me in for breakfast."

"What is going on, Olivia? This is not like you. I just got off the phone with the school. Mr. Perry wants to see us tomorrow afternoon. Do you know what it's about?"

"Yeah."

"And…?"

"And I kicked Brian in the balls."

"Testicles."

"Whatever." Olivia could feel tears crowding the back of her throat. "Mom, he stole my poster and ripped it."

"Well, that explains why you didn't get a ride from Patricia. At least you made a good decision to not walk to school by yourself. That rapist has us all rattled." Her mother paused. "I can't call you in sick. You know my rule." Another pause. "We'll talk when I get home tonight. But I'm very disappointed in you."

"Yeah, whatever." Olivia said.

She could hear her mother thinking out loud. "When I get home, I want to see that you have called your friends and gotten your assignments. You can show me that you have started your homework. Pull out the hamburger in the freezer. We'll have spaghetti for dinner. You can start on a salad before I get in."

"Yeah right. Whatever."

"Olivia. I can't talk right now. But we have a lot to cover, one of which is your tone with me. I'm not the bad guy here. I love you, sweetie."

The girl's stomach lurched, contemplating the meeting with Mr. Perry. Just like she thought. No help from her mom. But what about her dad? He got her the poster. He knew how rad it was. He would set them straight. After all, he was the village president. Except he wouldn't be able to set them straight. He was in New York.

CHAPTER 2
MR. FIX-IT

That same morning in 1996, Gordon could not be late for work. Clerise Harper, the store's administrative assistant, said the new store manager was some hotshot from the corporate office. The guy was a hatchet man with a reputation for mind-boggling transformation. She was plugged into the grapevine and had heard their U Do It was to be some kind of pilot hardware superstore.

The kitchen lights flickered to life, and while he leaned against the sink, rubbing his chin, the front bell rang, accompanied by a pounding at the door, which he opened to a mittened fist landing on his chest. Before him was the fist's owner, a girl, Olivia Dimato, he recalled. Someone who resembled his neighbor, Patricia Wrenowski, had wheeled a van into his driveway, demanding the girl get in. She then backed into the street, smacking his garbage can and tore off down the block.

He was thinking of a way to send the girl on her way when her terrified face made him hesitate. To his consternation, he found himself inviting her in for some breakfast.

The greater irritation was being in his pajamas and bathrobe, a girl on his doorstep the last thing he would expect that early in the morning.

She will have to eat quickly, he thought. Company was infrequent—if at all—for Gordon, and he didn't like to be surprised, let alone when he was on a tight schedule. Why he even let her in was beyond him. But he was stuck with her, glued to the task of playing host.

At last, he watched the bright daub of Olivia's pink hat disappear as she closed the door behind her. Within minutes, he stood in the foyer, rolled up the frayed cuffs on his flannel shirt, grabbed the U Do It apron from a limb on the coat tree, checked his pockets to be sure he had everything, and shook his asthma inhaler for signs of medication. What a strange morning it had been so far, his routine disrupted.

The door to the employee entrance slammed behind him as he passed through, the dull thud echoing his anticipation for the day ahead. He calculated how long until retirement—a little over two years.

Gordon made his way to the lumber department, the smell of wood intensifying as he drew closer. One of his subordinates handed him a clipboard with the latest packing slip as he lifted a length of trim to inspect it. The board brought back memories of when he had swept the family hardware store every day after school, the feel of the old broom's wood still living in the calluses on his hands.

"Not bad," he commented to the employee. "Nice millwork on this."

Next was to prepare for the tiling class scheduled at ten o'clock. He frowned, loading the equipment onto a cart. He had no illusions about why he worked at U Do It. His family business had been a fixture in this community, Carlson Hardware having sustained Forester for almost a century. He was like the little fish on those car decorations, swallowed by a bigger fish swallowed by an even bigger fish. The 1980s craze to restore the Victorian houses in Forester became a frenzy, with customers no longer patient enough to wait the week or so for Gordon's business to receive an order. Soon a national hardware chain, Superior Hardware, bought a nearby vacant lot. As the bull-dozer scraped out the new store's foundation, Gordon knew his family's business was going under.

His present employer, U Do It, had swallowed Superior Hardware in a vicious merger and expanded with excessive warehousing, replacing customer service with volume, voluminous space holding voluminous numbers of gadgets.

Gordon wheeled his cart onto the main floor, passing the aisle containing nails. He recalled the kegs in his family's hardware store. Near them had always been a couple of men leaning on the counter by the cash register, the smell of burning tobacco mingled with sawdust. They stopped by every afternoon. He still missed that.

As he reached the site for the tiling class, a fellow in a U Do It manager's jacket approached. "Carlson!"

"Yes?" Gordon stopped the cart.

"Carlson. Glad to meet you." The man stared at Gordon.

"Glad to meet you too." *This was awkward. He could at least tell me his name.*

"See you later. After the class." And the man jogged off.

A few minutes into his demonstration, Gordon glanced at the group's fringe where, leaning against a display shelf, was his new boss. Something about the manager's scrutiny, insolence emanating from his eyes, put him on alert.

Class over, participants dispersed, Carlson found himself ascending to the second floor for his introductory meeting with his new supervisor.

He gave a weak smile to Clerise, who was seated at her desk opposite the manager's door, shaking her head.

"Carlson." The man emerged, extended a hand, and escorted him into the office, enclosed by a glass wall overlooking the floor below.

What was he? Mid-thirties?

On the new manager's desk sat Gordon's personnel file, thick and a bit tattered. "Tell me about yourself, Carlson," he said.

Gordon eyed the file. "Well, I grew up in Forester. I went to Forester High School. I live in Forester. Not much else."

"I bet you're wondering about me. At U Do Its corporate office, I got the reputation for being Mr. Fix-It. I have a knack for turning things around." He had a grin like a saw blade.

"You must be very proud of that," Gordon gauged from his new boss' face.

"You bet I am. Anyway, I caught some of your class today. Nice job. Let's talk sometime. But you need to get back to work. So." Mr. Fix-It stood.

Gordon found himself standing before the administrative assistant. "Well, Clerise, that was informative."

Her eyebrows arched, and she smiled. "Yeah, I went in earlier. Did Hunter give you the Mr. Fix-It story? Do you believe it? He asked me if I spoke Ebonics and then wondered about a market-share benefit. He be bad ass muthah." She grinned, her brown eyes flecked with amber.

"At least you warranted an introduction. Hunter be first or last name?" Her deep laugh made him smile.

"Last name, sugah. He be Charlie Hunter." She huffed. "Something about him doesn't sit right. By the way, here's your paycheck."

Gordon glanced at the check, closed his eyes, and sighed. Shorted. Being on a tight budget and having his family's original house to maintain, he hoped the corporate office could straighten it out before his house insurance payment bounced.

Back on the floor, he passed the lighting department, where a crumpled chandelier sat in the middle of the aisle like a beached octopus. A high school kid swept up glass shards, and the boy's earnestness made him smile, until his heart clouded over as he recalled one afternoon at Carlson Hardware over fifty years ago.

He must have been about nine. Between the rasp of broom strokes and mutterings behind the cigarette smoke, a half-heard conversation occurred. Floor closure? That didn't make sense. Door closure. More mumblings. Something about a good man. Gordon had imagined a door slamming in front of someone's face just as he reached for the knob. At supper that night, he had asked his father what was so bad about a door closure. Didn't they sell all sorts of hardware for that?

He remembered his mother's amused eyes skewed in his father's direction, while the man pushed potatoes into his mouth. Gordon repeated the question. His father continued to chew seeming to ignore him.

Finally, his mother, Maude, said, "It's not 'door closure', it's 'foreclosure', dear. It happens when someone can't pay the bills. Usually the person owes money to the bank, but if he owes money to the bank, he owes money to other people too. Because the bank is big and powerful, it can foreclose, take property—a business or house even—to get the money."

Gordon had nodded as if he understood. His father's unnatural gruffness must've meant he was worried about the same thing. Years later, it felt prophetic.

Now, as he continued to his office, he wondered whether this kind of store with its multi-corporate structure would ever have to deal with foreclosure.

While his house had never been mortgaged, he still worried. If something happened, he could not afford to replace it. Insurance premiums had gone through the roof in recent years.

He'd lost his family's business, but he'd be damned if he would lose his house too.

CHAPTER 3
SIDE TRIP

Brian, what in the world got into you? What Olivia did was atrocious, but what you did was just as bad." Patricia, turning onto the main street that same 1996 morning, glanced sideways at Brian's beanie. "Do you see where this led? That poster was special to her. Don't you remember how excited she was?"

Stopping to pick him up at school the previous afternoon, she'd arrived in time to see Olivia kick him in the groin. Without hesitation, Patricia jumped from the van, grabbed her son by the elbow, dragging him toward the passenger seat, as he walked knock-kneed by her side.

For the next several hours, they had sat in the emergency waiting room, Brian protesting that he was okay, to which Patricia answered, "This is a serious incident. You could be damaged for life!"

She eyed her husband, Ray, who had slipped into a chair beside her, his face eclipsed by the day's newspaper. Next to her, Brian stared comatosely at some health video making its sluggish way through the second showing.

Amid the constant noise, the emergency doors opened to admit a woman about Patricia's age, supporting a sobbing girl in her teens. Beside them was a village police officer. The woman and girl disappeared into the ER's womb, the girl's hysterical cries trailing behind them.

Curious about what she'd seen, Patricia strode to the nurse's station where the police officer stood.

"…rape kit and the counselor." The officer bent her head to scribble on a small pad.

"We're on it," the nurse said eyeing Patricia, "May I help you?"

"My son, Brian Wrenowski, needs to be seen for a serious groin injury. We've been waiting for over two hours."

"Ma'am, I'm sorry for the delay. We've had a critical emergency that we need to deal with. Your son will be called shortly." The nurse gave a terse nod and lifted the phone.

Finally, Brian's name was announced. As the boy rose to go back to the exam rooms, Patricia and Ray stood to follow. A scalding look from her son, along with raised eyebrows from Ray, caused her to sit back down and make another call to the school's message system to remind the secretary of her two earlier messages regarding the urgency of seeing the principal, Mr. Perry, the next day.

Eventually, Brian emerged, slouched in a wheelchair pushed by a cute, young nurse. In the emergency entrance lighting, his face was pale as he rose from the chair, a bulge in his crotch. Ray had pulled his car around to the hospital entrance and opened the passenger door. Brian clambered in, holding his groin. Patricia stood stunned, realizing that she might never be a grandmother, the automatic door triggered by her failure to get out of the way. In a multitask move, her husband shut the car door, telling her beneath his breath that he'd take Brian home in his car, the boy was fine, the bulge was an ice pack.

The following morning, no longer afraid that Brian would be impaired for life, Patricia was more concerned with secondary issues.

"The point is you stole her poster."

"And you're defending her?" Brian socked the door handle.

"Without more information, what can I do? You think about this, young man: I want to see you being sorry when we meet with Mr. Perry this afternoon."

In response, Brian slammed the van door before joining the knot of smirking students at the bus stop.

Her route took her past the high school, and she realized she could have given Brian a ride. Oh well. Olivia's attack on her boy had left her scattered. Parked on a side street was a dark green sedan, but she was beyond it before she could read the license plate. Odd. What would Ray's car be doing parked at the high school? *It's a popular color, no doubt someone else's sedan,* she thought.

She passed Gordon in his station wagon and wondered about the outcome of Olivia's frantic door pounding. The girl must have been the first outsider to get inside his house in close to a decade. What she wouldn't give to see the inside as a realtor.

Turning onto a quiet side street lined with ancient elms, she had just enough time to check her real estate listing before meeting her client. What she found in the vacant house's newly carpeted bedroom disgusted her. Just below the window seat was a crumpled workman's tarp, and as she lifted it, the aroma of perfume drifted into her nostrils. Glued to the tarp was a used condom. A workman or one of the other real estate agents must be using the place for recreational purposes. She crammed the tarp into the closet. Thank God, she'd stopped by. That could have cost her a sale. At the next real estate agents' meeting, the members would hear from her.

CHAPTER 4
DETENTION

Each girl had a broom, a dustpan, and a wheelbarrow. Mr. Riley, the janitor, was taking great pains to outline their chore. Long and lean, he was tired and bent, as only a man can be who suffers from chronic back pain and lack of sleep. Olivia watched, wretched at the thought of the coming week of detention, followed by a week's suspension from school.

Her partner was Becca Toole, who led a group of losers even the teachers were afraid of. Olivia wondered how she got away with her dyed black hair, stiff with feathers of mousse. She had a hawk-like nose, topped by kohl-edged eyes, the effect like a bird of prey. Becca's pale knees poked through the torn fabric of her jeans, and Olivia wondered how she got away with that too. Olivia would have guessed she was older. Maybe she was. Maybe she'd been held back when she was little, maybe she'd flunked a year.

As Mr. Riley instructed them in the details of sweeping sand from the sidewalk, Becca spun on a black Converse sneaker and flapped her shoulders as if about to take flight.

"If I find you've just swept the sand into the grass, I'll make sure you get another day of detention. Got that?"

"Yeah. Yeah. Yeah. We get it." Becca took her broom and swept.

"See, we get it."

"Do you know what you're supposed to do with the wheelbarrow, little Miss Know-It-All?"

"Yeah, like, dump it. Like, duh!"

"You're this close to another day of detention, missy." Mr. Riley hefted one of the barrows. "Follow me." He headed toward the cyclone fence at the far end of the baseball diamond. "Here. You dump it here."

"What a load of shit," Becca said under her breath, walking about five paces behind the janitor.

"I didn't catch what you said, Becca," Mr. Riley growled.

"I said, 'You dump the load. That's it.'"

The janitor shook his head and escorted them back to the school's front driveway, waited while they took up their brooms, and watched for a moment. "I expect you to have cleaned off a space from here to here." He indicated a stretch of pavement, then headed toward the janitor's office. "I ain't no goddamn babysitter," he mumbled.

Olivia's broom skittered over the cement, leaving furrows.

"Hey, awesome, like one of those whatcha-ma fugi syanora sand things." Becca twirled the broom, making designs.

"I don't believe this," Olivia muttered. "You can't really mean that."

"What do you mean I can't really mean that?" Becca asked. "Haven't you seen one of those before? Oh, I know. It's a sand trap on the first asshole. Fore!" She swung the broom. Globs of sand flew a few inches and settled on the street.

"Just get going, Becca. Mr. Riley's going to be back out in a while."

"Chill, Olivia. That's your name, isn't it? Just chill. Jesus!"

"I am chill." Olivia could think of nothing else to say, so she kept her head down sweeping.

"You know why they're doing this, don't you?"

"Yeah. We got detention."

"No shit." The black kohl emphasized the whites of Becca's eyes. "We got this cuz Mrs. Shulty's out sick, so they didn't know what else to do with us. We shoulda been in the office copying dictionary pages. I've done just about the whole dictionary." Olivia rolled her eyes. "Cockamamie. Know what that means? No? As in ridiculous, ludicrous. This is Hairy Perry's cockamamie idea of improving our behavior. Sweeping instructions is Mr. Riley's cockamamie way of making sure all the sand gets off the sidewalk. See what you coulda been doing if Mrs. Shulty hadn't gotten sick? You'd get to do cockamamie dictionary pages with cockamamie sentences illustrating cockamamie words."

"Just leave me alone. You like doing this so much? Fine. But I wanna get this done and get outta here."

"Cockamamie! Cock-a-mamie!" Becca made a giant *C* in the sand. "Whatever," she said and formed an *L* on her forehead with her hand. "Loser."

The swoosh of brooms was the only sound now. Olivia's sand went into the wheelbarrow, Becca's onto the grass.

"Is it true what you're in for? That you kicked Brian Wrenowski in the balls?" Becca asked.

"Yeah. He deserved it," Olivia said.

"No shit he deserved it!"

"What? You saw him break into my locker?"

"Naw, I just think he's a big loser. That's so rad. You kicked him in the nads. That's so rad. You kicked him in the nads," Becca sang.

Olivia surveyed her companion, shook her head, and went back to sweeping while Becca danced, a kind of soft-shoe.

Suddenly, Becca screeched. "Yow!" She clutched the broom handle as if it were a mic. "Yeah! She kicked him in the nuts. She rammed it up his butt." Her face contorted. She jabbed the end as if at an imaginary Brian.

"What is your problem?" Becca's face scared Olivia, and Mr. Riley would be hurtling out of the janitor's office any second.

"Just chill." Becca stopped thrusting. The terrifying anger on her face dissolved. She giggled, leaned on her broom, and smirked. "You've never had detention, have you?"

Olivia met her gaze. "So?"

"A virgin! Like a virrrrgin," Becca sang into the broom mic.

Olivia's shoulders slumped, broom dangling. Indignant, she wanted to tell Becca to just stop already. But anything she said just made Becca determined to get them in more trouble.

"Don't you wanna know why I'm here?"

"No." Olivia heaved the wheelbarrow.

"I turned in my English paper. Late."

"You got detention for that?"

"And I wrote at the top that it was a majorly lame assignment. And I was late to class."

"Come on. Let's get this dumped. Can you help out here?" Olivia pushed the wheelbarrow toward the baseball diamond, her detention partner remaining behind on the sidewalk. From home plate she saw Mr. Riley standing next to Becca, but before she could reach them, the girl had her back to her, heading toward the street.

"You're done for the day, Olivia. Weren't you paying attention when I showed you? You dumped sand all over the grass."

"I didn't…" She stopped. No way she'd get Becca in trouble. "I didn't think it would hurt."

"You think again, missy. I'll make sure Mr. Perry adds another day of detention."

The rest of the week was no better. Each day brought another of Becca's friends. By Friday, she had an additional week to be served after her suspension. The week off now seemed pretty good.

CHAPTER 5
GORDON'S NEW FRIEND

At one o'clock, Gordon pulled into the driveway with soup for lunch on his mind. Beef broth vapors were rising from the saucepan, when he heard the doorbell like a sound effect from an old radio show. From the kitchen, he could see a face topped by a pink hat through the door's window. His memory of the previous breakfast along with his subtle dislike of Patricia egged him to answer.

"Patty chasing you again?" he asked.

"No. But I can't stand my house anymore. Can I come in?"

Gordon nodded and stepped aside, not sure he wanted this new friend. She settled on the breakfast nook bench and began to swing her feet. "I got suspended. For a week. And I gotta write an essay on how violence doesn't solve things. Last week I had detention all week. How bad is that?"

"In my day, girls didn't kick boys in the privates, so I'm not sure what would have happened if one did. What about Brian?" He placed a bowl and spoon in front of her, ladling a portion into her bowl.

"All he got was suspended last week. It's not fair. And I had to do detention with Becca." She slurped the soup.

"Becca?" Beef and barley took a satisfying journey down his throat to splash in a pool of anxiety. He wondered how to get her to eat quickly. Several times over the past few days, he'd spotted Hunter leaning against a rack or pile of lumber as if he were spying. His gut told him his new boss would be watching if Gordon was arriving on time or taking too long for lunch.

"Creeps me out. She did a terrible job. I got blamed for it and had to do more detention. With Becca's loser friends. They practically live at detention."

"Losers?" Gordon peeked at his watch.

"Yeah." She made an *L* with her thumb and forefinger on her forehead. "And she says I'm a loser."

"Loser, huh?"

"Just cuz I'm in the advanced class. Except now that jerk, Brian, is dissing me while I'm suspended. When I go back on Monday, everyone in my class will say I'm a loser." She began to sob.

Gordon handed her the closest thing, a napkin, hoping his suspicion about Charlie Hunter was off base. "We didn't have losers when I was your age. We had squares, but I think they were the same." Olivia blew her nose, her pale face splotchy. "Would it make any difference if I told you I was a square?" She shrugged and blew into a new napkin. "Squares were the unpopular kids. I was unpopular. Seeing Mom was a teacher, kids thought I got special privileges. I wasn't handsome, so girls wouldn't talk to me. Not only that, but I had asthma, so I wheezed a lot and was terrible at sports."

"I'm not popular either. I'm ugly and fat. Kids hate me cuz my dad is the village president. Teachers used to be nice cuz of Dad. Then Mom and Dad got divorced, so now I'm just fat, ugly, and a loser." She shoved her bangs aside with the heel of her hand.

"So all these people think these other people are losers, right?" Olivia nodded. "Who's Rebecca?" he asked, knowing he shouldn't. It would just prolong her visit. But he couldn't help himself.

"Becca Toole. Rebecca's a loser name. She's the leader of these kids. They get in trouble. A lot. Everyone's afraid of them, even the teachers."

"You got detention with Becca?"

"Yeah and we had to sweep sand. Then I had to sweep more sand the next day. Cuz Becca's loser friend kept pretending the broom was a guitar, he did nothing, and I got blamed for it."

"So why didn't you say anything?" What was this compulsion to counsel her?

"And rat them out? They're way bad. They'd kill me. Now I'm stuck at home all week, and I have more detention when I go back to school. Don't you work or something?"

"Yes. I just came home for a quick lunch," Gordon grabbed at the opportunity to direct the conversation, stepped to the coat tree, and picked Olivia's coat from the floor.

"Mom gets an hour, then she has to get back," she said, her voice muffled as she bent to put on her boots.

"Me too, but why don't you come by the same time tomorrow?" he said. He had no idea why he'd disrupt his lunchtime like that, other than he hated to leave her dejected and crying.

Within moments, he backed the station wagon out of the driveway, spitting gravel, the dashboard clock blinking at him. He knew the shortcuts, where traffic would be light at this time of day. When he got to the store, Gordon locked the car, jogged into the building, and dashed through the staff lounge. No Mr. Fix-It. With his apron on, he was out onto the floor in moments.

The following day, Olivia was waiting on the porch when Gordon arrived home. She perched at the table while Gordon made peanut butter sandwiches.

"I'm on a very tight schedule. I can't be late, so this will be quick," he said, knowing it was just luck that he hadn't gotten caught arriving late the day before.

"What am I going to do? I hate being suspended. I hate that I have to go back on Monday. And face Brian."

"What about your friends?" He kicked himself for opening the door to another topic.

"There's a table of us at lunch. We're the geeks. Brian's at that table too. I know he's been trash-talking me."

"How about a close girl friend?" The angst in his stomach didn't mix any better with peanut butter than beef barley soup. He could not afford Mr. Fix-It's suspicions about his timeliness. Hunter could fire him, and his boss didn't need a reason. Except this girl obviously needed to talk. She wouldn't be here if she had a lot of friends.

"Ashley. But she's hot for Brian. And now Becca knows about me. She loves to jerk people around. I just know she's going to mess with me. It's the worst."

"What about Ashley?"

"No way she's going to stand up for me. I'm all by myself! This so sucks."

Gordon eyed the clock on the wall. "You need to talk to your parents about how you're feeling. They might have some good ideas." He hustled plates to the sink and wiped the table.

"Doesn't do any good. I have to go to school by myself." She didn't move.

"Olivia, I wish I could talk longer, but I have to get back. Why don't you come over when I get home from work tomorrow?"

As he backed out of the driveway, he could see the hat's pompom bobbing its way along the sidewalk above Olivia's hunched shoulders. After the same frantic commute as the day before, he strode breathless toward the lumber department.

"You're late," Hunter said, rounding the end of an aisle behind him. "Do this again and you'll regret it."

CHAPTER 6
REPORTING

How's the essay going?" Gordon asked as Olivia took off her boots.

"Sucks big time. I'm writing about Gandhi. Like, could you picture him at our school? He'd sit cross-legged in a corner of the lunchroom while kids threw fruit cocktail at him. I started thinking about that. How is he going to help me? Then I thought about your mom."

Gordon led her to the kitchen.

"Maude's a legend. She wouldn't put up with any crap, so I'm going to write about her instead." She put her notebook and pen on the table. "Can I interview you for my paper?"

"I suppose so. Not sure what you want to know. Want some tea?" Gordon asked.

Olivia nodded. As the water rattled the kettle, he wondered what this strange girl was doing in his kitchen. *Wasn't she at the age of hating adults?*

"Olivia, I have to take care of my tomato plants." He gestured toward the door to the basement. "If you don't mind, could you conduct the interview there?"

Both tended mugs of tea down the steep, old stairs where he kept his seed starter and a workbench holding his tools, an acrid smell wafting to greet them.

Olivia lifted her pen, studied her questions with the seriousness of a rookie reporter. "What can you tell me about Maude Carlson?"

"Mom? Well," Gordon peered under the seed starter's grow lights, "she was a schoolteacher who didn't want her house torn down. She grew up on a farm. She took the measure of things without romanticizing it. Her father owned a piece of land north of here, where Tacos N' More is now. She went to teacher's school in 1930." Olivia scribbled the date and raised her head.

"She came back here, began teaching, and married my dad."

"What was his name?" Olivia leaned over to inspect the small, green foliage in the starter pots, as if they contained important information.

"Gus. The Carlsons built this house in 1894. We owned a hardware business." Gordon stopped for a moment. Olivia heard Patricia tell the story every summer at the Forester Days picnic. She didn't need to interview him.

As he pondered this, he thought of Gandhi, the facts of his life affecting so many people. How did his mom's story affect the people on this block, and how did it affect Olivia?

In a flash, he realized how irritated he was at Patty's ridiculous annual rendition.

"I suppose you remember Patricia's yearly re-enactment of Maude chaining herself to that old horse trough on the corner in order to save the block from being torn down?"

"No duh. Like we don't have to hear it every Forester Days block party."

"'Fraid it didn't happen that way. But it makes a good tale." Gordon gave a sideways smile, this time with a slight nod down, amused at her surprise.

"What? That's like the best part of the story. That's like the nonviolence thing." She crossed her arms, slapping them against her ribs.

Gordon felt the curve on his back deepen as he reached across the small seedlings. "She didn't chain herself to anything."

"But I don't get it. If she didn't do that, why does Patricia tell it that way every year?" Olivia put down the notebook and pen, her face exasperated.

"Oh, I don't know. You got to admit it's pretty entertaining. The truth is Maude understood that the guys who wanted to tear down the block weren't going to be stopped by her refusal to sell." He turned back to the vegetables.

"Can I help?" Olivia asked. Gordon gave her a pair of dingy gloves and showed her how to squeeze the seedlings out of their little plastic cells. They began lining them along the bench. He smiled as he watched her gently tease the roots apart.

"The part about the speculators is true. They were trying to buy up the block in order to turn it into apartments and a professional building," Gordon said, realizing how good it felt to talk about his mother's real heroics. "Maude's refusal to sell the house was correct." Gordon loosened the threadlike roots and anchored them with soil into the larger pot, the tangy smell of tomato stems curling to his nose. "Mom didn't give in. She phoned Pete Robb. She said Petey was one of her best students." Gordon watched as Olivia patted the soil around the seedling's new home.

"You mean that hotshot lawyer?" Olivia giggled, as they moved to the far end of the row.

"Yep. Petey's law practice was just getting started at that time."

"In Patricia's story, your mom walks back and forth in front of the village hall with a sign protesting the demolition." When Gordon shook his head, she groaned. "That's another rad part."

Gordon gestured her to a third bank of lights, where tiny curls of lettuce sprouted. He grabbed a bottle of water and showed her how to mist them.

"I suppose she didn't get hauled off to jail either. Or organize a hunger strike among the other inmates."

"Nope. Petey had discovered a pending application to put a large part of the village on the historic register, which explained why the speculators were so impatient. He was able to get our block added, but by that time, work had already begun on the apartment building next door." He nodded toward the complex behind his house. "You have to admit Patricia's is a better story."

He watched Olivia for a moment while she opened her notebook again, tilting her head to one side, frowning as she peered at her earlier notes with questions on blue-lined paper.

"She kept the house and saved the block and it was nonviolent. But I don't get what's so heroic about it," Olivia said.

He busied himself with putting tools away. He had often tried to imagine what it would have been like had his mother failed. He had never been able to conjure up an image. They climbed the stairs carrying empty tea mugs.

Olivia stuffed her notebook into her backpack. "Is that it? She just called a lawyer?"

Gordon considered. She had the expression children have when they learn there is no Santa Claus. "Yes, that's what she did. If it makes any difference, she also wrote a lot of letters to the editor at the *Forester Times*."

"But how lame is that? It's not at all like Patricia says."

"Does it matter? After all, everything's still here."

"Well, yeah, it matters. She's lying. Every summer, we have to listen to that stupid story, and she's lying."

Gordon could feel his shoulders slump as he watched Olivia's disappointment settle in. "Think about it this way. Maude saved the block. She did it in a nonviolent way, just like Gandhi. Both of them prevailed."

"If it doesn't matter, why doesn't Patricia tell the truth?" Olivia asked, stepping onto the porch.

Gordon watched her disappear under the streetlamps, her shadow trailing behind. He pictured Patty at the picnic each June, disquiet leaching into his arms and legs.

CHAPTER 7
AT THE MUSEUM

Saturday was the day Gordon looked forward to, his day at the museum. He descended the stairs of his home, grabbed the newspaper from the porch, and paused to take a quick puff from his inhaler. The walk through the chilly morning was pleasant. Not long now before spring.

He mused that his roots were in a community whose inhabitants nurtured their past. Nurturing was a paradoxical role for him: At his own home, it took the form of his garden, a cycle of birth, growth, death, and rebirth. At the museum, it meant stasis, lest some grain of memory fly off in the fierce weather for which this part of the Midwest was known.

Originally the Forestier family home, Jean-Luis Forestier would be content that his house had been preserved. After all, the founder, who gave his name to this village, had built the town to last.

Gordon mounted the museum's front steps. Compared to his house, Louis Sullivan's design was triple the size, possessing a deep veranda, camouflaged by ancient elm trees.

Some said the old house was still a populated residence, the family's comings and goings marked by a whirl of smoke or an errant wisp of mist. Gordon smiled at the thought.

As a boy, he once dared his best friend, Bubba, to approach the structure on Halloween. They were disappointed to creep up the steps, peer in the windows, and find a house in complacent sleep.

Key inserted in the brass lock, his shoulder and hip came in handy, urging the old door to give way and let him in. He liked its solid weight. He liked any solid door that kept out unwanted intruders, whether extreme weather or extreme personalities. Gordon maneuvered it closed, the outside world receding to dull, white noise.

As he switched on the light, he noted the crystals on the cranberry chandelier needed cleaning, as did the wall sconces. Before him, leading to the upper floors, was a massive mahogany staircase, the bannister carved with ornate art nouveau birds, griffins, and swirls, encasing brass stair treads and a threadbare carpet.

He crossed the marble floor and turned left, passing through the morning room. On the wall above the fireplace hung a portrait of Jean-Luis, his wife, Charlotte, seated by his side. The founder posed stiffly, his angled face like some Cubist painting. Charlotte's likeness was of a woman in severe, Edwardian clothes, her abundant hair meticulously dressed. To the townsfolk, she was known as Grand Lotty.

Gordon continued through the doorway to the breakfast room, the office for the museum. A group, he hadn't seen before called Native Guides, was scheduled to come through at 10:00 a.m. He liked interacting with children, seeing their enthralled faces as he took them through the house and talked about the founding family. Afterward, he'd have the solitude to pursue his interest in the historic, detailed lives of the original townsfolk, his project to index various letters, diaries, and newspaper articles stored in the third-floor ballroom.

The visitors arrived in the foyer with a whoop. The energy emanating from the dozen boys was palpable, while two chiefs propped themselves against the doorframe in a vapid attempt to guard the exit. Gordon surmised that the previous evening had left the men to deal with the lethargy of major hangovers. Guiding the children through the house would keep him on his toes.

A boy dashed to him. "Brave Carlson. We're the Sioux tribe. We bring you a peace offering." The young brave placed a dainty, decorated box in Gordon's hands: cookies. Some mother had traded culinary skills for a morning of peace and quiet. Then with high-pitched voices, the boys began a chant, dancing a circle around him until one chief raised his arm and wiggled two fingers. The boys stopped prancing mid-syllable, their arms shooting up in imitation. Within moments, the boisterous commotion trickled to a stop. Gordon's eyes widened at the spectacle.

"Say, Mr. Carlson," one of the chiefs called. "Is it true that Grand Lotty's son-in-law sold hooch from here during Prohibition?"

"Actually, her son-in-law, Rupert Sipe, sold moonshine from his farm, which was over where Tacos N' More is today."

The chief punched his companion in the arm. "You owe me twenty bucks, Chief Flaming Mouth." *Some bet from the previous night*, Gordon thought.

"Okay, boys, let's start out in the main living room," Gordon began, ushering the group into a large rectangular area. "Back then the Forestiers called this their parlor. How many of you have a parlor in your home?" Most boys raised their hands.

"Carlson, Carlson," Chief Flaming Mouth interrupted. "I had a teacher named Mrs. Carlson. Any relationship?"

Gordon's speech floundered as he turned toward the gentleman. "Yes, she was my mother."

"No kidding? I forgot she had a son, if I even knew." The chief moved to the center of the room and raised his arm. "Chief Flaming Mouth has important news. Many moons ago, Brave Carlson Squaw chained herself to a water trough to keep the cruel bulldozers from destroying our homes. A brave, wise woman, she offered her life for the tribe."

Gordon's head snapped back at how tacky and disrespectful the chief sounded. "It wasn't quite as spectacular as all that," he stammered.

"This brave with many facts speaks humbly," Flaming Mouth's friend chimed in. He raised his arm. "Squaw Carlson's son, we honor you." The men and boys raised arms wiggling fingers in some kind of salute.

"Squaw Carlson's son, tell us the story of how she protected our tipi homes."

Gordon froze. "She wasn't as brave as all that. Our village had much braver people. Take Forestier, the founding father. He was half Blackfoot. He crossed many rivers and mountains to bring back beaver pelts." He cringed, but this seemed like the best way to get back on track with the tour.

"Squaw Carlson was even braver than that," Flaming Mouth replied.

"Well, the truth is, she didn't tie herself to the water trough. She went to an even braver brave, a lawyer, who made the village sign a treaty to protect our homes." *Was this really coming out of his mouth?*

The high energy in the room deflated as the small faces turned away. "Boring!" a voice sang, and the tribe began to mill around the large room, the racket swelling again.

"Let's take a few minutes to check out what's in the display cases. Then we'll talk about what you saw." Gordon called, struggling to keep the boys in control.

One boy peered at old photos in one of the glass cases. Gordon stood behind his shoulder.

"You must be Michael. I work with your mom, Clerise."

"I know," he said.

"That's a picture of a picnic the servant staff were having at one of the Forester Days celebrations. Back then, the African American servants didn't get to have a picnic until later in the evening when their employers had finished theirs." Gordon had examined the picture many times, wondering about the people. The contrast had faded over time, so what remained were faces, whose expressions of surprise or dismay floated in the darkness. Michael made a small grunt and began to hop toward the other boys, the lone black face in the crowd of whites. Gordon contemplated what this must mean to Clerise.

Noise seeped through the walls, and he could hear voices in the formal dining room. Fear of the damage all that energy could create shoved Gordon forward at a jog. Deciding to cut the tour short, he raised his arm in the signal he'd observed, whereupon the chiefs first stared at him as if trying to decipher what it meant and then complied.

"Let's go to the morning room, where the family celebrated Christmas," Gordon said, taking the lead once more. As most children's favorite part, it would keep their attention for at least a few minutes. Then he could usher them out the door.

The morning room was not designed to hold twelve exuberant boys, two hung-over chaperones, and a museum guide. From their photograph, Grand Lotty and Jean-Luis stared at the far wall.

"People have reported spirit sightings, a shadow in that corner, where the family had their Christmas tree," Gordon began. A chorus of oooh's responded. "Some folks think it's the ghost of Jean-Luis. Some think little Violet is searching for her Christmas presents.

"Violet Forestier was only five years old when she died. On the far wall, you can see her picture with her sister, Minette." He pointed at two solemn girls in black dresses with white pinafores.

"At Christmas time, this room was decorated with a tree. One year Violet got a picture book and a beautiful glass ornament. She was so excited that when she ran across the carpet to show her mother, Grand Lotty, she tripped and fell.

"The ornament shattered and cut her arm. A few days later, the cut got infected. Can someone tell me what an infection is?"

Hands waved to answer. Now he had their attention. Nothing like a gruesome tale to engage young boys' minds.

"It's when you get hurt, like a cut or a burn, and it gets red and this yellow stuff oozes out, and then it gets green and pretty soon it turns black and your leg falls off. And then it spreads all over and you die!" one boy said, toppling over, his buddies joining in.

Gordon's arm shot up. With them being so distracted, the signal thing wasn't working. "Boys! Boys!" he shouted, wiggling his fingers. The din abated a bit. "Don't you want to know how she died?"

The high-spiritedness momentarily subdued, Gordon continued. "Within a few days, her arm became a nasty red color. Grand Lotty put a dressing on it, but the dressing got soaked with yellow pus. She called for the doctor to come.

"Little Violet's arm was puffy." Gordon had no idea if this really happened, but the boys remained interested. "The doctor unwrapped the bandage. Her arm was blotchy, swollen. The cut was ugly, turning black around the edges. She cried when he touched it." Gordon was now winging it. "He took tweezers, pulled away the skin, and it came off. Buried in her arm was a piece of the ornament. The doctor pulled it out. He said Violet would be fine."

Gordon paused dramatically.

"But Violet was not fine."

He looked from one rapt face to another. "Over the next few days, her arm got worse. The infection spread. The doctor said she would have to go to the hospital. To save her life, the doctors would have to cut off her arm. Sadly, she died the next day.

"Some say they've seen her ghost in this room, searching for her picture book. It was the last thing she asked for."

"What about the book? Where is it?" Chief Flaming Mouth spoke, leaning against the far wall.

"Good questions," Gordon replied. "The book began to fall apart, so now only the docents can handle it. But anyway, I'm sure you'd like to get outside into this lovely day." He led them back to the foyer.

Chief Flaming Mouth came forward and placed a headband on Gordon's head. "We Sioux tribe name you 'Truth Speaker,' who holds the sacred knowledge of our tribe." With that, the boys and two men snaked around Gordon chanting their way out the door.

Relishing the sudden contrast, he ambled toward the kitchen. He dropped the headband into the waste basket and made a mug of tea. That was the most bizarre tour he had conducted in his many years as a docent. Trying to center himself, he picked out a cookie and unfolded the newspaper, hoping for a distraction. The headline, "Rapist Strikes Community Again" jumped out at him. He scanned the article. Hadn't Olivia mentioned stranger danger the other day? Having no kids or grandkids, he had not connected her comment to this. He savored his tea and thought about what kids had to deal with nowadays. He shook his head. Would they ever be safe?

He climbed the stairs to the ballroom on the third floor, badly in need of renovation. Around him boxes held evidence of the history in which Gordon had grown up and lived. He had embarked on an indexing project to categorize these pieces of people's lives gathered and stored over the decades.

He thought about the troop of boys he'd just entertained. That was exactly what he'd done, entertained them. They had come to learn about the history of their community, and he had gotten carried away fabricating that outrageous tale about Violet. Their cavalier attitude about Native American culture had thrown him.

Olivia's opinion a few days earlier about Patricia's phony story added to his uneasy ruminations. How was his rendition of Violet's demise any different than Patricia parading the fiction of his mother? Each summer, she told the story as if it were the truth. Apparently more than just his neighborhood believed it. He wondered if his attempt to correct the misperception that morning would have any effect. Meanwhile, he had created another distortion.

That they were bold lies, as Olivia would have it, was not so clear. Johnny Appleseed was based on some fact. The tale of George Washington and the cherry tree was a piece of American folk history. But those boys and their leaders pretending to be from the Sioux Nation crossed the line. A niggling thought took root in his head that the whole truth did matter.

One of the crystals on the wall sconce shuddered imperceptibly. He was used to this occasional flutter of air, a wisp curling into the wallpaper, or an odd-shaped fog melding with his shadow as he ascended or descended the stairs.

The first time the phantasm appeared, he had been very young. His mother and he often visited Grand Lotty in her final years. The occasion was a summons to put on a starched shirt. Then he had to sit quietly, drinking tea—which he hated—while his mother chatted with the ancient woman.

One afternoon, he had offered to clear the tea things, his mother having already sent him stern glances for fidgeting, when an old woman came in, wearing a modest black dress and white apron. Grand Lotty dismissed him along with the maid, Harriet. As he trailed behind Harriet, he saw something hazy clinging to the wallpaper above the lamp. That first encounter had terrified him. He almost turned to run back to the safety of the parlor, but Harriet didn't seem to notice. Only later when he knew her better did he appreciate that he was not alone in seeing the apparition.

To him and Harriet, the truth was that some kind of specter existed in this house. The irony was that compared with Patricia's story and his exaggeration of Violet's death, a spirit would be the least believable.

Gordon shifted in his chair, reached in a box, and extracted an old newspaper article to index, deciding the issue was as evanescent as the stirring he'd just seen. Here were pieces of truth that hovered like ghosts in time until they were revealed. Whether they existed depended on whether a person was able to see them. That was the purpose of his project, to make them visible.

✦✦✦

Intent on the proceedings, Patricia leaned forward in her seat at the dining room table in the museum, where the Forester Museum Board, comprised of community notables, conducted its monthly meeting. Usually only founding family descendants got a seat on the board.

Forester had a three-class system. There were the aristocratic founders along with the families who settled the area at the same time. Her family was the latter, the common folk who made the businesses possible. Their names weren't on brass plaques in the village hall's entryway.

The newcomers were the third class, those rehabbers, who grabbed up Victorians and installed expensive renovations, skyrocketing the property taxes. They could donate their megabucks. They might even chair fundraisers, but they would never be allowed to join the board.

Getting herself onto the museum board had been a major coup. As far as she knew, she was the first in her class to break into this elite group. But quickly, she realized that while she could participate, she would never be president.

She decided to run for the village council where she would have a chance to become village president just like John Dimato, an outsider.

A discussion was in progress about the museum board's future projects.

"We can't save the trees from Dutch elm disease and restore the ballroom without a major fundraising event," the current president commented.

"Patricia, you've been unusually silent. What are your thoughts?" The treasurer turned to her.

"Well, I think we should renovate the ballroom. We could then generate income through renting it for private affairs like weddings, paying for itself and generating funding for other projects."

The president turned an indulgent smile toward her. "I'm sure you have the best intentions, dear. However, our community isn't built that way. Our museum is prized for its historic value and authenticity. If we restore the ballroom as an event facility, we would be corrupting that purpose. Do you understand, Patricia? Why, I'm appalled at what has happened to some of our neighboring villages. They're full of bed-and-breakfasts now. Rather than remain true communities, they have become tourist attractions."

"In that case, we could get some help from the village council. After all, this is a community issue. When I'm elected, I will champion the cause." Patricia met the president's eyes. She hadn't been so successful in the real estate business by letting some snobby woman intimidate her.

"What a great idea!" The treasurer jumped in. *Good, an ally.*

"Perhaps. But don't you think you're counting your chickens, dear?" The president ignored the treasurer.

"This is the kind of promise I can make to this community and see it through. I know a little something about houses." She paused, the chuckles pattering around the table. "You'll be amazed at what I can do. Don't forget to get out and vote next Tuesday."

CHAPTER 8
THE GREEN SEDAN

Monday morning, the day before the election, Patricia huddled with a group of campaign supporters at the intersection by the train depot. She'd been at it since 5:00 a.m., waving at cars, greeting neighbors as they jumped onto commuter trains, and reminding them to vote. She gulped a cup of coffee and the next moment dashed to the platform to mingle with the next wave of people. "A vote for me for village council is a vote to preserve your past, present, and future. Don't forget to vote tomorrow."

Over the past month, she'd kept an exhausting schedule, spring being the busy season for real estate. Campaigning had competed for her time.

With all this activity, she'd forgotten that today Olivia would return to school. Ray had had a good idea to shuttle Brian so that the two kids wouldn't have to ride the bus together.

+++

She knew this would happen only once: the drama as news trickled in Tuesday evening. All her campaign supporters gathered in the living room, a cheer when the news was good, groans when it wasn't. Her competition was stiff: the great-grandson of the first bank president was now in the lead. Never mind that he had the charisma of a garden grub. She flicked the underside of her acrylic nails, jumping up when the anxiety drove her to the kitchen for more coffee and ko-laches.

Then came a phone call from the village hall. Patricia was now in the lead by eleven votes. The jubilation was immense, but not as deafening as when Patricia received the call that she had won by seventeen votes. Her opponent demanded a recount, and so the evening dragged on, finally to conclude with Patricia's victory diminished by five votes. But twelve votes were twelve votes. She was on her way.

+++

The day after the election left Patricia logy, like after a New Year's celebration because—for her at least—it was a new year now that she had a seat on the council. Thus, she spent the morning dismantling the campaign machine she'd driven for the past few months, then hosted a luncheon for her crew, presenting them with small gifts. She'd need them again.

Dinner preparations found her stirring spaghetti sauce as she mulled over where she could have left her Polaroid camera. How odd. She'd always been so organized. As the tomato and sausage mixture began to burp, she thought she'd found the answer and reached for the wall phone.

"You think so? Okay, but you gotta promise she won't find out." A soft voice floated out at her.

"Mom, I'm on the phone," Brian's voice cracked.

"Oh, sorry, Brian." she stammered. She'd never found Brian on the phone with a girl before. Curiosity spurred Patricia to open the conversation at dinner. "Who was the girl on the phone just now?"

"Someone from class," Brian jammed a meatball in his mouth. "Her name's Ashley, if you have to be so nosy."

"Ashley?" Ray was suddenly alert. "Why is that name familiar?"

"Cuz she's on the swim team. How long've you been spying on me anyway?"

"We aren't spying on you," Patricia said.

"We're just interested in what's going on in your life," Ray added.

"Can't I have a private conversation without being interrogated? She's just a girl, that's all. She's not special."

Patricia remembered Ashley from the swim team. She was thin, leggy, shaped like a bullet. And the Cook County diving champion. Internally, Patricia was thrilled. And sad. Of course, Ashley was special. She was Brian's first love.

Ray gave a sardonic smile at Brian's tirade. "Then let's change the subject. Patricia, how was your first day as a village councilwoman?"

+++

Patricia was waiting for Ray when he walked in the door Thursday evening.

"Saw your car parked on the side street by the school a while ago. How come you were there?" She knew better than to pounce on Ray like this, but the sight had been like a blast of air conditioning in mid-winter.

"Finished work early." Ray's voice muffled while he hung his jacket in the foyer. "Haven't seen much of Brian lately, so I decided to give him a ride."

"He's in his room."

"He is?" Ray began to climb the stairs. "Just going to poke my head in. You know how elusive he is these days."

"Ray, this doesn't make sense." Patricia called after him.

He paused, turned, peering down at her. "I had hoped to catch Brian before he caught the bus and give him a ride home. Pretty simple."

"The bus had gone over an hour earlier."

"Honestly, Patricia, what's going on with you today? Did you lose a sale or something?"

"It was getting on toward six when I saw you. Why were you there?"

"Honey, I finished early. I decided to pick up Brian. I parked at the side street, so I could watch for him. I screwed up about the bus."

Ray's form disappeared as he rounded the landing to the second floor.

She stared at the empty stairs, decided Ray had made a timing goof and went to make dinner, trying to shake off the creepy feeling still clinging to her shoulders.

+++

Patricia's Friday started with a phone call from the owner of one of her real estate listings.

When she arrived at the house, he threatened to sue, to complain to the real estate board, and to make sure she never sold another house. The new carpet was stained with booze, and he had found a used condom in the shower.

While her insides churned, Patricia kept her face empathetic, reassuring. Was he sure it wasn't the workmen? She thought she had seen something fishy earlier in the week, when they were still working upstairs. To calm her client, she offered to have the carpet cleaned and promised she'd convene a real estate agent meeting.

In the van, she rolled down the window and lit a cigarette she kept for moments like these, seething that something so disgusting could happen. And this was the second time in not so many weeks.

Then on impulse she decided to stop at the bus stop, where she found Brian pacing, shoulders hunched.

"How was your day? What did you do?" she asked as her son buckled his seatbelt.

"Nothing much."

"What's that in your hair?" She pulled a kind of dried, red substance from a strand.

Brian jerked away and scowled out the window. "Food fight."

"Food fight? Where were the lunchroom monitors? They should've kept it from happening."

"Why are you always grilling me like I'm doing something wrong?" he exploded.

She put the car in gear, nosed toward home, deposited Brian, and dashed to the camera store to replace the Polaroid. How odd that it had not surfaced. On the return home, she passed a knot of girls. She frowned at the recollection of seeing Ray's sedan in that spot the day before.

CHAPTER 9
LOST DOG

Suspension had felt like forever. Then all of a sudden, it was Sunday night. Even if she could delay returning to school, Olivia knew Brian would just have that much more time to do whatever creepy things he was capable of. And she'd still have a week of detention to greet her.

Ashley had been uninformative the whole time. Any detail about what was going on at school that previous week had been sketchy.

Consequently, that Monday morning while Patricia campaigned, Olivia took her usual seat in the front row in advanced algebra class. Ashley's seat next to hers remained vacant until she spotted her friend walk in behind Brian. She clenched her teeth, her stomach a slurry of gelling concrete as Brian slipped into his desk on her other side.

Mr. Erstedt turned from the blackboard and surveyed the class, his eyes catching hers. "Just a reminder you have a math quiz tomorrow. I take it you have kept up with the assignments, Olivia?"

"We're on this page." Brian reached over planting a finger on Olivia's open textbook.

"Like duh. What do you think I've been doing all week?" she snapped.

"Just trying to help." Brian's eyes were round, innocent.

Erstedt glanced their way, an eyebrow raised. "Class, turn to page

110."

As they hustled to their next class, she grabbed Ashley's elbow. "Since when did you start hanging out with Brian?"

"He's really very sweet. You just don't give him a chance."

"Sweet? He's been at me ever since I won that contest. Did you forget he cheated? I could've turned him in, but I didn't."

"I knew you'd be like this," Ashley said. "What's the point of saying anything when all you're going to do is get mad?"

"How about cuz you're my best friend?"

"Some friend you are. You should be happy for me. That's why I didn't tell you last week that Brian called. And now I'm not going to tell you all about it."

"You're on his side?"

"Hey, I don't want to get in the middle of this. See you at lunch." She said, ducking into the restroom.

Stupid, stupid, Olivia thought, pushing open the double doors to the cafeteria, wishing she hadn't dumped her lunch in the trash. She grabbed a tray, inhaling the smell of rancid grease.

She snaked toward her seat through the noise and the gauntlet of tables, keeping eyes focused on her lunch, glancing to be sure she didn't bump into anyone. The cheerleaders and jocks smirked. Then came the skate boarders, hunched over their meals, pants sagged, wearing wool beanies. She could see Ashley's back, the vacant space on the end of the bench next to her, a seating assignment for the geeks.

A chorus erupted. "O-liv-ee-a! O-liv-ee-a!" Fingers clenched on the tray, she passed the new layer of noise where Becca and her band of losers chanted. She'd never realized how close they were to her group.

She approached Ashley to sit next to her and suddenly stumbled, her tray capsizing as Brian's foot dug into her shin.

"You uncoordinated pig," Brian said.

Olivia looked at the disaster cascading down her shirt and jeans, warm spaghetti sauce soaking into her legs. Around her, a roar emanated from Becca's table.

"I'll get rid of your tray while you go get cleaned up." Ashley stooped, gathering the dishes and utensils from the floor.

Staring at herself in the girl's bathroom mirror, Olivia wiped at her clothes with a paper towel. She would have to wear her coat for the rest of the afternoon, cocooned in souring milk and sticky spaghetti sauce.

+++

One good thing about having all that time to myself is I'm way ahead of the class, Olivia thought, handing Mr. Erstedt her math quiz the next morning. Not a warm person to begin with, he took the paper without a word, shoved his glasses to the bridge of his nose, and turned to speak with another student, leaving Olivia feeling rebuffed.

Ashley was uncommunicative other than to pass a note saying Brian wanted to sit by her at lunch. That left Olivia to plunge through the crowded cafeteria, her own lunch in its conspicuous brown bag, while her friend and Brian coursed through the lunch line.

She bit into her sandwich, closed her eyes, and opened them to see Brian deposit before her a bowl filled with food scraps from the garbage, smelling of rancid tuna fish. She gagged, spitting the doughy half-masticated bite of sandwich into the bowl, jumped to her feet, and tripped on the table leg.

"Su-ee, Su-ee, piggy, piggy," Brian crowed.

"Come on," she said to Ashley. Her friend's eyes shifted toward the exit but did not move. Olivia waited.

"Brian sucks! Brian sucks!" the kids at Becca's table roared, the noise intensifying.

"Come on, Ashley," Olivia's words a whisper. She left the lunchroom alone.

+++

"Olivia, would you stay behind for a moment?" Mr. Erstedt asked, class over that Wednesday.

She stopped, other students bumping her shoulder as they passed. Sweat sprang in the palms of her hands.

"It's come to my attention," he began, sliding his glasses up his nose, "that you may not have completed the math quiz on your own."

"Are you saying I cheated?" Olivia asked. She leaned against the desk, her mind numb.

"I hate to put it that way, but yes. After all, you were suspended last week, so you would not have been here. Yet you scored 100%, just like the person who mentioned it to me."

"How could I have cheated off Brian? Just cuz he sits next to me, I can't see his paper."

"So you were trying to copy his work." Was his tone accusatory or triumphant? "The school takes this kind of thing very seriously, and given your recent behavior, I want you to know that you will be seeing Mr. Perry."

Stunned, Olivia left the classroom, the rest of the morning filled with dread about being summoned to Hairy Perry's office. As the bell rang to signal lunch, she managed to catch Ashley in the hall. "I can't believe what that turd, Brian, did to me. When I see Hairy Perry, I'll set him straight."

"I told you, I'm not getting in the middle."

She and Ashley placed their trays at their usual table. Hamburgers and fries day, the burgers the consistency of mini-Frisbees, fries like tiny spears. Olivia had a pond of ketchup on her plate and was just dipping one when she felt Ashley scoot against her, shoving her sideways to the edge of the bench.

"Hey, Ash, I wanna sit here." Brian plopped his tray down and squeezed in. "You look hot today." He whispered something in her ear, which made her giggle.

Then a fry hit Brian's head. And another. And another. Over her shoulder, Olivia saw Becca's table laughing with each strike. "Asshole, asshole," they chanted.

"Just ignore them," Brian yelled. Fear scrambled across his face. "I've already been suspended once. Come on, but not you, Olivia, you cheating bitch." He picked up his tray, Ashley following, leaving Olivia alone, stabbing at her hamburger with a plastic knife.

The fry rain stopped as quickly as it had started, followed at the next table by whoops and high fives.

+++

All day Thursday, Olivia had expected a summons to the principal's office. *Maybe Mr. Erstedt didn't go to Mr. Perry after all*, she thought, making her way to the school's toolshed. One of her last days on detention would be raking dead grass.

"You know, you're not such a loser after all," Becca's black hair bobbed. "The rest of us think so too. You hear us?"

"Yeah, I heard you."

"Why is Brian being such a fart hole?"

"He's still pissed cuz he didn't win this computer contest and I did, even though he cheated. He told Erstedt that I cheated on Tuesday's math quiz." Olivia scooped a haystack of grass into the wheelbarrow.

"Yeah, yeah. Who gives a shit over some quiz or contest?" Becca played with the rake tines.

"I do and so does he. I won $500."

"Five hundred bucks?" Becca snorted. "Who's the girl you sit next to?"

"Ashley? A friend," Olivia answered.

"Some friend. I'd more than punch Brian's nuts if that happened to my friend."

"It's okay. It's not her fault. She has the hots for him."

"Like, psycho Brian is more important than you? I think she's more than a loser if she can't see that you're awesome."

The rake scratched and stalled as Olivia pulled it across the lawn.

"'Cept I could give a shit."

Olivia decided to change the subject. "Hey, why're you here to-day?"

"No big deal. I just didn't show up 'til lunch."

"Becca, why do you do that to yourself? This is, like, so old."

"No reason to." Becca tore pieces of dead grass and flung them.

"Yeah, I know what you mean, but what are the choices? Working at Tacos N' More for the rest of our lives?"

"Fuck you! My dad worked there."

"I didn't mean it that way. Sorry. I didn't mean to diss your dad." Olivia startled, afraid what might happen next.

"Gotcha! I don't even know who my old man is." Becca pranced around her rake. "Soon as I can, I'm going to work at Tacos N' More or some burger place. Free food and better than I get right now."

Okay Olivia thought, *this is too weird. So okay, she doesn't know who her dad is. So don't make her angry. So say nothing.*

"I heard your mom and dad split. Poor baby. Nobody loves you. Ashley doesn't love you. Brian doesn't love you. I wish I had it so bad. My mom's in some rehab program. Haven't seen her in a while. I'm living with my aunt, and you want me to feel sorry for you?"

"No, I don't want you to feel sorry for me. I just think you're so smart. You could do better than Tacos N' More. That's all."

"This is such shit. Ya think I even have a chance to do more than that? I don't have the village pre-si-dent for an old man."

"Well, yeah. If I can, you can." Olivia wondered how much con-viction her voice conveyed.

They turned in their rakes, hoisted their backpacks across their shoulders, and walked toward the front of the school.

"Olivia, we're the same. You need a friend who'll stand up for you. I need a friend who'll believe in me." Becca ambled toward the trees and around the corner, leaving Olivia in front of the bus, filling with late departure students.

She weighed her mom's anger at walking home alone against Brian's possible catcalling, or whatever else he may have cooked up for the bus ride. She chose the former. At first she didn't pay much attention to the phone poles or streetlamps that were covered with flyers. But as she stood at the stoplight, she recognized her face. "Lost Dog" was spread in a banner across the top. Below was her picture. She yanked the flyer from the pole, scanned the street, then ran along the boulevard snatching them down, until she stopped, her panting edged in sobs. Being a loser at school was one thing, but Brian was ensuring she'd be a loser everywhere. As she trudged toward home, she saw Gordon's station wagon in the driveway and turned toward his house.

"It's just about dinnertime. Isn't your mom expecting you?" Gordon asked as he opened the door.

"I had detention. Remember? I can be a few minutes late." He seemed happy to see her and hustled to get a kettle going.

"How'd your paper come out?" He placed a plate of cookies on the table.

"Okay, I guess. Don't know. Don't care." Olivia sighed. Gordon handed her a napkin. She felt plugged up inside, beyond wanting to cry. "School's worse than before I got suspended. Brian plastered the lampposts with these Lost Dog flyers. See? I tried to pull them down." She handed him a crumpled piece of paper.

"That's terrible. Olivia, why don't you report him?"

"Won't do any good. Besides I can't prove it." She took a cookie from the plate.

"Olivia, that's harassment!"

"And stealing my poster wasn't? The worst part is Ashley's done nothing, so now she's part of it too." She met his eyes, which appeared as sad as she felt. "She's my best friend," Olivia whispered. She sipped her tea and munched another cookie.

"I don't know how a best friend could stand by like that." Gordon shook his head.

"There's no one. They're all against me." She placed her mug on the table and made her way to her pile by the coat tree.

"If the principal doesn't call you in, go see him anyway or at least tell your parents," Gordon said holding her jacket.

"Won't do any good. No one will listen. Brian hasn't done anything other than call me a cheater, trip me, and put up a bunch of flyers."

"I know that saying it will all work out sounds pretty lame, as you would say. But I want you to know, Olivia, you're welcome here anytime." She passed through the front door while he stood in the doorway staring at Bubba's house next door. She really did appreciate his offer for her to come by anytime. But he wouldn't be able to save her from Brian or change the fact that she now had no friends, and everyone thought she was a cheater.

+++

"I'm sorry John can't be here," Perry said closing his door to the sounds of Friday's school day beginning.

"He sends his regrets about not being able to change his meetings. But he is available by phone," Donna said, taking the seat the principal offered.

Olivia eyed the velvet backs of photos arrayed across the principal's desk and wondered if Hairy Perry's kids were as lame.

"These are serious allegations," Perry said.

"Yes, they are. Mr. Perry, my daughter doesn't cheat," Donna said.

"Well, it comes down to the student's word against yours, Olivia. If I find that the student's allegations are true, you'll be expelled. You will also have to return your contest award and prize money."

"I know it's Brian and he's lying. He's been at me ever since I got back from being suspended."

"Olivia's right. She found these posted all along Boise Avenue yesterday." Donna brought out a flyer. "This is harassment."

Perry scrutinized the crumpled paper for a moment before handing it back. "That's more mischief than anything. You blame Brian, but you have no proof. Even so, this is a matter for the police. Do you really want to go down that road?"

"I don't want to be known as a cheater!" Olivia stood, her thighs bumping the edge of Perry's desk. She could feel her mom tug on the back of her shirt, pulling her back down.

"Mr. Perry, my daughter doesn't cheat."

"You must admit the allegation about Tuesday's math quiz is plausible. After all, Olivia had been suspended the previous week. A 100% is suspicious, especially seeing the concerned student also did as well."

"Well duh, I had nothing to do all day except study." Donna scowled at her. "I sit next to Brian, so we all know he's the one saying this."

"Good. Studying is what you were supposed to do. As for the other, our policy is to protect the anonymity of students, so they can feel free to bring this kind of thing to our attention without repercussions."

"What about repercussions to me?" Olivia shoved back her chair and stood. "He's being a bully, just like before."

"It'll die down, especially when we underreact. As for the student who brought this to my attention, he made an honest mistake." Perry smiled. "I think we're done. You may go to your math class, Olivia. I'll give you a pass."

Mr. Erstedt took the slip, sniffed, and pointed to an empty desk toward the middle of the room. "That will be your place from now on, Olivia. Now where was I?" He pulled on the end of his nose and returned to the blackboard.

The next period was no better. Just before lunch, the computer club president approached her. "Hey," he addressed Olivia's chest. "We think you should give back the trophy, so it can go to Brian. He should have won."

"Yeah, right. As a matter of fact, I saw Brian cheating, but I didn't tell on him cuz I won fair and square. He's making this up to make me look bad. So go to hell." Olivia spun and stomped toward the cafeteria.

The Becca table was quiet as Olivia took her usual place.

Brian started, "Ruff, ruff, Olivia. Anyone see the lost dog?"

She kept her head down, wondered if her mom had made a special lunch for her. She could sure use it. She began to pour from her thermos, which disgorged tomato soup, a dog turd splashing into the lid.

Brian standing, head craned to see her reaction, whooped with delight in the midst of booing from the Becca table. The jeering continued, and as Olivia twisted her body toward the noise, she caught Becca's eye, whose anger-flooded face softened.

Olivia grabbed her thermos and rose. In those seconds as she moved toward her nemesis, she pictured herself and her parents in Hairy Perry's office, knew what would happen. That after all the talk, nothing would change.

"You asshole!" she yelled, dousing him with its contents, then turned and walked over to Becca's table. "Got any space for me?"

CHAPTER 10
SEED STARTING
VEGETABLES

That Monday morning while Patricia campaigned and Olivia returned to school, Gordon made his way to the employee lounge for the first mandatory staff meeting in the short history of Hunter's U Do It management. He had just settled into a seat when his boss strode in, followed by Clerise. The manager halted in front of the vending machines and turned on his heel to face the group.

"This is the beginning of a new era at U Do It. We are going to rock this town. As a flagship store, we're special to corporate. We're implementing policies that will become the gold standard across the nation. We will make it happen."

Staff stared at Hunter. A chair screeched. Crackles of ripping cellophane surfaced from various parts of the employee lounge.

"Gordon, what do you think it means being a flagship? After all, you're the granddaddy of the hardware business."

"Well, seeing this is a first for corporate, I'm sure we'll be surprised," Gordon said. *Just another new manager asserting his dominance by choosing me.*

"Well, yes and no. Because the people who are going to be surprised are our customers. We're going to shake things up here. In the end, we'll be the envy of the hardware industry. How does that sound?"

Faces remained blank, heads bowed, staring at the table, at the floor, at some mid-distance. Finally, "It sounds like more work for us. What do we get out of it?" came from the back of the room.

"Glad you asked," Hunter nodded at the speaker. "You get to work as a team, being the best. Giving the competition hell. But we can handle it."

"Sir, in the spirit of giving the competition hell, the store opens in ten minutes and I still have my section to review." The woman speaking stubbed out her cigarette.

"Just hold on. You'll be out of here in time. I have a couple more things to cover. First, department managers, we're going to start meeting on a weekly basis. I've noticed we can tighten things up around here. Second, we've lined up some new vendors who will provide us with better quality merchandise at a better rate. The vendors'll be coming on board this week. Questions?" Hunter paused. "Okay, we're done."

+++

When his beeper buzzed on Tuesday morning, Gordon was pulling warped trim from a new shipment. Perplexed at what was so urgent, he made his way to Hunter's office. The man, concentrating on some printouts, gestured for him to have a seat and ignored him. Scanning the walls for clues to his new boss's character, he noted pictures of Charlie Hunter shaking hands or standing in a semicircle, commemorated for some accomplishment. Hunter continued to ignore him, so Gordon grabbed the opportunity to mention the lumber. "The shipment of trim from the new vendor is substandard."

"Then send it back." Hunter's gaze remained on the printouts. "I've been reviewing some data on work patterns. Help me out, Gordo."

Gordon's shoulder muscles spasmed. "I'll do what I can."

"You're department manager for lumber, right?" He closed the printouts.

Gordon nodded.

"Yet you teach all these classes. Good work by the way."

"Thank you."

"Why is that?"

"That I do a good job of teaching the classes?" Gordon decided to play with the man a bit while trying to get a better read on him.

"No." Hunter's tone was patient. "Why does the department manager for lumber teach all these classes?" He opened another printout. "Your area is lumber, and I see by the schedule you do at least one class each week." His finger stabbed the paper as he read, "'Wallpapering for Beginners,' 'Window Installation Made Easy.' Then there's this series, 'Renovating the Dream Victorian.' That one goes for eight weeks. So why is that?"

"Well, to cover all the topics to renovate a Victorian takes eight weeks."

"No, Gordon." He talked slowly, enunciating. "Why is it you teach all these classes that have nothing to do with your department?"

"Because I'm good with customers and I can teach. I know the subject matter, and it helps sales."

"Let's say that's true. Except you're the lumber department manager. That's the biggest area in the store, you have the most employees reporting to you, and yet you have all this time on your hands."

"It's never been an issue. My numbers are good. Staff is well supervised. I enjoy teaching the classes. Also previous management liked it."

Hunter's jaw muscles rippled. "That may well be, but as I said yesterday morning, I'm going to make some changes. When I saw all these classes, I decided to take a look at your area." He pulled open another spreadsheet. "Yes, your numbers are good, but I think they could be better. I appreciate that you are good at teaching; however, a man your age starts to slow down. For now, I'll let you continue as the department manager, but I'm watching you."

Gordon considered. What was Mr. Fix-It saying? That he was too old? That he shouldn't teach? That he was a bad manager? As he mulled this, Hunter broke in. "Fine then. We'll chat again soon."

Gordon left the second floor feeling as if Hunter had swung at him with a two-by-four.

+++

Wednesday found Clerise shaking her head at the continued mix-up with Gordon's paycheck. She was an exotic splash of color in the beautiful head wraps and caftans she sewed from African fabric. Elaborate gold earrings rimmed her ears, jiggling as she passed him the paycheck. She shivered. "I thought the old payroll system was bad."

"Now what? I can't just cash it. Fixing that will be even harder."

"I know. Mine's off too." Clerise's earrings glinted in the pale light.

"I just hope my house insurance payment won't bounce. Guess all I can do right now is get back to the floor to teach my class." He took the paycheck error form she handed him and descended the stairs.

Today was "Seed Starting Vegetables." He had enlisted a couple of the customers to help assemble the seed starter frame, and they were busy attaching the lights when Gordon spotted Charlie Hunter leaning against a stack of potting soil bags with a new employee by his side.

"Gordo, I've been doing some research and thinking," Charlie began, the last of the class participants leaving with an armful of gardening books. "You know, you are good at these classes."

Gordon's anxiety from the day before dissipated a bit. Maybe Hunter was going to be okay after all.

"But then, I noticed that your class customers are old like you. That's a problem when we're trying to target a younger market. I still think you could do better in lumber sales. Except you are so damn good at the classes." Hunter's smile streaked across his face as if drawn by a builder's pencil.

Of course, he was good at them. The Carlsons had made it their business to be good at helping people.

"However, I think you are starting to slow down, which explains the slow growth in sales."

"Did you consider that building starts have slumped? Any growth is impressive," Gordon stated flatly, reasonably, keeping his anger in check.

"Yes, Gordon, I did. I also know you're a pro. Of anyone, you have the ability to increase sales. I think you're being distracted by these classes."

"The classes offer me a chance to do cross marketing."

"Well, here's the deal. I think you have talent. I want you to train one of the younger guys. That way when he takes over, you'll have more time to concentrate on your department."

Gordon glared at him.

"You can continue to teach the deck-building class and any that'll help you sell lumber."

Mr. Fix-It glided off with the new guy in tow. Speaking over his shoulder, he added, "In fact, I'd like you to train Rick here. He has great potential, perhaps even to teach the renovating class."

+++

Is there a song about Thursday? Gordon wondered. *If so, was it upbeat or depressing?* He remembered a ditty from when he was a boy. "Monday's child is fair of face. / Tuesday's child is full of grace. / Wednesday's child is full of woe. / Thursday's child has far to go." How far did he have to go to get through the day? How far did he have to go to get to retirement?

That morning, Gordon waited on the loading dock, the truck's steady beep signaling the plywood shipment had finally arrived. The smell of wood wafted toward him as the forklift hoisted the flat and moved it toward the warehouse floor. He nodded, splitting his concentration between the clipboard's packing slip and the sheets of wood.

"Yo, Gordo. Wait," Hunter bellowed, fastening the chinstrap on his hard hat. "Hey, you're my main man."

"Our shipment's shorted," Gordon yelled, and pointed at the paperwork on his clipboard.

"Yeah, I know." Charlie gesticulated waving his arms. "Catch up with me when you're done."

As he arrived at Hunter's office, Clerise's eyebrows arched and she dipped her head.

"How's that boy of yours?" Gordon took the schedule from her.

She shook her head. "Don't know what I'm going to do with Michael. Maybe it's his age. I heard that when they hit eight or nine, they start to change."

Gordon's shrug said he guessed so. He scanned the sheet and could see why the high eyebrows from Clerise. The staff schedule he'd submitted had been changed. Significantly. "What is this?"

Gordon perched on the folding chair outside Hunter's office until Hunter breezed in.

"With all due respect, this is getting out of hand. My paycheck is usually off, I have to send it back for revision more times than not, and now this." Gordon followed him into his office and placed the schedule on his boss's desk.

"I can't have my best manager treated like this." Charlie frowned.

"Okay." He had expected some kind of Gordo routine.

"I'll make a few calls. This won't happen again. By the way, I reconsidered. I have something much more important for you. It involves all your experience and expertise."

"Okay. Shoot." Gordon met Charlie's eyes and waited for him to break contact.

"Well, here's the thing, my man," Hunter maintained his gaze. "I need someone with your ability and dedication to top quality and customer service. I did not ignore you when you mentioned the poor lumber from our new supplier. Corporate's concerned. I told them I knew just the man to help us out. Gordon Carlson."

"And?" Gordon stared at Charlie's glacier blue eyes.

"If we can keep our inventory to just what we need when we need it, we can offer more choices to our customers. More samples on the floor, more in stock. The success of our flagship depends on suppliers we can trust. That's where you come in. Quality control. Doesn't that describe you?"

"Yes, I do believe in good quality, but …."

"See, you're just the man. I want you to start quality control inspections for the whole warehouse."

"I'll think about it." He narrowed his eyes, waited.

"You have to. Corporate expects you to. And if you fail corporate, why … well, you get the picture." Hunter laughed, patted Gordon's shoulder. "Have Clerise set up a meeting. We'll talk about your new duties tomorrow. Later." Charlie waited a beat then flashed a knife-edged smile. "Gordo."

+++

At seven o'clock on Friday evening, Gordon pulled his station wagon against the curb in front of the Forester museum, feeling the need to focus on something other than his saw-toothed interactions with Hunter.

A battered pair of slippers resided by the inner door, and he felt more relaxed than all week as he shoved his feet into their frayed linings. He shuffled toward the kitchen to put a tea kettle on. While he waited for its whistle, he scanned the day's newspaper. The front page contained an extensive article about the rapes that had been taking place in Forester and the neighboring communities for over a year. Another incident had occurred. Police urged extra caution. *As if Olivia didn't have enough to worry about.*

The tea made, he tucked the newspaper under his arm to join its companions waiting for cataloguing on the third floor. At times, he felt overwhelmed, all that information with more added every day. If only history would just stop so he could catch up.

Now as he sat in the ballroom sipping his tea, a wisp, as light as a spider web in a breeze, curled around a wall sconce and disappeared.

Olivia's trials with trying to fit in had gotten him thinking. The Carlsons being a founding family, he'd always assumed he was part of Forester. The family belonged, but did he belong? In an uncomfortable recollection, the Native Guide tribal chief's comment that he didn't even know Maude had a son, came to mind, accompanied by a feeling of desolation. He'd become a ghost in his own community.

CHAPTER 11
SEPARATE HOUSES

Wrapped in the yellow light from a brass lamp, Gordon sat by the fireplace in his mother's old rocker. He adjusted his sweater, considering whether to light the crumpled newspaper supporting the wood.

He wished desperately he could retire. For a moment he imagined waking in the morning with nothing more important than his garden, repairs around the house, or volunteering at the museum. Bills, health, car and home insurance, food, heat. That's why he couldn't retire.

His dependence on U Do It was corrosive. For all those years after the family hardware store was gone, he was able to shrug off his job, collect his paycheck, and live a comfortable if Spartan life. Since Hunter's arrival, the months until retirement had stretched into strenuous sprints instead of short hops.

Gordon's new title was "quality control officer." What he had found was inventory coming in shorted or so flawed as to be useless. Mr. Fix-It summoned him on every whim. If his boss was in one of his moods, it could be several times a day. When he reported back, Hunter said, "Right on, Gordo." Hunter could disappear behind his sharp grin and eyes, making everything else about what he was up to just sawdust. Gordon couldn't quite put a finger on it, but something strange was going on. He monitored the shipments of inventory, but the number of vendor changes in so many departments was mind-boggling. And Hunter added more each day.

Increasingly, Clerise's gaze would drop and slide toward Charlie's door. She was careful about what she said, how she said it. But her face said a lot. Sometimes Clerise's expression said, "The man is a nut case." Sometimes, "I'd trust someone in league with the white supremacists more than this guy."

After a month, Gordon knew something was terribly wrong. Clerise's eyes said, "It took you this long to figure it out?"

Now in his rocker, Gordon turned back to the reports on his lap, a stack of computer printouts Clerise had given him. He didn't have authorization for these documents. Neither did she. Her eyes were wide, and her mouth pinched as she handed them to him. Both knew the consequences if they were caught.

The chill oozed from the hearth, invading the dark living room. Throughout the evening, he had added water to the teapot, the peppermint flavor now as distant as the day he had harvested the herb from his garden. He took a sip from the mug and flipped the pages back and forth, comparing columns of figures, amounts, departments, and dates with the incomprehensible number of vendors. Inventory was being sent back as spoiled. Lots of it. But with all the nuts, bolts, lumber, plumbing parts, and every other thing, managers expected a certain amount to be substandard or damaged. Except something kept grating his brain. That morning Charlie had arrived on the loading dock, he knew the inventory was short before Gordon did.

+++

"Lez be friends," Brian would whisper out of the corner of his mouth or elbow Olivia in the school hallway or say in class just loud enough for others to hear too. He'd taken to calling her lesbo.

Maybe she was. Except she'd never felt that way about Ashley. Becca fascinated her; she wasn't afraid of anything. She flicked detention off like no big deal. And suspension? Becca knew exactly what she could get away with and how far to push.

Olivia wanted to be like that too. She was tired of being lame. For her whole life, she had believed you had to follow rules and laws. If you broke them, you got some kind of punishment, whether time-out, being grounded, losing privileges, detention, suspension, expulsion, jail.

One of the rules was who she was supposed to be: a fat, smart geek who was always good. And everyone except Becca persisted in this image of her. She said Olivia was a wuss for being afraid of suspension or—even worse—expulsion.

Come to think of it, suspension was just being grounded. Being grounded was just like a time-out. After all, Olivia's parents had said they needed a little time-out as a way of explaining their separation and subsequent divorce. She figured being expelled was nothing more than getting a divorce from school.

Becca was someone who knew what crap it all was. Her friend's anger had broken down the bullshit rules. And the result was the best part, elbowing through the crowded hallways with Becca, the losers parting to let them through.

Just that Becca sometimes made her flinch. Once in a while, her face would turn so angry. Then she would do something outrageous. Later, she would say she was sorry, that she didn't mean it, that she had been in a bad mood and that her old lady was acting up again. Olivia was learning how to be around her because Becca really did care.

She was thinking about that as she watched her transformation. She sat in the upstairs bathroom with a towel draped around her shoulders, Becca studying her, occasionally lifting a lock of hair, and scrutinizing it. A bottle of hair dye the color of midnight rested in her hands, the tip poised. The touch of Becca's hand sent a tingle to Olivia's toes.

The Olivia in the mirror stared back at her. The kohl made her eyes jump out against her pale skin, giving them a mesmerizing quality. The effect catapulted her away from nerd status, and all she had to do now was regard someone with eyes that said, "Don't mess with me."

"Mom's gonna shit bricks," she said to Becca's reflection.

"So?" Her friend tipped the nozzle down, depositing cold, blue-black islands on her scalp. Olivia closed her eyes and took a deep breath, her shoulders relaxing.

"Okay, now we wait." Becca covered Olivia's head with a plastic bag then opened a window, leaving a smudge of black on the lever. She threw the gloves in the sink and fished out cigs and a lighter from her backpack. "Want one?"

The girl in the mirror was bold. "Sure."

Actually, smoking wasn't as bad as she'd heard. She coughed and felt dizzy. Becca howled, but what's that compared to telling Becca she didn't want to get cancer? Besides, she'd rather do this here than try it out in front of all her new friends. She'd really get laughed at. But she knew that when their laughter died, they'd let her know she was okay. That she was okay. That she belonged.

Becca stood by the window, taking big drags and exhaling, staring through the tree branches, now fully leafed out. She flicked the ash where it landed like a bird dropping on the sill. "Brian lives over there?"

"Yeah, little shit." Olivia craned her neck to see the top two stories of the Wrenowskis' house.

"Ever thought of getting back at him?"

Olivia heaved herself up and edged toward the window. "I tried. Didn't work."

"You weren't brutal enough." They watched Brian and his dad get out of the car.

"It's got to be something he'll never forget." Becca flicked her cigarette butt onto the lawn below, Olivia's following. The timer rang. "Come on, let's rinse this stuff off."

As the two girls left the bathroom, Olivia noticed the spatters of black on the wallpaper. "Mom's gonna shit."

"Why you keep bringing that up? Big fucking deal."

The fridge door's opening and closing could be heard as the girls clattered into the kitchen.

"Hi, Mrs. D," Becca said, flashing her magic smile.

"Awesome, isn't it, Mom?" Olivia examined a strand.

"Well, it's different." Her mother's jaw muscle twitched. "Becca, I'm sure your mother must be wondering where you are. Do you want to use the phone and let her know you're on your way?"

"Thanks anyway, Mrs. D. I live with my aunt. She won't care. See you tomorrow, Olivia." Becca slung her backpack over her shoulder, Olivia wishing they were still upstairs, that Becca would stay, that she wouldn't have to deal with what was coming after her new friend left.

Donna stood with her arms folded in an obvious struggle to keep her face neutral. "I think we have a difference in our definition of minimal," she finally said.

"That is so lame. You never let me do anything. It's my hair."

"And this is my house. I have rules in this house."

"This has nothing to do with your house."

"This has everything to do with it. You agreed that if I let you wear makeup, you would keep it minimal. Then you started wearing all that black eyeliner—"

"Kohl."

"Okay, kohl. But this is beyond what we agreed to."

"It's my hair."

"We had an agreement."

"It's my hair. What's the big deal?"

"The deal is that it could look better. Have you seen how patchy the color is?"

"Yeah. It's supposed to look like this," Olivia again felt her own disappointment at the finished product. "You never let me do anything. No wonder I'm such a loser."

Her mother's body deflated. "This is going nowhere. Let's get dinner started."

Later that evening, Donna called from the bathroom, "Olivia, you've left an absolute mess in here. And you ruined my wallpaper."

"You're just trying to find something to ground me for. It doesn't even show."

"The walls look like someone threw permanent ink in here. Do you know how much time I spent wallpapering this bathroom?" she asked, pointing to a smudge. "This will never come off. Here. Or here. Or here." She roamed the small space, spots and drips reproducing with each gesture she made. She pointed at the porcelain sink, tarry with residue and containing Becca's tossed gloves. She opened the shower curtain surrounding the bathtub, where drizzles of black water like acid rain stained the vinyl liner.

Donna stopped the inspection, massaged the side of her cheek. "If I ground you, that's not going to do anything except make life miserable for me, and you won't learn anything."

Oh, God, here it comes. All that parenting crap, Olivia thought.

"If I got back at you and trashed something you liked, what message would you get?"

Olivia scowled as her mom put the lid down on the toilet seat and sat. *She's waiting me out. Well, I can be just as silent.* She leaned against the wall and slid to the floor. *God, I hate this.* The nine o'clock train sounded in passing. A rim of orange sky from the streetlamps sluiced across the window. Her butt bones began to complain as the cold linoleum seeped through her pajama bottoms. "I still have some homework to do," Olivia mumbled.

"You haven't answered my question. Do you think it would do any good if I threw ink on something of yours?"

"It's not ink."

"That's not the point. Do you?"

"No."

"Okay then. That's not going to solve the problem. If I ground you, do you think it will change things?"

"Okay, Mom. What will solve the problem?" *God, would she just get to the point?*

"I think you should help repair the bathroom. We'll have to remove the ruined pieces of wallpaper. I've got half a roll left from the project." She sighed.

Olivia rose, her butt flat, cold, and numb, leaving her mother still sitting on the toilet seat.

+++

Olivia's job was to call Becca as soon as the Wrenowskis' house was vacated, a task made harder now that she no longer hung out with Brian or Ashley. She knew Brian played baseball, and the Wrenowskis usually went someplace after, so he'd be gone Saturday evening.

She and Becca hid against Wrenowskis' garage, coddling cartons of eggs. As the first one hit, the crack of shell against clapboard sounded like exploding firecrackers. Becca's aim was deadly as she methodically coated the windows in shattered shells and drippy yolks. She would've been awesome on the girls' softball team. Olivia's first throw landed on the back door. The sight of it hitting, knowing Brian would be the one cleaning it up, was thrilling. By the time they threw the last of the eggs, she was lobbing them onto the peaked roof, where they would bake in the sun. The girls crawled over the neighbor's fence and darted across back yards until they reached the adjoining street.

In the interlude between daylight and night when the streetlamps were still dim, the girls danced and whooped. As their jubilation subsided, Becca smiled. "See what I mean?" A stream of cigarette smoke shot out of her mouth. "Feels pretty good." They leaned against the lamppost as the shadows sharpened.

What felt even better was standing in her foyer later that night as Patricia related that someone had thrown eggs at their house. In the tense moments following her pleasantly phrased accusation, Ray stood mutely, Donna stared back, mouth so firmly closed as to disappear. John, irritated at having to drive from the Loop for something so trivial, was insulted by the insinuation. The topic changed to his upcoming departure as village president.

+++

Thus, Olivia started her summer vacation early. She tossed notes from her teachers along with failing papers in the restroom wastebasket. She made a point of unnerving her classmates with her patchy black hair, kohl-rimmed eyes, and lipstick. A black smudge in her seat, she picked at her nails and never raised her hand, enjoying the teachers' raised eyebrows as she shrugged when called on. By late May, her grades were tanking.

Her biggest pleasure was Brian's pathetic hand-waving, realizing the snorts, rustling papers, and scraping chairs had also occurred when she was as lame. How odd that she had never tuned in to the constant white noise of bored students. Now, when Brian or any of the others happened to meet her glance, she made an *L* on her forehead with her thumb and forefinger. They would point at her, making the same sign, the dumb shits, and mouth lesbo.

As the weather became warmer and more humid, she monitored the Wrenowskis' front lawn. She and Becca had spent an evening hammering frozen hotdogs into the soil so that within a few days, a stench began to bloom. By midweek, Brian and Ray had to dig out the disintegrating meat and then lay new sod.

Final papers came due. Exams loomed a short week away, whereupon Olivia found herself in Hairy Perry's office again, this time both parents positioned like bookends in the uncomfortable chairs.

Perry pulled out her grades and examples of her tests, supported by records of her missing homework. Then, on cue, the school counselor,

Tony Mahoney, concerned about what was going on, came in to talk about consequences and options.

Both the principal and the counselor said she would have a chance to remain in the advanced classes the following year if she would study hard, make up the homework, and bring up her grades. As the bookends left the office, Olivia in tow, the counselor pointed out that Olivia thrived on association with the brightest, with students like Brian Wrenowski and Ashley Sidell. Hearing that, Olivia made a decision.

CHAPTER 12
BETWEEN THE LINES

Gordo, my man. Have a seat. I want to run something by you. What do you say we start another department?" Gordon arranged his mouth so that his expression was impassive. "I'm going to enhance the home décor aspect. We'll carry lines of decorator fabric and an interior decorator service. I'd like someone to run it who's more inclined to that. You don't know anyone who's inclined that way, do you?"

"What way?"

"Why, the gay way. We need to get them in here. I hear they drop a butt load."

"Can't help you there." *Was he hearing this?*

"Do you think Ted's that way? I've seen the way he walks and checks dudes out."

"It's not something I ask about."

"Could you find out? You know, go in the can when he does and see if he's checking."

"Charlie, I—"

"Okay, Gordon, you're right. We need to be more discreet about this. How about Clerise? I think she'd be great. But then again, she doesn't represent the target segment here. You've been around this town so long, whatcha think?"

"Charlie, I can't—"

"You know if we get the interior dec crowd, we could start offering a line of furniture."

"We might as well sell toys," Gordon said.

"Toys?" An eyebrow shot up. "Not sure where you're going with this, old man. Are you thinking Christmas, in with the Christmas decorations?"

"I was being facetious."

"Gordo, you old buzzard. Of course. Winter stuff, like snowmobiles. We'll call it Winter Wonderland. In fact, you're going to be in charge."

"Charlie, uh, this is making me very uncomfortable."

"Uncomfortable? Well, good. We can't get too complacent. You snooze, you lose. So, go to it, man. Be uncomfortable. That's where change happens."

"No, Charlie. That's not what I meant. I'm uncomfortable with your references to people. It's belittling."

"Belittling? Belittling! Are you crazy? I'm offering great opportunities. Clerise is going nowhere where she is now. She'll just type her buns off. And at the end of the day, I'm the one person who'll know what a gem she is."

"Charlie, I don't like the idea of you stereotyping people."

"Gordy, I am deeply offended. I am really deeply offended. I thought you knew me better. I've accorded you great respect because of your age and wisdom, and you tell me you think I stereotype people."

"Charlie, that's what it is."

"They're not stereotypes. They're representative of their market. What they do benefits them and benefits us. Clerise has potential. Despite being a single mom, she can make connections, get herself out there. In the process, she'll bring in customers we haven't had before."

"Charlie, I will pretend we didn't have this conversation. We obviously do not agree. I need to get back to the floor. And don't bring this kind of topic up again." He shoved the chair back and left without closing the door.

For Gordon, his own boldness took him by surprise. But so did Hunter's in this day of political correctness. Perhaps his boss was just an idiot who lacked the skills to hide what so many hid between the lines. As he passed Clerise, they both glanced toward the open office door.

From beyond, just barely audible, they heard, "He crosses me, he doesn't know what he's dealing with."

+++

Gordon tugged apart the museum ballroom's gold brocade curtains. A blazing shock of late spring sunlight toppled through the dust and onto the oak floor. He contemplated the view and how satisfied Jean-Luis Forestier would have felt surveying his creation. Below him, stretching toward the horizon were the roofs of houses like children's heads.

Despite its size, the room felt intimate, perhaps because he spent so much time there. In a corner, rickety wooden file cabinets created his cataloguing project space, an anomaly against the elegant tones of the ballroom.

The chair creaked as he shifted his weight. He scooted toward stacked boxes of Forestier memorabilia, documents from other notable families and events, as well as from village board meetings throughout the years. Indexing and arranging the contents into a logical order was, in many respects, like running a hardware store. Lots of bits and pieces that needed to be accessible and to make sense. Gordon nodded at what an impressive collection the museum would have once he arranged and organized it.

He removed the lid to a box containing a diary belonging to Charlotte Forestier, whom most people knew as Grand Lotty. A well-known public presence, and not a woman to be contradicted, her life had been decisive and big. Gordon put on a pair of white gloves to protect the pages and opened her diary to a new entry:

Tuesday, 22 April 1930

I quite fail to understand this custom of dropping in on people. I much preferred it when one had hours that one kept for receiving visitors. Nevertheless, M. rang the other day and asked if she might visit in the late afternoon. I was more than a little perplexed. She does not visit on her own, usually coming for luncheon on Valentine's Day.

In any event, she arrived promptly at 4:00. I noticed the change in her immediately. She wears her hair in the style that is quite the rage these days, which is actually becoming on her. It is disgusting when ladies dress beyond their age. I was pleased to see she has not taken to painting her face. She'd look like a harlot.

M. now wears spectacles, which I believe does not have the negative connotation it once did. We chatted for a few minutes. She remembers her manners well, despite that godforsaken family. The ability to carry on a decent conversation gets no exercise in R.'s household. The family seems to be coping, although that horrible son-in-law is the same, regretfully.

When we were on the subject of family, I noticed a change in her expression. M's mouth grew pinched. She had a kind of wariness in her responses, taking a moment too long to weigh what she would say, how she would say it. I have always loved her dearly, and I sensed something terrible is happening.

She was nervous and made small talk. This circling the subject is not like her. Finally, she asked if she might have a loan. At first, I didn't hear her as she was speaking into her hands. So that's why the creeping around! I had been down this road before. Inevitably it had to do with a debt R. had acquired. It enrages me to think that skunk would send her over. When I didn't say anything, she rushed on. She couldn't stay there any longer. R. was getting worse, especially at night, when all were supposed to be asleep. She appealed to me to please help her get away. This is not someone who is used to begging. For that character trait alone, I would give her the money.

I replied I needed time to consider. I asked her to call again on Thursday. She agreed, but I could tell she was crestfallen. I suspect it took a considerable amount of courage to come.

Thursday, 24 April 1930

M. was punctual today. I came to the point immediately. I said I could give her a small loan. My biggest concern is R. could get a hold of it. The condition is that I will not give her the money right out. I will therefore make the arrangements on her behalf.

I do worry about her. Who could have predicted the damage R. has done? I could never be as hard and unyielding as J., may the dear Lord look after him.

Gordon opened the word processing program on the museum's newly purchased computer to make entries for Charlotte Forestier, Jean-Luis Forestier, their daughter, Minette, and Rupert Sipe. Very little existed about Minette. Perhaps more would turn up in the other boxes. Information on Rupert came mostly from police reports referring to his illegal still.

Gordon pondered the way meaning was conveyed in these old letters, what the terrible thing was that Grand Lotty feared. Most likely, Minette was being beaten or perhaps raped, although back then wives weren't considered to be assaulted by their husbands. Even in private, people did not come right out and say what was going on, harboring it in reference. What was not said was a language of its own. In many respects, Charlotte's diary was a Rosetta Stone. The difference was having to translate the space between the lines, rather than the characters.

He thought of his recent meeting with Hunter and the man's astounding disregard for individual differences. Why this sudden expansion of departments and his absurd decision to add winter rec-reational equipment to their inventory? Or the eye language Gordon had with Clerise, a Morse code of blinks and nods? Or decoding the U Do It spreadsheets? Gordon remembered the old adage about not airing one's dirty laundry in public. Something was certainly being laundered at U Do It.

CHAPTER 13
DEAD VIOLET

And so Forester Days arrived. Each June, the Forester community honored its founder, Jean-Luis Forestier, with a big parade followed by block parties, a tradition going back to the days when Jean-Luis presided. This year, Gordon would host the open house at the museum while Olivia perched on a convertible's backseat and Patricia in her own convertible made her debut as a village councilwoman.

In the early morning, Gordon opened his great-grandfather's trunk to retrieve a pair of trousers. Stooped as he was, he was still a good six feet tall, his legs clearing the bottom of the britches to reveal his ankles and feet encased in a tangle of blue veins.

He paused on his porch to take a quick puff from his inhaler, pollen being a problem at this time of year. The air would be heavy before the parade completed its route. He strolled toward the museum through the tepid morning, passing neighbors swaddling their homes in bunting. Gordon soon crossed the museum's veranda, inserted the key into the ornate brass lock, and entered. The slight thumping of a marching band seeped through the walls while he settled himself at a card table in the foyer—pamphlets at the ready—and opened the newspaper. The front page carried a story about the new village council and John Dimato stepping down. He was just wondering how

Olivia was doing when the front door opened, admitting a sudden blast of music. A young man approached, head tilted back to gaze at the magnificent chandelier. Gordon raised his eyes hoping to give a tour. But the fellow was lost and wanted to use the bathroom.

Visitor departed, Gordon glanced toward the parlor. Beyond the rippled old glass windows, a muted whoop went up. *Must be the village president with his family.*

At noon, the brass key clicked to lock the door, and Gordon headed home to the block barbeque, content that so far the day had gone smoothly.

+ + +

Meanwhile, as a newly elected village council member, Patricia roosted on top of the backseat of a convertible, its sides carrying a sign from her campaign slogan, "I'm here for your past, present, and future. Count on me."

The Forester High School drums syncopated in a holding pattern, the bandleader's whistle picked up the beat to signal the band's rendition of the school fight song while the drill team began to spin its flags like blue and gold whirligigs. With tubas, horns, and saxophones swinging, they marched forward.

As a high school student on the drill team, Patricia had envied the beautiful girls in their frothy gowns and tiaras, gliding on some float or convertible, while she mopped sweat from her eyes trying to remain in formation. Focusing on the routine had kept her from enjoying the cheers and attention as they marched. By the last part of the two-mile route, her flag drooped dejectedly as she limply maneuvered it through intricate circles and dips.

Her sixteen- or seventeen-year-old self would have given anything to be riding atop a convertible, cruising along the streets, families watching from lawn chairs on the parkway. Vendors strolled along the curbs selling top hats, bonnets, and raccoon caps. Other vendors sold sodas and over-priced snacks.

She waved, calling to people she knew, imagining herself as village president someday, Ray and Brian at her side.

But she was also scanning the crowd. For whom, she hadn't a clue. Whoever was vandalizing her home must be a kid, given the nature of the pranks. But this was getting to be more than pranks. The eggs maybe, but the hotdogs in the lawn and now bleach on the new sod. She'd spent the early morning maneuvering picnic tables to try and cover the scorched grass where someone had written "Fucker." The whole front lawn would have to be replaced. Again.

When she'd mentioned her suspicions about Olivia, asking if Brian had done anything to antagonize her, he became angry and accused her of blaming him for everything. He wasn't the only one who had enemies. What about one of the people she beat in the village council election? What about that old lady from the museum board she was always complaining about? What about an irate customer? At that point, Ray walked into the kitchen, whereupon Brian suggested that maybe someone, maybe a pissed-off computer nerd, was mad at his dad. The conversation became so ludicrous, Patricia dropped it. But when she climbed the village hall steps to be sworn into office and saw Olivia standing next to Donna and John, who were pretending nothing was out of the ordinary, she wondered if she'd been right.

+++

Earlier that morning, Olivia had stood in the doorway to the master bedroom. "I told you last year I wasn't going to do this. You said all right, but now you're making me do it anyway."

"That's not what I said. I said we'd see how things turned out." Her mom adjusted her heavy gabardine skirt.

"You didn't. You said I didn't have to be in the parade anymore."

"You must've misunderstood, Olivia. After the barbeque, you can spend the rest of the afternoon in your room, seeing you don't want to participate."

"I won't be ready in time," Olivia said following her mom to the foyer. Her dad would make this year even worse with another of his stupid speeches.

"Go put on your white shirt and that black skirt. You can meet us at the docking site," Donna called and pulled the front door shut.

As usual, the morning would start with a parade through the streets, the village council members riding in convertibles, the president and his family costumed like founding family members. Floats from various clubs and businesses would punctuate the event, along with bands and drill teams from surrounding schools.

By the time Olivia plodded to the car at the docking site, everyone was waiting to join the parade. Her dad represented the elderly Jean-Luis, her mom was an elderly Grand Lotty, the new president was costumed as a younger Jean-Luis, his wife a young Charlotte. Their son was Jean-Louis in his youth, and the small daughter dressed as Minette.

Olivia eyed her parents for a reaction to the black kohl and lipstick, but the only emotion was the telltale twitch at her mom's jaw, her dad's expression hard to read beneath the latex beard on his chin.

The new president raised an eyebrow to his wife. The kids asked, "Daddy, who is she supposed to be?"

"Violet," Olivia answered.

"But Violet didn't look like that." Both children cocked their heads, shifting their feet.

"How do you know how she looked? I'm dead Violet."

Olivia found herself wedged in the back seat, out of sight and between her parents, who perched on the top of the seat, the new president and his family seated in the convertible behind.

The car made snail progress, ducking in and out of shadows, John's face beginning to drip, Donna fanning herself with a shopping list. Finally, the convertibles pulled before the village hall, where the old Forestiers, the young Forestiers, and dead Violet spaced themselves across the front stoop, the village council members pretending not to notice Olivia as were her parents, while the children stared.

Her dad began his speech, substantially shortened since his practice run in the kitchen earlier that morning. Despite the awning, the heat crept across the landing and bounced off the front windows. John's beard began to slide, Donna barely managed to keep her old lady makeup from melting, and Olivia's kohl merged with her lipstick.

The new village president raised his hand to be sworn in, heavy ellipses of sweat under the arms of his gabardine suit. Then moments later, Olivia tore down the steps and across the parking lot toward home.

Several minutes later, her father stood before her on the veranda. "That was extremely rude just now, Ollie. I don't know what's come over you with this get-up you have on. You embarrassed me and your mother."

"We made it clear what was expected of you this morning. Can you tell me why you ruined this last ceremony for your father?" her mom asked.

"Dunno."

"As I said, you can spend the rest of the afternoon in your room after the picnic. Now go change your clothes," her mom concluded.

+++

At one o'clock, Gordon descended the front steps of his house, bearing his usual contribution to the barbeque: a salad and homemade dandelion wine.

In the years when Maude had hosted the picnic on their front lawn, the bowl was in the center of an aluminum picnic table covered with vinyl tablecloths, spotted from many years of use. Maude sat at the head, not to preside, but to have easy access to anything a guest might need. The table was crowded with arms and hands scooping, dipping, reaching for bowls and platters overflowing with barbeque, casseroles, and salads. At the end of the bench was his wife, Lara, in animated conversation with their next-door neighbor, Bubba. One of his last memories of her was her smile, eyes crinkled shut, thick brown hair in braids.

Patricia Wrenowski became his mother's successor and the block's matriarch. If she'd been alive, Maude would not have had much truck with Patricia's sloppy, inaccurate rendition about how this particular block came to be on the Historic Register.

It did not escape anyone that without Maude, these houses, their nest eggs, their key to retirement, would not be here. As Gordon approached Patricia's front yard, he knew it definitely didn't escape her, since as a real estate agent, she had profited during the big gentrification madness of the 1980s.

Gordon was as much a tradition as everything else, his latest batch of dandelion wine made from harvest along the parkway. On a street replete with customs, this one was sacred: No one could spray their lawns with insecticides or weedkiller.

His bottle splashing into the cooler always marked Gordon's arrival, although he was rarely noticed. In the years since his mother's death, he had perfected a precise timetable for arriving, eating the meal, and leaving.

"Gotcher wine, Gord?" Bubba asked. He was the only other person on the block who wasn't teetering on some rung of a corporate ladder. His family had opened the first gas station in the early 1900s. Like Gordon, a conglomerate had guzzled up the family business. Unlike Gordon, the conglomerate needed the little gas stations dotted around the country to sell their gas, so now Bubba owned a couple of the local mini marts.

"That's yours." Bubba motioned to the empty lawn chair next to him and handed Gordon a bottle of beer. "To yer Mom," he said quietly.

Truth be told, this big robust man with a laugh that enveloped the whole yard was the reason Gordon didn't blow off the annual event. Bubba once told Gordon he showed up every year because it was a party with lots of beer, and he loved to sit next to Gordon uttering side comments as Patricia did her history spiel. As the night blossomed, the party would move to Bubba's front porch, where the laughter fluttered the curtains at Gordon's bedroom window.

When he returned to his seat with three helpings of dessert, Gordon caught a glimpse of two pairs of feet behind a pyramid bush. For a moment, he saw Brian's head show itself, then retreat into the shadows. Attached to the other feet was a pair of pink sandals.

At the far end of the lawn almost on the sidewalk, Olivia stood alone, attending a sagging paper plate. Her unusual hair and black clothes were at odds with the girl who had helped him in his basement just a few weeks ago.

From the corner of his eye, Gordon saw Brian and the owner of the pink sandals step into his line of sight. They wove around groups of neighbors, holding hands in the casual way that told Gordon they'd been dating for a while. He was intrigued by Olivia's reaction as they joined her. The triad had an adversarial stance to it, Olivia on the sidewalk, the couple's toes at the edge of the cement.

Brian gestured toward some sod under a picnic table, which until that point, Gordon hadn't noticed. From his position in the lawn chair, he could see curves of dead grass and surmised Patricia had deliberately placed the table in that spot. Olivia shook her head, whereupon Brian stepped forward into Olivia's space, sweeping his arm toward the house. The pink sandal girl, no longer holding Brian's hand, stepped back, leaving Olivia and Brian facing off.

By now their voices had escalated enough that nearby people stopped conversations to stare. Brian grabbed his girlfriend's hand, jabbed at Olivia with his free one, and the two crossed toward the grills.

Gordon wondered how much the parents knew about their kids' interactions, especially Patricia, who had taken her customary place on the porch. He prepared himself for her annual recognition, Bubba nudging him to indicate he was ready to make his commentary.

"We all know—" Patricia began.

"That's not the way it happened," Olivia called from her place on the sidewalk.

Patricia surveyed the crowd, not having registered Olivia's outburst. "—that had it not been for Maude—"

"That's not what happened," Olivia called again, moving onto the grass.

Neighbors turned their heads toward the girl as she navigated between the chairs. "Why, Olivia," Patricia smiled, tight lipped.

"Maude didn't do those things. She didn't chain herself to that stupid horse trough or get arrested."

"Olivia, let's you and I chat as soon as I'm done, okay? People like to hear this every year."

"But it's a lie. A stupid lie."

"Hear! Hear!" For a micro-second Gordon wondered if someone else had blurted it. But surprised faces at the neighboring table swiveled in his direction. He froze, eyes darting, composing his face as if he were just another neighbor who had not uttered a word.

"Gee, Gord. Beats anything I coulda said." Bubba leaned toward him.

Gordon grimaced. "How about you get me another beer?"

John Dimato took Olivia by the elbow, eased her past the neighbors to Donna, and escorted them to their own porch where they disappeared through the front door. And then reappeared without their daughter.

Soon the sun's rays angled along the asphalt and trimmed lawns. Lunch had been over for quite some time, Patricia's speech derailed and not salvageable. Men and women trundled back and forth. Some brought steaks, some brought ribs, some brought potatoes and corn, the makings of a barbeque dinner.

Usually Gordon would have left a long time ago, but he remained, enthralled with the conversation. The corporate climbers were clinging by their nails on the career ladder, hoping the winds of reorganization wouldn't fling them off. Businesses were not the right size anymore. Layers were being upsized, downsized, resized. "Lean and mean" was the catch phrase.

Bubba elbowed Gordon. "Cheers!" and they clinked beer bottles.

+++

Olivia's room was a convection oven, the central air conditioner turned to tepid. She surveyed the walls that were in transition from girly-girl lavender to teen angst and yanked the wall art, Beauty, the Beast, and the dancing teacups, leaving holes from the screws.

Her mother had some pinking shears, which she grabbed to re-design her clothes, shearing off sleeves and pant legs at odd lengths, inserting holes in the knees and tops, leaving gaping mouths in the fabric. Her triumphant hoot came out as a sharp bark.

In the distance, high laughter punctuated the babble of conversation, and from the bathroom window, she could see her neighbors. She thought her dad or mom would have come back to see how she was doing, but neither showed up.

Then beneath the canopy of elm trees, she spotted Ashley with Brian's arm draped across her shoulders like a scarf. Olivia picked up the phone.

"Hey Becca," she said.

+++

Fireflies glittered the bushes surrounding Bubba's veranda and the cooler had just been loaded with fresh ice, when Gordon climbed the stairs. Mothers balanced children on their hips to head home as the party now moved to the new location. His friend made a space for him next to the railing. "Gord, you decided to come. Did ya bring some more er yer dandelion wine? I got beer."

In the dark, beer shushed as Gordon pried off the cap and took a swig. Small orange circles of cigarette ends glowed, talk ambling nowhere in particular.

A voice, "Say, Dimato, how's it feel not being the big shot any-more?"

"Pretty damn good. Fact is, these last few months've been hard. Donna's been on my case, the council could give a shit …" John said.

"Man can't get no respect." Laughter all around.

"Hey, Dimato, Donna looked pretty hot …"

"She was, that damn wig …"

"What's with that daughter of yours?" Ray asked.

"God knows." John said.

"Leave 'im alone, Ray." Bubba said.

"Well, what's with that sonner yours?" John asked.

"God knows, Dimato. Won't happen again, man." Ray's voice traveled from the other side of the porch. "We good?"

"Yeah."

Gordon remembered Olivia perched in his kitchen, swinging her legs, crying, then the interchange she'd had with Brian a few hours ago.

"Gord, why didn't you say nothin' before when Patricia did the speech thing each year?" Bubba's cigar end sparked, smoke discharg-ing. He was the only person Gordon didn't mind calling him by a nickname—the only person living, that is.

"Why should I?" Gordon asked.

"Because it's so damn boring." Bubba reached in the cooler for another beer. "Where did she get that thing about the horse trough? No disrespect to you, Ray."

"Don't mind me. I just live with her." Ray's voice shot from his corner, followed by a raucous chorus of laughter. Gordon began to understand what caused the noise to float into his bedroom.

"I don't think it's so boring. But that's cuz I get a play-by-play interpretation every year. Bubba, I think you should do the speech," Gordon said. Hoots and howls flew off the porch, the kind that would have wakened him.

"Holy shit, Ray. See that little whatsername Brian was with?" Bubba asked. "You're in for it."

"Yep, just like his old man. I remember when I was his age …"

"We all do. Good times, those." Bubba puffed on his cigar and exhaled.

A while later Gordon was just unbuttoning his shirt to get ready for bed when he heard thumping. *Could be squirrels in the attic.* He'd have to bait the safe trap and relocate them. The sound moved to the front of the house, followed by the ca-ling of the bell. Definitely not squirrels. Then through his open bedroom window, he heard a small voice at the kitchen door.

Gordon peered out the backdoor window to find Olivia, appearing as if she had been on military maneuvers and not dressed for it. He opened the door, the slice of light falling on her, the rank smell of vomit and booze rushing in.

"Gor'n, I come in?" she wavered on the steps.

"Olivia, where have you been? You better go home. Your folks must be very worried."

"Can't. I gotta pee."

"You're almost there. You can use your own bathroom." A drunk teenager. He was definitely in foreign territory.

"Can't. I gotta pee real bad." She floundered against him. Gordon stepped back; the smell was overpowering. She fell, and he found himself sitting on the floor, Olivia half across the threshold and sprawled across his knees.

"Okay, but only to use the bathroom." While the girl bumped her way into the powder room, he pulled out the phonebook in the front hall and dialed the Dimatos. He was brewing coffee when she listed back into the kitchen.

"Have a seat. When did you last have something to eat?" He placed a plate of bread, a bottle of aspirin, and a glass of water on the table.

"This won't keep you from feeling like hell tomorrow, but it'll help you feel less bad."

"I puked in your bathroom." She lay sideways on the bench.

"I heard."

"All over the toilet."

"I'm not surprised. Awful, isn't it?"

Olivia grabbed the edge of the table to steady herself. Her hands shook as she took small sips. "Gor'n, what 'm I gonna do? I can't go home. Can I stay here?"

"Sorry. The deal was for you to use the bathroom. I'm trying to get you in condition to get you home." *And then clean up the mess.*

"They'll kill me. I was s'pposed to stay in my room. I wouldn't put on my costume today. They're mad cuz I told people I was dead Violet and ruined Dad's going-away speech. I also scared some little kids. Then I pulled Beauty and the dancing teacups off the wall. And then I did this." She pointed to her clothes. "I'm going to puke again." Gordon handed her a wastebasket and held it while she heaved, tears running down her face.

"Olivia, do you think running away is going to make this any better? Where would you go?"

"Dunno." She leaned over the wastebasket again. "I jus' wanna sleep."

"Want some coffee or more to eat?" She shook her head. "How about I walk you home now?"

As they made their way down the block, Gordon asked, "So where were you?"

"Anderson Park in the bathroom."

"Yeah? That's where I used to hang out and smoke. My buddies and I just about burned the place down. We dropped a lit cigarette in the garbage can. The fire department had to come and put it out. The fire singed the side of the building and spread to some of the elm trees. You can still see it if you know where."

"Did you get in a lot of trouble?"

"Yep. I spent the summer picking up litter for the Parks Department." Gordon helped her onto the porch, wondering what kind of summer this evening heralded.

CHAPTER 14
SUMMER

As the summer began, her parents made it clear she would have little free time. Olivia found herself enrolled in summer school in a classroom smelling of incense, furniture polish, and mildew. They also signed her up for the Forester swim team—against her will—and arranged with Ashley's mother for rides to and from swim practice—also against her will.

When the girls got to the pool for the first practice, Olivia's legs spasmed as she fought the urge to bolt. The swimsuit's scooped-out arms and back just encouraged her rounded shape to escape out any side that was available. Without her black makeup, she felt naked. She and Ashley were sitting on the pool's coping when Brian swam to the edge. He flicked his head, droplets landing on Olivia's arms.

"What're you doing here, cow?" He shielded his eyes with his hand. "You are so out of it if you think anyone here is gonna protect you. Not so tough without your girlfriend, are you? Come on, Ashley. Let's go practice our dives. Besides, I bet this pig here pees in the pool."

"Brian." Ashley drew his name out and pouted. "Olivia's new. I'm supposed to make her feel welcome."

"Well, she's welcome to sit right here on her ass all day, for all I care." Brian grabbed Ashley's ankle and pulled, the girl toppling in with a delighted scream.

The sound of a whistle cut across the water. Olivia glanced over to see Ray by the diving boards. "All right. Let's get going. Our first match is in two weeks. We've got stiff competition this year," he said clapping his hands.

On the succeeding mornings, the routine became predictable. Olivia had to admit that Ashley tried to make sure she was included. But soon after arriving, Brian would saunter over, lob some insult at Olivia, and then he and Ashley would wander away, leaving her by herself.

At the beginning of July, Ashley dragged Olivia into the girls' locker room. Brian had broken up with her. She wasn't sure why. He just stopped calling or talking to her or coming up.

"Ashley, at the last swim meet, you aced your events, and Brian blew it big time. You went home with first place ribbons and a trophy. He went home with nothing."

Ashley countered, "That's silly. He isn't the type to make such a big deal."

"Yeah right. And he was so chill when I beat him in the computer programming contest." Olivia noted Ashley's frown and knew she'd made her point.

A few mornings later, the two girls sat on a bench eating chipped-ice cones, their tongues stained blue and red. The air sagged under the weight of approaching thunder and lightning, mingling with the smell of chlorine. Swimmers leaned against the cyclone fence, exotic water bugs wrapped in carapaces of soppy beach towels, swim goggles perched on their heads as if they were just-emerged dragonflies.

"He's such a great kisser." Ashley pointed to Brian, who was helping one of the kids out of the pool, the child noisily resisting the directive. "See how kind he is? And he was so sweet the way he'd carry my lunch tray. I remember one time …" Ashley blew her nose in her towel.

"Could we talk about someone besides Brian? I mean he's a major butthead for dumping you and being such an asshole to me."

"Well, gee, Olivia, maybe we could talk about you. Some friend you are. So why did you do it?"

"Do what?" Olivia's breathing quickened as she pictured Wrenowskis' lawn.

"Dye your hair black. It was rad before you did that."

"Cuz I felt like it." At her mother's insistence, her hair had been re-dyed a color close to her own, but the constant chlorine wash was turning it an awkward shade of green.

The trees shuddered in the oncoming storm, the wind beginning to pick up. The whistle blew, and the pool closed, Olivia deciding to walk home rather than continue a conversation that was careening into an argument. For a moment she thought about heading to Becca's house, but she had gone to stay with her mom in Iowa. When she turned onto her block, the weather broke. She took shelter on Gordon's veranda and was sitting on the steps when he pulled into the drive, the storm now passed. She stood as he cut the engine, her baggy shirt sticking to the wet suit underneath.

"Well, Olivia. How've you been lately?"

"Okay, I guess."

"That's good to hear. I'm just home on the run today. But you're welcome to a quick lunch."

He slapped sandwiches together, grabbed a jug of lemonade, and headed for the door to eat on the stoop.

"Gordon, I'm sorry about Forester Days." Olivia wondered if he'd lecture her about the evils of drinking, that she was too young. Whatever.

"It's forgotten." As he stood he said, "Well, I've got to get going. I'm leaving the lemonade and the last sandwich for you. Just leave the dishes on the step. I'll get them when I come home tonight."

Now what? She helped herself to the sandwich as Gordon pulled out of the driveway, then perched on the stoop, relishing the cool cement on her legs. Before her was a small truck garden, every available inch devoted to growing. At her feet were rows of tomato cages, miniature skyscrapers—Hancock Buildings or Sears Towers—with green vines and leaves erupting out the tops and sides. Dotted among the leaves were yellow, star-shaped flowers next to small fruit in various phases of maturity. She ambled over to inspect further.

+++

At first, Patricia had obsessed over finding who vandalized the lawn. Everything pointed to Olivia, but she had no proof, and when nothing further happened, she turned her focus to supporting the swim team. During all those seasons, Patricia had gone to every swim meet, cheering Brian's progress. She longed for those enthusiastic days, when he danced on the poolside cement, elated to have her there. Now she was relegated to the picnic tables with the other moms, also contending with creatures who had once been loving and lovable. From under the trees, Patricia and her friends comforted themselves by sipping strawberry daiquiris and sneaking cigarettes.

As she watched, Ray, the assistant coach to the girls' swim team, huddled with two girls in preparation for the next event. He draped an arm over each girl's shoulder, his head bobbing with some intense last-minute instructions. The three raised their heads and did an intricate handshake routine. Ray concluded with a pat on each girl's shoulder, trailing his fingers down their spines to rest on the small of their backs.

Patricia gasped, her plastic cup toppling into her lap as she sprang and ran to the cyclone fence, the red stain running down her legs. Across from her, Ray crouched on his haunches. For a moment, he raised his chin and glanced her way with a quick drop of his eyelids. She thought she saw contempt swim across his features. Then he refocused on the girls.

Swim meet over, Ray opened the door to the house, ushering

Patricia and Brian toward the kitchen. "It's a shame Ashley biffed her dive," he said. He had jubilantly hugged the two girls when they placed in their events, and now walked with a slight swagger, mentioning steaks on the grill and baked potatoes for dinner. The memory of Ray at the pool caused Patricia to dart toward the fridge.

"Good job, Brian," she said, grabbing a bottle of wine. An answer other than a grunt would have been unthinkable. But she knew from his high fives at the awards ceremony that he was ecstatic. "You and Ashley break up? I notice you didn't go comfort her when she blew her dive."

"What of it?" Brian mounted the stairs with his trophy.

Patricia remained in the foyer, trying to sort out another instance of Ray's strange behavior in the past few months. He was, after all, on the other side of the pool, and the girls must have moved, making it look like he'd run his fingers down their backs. She held her breath and closed her eyes as if that would erase the images.

+++

Once Olivia decided, getting out of going to the pool was easier than she had thought. She told her parents that because she lost, she would no longer be competing, and they didn't need to go to the meets anymore. That taken care of, she told Ashley she had some papers to write for summer school, got grounded, and couldn't finish the swim season.

Gordon didn't seem to mind finding her working in his garden when he arrived home for lunch and soon there was a routine, which Olivia liked, especially once summer school was over for the year. She liked being alone in the heat, listening to her boom box, chasing the shade, hoping for a bit of breeze. She liked the sound of tires on gravel, which meant Gordon was home for lunch, a sandwich and a quick gardening lesson. She liked that he concluded the lesson by picking two small ripe tomatoes and tossing one over. Then he grabbed the hose, brought it over, and sprayed the fruit, the hose water hot from sitting in the sun. The tomato tasted deep and sweet, with a tangy fragrance that attached itself to Olivia's fingers, lingering like a good Italian dinner.

Most of the time, Olivia made sure she was there at the end of the day because he invited her in for lemonade. The two didn't say much. Gordon never asked her to do any of the gardening. He didn't seem to expect it. He just seemed pleased and delighted to see her.

+++

The radio news had been full of the record-breaking temperatures, and that day, Olivia worked through the coolest part of the morning, but even the hose failed to give her much relief. The sunshine sprawled across the house's roof, lighting the back of the yard and beginning to scorch the side of the garage. She turned off her boom box, decided not to wait for Gordon to come back for lunch, and had just parked the wheelbarrow, when her back and shoulders began to tingle. Had she heard something? With no breeze, the humidity was like pudding. Olivia reached to lift the boom box, glimpsing the smallest patch of orange in the space between the branches of a pyramid bush across the street. She turned in time to see the bush jiggle. A figure dashed between two houses. Brian. Shit. Now what? Spooked, she watched him emerge.

"Olivia, you bitch! Ashley and I got back together. But because of you, she broke up with me. You think what I did to you at school was bad. You're gonna wish you'd never crossed me. Whatcha gonna do now? Hide behind some old fart? He's not even here. You're all alone." He turned and sauntered down the sidewalk toward his house.

She scanned the length of the street, cold fingers of sweat crawling down her back to her toes.

All the next morning, she was alerted by any noise that might mean Brian was lurking. Having run out of tasks to do for Gordon, she wandered to the tiny garage, barely able to hold one car, let alone Gordon's massive Oldsmobile. The white paint had long ago lost to the weather, the clapboards now pale gray, the roof bowed from many years of too much snow. Olivia pulled on the catawampus door and squished through the small opening. Inside, the dirty glass window emitted yellow light, the faint sound of her boom box sifting through the cracks. Work benches edged the walls and pegboard held tools, neatly organized. A gas can with scraped green enamel waited under one of the benches. In the far corner was a barrel with black, stained rags. The smell of decrepit, heated wood was suffocating. As Olivia began to edge her way out, a movement in the backyard caught her eye. By the back stoop, she saw Brian's muscle shirt stooped over her boom box. The radio dial began to shift stations, half notes and half words. She froze.

+++

Gordon backed out of the parking lot at U Do It, hoping to have lunch with Olivia. He anticipated finding her bent over a tomato cage or waiting on the stoop. She had been gone the past couple of days, but he knew how hot it had been. The ensuing quiet on those days had created a hole. She was a welcome break from Hunter and his obsession with opening the Winter Wonderland Department by Black Friday. She didn't seem to mind the gaps in conversation. She was enthusiastic and curious about gardening. Frequently, he had wondered if his lessons at the warehouse had any effect on the little groups he taught. Folks would arrive, sop up what he had to say, buy books, tools, seeds and plants, then disappear to their fenced back yards. To do what? Create Edens, truck farms, toxic dumps of too many chemicals? With Olivia, he could see her progress, that she was benefiting from her interest and his desire to share what he knew.

He pulled in the driveway and saw where she had dispatched fledgling weeds into the wheelbarrow. As he stopped the car, she crawled out of the shed, her hair like drenched bulb roots, her face red, her clothes soaked. The garage must have been well over 100 degrees and God knows how much hotter with the humidity. Fearing heat stroke, he sprang toward her, leaving the driver's door gaping.

"Olivia, we've got to get you inside. Lean on me." He all but lifted her into the kitchen. From the fridge, he pulled out Jell-O, watermelon, and ice water and laid them before her.

"I wanna throw up," she said, slouching against the wall.

"We've got to get you cooled down." He felt her forehead, ran to the sink, drenched a dishtowel, and wrapped ice cubes in it. "Tuck this in your arm pit."

"But you'll be late for work." She was hardly coherent.

"That's not important right now." Gordon monitored her as the cold towel and liquids began to work. After a while, he called the store to say he had an emergency and would be late. When he could perch across from her at the table, he said, "I need to call your mom."

Olivia shook her head, her voice thin, "Mom doesn't know I'm here."

"Olivia, what? Don't you tell her when you come here?" Then it all came out: The humiliation of having to go to the pool, of people watching her fail, of the snide comments she heard just out of earshot. And now the latest, why she was hiding in his garage.

Gordon sat for a long time, rubbing his neck. He anxiously watched her head drooping as she picked at the watermelon. Finally, he said, "Olivia, don't you worry about this. I'll take care of it. But I want you to stay home tomorrow."

She met his gaze. He remembered how ordinary he had been as a boy, and what it was like to be invisible—or to be visible only when kids made fun of him.

+++

The next day, as he pressed flat against the side of the house, Gordon heard Brian advance with his second bucket of garden waste. In its usual place in the shade sat the boom box, now topped by a mound of putrid, green muck. From where he stood Gordon could smell the foul slop, rotting vegetable matter disintegrated beyond recognition.

"What the hell are you doing with that? And what the hell did you do to this boom box?" Gordon rounded the corner as Brian raised the bucket in his direction.

The boy faltered and stepped backward, the glop falling at his feet. He turned to run.

"Won't do you any good. Patty Wrenowski's son, aren't you? Might as well come back." Brian retraced his steps. "The way I see it, I could report you to the police for trespassing and vandalism. I could also bring charges for attempted assault."

"I'm sorry, sir. It was just a joke. I didn't mean any harm." He stared at his feet.

"Maybe you can explain to me what is so funny." Part of him felt like a bully. But this was about Brian's misuse of power. The boy needed to learn a lesson or two.

"Nothing, I guess," Brian mumbled.

"Did you think I would laugh if you ruined the boom box?"

"I dunno."

"Maybe you didn't think this through."

"Guess not."

"Here's the deal. I'm going to contact your mother. You will replace the boom box with one I choose. If you even think about coming on my property ever again, I will have you hauled off so fast you won't know what hit you. And it won't be this gunk. You get it? By the way, Olivia Dimato is doing some yard work for me. If she reports that you are anything besides courteous and respectful, I will take action. Understand?"

"Yeah."

"Now get out of here." He went in to make some lunch and then lifted the phone's receiver.

CHAPTER 15
THE GREAT SQUIRREL RELOCATION PROJECT

Gordon loved late August. He could feel and smell the change of season. The sun's movement was a golden caress, a message to him that it would soon depart for long stretches of time. Now in his own autumnal years, he savored the end of summer. Harvesting vegetables from the garden, preparing for winter, and recognizing his hard work felt right to him. His life was run by the seasons. A hardware business is just an offshoot of the agrarian life.

Gordon loaded his station wagon for a trip to the family cabin for Labor Day weekend. Soon he would pick up Clerise and Michael. And he was nervous. The cabin had been his refuge, but when he saw Clerise's careworn face, the invitation was out of his mouth before he could stop himself.

Now that Charlie Hunter had relocated Clerise out of her clerical position to the kitchen design section, they took their breaks surrounded by mini displays of remodeling possibilities. Sometimes they just sat and talked. Sometimes they grabbed a cup of tea. Sometimes they took a walk. The day he invited her and Michael to the cabin, they were drifting on an elliptic route skirting the parking lot.

Michael's summer was coming to an end. He'd spent most of it at the Boys and Girls Club. Lifesaver that the organization was, Clerise was aware that on the first day back at school, kids would compare their vacations, and Michael would have nothing to talk about. She was trying to figure out how she could take him someplace exciting on her small income, something that would be fun for him and give him bragging rights.

Gordon could picture Michael on that first day of school. Suddenly he was Michael's age, and he began telling Clerise about the family cabin in Michigan. He described the fishing, the frog catching, and the sound of squirrels chirping in the trees. He could smell the lake, the early mornings, and the campfire smoke that never seemed to quite leave his clothes and hair until the end of September. Before he knew it, he had invited them, and Clerise had accepted. She grabbed his hand, then his elbow, her garments moving gracefully. In a swirl, she hugged him.

Friday evening, Gordon made his last-minute inspections of the tires, brakes, and oil. The backseat was ready to hold their luggage. Three sets of seatbelts were in good shape in the front. And then he was at Clerise and Michael's apartment. He had never been to their place before and didn't quite know what to expect.

He thought Clerise would float to the car in one of her caftans, so he was surprised that she wore a T-shirt and jeans, her close-cropped hair caressing her head. Her demeanor was awkward, making him feel awkward too. Michael was engrossed with some handheld electronic game. She chastised him. Where were his manners? She appeared as nervous as Gordon.

She jogged to the tailgate of the wagon. As she reached for the lever to open it, she stopped and peered in the window. "Gordon, what are those metal cages doing in the back? And what are those animals?"

Gordon began to stutter. "S-S-Squirrels." This wasn't going right.

"Yes, I can see they're squirrels. What are you doing with squirrels in those cages?"

"They're safe traps. I'm taking them to the woods by the cabin."

"But they have trees here." She was nonplussed.

"Clerise, they're rodents. They invade houses, damaging them." He felt backed into a corner. "See?" Clerise shook her head and placed the groceries in the backseat, grabbed Michael's hand, and climbed in the front.

To the sound of squirrels rattling and chattering, Gordon maneuvered the on-ramp to the highway. Before long, the car's movement calmed the animals and the noise quieted. They could finally talk without having to yell. He was pathetically out of practice in small talk, so they rode to radio news and traffic reports punctuated by bleeps from Michael's game.

When the car inched forward at a tollbooth, Michael raised his head. "How come you're not married?"

"I was. She died."

"Oh." His head went down and back to the game.

Clerise turned toward him. "Died? Oh, Gordon, I'm so sorry."

"It was a long time ago." The toll light turned red. He started to roll and tossed his coins in the catch. He could feel her still staring at him. She expected more. "Her name was Lara. She was an army nurse."

"An army nurse?"

More. She expected more. "She believed she should support the boys fighting in Vietnam. And she died."

"Were they able to bring her home?"

"Yes." These kinds of trips bring these kinds of questions. "Did you grow up here?" He tried out the question.

"No. Back east. Near Pittsburgh."

Why was he struggling so hard to get her talking in the car when at work it was so easy? Gordon pushed on at a steady speed. Traffic thinned. By the time they crossed into Michigan, Michael had fallen asleep in Clerise's lap. Her voice was low, and from the corner of his eye, Gordon could see the outline of her hand stroking her son's head.

"What was she like?" Gordon had been waiting for the question.

"Well," he scratched his neck, staring at oncoming traffic, "she was very passionate about her beliefs." He checked the speedometer. "She was a nurse at Cook County Hospital. She said once that Hanoi couldn't be any less safe than the emergency room at Cook. I think she was trying to make me not worry."

Clerise patted his shoulder. "Gordon, this has got to be a record. You monopolized the conversation for thirty seconds." He smiled. The drive was becoming easier.

At close to midnight, the Oldsmobile headed past the trickle of buildings that was the small town of Freelak. Gordon had just cleared the "Thanks for Visiting! Come Back Soon" sign when flashing lights illuminated his rearview mirror. As he parked the car on the grassy shoulder, the squirrels began to jostle their cages, and Michael sat up.

"Good evening, officer." Gordon handed him his driver's license and the registration documents he kept clipped to the sun visor.

The patrolman circled the wagon peering in the windows, then stopped for a moment and examined the cages. "Step out of the car, please." Gordon complied. "Going a bit fast for a congested area, wouldn't you say? Do you know how fast you were going?" he asked.

"Twenty-five miles per hour, I'd say."

"You were going twenty-nine. Mighty awful racket going on. What's in the cages?" He peered at the occupants in front and back.

"Squirrels, sir," Gordon said.

"Squirrels. Don't they carry rabies or something?"

"Not usually."

"What're you going to do? Cook 'em?" The patrolman smirked for a moment.

"Actually, officer, my son's working on a science project." Clerise joined them. "He's learning about the environment and ecology. He's been studying urbanization's effect on animal life."

"Urbanization and animal life," the trooper repeated.

"Yes, sir. Because of increasing population density, they are vermin, rodents. In the wild they're … squirrels. My son is relocating them to our friend's cabin where we will observe them in their natural habitat."

The patrolman shone his light in Gordon's face. "That so?"

"Yes, sir." Gordon's eyes blinded in the glare. "We'll come again in the next week or two to be sure they've settled in. We'll be back at Thanksgiving and in the winter." Feeling winded, he reached for his inhaler.

"Environment and squirrels, huh?" The officer scribbled on a white form, then handed it to Gordon. "Have a good evening."

Gordon put the speeding ticket in the packet on his sun visor mirror and eased off the shoulder. From the side mirror, he watched the pair of headlights follow them until he turned the station wagon onto a soft dirt road. Like air escaping from a tire, both Clerise and Gordon burst into laughter, increasing the volume of chattering in the back. He could sense her leaning back with contented after mirth, now a silhouette illuminated by the interior console, Michael fitting into her contour. The car and its noisy occupants crawled down the pitch-black road, the headlights catching the white bark of birch trees.

At the cabin, Clerise tumbled Michael into an old sleeping bag on a bunk bed. The two adults spent the next while unloading squirrels, some more docile than others. "I often see ones from previous years, especially when I leave out peanuts," Gordon said as the last of them scampered into the night.

The next morning, sunlight nosed across the treetops and gold-infused mist hovered above the small lake as Clerise and Gordon sat on the front steps. In the daylight, Gordon was acutely aware of how the log cabin must look to Clerise. The place had been a destination for the family when he was young and a get-away when Lara was still alive. While habitable and in good repair, it sufficed as his refuge. But the cabin was not guest worthy.

In the far corner on the bottom bunk bed, Michael was still

comatose, the lip of the sleeping bag resting against his head. Clerise had slept in the one above while Gordon had taken the lower bunk of the second pair. A decrepit foldout couch sprawled before the stone fireplace, where Clerise and Michael would sleep tonight, if it was in any condition for a back. And where he and Lara had slept. *Don't remember that right now,* he thought.

The kitchen occupied one whole wall of the cabin, the porcelain sink, now feathered in rust, the yellow countertops displaying the patina of many summers. The ochre fridge was the same vintage as his appliances at home. Actually in better condition.

"What is this place? Mom, it really stinks!" Michael raised his head from the sleeping bag.

"A very old cabin, Michael, which my family built before the Civil War," Gordon replied. This had been a bad idea to invite them.

"That why it smells so bad?"

"No, it's just what happens when a cabin isn't used often. Let's see what the problem is." Michael raised the ancient sleeping bag for his inspection.

"Gordon, if Freelak has a laundromat, we can drop the sleeping bags off. Michael, you can take your roller blades," Clerise said, rubbing her son's back.

Gordon nodded. The errand would get them out of this embarrassing place for a while.

As they parked at the laundromat, Clerise asked, "Does Freelak have a thrift store? To dry clean these sleeping bags and blankets will cost more than buying some good used ones. We can try getting the mildew out of the sheets and towels. If not, what would you think about buying some used linens too?"

Gordon quickly assented. She was being such a good sport about such a disastrous weekend.

Later, Clerise and Gordon sat in the window of the café where they could keep an eye on Michael in his rollerblades as he navigated the rough asphalt of the high school's basketball court across the street.

For a moment, the two turned their attention to picking at the shriveled ends of fries in the basket. The white T-shirt and jeans suited her. "Those African caftans you wear to work are beautiful. I was surprised you weren't wearing one when I picked you up."

"Well, I was surprised to see that you wore what you wear to work every day." Her laugh was throaty. "Actually, I wasn't. But you are more than your jeans and old plaid shirt, just as I am more than my African clothes."

He watched the crinkles around her eyes deepen and fade. For the second time in as many days, he made more sound than a chuckle. He slurped the terrible café tea, feeling his neck muscles relax, filtering down to his shoulders and arms. Crowding their feet were grocery bags stuffed with blankets and towels they had found at a garage sale.

Across the street, another boy, close in age to Michael, entered the basketball court. He wore a loose jersey over a T-shirt that had once been white. In addition to his rollerblades, he manipulated a hockey stick and puck. At first, the hockey stick boy moved the puck in small circles by the hoop. Michael continued to practice his jump near the side of the building. The hockey stick boy widened the circles, and as Michael began to move toward the center, the puck came shooting over. Both boys dug in their toe brakes, stopped face-to-face. Posturing and head scratching commenced. Shoulder shrugging followed. Then the boy handed his stick to Michael and pointed at the puck, demonstrating with the blades how to weave back and forth.

Tea finished, Gordon and Clerise headed toward the grocery store, returning to the school later in the station wagon. Michael climbed in the backseat and removed his skates.

"Mom, I need a hockey stick."

"Honey, whatever for?"

"Isaac asked me to play tomorrow. I'm going to join a team when we get back."

"Michael, I don't want to be spending money for something you want to do now and then have the unused equipment sitting in the closet taking up space."

"Mom, it won't sit in the closet. I promise. Isaac says I could be a great center if I practiced a little."

"You know, Clerise, I've been worrying that Michael would be bored and with nothing to do. What do you say I drop you and Michael off at the laundromat? I'll run over to the general store and pick up a stick and puck. When I was a boy, I used to play sand hockey in the summer."

"So did you have a good time today?" Gordon asked that evening.

"Okay, I guess. It's just that Isaac's kind of dumb. The first thing he said to me was that I was probably really good at basketball. Just cuz I'm black, and my name's Michael." The boy took a bite of hamburger.

"And what did you say?" Clerise asked.

"I told him I'm my school's chess champion. He said they have super chess champions at his school." Michael shook his head. "He asked why I have a white grandpa and a black mom."

"Then maybe you don't want to play roller hockey tomorrow," Clerise said.

+++

Michael, still wearing his elbow and knee pads and clutching the hockey puck, slept most of the way back to Forester the next evening. A few miles from the exit, he woke. "What happened to the squirrels?"

Gordon looked in the rearview mirror, the boy's head backlit from the traffic. "They're making themselves at home. I left a bag of peanuts strewn around. Why do you ask?"

No answer. Gordon supposed Michael shrugged. "I'm going to the cabin again next weekend to see how they're doing. Clerise, would you and Michael like to come? We didn't get much of a vacation, seeing you and I have to work Labor Day, and we spent most of the time getting the cabin livable."

"When I told the officer you come up to be sure they're all right, that's what you do, just not as a science project." Her tone said she was more than surprised. "And yes, we'd love to. It felt great to get away."

The next day, Gordon was reviewing the draft Winter Wonderland layout plan, when Clerise rounded the corner.

"Gordon, I have a big favor to ask. Michael could not stop talking about the weekend, Isaac, roller hockey, and especially the squirrels. Would it be possible for him to do that as a science project? He'd like to enter the experiment in a contest. The prize is science camp next summer. I'd pay for gas and groceries. Peanuts or whatever."

Gordon busied himself rolling up the plan. Having them come to the cabin had been fine for a weekend, but he liked the solitude, and yet …. "Sure," he said.

CHAPTER 16
WHAT'S IN A NAME?

Patricia, Brian, and Ray sat at the kitchen table. "Do you know how embarrassed we are? You vandalized Gordon Carlson's property, and from what he says, you were about to chuck rotten yard waste at him. Brian, what were you thinking?" Patricia's voice squeaked.

"I dunno."

"Can you tell me why you chose Gordon to harass? I played pranks as a boy, but the guy was an old grouch," Ray said.

"Well," Patricia craned her neck forward, "you must have something to say."

"I don't," Brian said.

"In that case, you're going to go down to Gordon's house and apologize to him. You will deliver the new boom box, and you will pay for it out of your savings. You will also ask Gordon what else you can do to atone for this. He said this had something to do with Olivia. That means you'll apologize to her too. And you're grounded for two months," she called as Brian bolted from the table.

Alone now, she leaned her forehead on her arms and closed her eyes. She hadn't been called Patty in ages. When he called, Gordon using her childhood nickname represented everything she never wanted to be: Ordinary. As a kid, she had had ordinary straight brown hair and hung around with ordinary kids, whose ordinariness made them invisible.

Not only that, but Gordon was Maude's son, and Maude Carlson was anything but invisible. Patricia remembered the weight of her chin on her arms, when Mrs. Carlson read to the class after lunch. She could imagine being interesting for a little while, like Anne in *Anne of Green Gables*, who had carrot red hair and was brave and spunky. As Mrs. Carlson read, Patricia began to believe she could be somebody too.

But then junior high and high school came, and she was in the same boring group. She joined the drill team but got lost in the flag she had to manipulate. She was never beautiful, smart, or popular enough to be on the homecoming court.

After graduation, she joined the students trekking toward an associate's degree. As the final quarter approached, she realized she would become just one more in a legion of secretaries in a pool.

Still, she thought of *Anne of Green Gables* and of Anne's carrot hair. She longed for something or some event where she could become extraordinary. She saw an ad for real estate classes and a glimmer of hope went through her. This could be it: a career in real estate. For all those years she had been invisible, she realized that although other people didn't see her, she saw them. She saw them, observed their ways, their style.

The transformation began. She bought a suit, silk blouses, shoes, and a piece of nice gold jewelry. Now for her hair. She permed and dyed it carrot red. The big-hair look was right. But her name, Patty, was too mundane. She needed a name that would make people take notice. She applied for her real estate license as Patricia Lane.

Gordon's phone call had reminded her of what it had been like to be ordinary. He commented he was sure Brian was an ordinary adolescent, testing the rules. All parents go through it, he'd said. But she wasn't all parents, and she was making sure Brian was not an ordinary kid.

In that moment, she remembered the old saying, "Be careful what you wish for." She was learning that something about Ray was definitely not ordinary, either.

+++

Olivia had failed summer school, so she could be in the same classes as Becca in the fall. That first day of sophomore year, she found out she had only one class with the girl. Her parents were pissed, and she would probably be grounded for the rest of her life.

Well, she got what she wanted, Brian missing from all her classes along with anyone else she knew. By working so hard at blowing everything, she had earned a place with students in the slower-paced classes. Their track—and apparently now Olivia's—did not include advanced placement in their senior year. Like a parallel universe, everything appeared the same, but all wrong.

This new universe's substrata included kids with learning disabilities, for whom special programs were developed to help them improve, who struggled and worked hard. Progress was a true victory. Kids just marking time until they could drop out or be kicked out or be passed along to become someone else's problem inhabited this universe as well. Like the raucous group Becca led or the kids with heads on desks, asleep.

She'd really screwed herself by screwing up her grades! Searching the hallway for her homeroom, she saw Brian duck into a classroom with a gaggle of other accelerated students. As he turned in profile, the memory of the slime onslaught in Gordon's back yard came vividly to life, and she hated him as intensely as ever.

She walked into the classroom for the one period she shared with Becca, who, seated in the last row, turned her back to talk to someone else.

Now what? These first few days were critical, jostling for position in the pecking order. As usual, she headed for the front couple of rows, but her gut told her this was not where she should sit. She strolled back and forth, scouting a seat, then settled on a vacant desk in the middle of the room. She could feel everyone's eyes on her, and she knew they wondered what kind of loser she was. She didn't even fit in with the loser crowd.

The desolate day now over, Olivia trekked toward the bus stop knowing the next day would be no better. At least the new route meant she wouldn't be dependent on rides like last year. As if there was anyone she could be dependent on now that she no longer had any friends. She felt the scurry before she saw the face, Ashley, pink-cheeked from running.

"You bitch," she panted. "You awful bitch. You just had to keep digging at him. You couldn't just let it go."

"Ashley, what are you talking about?" Olivia squinted her eyes, as if emerging from a dark room.

"Yeah, like you don't know. Cuz of you, Brian's grounded, so we can't go to homecoming."

"Go to hell, Ashley. I didn't do anything. I haven't even talked to him since August."

"You didn't need to talk to him. You just got him in a whole bunch of trouble. His mom got a call from some old guy. Brian says he's totally demented. Has some crazy idea Brian's out to get you, and if Brian doesn't apologize, he'll call the police and file charges. Whatever you did, Olivia, I hate you!" she screamed.

"Brian's a major liar and he trashed my boom box." Olivia's voice matched Ashley's pitch.

"You're making that up. I bet you lied to that old guy too. You're just jealous."

Olivia scrutinized her ex-friend. "Why're you here, Ashley?"

"Because Brian has to apologize," she sing-songed.

"That's it? That's the apology?" Olivia blinked.

"Well, duh," Ashley cocked her hip, crossed her arms.

Olivia began to laugh, laughter that rebounded from the limestone walls. "Tell Brian to go fuck himself." Ashley recoiled as if smacked. "My name is O, get that?" She stepped around Ashley and strolled off.

+++

Gordon, lost in thought about the recent trip to the cabin with Clerise and Michael, didn't hear Olivia come into the garage until she was at his side.

"Hey, Gordon," she said.

"Olivia! How's school?" He held a rag saturated in disinfectant.

"Awful. I hate my classes. I don't know anyone. Everybody knows what they're doing except me. And my hair and clothes suck."

"I wouldn't like that either." Her hair did look rather mangy. He couldn't figure out whether it was intentional or not. Better not comment on it. To him, her clothes seemed just fine. Better not comment on that either.

"I saw Brian today."

"Did he say anything? Like an apology?" Gordon wiped the bottom tray of a squirrel cage.

"He sent Ashley, the jerk. What a loser."

Gordon grunted and shook his head. He wondered if Patty knew what a twerp she had for a son. Probably not.

"What're those?" Olivia pointed at the wire cages.

"Safe traps for squirrels. I took some to my cabin last weekend to let them loose in the wild." He tested the latches. This young woman was such a puzzle. He could still picture her that past summer when she stumbled out of the garage. She remained by his side, opening and closing the cage doors. He worked on, cleaning the traps, saying nothing.

"I decided I want to be called 'O' now." She had such an earnest expression, her eyes traveling over his face.

"Oh."

"Yeah, O."

He was at a loss. One of the traits he most admired about his wife was she had never seemed flustered. For the umpteenth time, he wondered how she would have dealt with Olivia.

"Well, I better go home," she finally said. "Hope you had a good time at the cabin."

From the open garage door, Gordon watched her turn back to the sidewalk. He closed his eyes for a moment, opened them, then inhaled at his helplessness and dipped a rag in the cleaner.

+++

Now nearly the end of September, Charlie studied the store plan marked with the new department.

"How's progress going on Winter Wonderland, Gord?"

"The new sign, 'Toys for Good Girls and Boys,' has arrived and is in storage when you want to check it out." Gordon consulted a clipboard.

"Are we on track?"

"Yes, the ads are going in for the grand opening next week."

"You my man, Gordo!" Hunter raised his hand for a high five.

Gordon eyed the fingers for a split second before tepidly upping his hand and meeting Charlie's.

"You don't like high five, or was it after your time?"

"I wasn't thinking about that," Gordon said.

"Oh, well, what were you thinking about? I know older people have 'senior moments.' Were you having one of those?"

"No, it was not a senior moment. I was wondering about you."

"Having a senior moment? No, Gordy, I'm too young," Hunter explained as if Gordon were a two-year-old or indeed suffering from dementia.

"I wasn't wondering that. I was wondering when you were going to get my name straight."

"What do you mean? I do have it straight."

"I prefer to be called Gordon, Chuck."

117

"Chuck? Oh, that's good."

"Charlie, we all have names we like to be called. You like Charlie or Hunter. I like Gordon or Carlson. Simple as that. And I'm reminding you that I like to be called Gordon. Perhaps I haven't been clear."

"Note taken."

Charlie concentrated on the papers in front of him. Gordon sat for a few minutes.

"Anything else?" Gordon asked.

Hunter raised his head. "Uh, no. Thought you'd left."

+++

The major agenda item at the managers' meeting was the upcoming sale. As Charlie concluded, he added, "By the way, it has come to my attention that Gordon here is sensitive about his name." He cut a hard look at Gordon. "All of you, do not call him Gordy or Gordo or Gord or any other permutation. His name is Gordon. Okay, we're done."

"So Gordo, what's that all about?" Clerise punched him in the arm as they left the room together.

"Respect."

CHAPTER 17
NUTS AND BOLTS

Patricia's mission that September day was to go through Ray's wardrobe, find things he never wore, and give them to the local thrift shop. The second-floor hall closet, which had once housed linen, now contained his clothes so she could have the one, small closet in the master bedroom. She yanked the cord to the naked light bulb. It flicked on and for a moment shadows danced around the tiny space. She threw some short-sleeved shirts over her arm, followed by several slacks, and tossed them onto a heap in the hallway. Then she spied old running shoes, caked a bit with recent mud. Taking them would cause a ruckus, so she left them alone. The back part of the closet hidden in shadows was a good place to find unused junk.

For a man who was so good at the tedious detail of computer programming, he sure was a slob. She crawled toward the nether regions, where her hand fell on a floorboard that groaned and moved a bit. Odd. She pressed the board to determine how loose it was. Termites? Oh God. Once in a home, they invaded adjoining houses, a sure way to alienate neighbors, the block, the whole neighborhood.

In the bathroom, she scrabbled in the vanity drawer until she picked out a nail file. On her hands and knees once again, she wedged the file between the cracks in the boards and pushed to leverage it. Nothing. She leaned her weight again, and the file snapped, the end gouging the heel of her hand.

Sucking the blood from the ragged tear, she scanned the wood for another place to jimmy. At the other end, she saw what appeared like a bolt protruding about a quarter inch. Her nails closed crablike around the metal stem as she pinched and pulled. The bolt lifted as if housed in something. As it rose, the board revealed its ability to swivel. Had she found a secret storage cache?

The fun part of owning an old house was little glimpses into the lives that had preceded hers. As the board turned, Patricia peered into the dark, termites still a possibility. Next, she got a flashlight from the medicine cabinet, her eyes following its beam into the space below the floorboards. Well, at least she didn't see any wood particles from termites. Confusion followed relief as she saw the contents. A shoebox? The top declared Ray's favorite brand.

Already she was thinking about whether to let Ray know she knew about his hiding place. How weird. You think you know everything about someone you've been married to all these years.

She pulled up the box—the contents slapping against the sides—placing it on the floor by her knees to examine later. She half smiled. Old love letters from some former girlfriend perhaps. She plunged her hands in again and pulled out a Polaroid camera. Her Polaroid camera.

Patricia frowned at the box on the floor. Jagged spikes of worry jabbed her stomach, a fear that had no name yet. She tore off the shoebox lid. A picture. No, lots of pictures. Polaroid pictures. Patricia turned the top one over, able to focus on only pieces of it. A face and dark hair. The photo had a bleached quality as if the flash were too close to its subject. A woman? No, younger, but developed. Breasts. The frame ended just below her waist. Eyes half-mast. Head tilted back. Patricia lifted it closer, hand shaking. Was that something glistening on her belly? It slipped from her hand. The next picture was from the waist down. Legs spread, shot from above. Dark pubic hair.

"Oh, my God! Ray? Oh, my God!" she crawled backward, the

shoebox tipping over. Photos spewed across the dusty floor. "Ohmygod, ohmygod!" Bile burned her throat, stung her nostrils, and stained the front of her sweater.

She retreated for a fraction of a second, then lurched forward, grabbed the box, shoved the pictures in, and slapped the lid shut. *Not in my house.*

Holding the box at arm's length, Patricia tore down the stairs, flung open the back-porch door, ran toward the garage, to the garbage can, opened the lid, and hurled it in. Exhaling sent the terror out and inhaling brought fury. That bastard. She ran back to the closet and grabbed the Polaroid camera. He'd stolen her camera! That pervert. The camera landed with a clatter next to the box in the garbage can.

Back in the closet, the light cord swung in circles, making frenzied shadows around the walls, the shirts, and the pants on hangers. She took a deep breath. First, close the floorboard. A little tricky, but the nail dropped into place. She scooted toward the doorway as if the floorboard would open again and disgorge more. Then she stood, fished for her cigarettes and matches in her pocket, and broke her own house rule. A spark from the lighter, then the flame, and the tobacco took hold. She dragged deeply, the smoke scalding her raw throat, she exhaled the fear and let the fury get another foothold as she yanked the cord.

CHAPTER 18
OUT OF THE ASHES

Patricia stubbed out her cigarette and surveyed its companions crouched in the ashes. She stuck her index finger among the stand of butts and twirled the saucer, watching them topple and spill onto the kitchen table.

Brian would be home soon. Getting rid of this evidence was easy. Lying when he smelled the smoke was also easy. But the other? Ray must've been at this for a long time, considering all those photos. Why? "Why" didn't matter right now. How could he do this? No, he couldn't have. Not Ray. Even if Ray hadn't done it—even if someone else did—that Polaroid was her camera. He was there. And even if he wasn't, he knew, participated in some way.

Of course! Ray was keeping them as collateral. Someone had something on him, was blackmailing him at work. His job was at risk, and those pictures protected him from this gross, unscrupulous superior. No, someone who wanted his job, some greedy kid, who was ruthlessly climbing the ladder, and Ray was in his way. Yeah right.

She should have seen this sooner, the clues, changes in his behavior. Unless. Unless he'd always been doing this.

What to do? Who else knew about this? That sick moment at the swim meet, Ray running his fingers down the girls' backs. Damn you, Ray! The self-centered bastard. Brian would find out, and during such a critical phase in his development. He needed male role models he could emulate, not some pervert. How could he develop a proper relationship with a woman with this filth and because of this filthy man?

Her political career would go down the drain if Forester found out. She and Brian would be banned. They couldn't walk down the street. She could picture her business as word got out. All her hard work. That bastard.

What to do? Move away? Divorce Ray? Kill him? She had a vision of digging a hole in the backyard, his body in the shadow of an elm tree.

Action. That's what she needed. She hadn't become a top real estate mogul from sitting on her hands doing nothing. A plan began to galvanize her. Who were the young women in the photos? And how likely were they to tell? Maybe this happened a long time ago, and she could prove to herself Ray wasn't involved.

Sitting here wasn't going to get her answers. She glanced at the clock's pendulum swinging back and forth. Brian was due in about five minutes, and he would be moving the garbage cans to the parkway. Get the box and camera!

Out the back door, she jogged toward the garage, her soggy slippers leaving a wet kiss on the concrete floor. The aluminum garbage can lid clattered on the cement as she reached in to snatch the box. She spied a sack in the corner where she could put the stash for now, then put them back in Ray's hiding place in the linen closet later. Like some obscene relay race, she dashed to dump the box into the sack before time ran out and Brian was standing at the kitchen door gazing quizzically at her.

The trail of wet slipper prints smeared toward the corner like smudged lipstick. With a thud, the camera landed on the box, and she knotted the gunnysack cord.

Patricia had just returned to the kitchen door when she heard Brian's voice behind her. "Mom, how come you're outside in your slippers?"

"Isn't it trash day tomorrow? How was school?" She sounded pretty nonchalant, considering.

"The house smells awful. Were you smoking in here?"

"No, a client was." Patricia swept the ashes and butts into her palm, deposited them in the trash, and turned to start the stove for dinner.

CHAPTER 19
ARRANGEMENTS

As the third week of school began, Olivia could navigate to her classes without disaster. She could even recognize other kids at lunch tables. Best of all, she could pass Becca in English, go to her seat, and exchange a few words with the girl next to her. While not ideal, she could see school was getting better.

Class over, the bell rang, chairs scraped the floor. Olivia put on her blank face and shuffled toward the door.

Becca grabbed her sleeve. "O, I gotta go do something. Get me a cheeseburger and save me a seat in the lunchroom."

Olivia found herself, tray in hand, grabbing two cheeseburgers, scouting a half-filled table, and claiming two seats. When Becca finally strode in, the room was practically empty. She knew reaching her next class in time would be sketchy.

"Hey, thanks." Becca snatched the cold burger, wrapped it in a napkin, and headed out. The next day, Olivia found herself babysitting a grilled cheese sandwich until Becca ran in, beamed at her, and stuffed the sandwich in her mouth. As she dashed toward the hallway, she called, "I'll pay you back tomorrow."

"Tomorrow's Saturday," Olivia shouted after her. Over the weekend, she stewed. She was out a bunch of money and didn't expect to see it again. By Sunday night, she was practicing saying no in case

Becca asked for anything the next day.

That Monday, as Olivia left English, Becca tugged her jacket. "Here. For lunch. O, what the hell? Do you like sitting in Buchard's lap? You sit with us."

Short a couple of bucks, but better than nothing. "There's no place to sit back here."

Addressing a boy next to her, Becca said, "I'm doing some rearranging. Spider, you sit next to Dank. This is O's from now on." She snatched his notebook and tossed it at him.

"Yeah. Whatever." Olivia eyed Spider, whose head was a mass of black braids, while his thin arms and legs extended from a bulbous, black sweatshirt. The other boy, Dank, was tall, his skin a mosaic of acne, pale skin, and chin stubble. She remembered them from detention.

"Come on, we're hanging with Lauren at Tacos N' More for lunch." Becca said.

Olivia trailed Becca, Spider, and Dank into the fast-food place, certain that someone would report her unauthorized leave from campus. Lauren lounged in a far booth, exuding a definite warning not to get too close. A tray of tacos sat on the table, and she made room for Becca, a smile passing between them. Olivia, Spider, and Dank perched opposite.

"The aunt's in a pisser mood. Something must be up with the old lady." Shredded lettuce escaped to her cheek as Becca chomped on the taco. "She is so mental. Last time we went to court, so the aunt's been on my case about homework and curfew. It's the whole unfit mother shit. Here." Becca shoved a greasy taco at Olivia.

"So, what's comin' down?" Spider asked.

"Nothin'. I got it covered," Becca said, stood, and grabbed a taco. "I'm outta here. Let's go, O. Business to take care of."

"What's with your mom?" Olivia asked as they left Tacos N' More. She noticed Ray Wrenowski chatting with some girl at the counter and held her breath. All she needed was that snoop Patricia calling her mom.

"God, do you have to drill me? You sound like Tony Baloney."

"You see him?" Olivia wasn't as surprised about Becca seeing the school counselor as that she admitted it.

"Of course. He sees anyone. What a prick." Becca led the way toward the woods. Within minutes, they were in the interior at a half-circle of thicket strewn with flattened beer cans and wrappers.

Before them was a small group. Jocks and kids who'd been in her advanced classes last year and were still on the advanced track. The deal was done within moments. Baggies and money exchanged, they scrambled toward school. She'd just make it before the bell. At the end of the day, she could still feel the sting from the high-five with Becca, but as she crossed Boise Avenue, the full impact of what had come down hit her.

+++

On the next trip to Freelak to check on the squirrels, Gordon had awakened in one of the bunkbeds, his back aching as if he'd torn every disc. Clerise had pointed out that if they planned to go throughout the fall, at Thanksgiving and in the winter, he might want the cabin to be in better condition. It needed to be renovated. He averted his eyes as he thought about what could happen to his place, his family place. The memories, especially of Lara, were in the walls and furniture. If the cabin were renovated, where would those memories go?

Trapped between his inability to begin updating the cabin and his need to honor the offer he made to Michael, Gordon began to avoid Clerise at work. Thus, throughout September, they continued to follow the project's schedule with Michael writing observations about the squirrels and their behavior, while Clerise said nothing about the cabin or its habitability.

Then in early October, she insisted on meeting Gordon for dinner at a small café featuring tablecloths of butcher paper and tumblers holding crayons for artists of all ages.

"Gordon," she began, "I don't think we can continue the experiment. This doesn't seem to be the kind of arrangement you had in mind. I'm sure you never imagined having to insulate and make changes to the cabin."

Clerise doodled swirls in yellow and red, orange and green. Gordon grabbed a blue crayon and drew a box.

"Gordon, you have been so kind to agree to this project. But we still have to be able to go to the cabin in the winter so Michael can see whether the squirrels are hibernating. You may be able to tolerate those conditions—and God knows your ancestors did—but it's not good for a ten-year-old boy. Michael has just started his project. I could explain to him that we can't make the cabin winter-proof."

Gordon sensed she wanted a discussion, some comment. These occasions, where he was expected to think on his feet, made him so tongue-tied, he could think of nothing to say. He just wanted to get out of the café, but dinner was on its way, so he'd just have to slog through the meal. But then what? His own silence felt excruciating.

Picking at her entree, she said, "Maybe we didn't think it through. Give it some thought, Gordon. It's okay if we cancel the project."

Clerise became elusive at work. He saw something in her face as if she were shutting a door when she said she and Michael wouldn't be able to go to the cabin that weekend. Gordon went anyway.

The drive to Freelak was gloomy without the smell of her perfume, the occasional contact of her shoulder, and the bleep of Michael's electronic toy. He surveyed the interior of the cabin, a musty, dilapidated structure. What was he holding onto? His space. During the past few weeks, that space had filled with laughter, chatter, and the mundane made memorable once more. If he updated the cabin, what could he expect after the project was over? He'd get his space back, but it would be changed. He would be changed. If he didn't update the cabin, he'd get his space back, but he still would be changed. He already had been.

And so, a few days later, he arrived at Clerise and Michael's. He didn't have to do this. Yet ….

"You know, I'm curious to see how things turn out," he said when Clerise reached the station wagon, "I mean. I mean, because of you, I didn't get hauled away as a lunatic, let alone given a huge citation for transporting wild animals across state lines."

Clerise's laugh was quiet and deep. She seemed genuinely tickled at the image.

"I mean, what an interesting experiment. What I'm saying is …." Gordon began to flounder. "What I'm saying is that we should complete Michael's project. After all, we're talking about his future here. A science camp is at stake." He opened the back of the Oldsmobile, packed with rolls of insulation.

CHAPTER 20
GHOULS

L ike I said last spring, you aren't being brutal enough. Brian ruined something of yours, you ruin something of his," Becca whispered. She poked a coat hanger down the window by the car door's lock and pulled. "Open the gas cap, O."

"Yeah, but what's being brutal got to do with Ray's car?" Olivia placed the cap on the sedan's roof, gas leaving an oily smell on her fingers.

"Shit, O. Brian trashed your boom box. You almost died. Who bought you the boom box in the first place? Your old man." Becca nodded toward the front of the Wrenowskis' house. "Lauren, leave that back door open. Spider, Dank don't let go of those cats."

"I get that, but Brian got me a new one, and I didn't die." Olivia took her time opening the box of sugar.

"Brian got me a new one," Becca mimicked, untwisted the cap on a small tube. "If he'd got the message we left on his lawn…."

"Becca, this is way not cool. Couldn't we do something else?" Olivia asked.

"You wanna get back at him so he never messes with you again. He'll know it was you. And me. And Lauren. And Spider. And Dank. We got your back. And nothin' he can do about it. You'll be back in your room like you never left. 'Sides, you'll feel so awesome. Even better than last time."

She motioned for Dank and Spider to bring the cats and moved next to Olivia. "What the fuck, O? Just dump it in. Lauren, you done with the razor blade? We're outta here."

Becca was right, especially when she remembered how terrified she'd been in Gordon's garage. Brian getting grounded was not good enough even if he had apologized himself. Which he hadn't. But the most awesome feeling came from laughing and jumping and hugging her friends under the streetlamp. They'd had her back.

Later that evening, Olivia sat motionless at the kitchen table in case any movement might change her dad's mind about the culprit. John leaned against a counter, bundled in a raincoat and scarf, not going to stay long. "Well, I had a chat with Ray. He's going to call off Patricia. I can't believe she'd blame that on you, Punkin. How could they even dream you'd be capable of super-gluing the car locks? I pointed out someone could be out to get her. She's on the council, maybe some sorehead."

"John, I'm afraid gang activity might be moving in, although why someone would target the Wrenowskis is beyond me." Donna shook her head, arms folded. "We could be at risk. All that graffiti scratched into the paint."

"If it'd been gangs, they would've stripped the car and not left cats inside. Ray insisted on showing me. Cat piss all over everything. There's sugar around the gas cap and on the ground, so even with that alone, the car would've been totaled. Not our problem, but either of you have any idea who'd want to do that?"

Olivia stared at her shoes. *You weren't there for me. Becca was.* She focused on her dad's hat to avoid his eyes and shook her head.

+++

Patricia's mission to find out who was in the pictures had stalled. Keeping a vigil for the girls in the photos, she edged the van along the street as if lost, while she chauffeured clients to view houses, and her clients were perplexed. She now gave Brian a ride from school each day, hoping she might spot someone. If she arrived fifteen minutes before the dismissal bell and parked across the street from the entrance, she could watch students as they left. Visually disentangling the tight knots of girls to see if anyone looked familiar was tough. They moved quickly, shielded by their backpacks. Her strategy lasted about a week until Brian failed to turn up. At home that afternoon, he ranted about what a loser he was because she picked him up from school.

Next, Patricia cruised the streets, following groups of girls until they began to glance nervously over their shoulders at her creeping van. She needed a better plan.

The box and camera's presence in the linen closet drew her. Her compulsion nauseated her each time she breached the floorboard cover, increasing the likelihood Ray would know. Thankfully, no new pictures had emerged, and the news hadn't mentioned any current incidents, but she wondered if he pawed through the old ones anyway.

When she had a chance to calm down, Patricia implemented a plan to do damage control. Brian would not be home with Ray any more than possible, so he had soccer, debate club, computer club, and anything else she could think of to fill his spare time. Fortunately, he'd had this kind of schedule for years. Being home in the evenings was anathema to her, spurring her to revise her schedule, showing more houses at night, and going to libraries.

Fall was busy for real estate. Patricia knew she was crazy to spend time in this hunt, but she figured she might spot some of the girls in yearbooks. She copied the Polaroids and made a file, which she took to the libraries and combed through yearbooks in hopes of matching her pictures. But often years were missing.

Having no luck, she went to high school libraries. The librarians, probably from years of policing students, kept her in close scrutiny, which made her nervous. She couldn't bring out the pictures without being seen. When she asked if she could check out the yearbooks, the answer each time was that school policy prevented it. She couldn't concentrate and so she struck out.

+++

Halloween approached. Olivia surveyed the classroom from her post in the last row next to Becca. She'd never been able to figure out why kids wanted to sit in the back. Well, duh. How did she not get how vulnerable she'd been? In the past, she hadn't been able to see who could ambush her from behind. Her scalp stung as she remembered the crap she had been hit with over the years. Here, there was no behind.

The bell rang. Becca slid in next to her. "Hey."

"Hey. Wazzup?"

"Usual."

"Yeah."

Then Buchard began scratching across the chalkboard. "…due Wednesday. Two pages … rough." Olivia squinted at the board, opened her spiral notebook, put a date at the top of the page, and started to write down the assignment. Becca cocked her head, raised an eyebrow. Olivia slid her eyes back to Becca. "What?"

"As if."

"Whatever." And Olivia stopped writing.

"Spider was totally wasted last night." Becca's voice registered just below the rustling.

"No lie?" Olivia scrawled across the notebook.

"Why'd you leave?" Becca asked.

"Had to get back before I got caught." Olivia picked at her black nail polish.

"Surprised you're not grounded."

"I moved to the downstairs guest bedroom," Olivia whispered.

"You shitting me? Sweet."

"The shrink told the parents to give me a little space. I'm at an age where I need to discover who I am." Olivia made a face.

"Can't believe this class is so lame," Becca said.

"Ms. Becca speak up, so we can hear your contributions to this enlightening discussion. I'm sure you have something interesting to say," Buchard called.

"Not really."

"It must have been something. You appear so engrossed. Pray share it with the rest of us."

"I said, 'I can't believe his name.'"

"Heathcliff?"

"I love doing this. Fucking with his head," Becca said under her breath.

"Ms. Becca, you will have to speak up." The teacher pressed his back against the board, smile frozen on his face, eyes boring into her. "I'll send you to the office if you said what I think you said."

Becca raised her eyes and gazed back. She tilted her head sideways, appraised him. "I don't know what you mean. I just said, 'I have a cold stuck in my head.' I can't hear so good myself."

The teacher nodded. "Then you can move closer so you can hear. Right here." Olivia smirked. Buchard was pointing to the front row.

Becca shoved her desk back, the metallic screech shooting across the classroom, dumped her books on the floor, and with broad gestures retrieved them. All the front-facing heads craned back at her. Some just stared. Others laughed.

"My apologies, sir," Becca said. She grabbed the strap on her pack and flung it over her shoulder, hitting Dank. "Ohmygod. I am soooo sorry. I am just all clumsy today." Becca giggled.

"Becca, you have ten seconds to get up here, nine, eight—"

"All right. All right. I'm coming."

"What an ass wipe," Olivia said as Becca sidled by.

"Olivia!" Buchard's voice cracked through the room. "That's it. Out!"

"But …," Olivia started to exclaim, then stopped. "Yeah, whatever."

As she left the classroom, she could hear Mr. Buchard on the phone: "… on her way to the office. Insubordination."

+++

The avenues had been a forest of orange lights, pumpkins, skeletons, and bats for a month. Forester knew how to celebrate the holiday. But Halloween was unusual that year, the evening balmy, as if the seasons had somehow confused themselves. Normally, the frost had staked out the early mornings, soon to be followed by subzero weather that turned the lawns to concrete.

For the first Halloween in many years, Gordon sat on his front step, a thick glass bowl at his side, recognizing children who had toured his museum as he dropped a handful of candy into their bags. The evening wore on, trick-or-treaters now infrequent and comprised of older kids. *It is truly an Indian summer*, he thought.

That serenity he relished stole over him. The quiet was an island engulfing his front porch. Peaceful.

The time of night to be watchful arrived. On more than one All Souls' Day, he had wakened to a blizzard of toilet paper, his windows frosted in soap. He had played those tricks himself, except these days, he noted graffiti on walls and buildings. The tricks were more like vandalism.

A large, hulking shape shambled towards his stoop, which Gordon didn't recognize until the figure was directly opposite. Bubba waved a six-pack.

"Thought you could use the company," he said as he wiggled a beer out of its plastic loop and handed it to Gordon.

A cluster of shadows slid in the direction of the Wrenowskis'. One like a decaying crookneck squash on legs caught Gordon's attention as he took a swig, but Bubba appeared oblivious.

He began to describe Michael's science experiment, laughing

along with Bubba at the police incident and Clerise's quick thinking, for a brief moment picturing Clerise, Michael, and him by the fire at the cabin.

A couple of beers later, Bubba's back receded toward home, and Gordon checked his watch. Late. Almost the witching hour. Achy from his vigil on the front steps, he hauled himself up and retreated to a lawn chair in the shelter of the porch.

He waited.

Patience. Gordon was good at that. Patience was sitting in the recess of the veranda, alert, despite arthritis and longing to lie down. Patience was waiting out the deep grief and guilt in not being able to stop his wife from wanting to go to Vietnam. Patience was riding out the regret in losing the family store. And most certainly, patience was clocking in at U Do It every morning. So there he sat in his lawn chair.

The witching hour came. No ghosts or ghouls like Michael's school drawings, just a chill some might think was someone walking over his grave. But it was only the night chasing the Indian summer.

Then he saw the black squash appear under the streetlight at the end of the block and turn onto his street. Gordon left his post and moved to the front steps.

"Olivia," he said as she passed. Startled, she dropped a can of spray paint, grabbed it, and hid it behind her back. "You're out late."

Her hands were black. Gordon could imagine her trying to get the paint off. She'd be marked for a few days.

"Looks like you got an empty spray paint can. You can put it in my trash." She backed off a few steps. "Olivia, come keep me company for a couple of minutes."

She hesitated as if about to run but then approached up the path and sat on the cool concrete step.

"Why don't you give me that can?" he asked.

"Uh, thanks. I found it on the sidewalk." She jerked her head toward the streetlamp.

Gordon took the spent can and placed it in the glass bowl. "Must've had quite a bit of paint on it judging from your fingers."

Her hands disappeared into the black fabric of her lap. "Yeah."

Speculating what might be going on, Gordon made small talk. He struggled. He could ignore it and let her parents deal with her. He could treat her like the adult she wanted to be and tell her his concern. More small talk.

"Olivia," Gordon said. She jumped. "This is your spray can, isn't it?"

"Yeah, what of it?"

"Well, this stuff is permanent. If you sprayed anything, it'll take someone a lot of work to get it off. If they can. They may have to spend a lot of money to repaint."

"Uh, uh. Becca said it would come off with paint remover."

"Becca."

"Yeah, she's my best friend now. We hang out together."

"She can't be much of a friend. You understand what'll happen if you get caught?"

"Yeah, but I won't. We were just playing a trick." She twisted toward him. Gordon kept his face impassive. "You know, I was forced to do this. I didn't have a choice."

"It may not seem like it, but you did have a choice. This time you made the wrong one."

"Well, I don't think so. You are so lame." Like a spring pushing her, she was on her feet. "We were just having a little fun. I don't care what you do. Call the cops. Call my folks. You're just like everybody else."

She ran down the steps and toward home.

Gordon watched her disappear and sighed. He took the depleted can to the trash. In the garage, he rummaged until he found a jar of paint remover. He shambled along the avenue and deposited the jar on Dimatos back porch. Turning back toward his home, he saw Patricia climb the steps to her veranda, the decorations going dark in her wake.

Restless from his encounter with Olivia, he took up his vigil on his lawn chair once again. Along the block, houses' first floor lights flicked off, followed by upstairs bedroom windows darkening. Soon just a row of porch lights lined the street. Ray's new green sedan curved onto his driveway. Intrigued at his neighbor's late-night return, Gordon craned to see if Ray had on a costume, but nothing from his attire at this distance suggested it.

The evening advanced. Shadows and ghouls and something more sinister.

+ + +

Patricia had leaned over each pumpkin staggered up the steps to the front door and blown out the candle stubs, the smell of singed guts slipping up her nostrils. The jack-o-lanterns' grins sagged with age. She knew the feeling. While this was her favorite time of year next to the Forester barbeque and Christmas, she had ended the evening emotionally off balance. She gathered the full skirts of her Glenda the Good costume, the white tulle fluttering in the breeze. The weather would be cold tomorrow. By then, the squirrels would turn the pumpkins into masses of gnawed flesh. On the porch, she pulled the plug to the orange-lighted decorations, seeing black loops on the clapboard, the kind she sped past in certain areas of Chicago.

The patrol officer she called was unconcerned when he heard nothing had been stolen and no one was hurt. Someone would be out in the morning. They were busy with a more urgent matter. Brian was ostensibly in bed, and Ray had yet to walk through the door.

Smoking and wine were the only things that could help. She settled in a living room wingchair to wait for her husband, the bottle on the end table next to the ashtray, her Glenda the Good wand propped against the chair's legs. As the level of the wine bottle crept down, she scolded herself. She knew damn well Ray was on the prowl. If she didn't act, he would get caught and everything would explode. Her thoughts ricocheted from the village council to Brian to work to anger at her husband. Ambivalence had balled her up, and she had yet to think of a plan that would protect her son and not sacrifice her political career and business.

Finally, she crawled into bed, playing her part in the ruse, expecting Ray would sleep in the guest room as he had taken to doing. But a movement, like a sudden gust of frigid air, startled her from sleep. She could feel the slight fluff as Ray slid under the sheets. His smell carried the remains of the day, and her nostrils flared at the floral scent clinging to his skin, sending her scuttling to the bathroom and barely making it before the burgundy contents of her stomach erupted. She huddled on the cold tiles in the bathroom while vomit dripped from her chin.

CHAPTER 21
THANKS

Olivia found herself trailing behind Becca and Lauren, listening to the conversation tossed back to her. At the town's resale shop, the two girls formed a screen while Becca exited stiff-legged with golf clubs. Olivia knew better than to ask why.

"People are so freaked when they see us, they won't see the clubs." Lauren talked over her shoulder to Olivia as she and Becca walked, arms wrapped around each other's waists, the clubs wedged between them.

She felt like the last person in a parade, and thanks to Lauren, the only time she could talk to her friend alone was in class. Even then, it was hurried or through passing notes. She ached watching Becca and Lauren. She'd always thought of gay women as being masculine. They were muscular and never wore anything but jeans and plaid shirts. She tried to think of girls she knew besides Becca and Lauren. There were celebrities like Ellen DeGeneres and Rosie O'Donnell. But who her age?

+++

"Can we talk?" Olivia passed a note to Becca.

"We talk all the time."

"No, I mean alone. Without Lauren."

Becca shrugged.

At the end of the day, Olivia caught up with her at Tacos N' More, praying Lauren would be late. What would she say? That she hated that Lauren monopolized all of Becca's time? That she liked it when the two of them did stuff together alone? That she was confused?

"Well?" Becca's face made Olivia's stomach turn to hard clay.

"Like I've been wondering," her pasty tongue glued the words together. "Are you and Lauren going together?" There, she spit it out.

Becca raised an eyebrow. "That's so lame. Are we going together? Gee, O, did I give her a ring?" she minced. "I don't go with anyone. But, yeah, I like Lauren. So what?"

"I … I was just wondering." She spotted Lauren in the restaurant's doorway. "Uh, I'm going to New York with Dad for Thanksgiving, and I wanted to bring you something. That's all."

"Are you jealous?" Becca grinned, the kind when she had an idea. "Well, sure, O. Bring me back something. Give me a call when you get there. Your old man loaded?" She cocked her head, looking over her shoulder as Lauren slid in next to her. "Hey," she cooed, enveloped the girl and kissed her.

+++

Patricia's script, usually round and loopy, jagged across the legal pad while she pretended to take notes at the village council meeting. Before her, a village police officer fussed with an overhead projection about the rapes in the vicinity. Behind him stood two other individuals representing a local group, Communities Are for Safe Streets or CASS. CASS came into being to avenge the assault of a young woman. According to the presentation, the young woman had been drugged and raped. The men from CASS wanted to generate a list of dates, places, and pretexts used to isolate subsequent victims. Patricia squirmed, thinking of her evidence. She could feel the sweat gathering at the base of her neck and lifted her hair away from her collar. The CASS members concluded by asking the village council to donate funds in order to form a task force with the police.

After the presenters left, Patricia scanned the members' faces. No one leapt forward to comment. "Well, I don't know," she said. "What exactly is CASS going to do with the money? God knows how much funding goes to the schools every year for stranger danger education, letters home to parents, PTA support, and community involvement." Internally, she cringed at what she had just said. "I mean, we also need to consider the rising vandalism in our community. In the past three months, our lawn has been destroyed, my husband's car ruined, and our house tagged with gang graffiti." She fought to keep her tone level, reasonable enough to imply their budget should be used for other pressing issues.

The president cleared his throat, scowled at her, and raised an eyebrow. "You might be some kind of target. And you want to divert precious dollars for your benefit?"

Patricia gulped. "Absolutely not! I expect others have been vandalized too. But while there may not be any connection to the rapes, there may be, and the council must take that seriously. I think we should partner with CASS. I volunteer to head an ad hoc group. I'll keep the council informed on CASS's progress and coordinate any support we wish to give. Who wants to help?"

Her request for volunteers was met with awkward paper rustling. A vote approving the move to form the committee was seconded and passed. With Thanksgiving just days away, the council adjourned until the new year, and Patricia left the meeting chairing a committee of one.

The chance of someone discovering what Ray was doing before she could think up a plan now became somewhat less risky. She'd have access to information she could use to protect herself and Brian.

A few evenings later found her in her dining room, chipping away at the dried wax on the side of the candelabra. A halfhearted turkey carcass roosted in the center of the table, flanked by a dented mountain of mashed potatoes and peas drowning in a pond of solidifying butter.

She sat alone, studying the gravy stains on the linen by Ray's plate, as if they could give a clue to the internal workings of her husband.

Ray had scraped the chair legs against the newly refinished oak floor. She knew the act was to spite her and to push enough buttons to start a fight. Within moments, they were hurling insults at each other with practiced proficiency. The real issue was who would stomp off first.

Brian concentrated on decorating his mashed potato mountain with peas and blobs of cranberry sauce, much the same as when he was three and built food sculptures and then refused to eat. She listened to Ray's continued protestation as he climbed the stairs. She hardly heard her son stand and leave the room.

In the buffet drawer, she had stashed a number of cigarettes in the silverware box. Lighting one, she took a deep drag, not caring anymore if she got caught. They probably knew anyway. Inhaling all that tar and nicotine was so satisfying that for a moment she forgot why she had ever decided to quit in the first place. Right. Brian had become "born again" in fifth grade, thanks to a drug and alcohol prevention program at school. He was convinced Patricia would die soon. He would follow after taking a downward spiral into marijuana, alcohol, and crystal meth, culminating in HIV/AIDS from sharing contaminated needles in some murky hallway of a decomposing building.

In the buffet cupboard were the liquor bottles. As long as she was going to feel sorry for herself, she might as well feel really sorry for herself the following morning when, with a raging hangover, she faced her angry husband and son.

Patricia now grabbed a bar glass and shoved bottles around to find something that would go with pumpkin pie. She spotted the Frangelico and poured a finger's worth. Another finger paired with a second piece and whipped cream. The next shot was capped with whipped cream, making her woozy and sleepy. She pushed back the chair and decided she would deal with the dishes in the morning. The turkey had managed to get wrapped and refrigerated sometime between the second and third drinks, as had all the uneaten vegetables. The plates remained at their places like a suddenly evacuated gathering. If this room were to be buried in volcanic ash, what would future archaeologists think? That they had been enjoying a traditional Thanksgiving feast when all of a sudden, the festivities were dramatically interrupted? Patricia re-positioned her chair.

The house felt sullen, the low energy like fog. On the second floor, Brian's door was closed, and she could hear noise from his TV or a video game. At the top of the stairs to the attic, she saw a slit of light underlining the door. Ray must be doing something up there. Was this where he was hiding more stuff?

She collapsed onto the bed, relieved that he had moved into the guest room permanently. Sometime in the night, she roused, the bedside lamp still burning, switched it off, turned over, with the thought that Thanksgiving was over for another year and December's rush was just beginning.

And then she was wide awake, the memory of the lighted crack under the attic door slicing open her consciousness. She had to get this under control. That meant confronting Ray.

+++

The Thanksgiving feast at the cabin was simple but had the essentials. The smell of roasting turkey wafted around the newly insulated walls while Clerise prepared sweet potatoes, a very important part of her family's tradition, she assured him. Gordon had never been crazy about the vegetable, but she swore next year he would be drooling for them. Michael countered that his mom was exaggerating, then grumbled about going back to Forester and the adults having to work on Friday.

Gordon had been through too many Black Fridays to be rocked by nerves, except Hunter's behavior and the opening of the Winter Wonderland Department bored into his brain like a drill. His boss had insisted he take Wednesday off, adding that he wanted the assistant department manager, Rick, to get some experience. Besides, Hunter had concluded, things were under control. What could his assistant do while Gordon was away? *Major damage*, Gordon thought. But he said nothing of his misgivings to Clerise so that at least two people would fully enjoy the holiday.

After the meal, Gordon and Clerise sat at a picnic table in a park at Freelak, drank tea from a thermos and watched Michael and Isaac shoot down the toboggan run. They could see the pompoms of the boys' caps as the line to the run wiggled and lurched forward, people crowding the park in this first real evidence of the snowy winter ahead.

"I'm trying to remember if this run was here when I was a kid," Gordon mused. "But somehow it escapes me. Dad was busy at this time of year, making sure the Christmas inventory was in."

"The town where I was a kid had a small hardware store," Clerise said. "Part of a chain of shops you accessed through doorways in various locations, like a maze. The hardware store had a doorway to the women's apparel shop, and through the back was the children's store with a doorway to a pharmacy, and then the men's store. Boys hated the layout as they got older and wanted to buy rubbers. The risk of someone recognizing them no doubt contributed to a bunch of shotgun weddings." Clerise chortled.

Gordon watched Michael and Isaac just visible above the run's wooden sides, the toboggan shooting toward the end. "Beats me how my great-grandfather and great-grandmother lived in that cabin, but they did. You can still see the garden where they raised crops."

"My lord, you are chatty today, Gordon," Clerise patted him on the shoulder. "So when and how did they get to Forester?" From a distance, Michael gave a thumbs-up sign.

"After the Civil War, lots of folks moved to Chicago. My great-grandfather opened a hardware store there. Then my grandfather saw an ad in the paper for a new village near the city with promises of jobs and growth. That got old Carlson started. What brought you to Forester?"

"My husband landed a great job in an accounting firm. I wasn't a-counting on him landing other things." She burst into laughter at her own joke. "Michael was a baby when his father and I split, and I had just finished my B.A. in business."

"You have a business degree? What are you doing working for such a nincompoop as Charlie?"

"Well, I researched, and the schools in Forester are good. No way could I afford to buy a place. No way this black woman be getting any kind of management job here, yes suh. Thanks to U Do It, I can be close to the school. I get some child support and we be comfortable."

Clerise brightened. "Michael and Isaac are placing the toboggan. They're going again."

He reached out a glove, put it on hers, and as Gordon turned to watch the boys, he saw others look away.

Clerise eased her hand into her lap. "Oh Gordon, you are such a wonderful man, but it's still there, just gone underground. Where do the African Americans in Forester live? Where their servant predecessors lived. Granted, the homes are now upscale. But it's still there."

The chill, where her warm glove had been, crept up his arm and froze his unspoken thought, the thought that when the squirrel experiment was over, at least he had this day.

And then as if he thawed, he wondered how he had forgotten something so important. "You know, our family was part of the underground during the Civil War. The cabin has a root cellar under the floor where we hid runaway slaves. Haven't been down there in decades."

Back at the cabin, Gordon rolled back the tattered rug. Squatting on his haunches, he studied the floorboards until he pointed at the small indent, the trap door to the cellar. With a flashlight, he and Michael clambered down the ladder.

Michael sneezed, and Gordon took out an inhaler. "I forgot how dusty and musty this cellar is." Along the walls were wooden shelves used to house canned goods as well as cold-storage vegetables. Gordon moved his hand along the walls and found the gap, so slight as to be invisible. Next, he felt along the wood until his fingers landed on a small shim. Edging that out, he was able to pull open the door to reveal a room big enough to hold about four people.

"This is where slaves escaping to Canada could hide if bounty hunters came by and searched the cabin." Gordon pulled out his inhaler again and took a big puff.

Michael stood in the small dirt room. "How did bounty hunters find this place? It's in the middle of nowhere."

"Apparently they did or else it wouldn't be here. This is wreaking havoc on my lungs. Let's go back upstairs, okay?" The boy was already placing a foot on the ladder.

Thursday morning, Gordon steered the station wagon home and wondered what disaster he'd soon be steering through at U Do It.

+++

The Friday morning after Thanksgiving, Olivia and her dad caught a cab in New York's Midtown to go shopping. Because he had a business meeting on Saturday morning, Becca said Olivia could take back the clothes and get cash, so to remember their route.

The cabby sounded like someone from a TV show. "So d'ya see the Thanksgiving Day Parade?" He put the car in gear, glancing at them from his rearview mirror, and elbowed into traffic.

Her dad leaned forward, "Yeah. I loved it. You go every year?"

"When I can. How'd you like da balloons? Little ones love 'em, 'specially Garfield."

"Boring." Olivia, muffled in a black scarf, pulled her chin out. "What a waste of time. I got up in the middle of the night to go stand in the freezing cold behind a million people, and I couldn't even see anything."

"Ya' woin't lookin' high enough." With his right hand, the cabby manipulated the wheel and kept another taxi from cutting in front, winning a precious few feet. "Yeah, yeah, the floats is okay, but gimme da balloons. Talk about grand, the way they goes down the street an' all the folks that gotta hold onto 'em." He hunched forward in a shabby, red jacket with an oil spot on the shoulder, honked at pedestrians crossing against the lights, scrambled through the inter-section, and careened to a stop. "Ya been to da Twin Towers yet?"

"I'm taking Olivia to see them tomorrow afternoon. They're some-thing, aren't they?" her dad said.

"Yeah, right. A big building's a big building. We got plenty of them in Chicago. Ever hear of the Sears Tower?"

In the rearview mirror, the cabby's eyes crinkled above a bulbous nose. "Yeah? How old are you? I got a daughter 'bout your age."

"Fifteen."

"Yep, 'bout the same age all right."

"Okaay, Punkin, we're at Macy's."

"We got one in Chicago."

The cabby scooted behind other yellow traffic bullets and slammed on the brakes. "Enjoy da' Big Apple."

"Like here's any better than the Windy City." Olivia pulled up her muffler and pulled down her hat.

"Well soochyerself." The cabby nodded.

Once in the store, her dad let the sales associate know this was a shopping spree so that his Ollie could get some new outfits. After all, she was not a little girl anymore.

The Olivia in the changing room mirror resembled various flam-boyant beach balls. In frustration, she threw the clothes on the floor, dressed, and crowded past her father, who was seated in a waiting area. He trailed after, gesticulating that he didn't understand what was so wrong. Tell him. Let him help.

She pushed through the exterior doors and down the packed

sidewalk. Just about at the corner, she stopped. Had he followed? She focused on the display window at some dumb Santa scene with fake snow and reindeer. In the moment he approached her, she made sure to turn her back and round the corner. She slowed her pace, halted, and wiped her eyes with her hand, then pretended to search her pockets for her gloves as he reached her side.

They walked to her dad's nonstop commentary on the street, about the stores and people until from a distance, she spotted a store window crammed between the glitter of white lights and enormous displays. A fluttering in her stomach drew her toward it.

"Dad, awesome! This is so rad. Can you believe it?" Before them was a toppled, silver Christmas tree, decorated in jet ornaments, a black star cocked sideways in the process of falling to the floor. Splintered ornaments displayed shiny silver centers as if a robot squirrel had noshed through them. Crushed white and black boxes were testament to someone drunkenly listing around the room in the wee hours of the morning. Rats squatted in the corner, peering at a young mannequin woman dressed in a flour sack. Another mannequin sprawled on a dilapidated couch. And in the window was a large placard, blood red on white, "Season's Greetings."

Olivia shoved through the door, on which was painted in jagged letters "Shattered." And stopped. The shop's flat black walls swallowed intense halogen lights. Shoppers rooted through stacks of black T-shirts. Army fatigues followed each other in close formation on circular racks. Others contained circles of black jeans. In the center, haloed in white light and surrounded by lucite boxes, was the cashier's square.

Taking a couple of steps forward, she inhaled with satisfaction. A young woman with white makeup, her features enhanced by black lips, a nose ring, and a dog collar around her neck, approached. "Yo, whatcha need?" she said.

"Clothes." She could feel her dad behind her. "You know, jeans, tops, jewelry. Stuff.”

"Yeah, what size?" The sales associate appraised Olivia's figure.

"Thirty-six, thirty."

"Gotcha." The clerk shouldered her way to the back, Olivia following. "These just came in. I think you'll need a twenty-nine leg," she said.

Olivia held the jeans to her waist and nodded. "What else ya got?"

"How's it going, Punkin?" Her dad elbowed his way through the racks to her side.

"O!"

The woman guided them to the other side of the store where ottomans, splattered in paint, created a shoe space, then departed, mumbling Olivia's shoe size.

"You gotta get these." She staggered back with a tower of shoe boxes. By now they were old friends.

And then her expert fingers entered digits into the cash register, diminishing a substantial pile into black sacks. "You go back to Chicago and show those losers at your school what you're about, girl." The clerk paused. "Know what? Just a suggestion, but you're kind of out of it with only one piercing. You should get a set up your ears." She lifted a hank of hair to show Olivia. "We got someone here can do that."

Sometime later, father and daughter burst into the glare of the street, lugging several shopping bags, Olivia carrying a hand full of alcohol wipes in her pocket for later.

"These are great duds, Punkin, I mean, O. You're sure that the school will let you wear them?"

Olivia thought for a moment. "You know, you might be right. I should get a variety of clothes just in case. Let's go back to Macy's. I'm sorry about earlier."

The city was a mash of lights scaling the skyscrapers and illuminating the night as they rode back to the hotel, replete. John closed the privacy glass in the cab. "Olivia, what's this about?" He pointed to the new piercings on her ears. "You show up for Thanksgiving in jeans that look as if they'd been worn by a homeless person. While I think you got some cool stuff at that shop, are you sure kids are wearing this?"

"No duh, Daaad. You think I'm going to get a bunch of loser clothes?"

"It's just that it's not like you, Punkin."

"I'm. Not. Your. Punkin."

"Right, honey, I know that. You're growing into a lovely young woman. I'm trying to get used to that. But sometimes I don't recognize you."

"OOOOkaaay, Dad." She clenched her jaw.

"It's just that you're fifteen. It's normal for you to want to try things at this age, O."

At the word "normal," torrential anger filled her. "OOOOkaaay, Daaad."

"O, as I said, it's normal."

Olivia continued to apply the Accident Chrome lipstick she'd just gotten, her lips like teeny bumpers in her compact mirror.

Past dark when they got back to the hotel, Olivia grabbed the mint on her dad's pillow and made her way to the sitting room. She dumped the bags where their contents cascaded onto the small table, then turned on the TV, channel-surfing through *Beavis and But-thead*—those dinks were so much like Brian—and stopped when she spotted MTV. She glanced through the curtain sheers at New York City, the flash of TV sets in apartment after apartment after apartment, flickering like forgetful Christmas lights.

A wisp of conversation came from her dad's bedroom. She tiptoed to the door where she could hear.

"Donna, you'd … same thing." After a pause John's voice dipped. "… that bad, and you won't notice it with her hair." Her ears pricked at the edge in her dad's voice. She remembered the drill from before the divorce, their voices rising and circling each other like hawks. Often she had put her hands to her ears, or pretended to be asleep, or left the room. One time, she went for a walk and returned to find their voices in full attack mode.

In her bathroom, she grabbed a washcloth and cleaned off the makeup. She put on tiny, sparkly earrings from the day's purchases. In the bedroom, she pulled on the new stirrup pants and striped sweater from Macy's, brushed her hair, and made sure her new piercings didn't show.

Back at her father's door, she rapped and could hear, "I'll drop her off around noon. See you then."

Olivia stood in the doorway.

"Here's the young woman I know! You look beautiful."

"I do?" Her throat constricted.

"Yes, honey, you do. Let's order room service. We've had a big day. I'm pooped. And I want to see you in your new duds." His smile was eager, the one she remembered from when she was little.

They ate dinner in the sitting room, each with a glass of pink wine, way cool to be sitting so high in a posh suite. She wouldn't be able to brag to Ashley or Brian, and they would have gotten the significance. She could tell Becca about some of it, but what it was like right now, she couldn't.

Later that night, her dad having closed the door to his bedroom, she shoved the purchases she was going to return back into the bags. He'd acted so proud as she paraded her girly new clothes. But Becca was expecting jeans and tops. She grabbed one of the pastel sweaters from the heap and then noticed the necklace and flower earrings her dad had admired and snatched those out of the returns too.

Riding the elevator to the lobby the next morning, she told herself this was no different than Chicago. She'd been to the Loop many times to meet her father. She steeled herself, remembering Lauren with

Becca, stepped up to the doorman, and asked him to hail her a cab.

+++

When the limo parked in front of Olivia's house at noon that Sunday, Forester families had been busy decorating their gingerbread eaves for a Victorian Christmas. She glanced for a moment in the direction of the Wrenowskis' house, her brows wrinkling at the sight of cracks striating their first-floor windows. Donna stood on the front porch. She watched her mother take in the effect of her winter camo parka and the dog collar around her neck. On her hands were gloves with the fingers clipped off. Her polished nails shone in gunmetal.

"John, what the hell did you let her do?"

CHAPTER 22
BIG DEAL

Upon arriving at U Do It late Thanksgiving afternoon, Gordon came the closest ever to clobbering a living soul. Rick, the assistant manager, exercising his sudden managerial power, had decided to reconfigure the Winter Wonderland Department so that the display was at the back of the store. But the move was only partially completed.

Something like this was bound to happen. The prospect that had squatted in Gordon's brain for the past two days materialized.

Hunter's oversight of the Winter Wonderland project was a disaster. Initially, plans had progressed uneventfully until inventory began to arrive. The one successful change Hunter had accomplished was in the department Clerise oversaw, which Gordon now knew was due to her business acumen and sheer drive. Then the first glitch occurred. Their shipment of snowmobiles had gone to Massachusetts. Confrontation over whose order it was delayed critical deadlines. So Hunter assigned Rick to assist Gordon in untangling the mess even though the boy had decimated the do-it-yourself classes. The assistant bungled his new role, angering Gordon's contacts, whose cooperation meant the difference between success and failure, thus adding hours to his overpacked day as he finessed a situation that threatened to topple the project. Then just before Thanksgiving, Hunter temporarily reassigned Clerise to her old secretarial position on the second floor, stating her wild African garb during the Christmas season would clash with the colors. She found piles of correspondence that had not been sent, documents not signed, and the filing system trashed by the secretary Charlie had hired and subsequently fired.

Thanksgiving afternoon, Gordon stood on the lunatic fringe with sixteen hours until the early-bird sale. The first order of business was to halt the action and send Rick home. Then he'd need to return the Winter Wonderland Department to the original layout. The catch was it would take the rest of the night.

Moving and organizing went without a hitch; however, Gordon was superstitious: Something needed to go wrong to ensure the sale went right. And it did. At 4:00 a.m., Gordon heard a huge crash coming from the back of the store. A forklift driver had slammed into the shelving, toppling stock and creating dominoes of shelves that plunged into each other all the way to the back wall.

Miss DuPont Junior College arrived at 6:00 a.m. to take her place on the snowmobile, where she would perch on a special dais behind a fraternity boy who was at the wheel of the machine.

By 6:30, the night crew staggered out, the morning staff staggered in, and Hunter arrived to assume command. He scowled at the snow vehicle display. "What the hell is this doing here? When I left Wednesday night, the snowmobile was being moved to the back. And why is she in that?" Hunter pointed at the young woman who stood in a snowmobile suit, her ribbon cut tight across her chest between two ample breasts. "She should have on her tiara and her contest-winning swimsuit."

The beauty pageant winner backed away taking refuge behind Frat Boy.

"First off, the display will be totally wasted in the back," Gordon responded.

"I thought Rick's idea was a good one. What? Were you here all night undoing his work?" Hunter raked a hand through his close-cropped hair.

"Employees would have been here all night anyway. The boy mis-gauged the amount of time it would take to move the display. He had created a mess by the time I arrived. Everything was scattered throughout the store. If the display had been moved to the back, no one would see it."

"The whole point, Gordo, was for shoppers to go through the store. It's the special sale item. Do I also have to teach you marketing?"

"You approved my configuration plan. You agreed that putting the snowmobile display at the front would entice people in. I think mine's the better plan."

"Well, I changed my mind. Let's continue this in my office." Hunter marched to the back and up the stairs. From his window, the two surveyed the floor below.

"Rick reported to me. I gave him no instructions to do this. As for those two," Gordon pointed at the couple below, "did you honestly think she was going to sit on a snowmobile in a bathing suit?"

"Look at those racks. See? See what your meddling did, Carlson?"

"Rick overstocked the racks with inventory on top of empty boxes that shouldn't have been there." Gordon pointed to a twisted rack that resembled an earthquake calamity.

"Jesus Christ!" Hunter's voice spattered like shrapnel.

"I'd bet money that snowmobile display is exactly where it should be and set up the way it should be."

"Okay, you're on. If today's sales numbers exceed projections by ten percent, you win and I bring you tea every day for a month. If not, I win, and you bring me coffee every day." Hunter extended a hand.

"Fine." Gordon shook and headed toward the toppled racks. What he couldn't figure out was why so many empty cartons got mingled with the back stock.

As the store opened, employees in bibs, elf hats, and pointy felt elf shoes over their work boots stood at the door and at the aisles. Pinned to their bibs were badges that read "Treat the Elf in yourself. I'm (Employee name). I'm here to help."

At ten o'clock, Charlie arrived in a Santa suit riding a forklift, waved, and stopped at the snowmobile display. Santa Hunter announced a drawing on Christmas Eve to give away a snowmobile to some lucky girl or boy.

Eleven hours later and thirty-six hours since he had last climbed out of bed, Gordon stood in the main aisle scouting the store. Black Friday was over as straggling shoppers dallied toward checkout. He knew the day had definitely been black. With all the cash registers busy, even the customer service desk was handling sales. He grinned, the kind that stretched and wouldn't stop. He pictured Hunter proffering a cup of tea until he remembered whom he was dealing with.

+++

As Friday began, Patricia dialed the number for the window repairman she used in her real estate business. Late the previous night, someone had thrown hot coffee on all the first-floor windows.

"You know, Mrs. Wrenowski, you've got some serious vandalism going on here. Has your son changed his group of friends within the past few months?" The window repairman ran a glove over the cracks.

"No, he's got the same ones as always. Anyway, why would kids want to target me?" All the damage since the previous spring was the kind of pranks kids would play. Adults would be more subtle: rumor, back-stabbing to make sure she wasn't re-elected. Kids. Olivia? She was in New York. Then it hit her. Someone figured it out. This wasn't aimed at her. Or Brian.

+++

Becca nodded approval at Olivia's Christmas gifts. She fished out another pair of jeans from the black sack, held them against her stomach, and stuffed them in her backpack. In the cold, she'd shrugged off her jacket and put on a black T-shirt, the front reading, *I Dare You.* On the back was, *And See What Happens.*

157

"How come you didn't get me one of those?" She pointed at Olivia's dog collar.

"I ran out of money." Olivia's happy anticipation sank a notch. "But I got you this." She handed Becca a little box containing a friendship bracelet.

"What?" She examined the aurora borealis beads. "I'd rather have a dog collar."

"Then take this one."

"Hey, thanks," Becca shoved the bracelet in her coat pocket before fastening the collar. "Well, I got you something too." She hopped a bit, pranced.

Olivia hadn't dreamed Becca would get her a gift. "Wow. So what is it?"

"The best thing I could've gotten you."

"Rad, like, where is it?" Olivia brightened.

"Are you blind? Didn't you see Wrenowskis' when you got home?" Becca danced, raising her arm in victory and sang. "I did it! I did it!" She made a rotating motion with arms and fists.

"You did that?" Olivia's chin raised, her eyes widening.

"No, duh, who'd you think? Best thing I've done yet. The sound when the coffee hit the windows was awesome."

"God, Becca!"

"You fat bitch. I do this for you. I do this so he doesn't forget, and that's how you say thanks?" Becca landed hard on her feet, her body expanding.

"No, not that, Becca." Olivia struggled, knew her face said it all. If she didn't change her expression, Becca was capable of anything. "Just that you could've been caught. I was afraid for a moment. You've paid Brian back and more. He'll never forget. He'll leave me alone now. Thanks, Becca. This is the best gift." She beamed.

"Too late. You ruined it for me, O, you pig."

Two days later, Lauren cornered Olivia as she reached the street.

Then Spider and Dank flanked her. She knew her defaced locker was their work. Her stomach like cottage cheese, she put on a fierce face and scowled to hide her anxiety. They closed in. No Becca.

"Word is you ratted out Becca for Thanksgiving," Dank said.

"What? Why would I do that?" The ranks tightened. She could feel the heat and smell of unwashed clothes wrapping around her like a rancid cocoon.

"What do you think we are? Mind-readers?" Spider jostled her.

Lauren, in front, stopped, Olivia crashing into her back.

"You pushing me? That what you're doing?" Lauren whirled. "Don't fuck with me, O. I'll bring you down." Olivia felt a hard punch on her shoulder.

"What the hell are you talking about? I'm …." The blow to her stomach buckled her knees.

"This is nothing compared to how we'll handle you if you even think of going to the cops. Got that, bitch?" Lauren sneered. From behind, in quick succession, came an awful pain in the small of her back from a boot, then the hard cement on her forehead.

Olivia kept her face to the ground for some minutes after the last footfall. Her face stung, and her back throbbed. She rolled over, crawling forward to find her backpack had vomited across the sidewalk and into the street.

As she wiggled the key in the back-porch lock, she noticed the kitchen light was on.

"Mr. Mahoney called me at work this afternoon," her mom said emerging from the foyer.

"Yeah, what of it?" Olivia fluffed her bangs to cover the scrape.

"He wants to see both of us tomorrow. Any idea what it might be about?"

"Haven't a clue," Olivia said.

"He's concerned about some activities that seem to be having a negative effect on you. Know what that would be?"

"Nothing's having a negative effect on me. You know it's not necessary, Mom."

"I'm going to take the morning off from work and keep the appointment. Whether you come or not is up to you."

"Jesus, Mom, aren't we getting psychobabbled enough? I mean, we see a shrink every other Saturday, which sucks. And then I have to check in with Mahoney."

"First of all, you know how I feel about that kind of language. Secondly, you know very well I'm not one of these absentee parents. So deal with it."

+ + +

They sat in Mahoney's office on the couch, her mother prim in her gray suit and white blouse, sitting straight-backed next to Olivia.

"Nice to see you both, and thank you, Mrs. Dimato, for taking time out of your busy day," Mahoney said, glancing at a notepad on his lap.

"I'm always available where Olivia's concerned. So how can I be of help?"

She's not wasting any time, Olivia thought. *Good, we'll be out of here sooner.*

"O, would you describe what's been going on?"

"Mr. Mahoney, I'm not sure I know what you mean."

"Perhaps you might help us understand the reference in black, permanent marker on your locker door. I see from your expression, Mrs. Dimato, that you're not aware. O's locker was vandalized."

"Mr. Mahoney, I'll clean it off."

"Someone wrote 'snitch' in black marker. The school takes this kind of thing seriously. O, do you know of anyone who'd want to do that?"

Donna interrupted, "Not again. Olivia, why didn't you say anything? I had no idea this was happening to you."

"It's no big deal, Mom. Honestly, Mr. Mahoney." Her eyes skittered between the two. Lauren and the others would know she was in here. By tomorrow, she'd be dead meat.

"There's usually a reason. Mrs. Dimato, you said this happened before?"

Olivia cut in, "It's no big deal. Remember, I just need to ignore it. I didn't do that last time."

"I'm afraid so. It should be in her file," Donna said. Mahoney flipped through the pages in the manila folder.

"Remember, Mom, everyone said that when someone is a bully, you just ignore him, and he'll go away. So that's what I'm doing." She prayed that's what they would decide.

"You are right, O, but vandalism is not tolerated in this school. We need to get to the bottom of this."

"I don't see what this has to do with anything," Olivia pleaded. Both of them scrutinized her, waiting.

"Let's start with what happened before," Mahoney urged.

She shut her eyes and repressed a small whimper. Fists and boots floated before her.

"Oh, all right." She heaved a sigh, seeing a way to not get the shit kicked out of her. "Are you sure, Mom, that this won't just cause more problems?" Her mother nodded for her to continue. "Brian Wrenowski broke into my locker last year and stole a poster of mine. Because I kicked him in the … in the… in a place I shouldn't have. We both got suspended."

"Can you think of why he'd want to continue this adversarial relationship?"

Baloney sounds like something off a TV psych show. "Well, I don't know, Mr. Mahoney. I thought that was the end of it. But he did something weird last summer." Olivia could feel her mother's eyes riveted on her. She could just imagine what she was thinking. "There's this neighbor, Mr. Carlson. He's old and he has a garden. I was helping him out, well, cuz he's old and all. Anyway, there were a couple of days when Brian was standing across the street, calling me names. I tried to ignore him. But then he threw garden shit on my boom box."

"Olivia, watch your language!" Donna said.

"Okay, he dumped garden waste on my boom box and broke it. Mr. Carlson made him buy me a new one."

Mahoney leaned forward, his pad falling to the floor.

Her mother turned toward her, her face betraying confusion and despair. "Honey, why would he do that? We've known his family for years."

This was kind of rad, like telling a story, but better because she was the star. "He said something about it was my fault Ashley broke up with him. But they got back together."

"That doesn't make much sense." Mahoney's notepad filled with black ink as he wrote.

"Then at the beginning of the school year, Ashley came up to me one day after school. She was really mad. Brian's mom grounded him for throwing rotten weeds at Mr. Carlson, so he couldn't take her to homecoming."

"Rotten weeds? What? This is getting to sound like one of those teenage soap operas that take place in California," Donna said.

"Yeah, but I'm not making this up. Anyway, like you said, if we ignore this, he'll go away."

"I wonder if Brian's taking his punishment out on Olivia," Donna said.

Mahoney's notepad was now a mass of black scribbles. He put the pen down. "The school will follow up. O, I want to thank you for having this candid conversation with your mom and me. As I said earlier, we take vandalism very seriously. And Mrs. Dimato, I want to thank you for caring enough about your daughter to meet today. You'd be amazed at how many parents don't." Mahoney rose and opened the door to his office.

What a load of shit. They care more about their fucking lockers than the kids. Olivia met Baloney's eyes and let a slight smile spread across her face.

"I'm very proud of my daughter, Mr. Mahoney. Through all this, she has tried her hardest to do what's right." Donna said.

As they walked toward the school's entrance, she turned. "Olivia, I have to get to work. Do you have enough money for lunch?"

"Yeah. I'll see you at home." She paused at the door and watched her mom descend the steps, walk briskly toward the village and commuter train station. She huffed a sigh, wishing she could just continue walking with her. A bell rang, the hall filling with students headed toward the cafeteria, and she allowed herself to be pulled by the stream.

"Heard you got Brian blamed for our message on your locker." Lauren materialized before Olivia, who was eating lunch alone in the most obscure corner of the cafeteria she could find.

"What? Oh, yeah."

"Right on. You lucked out. But you do that again, we'll make sure you end up in the hospital. Got it?"

"Do what?" Olivia called out, but Lauren waved her middle finger and merged into the crowd.

When she arrived home from school, Donna was in the kitchen, her expression the same as earlier in Baloney's office.

"Olivia, I just had a very strained conversation with Patricia Wrenowski. My goodness, she was storming mad. She said a permanent marker like the one used to deface your locker was found in Brian's. One was also found in Ashley's, so the vice principal believes both of them may be to blame. She claims you planted it and have it out for Brian."

"Mom, they are majorly crazy over there."

"I don't know what's to be done. When will that boy leave you alone? And I don't think we can expect his parents to be reasonable. Thank God, the bus now drops you off down the block, and we don't have to rely on Patricia to ferry you. These days I'd be afraid to have you get in a car with her."

"I think I'd rather take my chances with the rapist," Olivia said.

"Don't even joke about that, sweetie."

If you had any idea I haven't ridden the bus all year, you'd shit bricks.

+++

The phone call from Mr. Perry regarding Brian's locker contents had sent Patricia spinning. She could feel herself verbally bouncing off the walls, not caring what she said. Brian's response was to slam doors and sequester himself in his room. All the psychology self-help books said this was the age when adolescents were testing limits and developing a stronger sense of right and wrong. But was lying to be expected?

She wondered if Ray had started, as a teenager, that he'd been lying all along.

When Brian was little, dealing with him had been easy. All she had to do was threaten no cartoons for a week. She thought about taking *Beavis and Butthead* privileges away, groaning at the absurdity of it.

Patricia was beside herself. Ray was no help, contending the prank was not worth the fuss. Brian continued to protest he was innocent. Ashley, who was more reliable, stated that neither of them had done anything. Her parents supported their daughter. The school was stymied. The principal had to concede there wasn't enough proof. But Brian battled and stomped more than ever, furious his mother even thought he was at fault.

The Dimatos had been friends for a long time, not close, but good enough to help each other out and lend yard equipment. Olivia and Brian often played together when they were young. Patricia remembered the two of them pumping away on the swings in the backyard. Serious business. She could picture their little faces, Olivia's round dumpling and Brian's delicate features, both of them so intense. She could never figure out why. They had both been temperamentally similar—studious, smart, not too prone to spontaneous laughter. How did all this animosity start?

+++

Between classes, Becca had shoved a ripped piece of notebook paper at her before evaporating into the crowd. Hands sticky with sweat, Olivia teased the folds apart: A summons to meet after school by the woods. She'd thought the marker thing had put her back where she'd started in September without any friends. She'd been relieved. Retaliation against Brian had become way more than she wanted.

At the meeting spot, Spider sauntered toward her, nodded, his long fingers claw-like around a joint and lighter. Soon Lauren appeared with Becca, who ducked into the woods, the others in a close line on the narrow path. At the place, Olivia bummed a toke from Spider and asked where Dank was. Spider's eyes darted with a subtle gesture to shut up.

"Who's been here?" Becca scowled, pointing to the litter and bushes.

"Some homeless dude?" Lauren volunteered.

"In December? They're sleeping in church basements. No, someone's spying on us. I can sense it. We may need to find another place." She nodded at them. "Anyway, I got some great new shit." Olivia peered at the baggie, the contents hard to see in the bleak light. Judging from everyone else's response it was pretty rad. She watched Spider to take her cue as he extracted a small amount and handed her some shredded material, spongy. He chewed and swallowed, so she did too. She relaxed, and after a while, Spider said something so hilarious she thought she'd pee her pants.

Like most of that late afternoon, time stretched and snapped. Then something very important happened. Becca said something or didn't say something.

As Olivia made her way home in the dark, she had no idea of the time. The streetlamps had an eerie, green outline that oscillated between dim and bright. She approached her block, which felt familiar, but somehow different. Oh, well. She giggled and lifted her foot as if sticking her toe into very cold water. She took a step and stopped. Took another step. Too weird. She continued hesitant footfalls toward her house with its huge ancient tree.

She was marveling at the elm, so beautiful with its black branches and twigs, when she heard Donna open the door and step onto the porch. "Olivia, what are you doing? Do you know what time it is?"

Olivia pulled back her coat sleeve and scrutinized her watch. "Let's see. It's 7:15. No, it's … 7:16 and …." The second-hand kept wobbling. She paused. "And forty-five, no wait, forty-seven seconds. Wow, Mom, I'm late, aren't I?"

"Olivia, what is going on? You are to be home when I get home."

"Oh. Well." She considered. "I lost track of the time."

"What were you doing, and why didn't you call?"

Mom is really pissed, she thought. *Okay, where was I and why didn't I call?* "I had a … project I had to do. An assignment I had to work on with someone in my class. I guess we just got into it, and I forgot about the time. Sorry, Mom." *Okay, she's motioning me inside.* Olivia stepped tentatively across the threshold. *Okay, like, everything's cool.* She placed her backpack on the stairs to the second floor.

"Olivia, you said you'd be home right after school. I had no idea where you were. You didn't call. I didn't have a phone number to reach you. I was worried with the rapist and all." Her mom ticked points off on her fingers.

Olivia hung her coat on the tree and moved into the kitchen. "I told you. I have an assignment I had to work on. We were at the library. Her mom gave me a ride home."

"You sure have had a lot of assignments lately. You could have told me. So why didn't you?"

"Because I forgot." Olivia wondered how the overhead lights had gotten so bright. Her mother loomed, a major obstacle to her bedroom.

"Aren't I allowed to forget once in a while?"

Olivia opened the fridge door to blockade her mother's advances. She peered, fascinated by the world within. Orange juice was on her mind. The metal was delightfully cool on her hands. Her attention was caught by stacks of pearlescent plastic storage containers, capped by semi-translucent lids, glowing in the fridge light. She lifted one the color of gelatin, containing tuna salad and wondered how long she'd been gazing at the contents. Her mom was saying something about dinner.

"I don't have time to eat," she said guessing at her mom's question. "I still have some stuff to do, so I'm going to take the tuna salad to my room." Olivia encircled her mom and hugged her as she made her way toward the stairs. "Mom, you're the greatest," she called.

+++

No more waiting. Tonight Patricia would give Ray the ultimatum after dinner. They would go to the lounge at the old Hudson Hotel, ostensibly to celebrate her latest sale. She would present him with a little show of her photocopies. Either he would move out and divorce her or the pictures would go to the police. He couldn't protest in public. Brian would be at home, so he wouldn't hear them.

Before going to the hotel, she went into her office to retrieve the copies, hidden in a file titled "Real Estate Listing Photos."

Gone. The whole file. Patricia clawed through the drawers and their contents. Nothing.

The precious copies of the pictures were gone. No question he knew she knew. Her dinner threatening to spew over the file cabinet, she paused and took a ragged breath. She would go ahead with the plan anyway and bluff. She grabbed her coat and walked to the hotel.

"So what great sale are we celebrating tonight?" Ray slid into the booth at the hotel lounge.

"That couple from Massachusetts. The sellers got back right away. Everybody's happy, especially me. Can't believe I spent so much time on them." Patricia took a gulp of her drink, gauging her timing.

"Well, honey cake, you just amaze me at what you can do." Ray was being charming in his nerdy way. Except he wasn't charming. Not that evening. Maybe not ever again.

"Oh, and guess what?" It was now or she'd lose her courage. "I found my Polaroid camera." His face was quizzical. "Remember how I thought I'd left it at a listing?"

"Your camera? No, I don't." Ray cocked his head as if trying to place the incident.

"Well, you should. I found it in your closet."

"My closet." His voice was flat.

"Funniest thing. I was throwing away clothes you don't wear anymore, and I found this cubbyhole. And my camera was in this cubbyhole. Can you believe it?"

"How strange. You found a cubbyhole in my closet and your camera. Are you sure?" His voice was low, as if it were any mundane conversation.

He knew, and he was pretending? She took a swallow of her bourbon, squelching the urge to screech. "Not as strange as what I found with it. A shoebox full of pictures." The words in her mouth, jagged.

"What are you talking about Patricia? Cubbyholes, cameras, shoeboxes with pictures?"

"I can't believe you're denying this, Ray. They were in your closet. I can't believe you'd do that kind of thing. It's disgusting!"

"What were you doing snooping among my things? How sneaky. What did you think you were going to do tonight? Embarrass and humiliate me? You know what's wrong with you? You jump to conclusions without checking out the facts. You just assumed."

"I didn't assume anything." Patricia felt as if she were verbally trying to shove him into a corner. "What do you expect I'm going to think? You hide this perverted stuff in our home where our son could find it."

"Look, Patricia, they're not mine."

"Then let the police sort it out. I'm sure they'd be interested, given a rapist is on the loose." Her voice caught. "My god, you're the rapist, Ray." Whispering it out loud felt like a punch in the solar plexus.

"Patty, honey cake. They're not mine. I'm hiding them for this guy at work. And you were never meant to see that stuff. I found those pictures in his cubicle, and I've been urging him to get help. I'm using the pictures to be sure he follows through."

"Do you think I'm an idiot? One of them was taken at one of my listings. I recognize the carpet, so that meant you stole my entry combination. And now you lie about it?" Patricia drained her drink, motioned to the server for another one.

"Oh, Patty Cake, it was somewhere else. Lots of people have the same carpet."

Patricia tried to light a cigarette, her hands trembling so much Ray took the lighter and held it for her. The drink arrived, and Patricia took a swig, the bourbon fighting its way past the knot in her throat. Tears started to escape. She had vowed not to cry. "I don't know how you could insult me. I know you took the copies I had in my office. If you weren't guilty, you wouldn't have done that."

"Because, my honey cake, I promised George I wouldn't let anyone know about what he's done." Patricia was silent, taking several drags, watching his eyes dart. "Patty Cake, honest. That's what happened. Why would you think I'd do something like that?"

"Because the rapes are happening here."

"So?"

She nodded, rose in the dim light, and made her way to the bathroom. Another bout of diarrhea scalded her buttocks. When she returned, Ray was sipping his gin and tonic.

"Are you okay?" he asked, making puppy eyes that in the candlelight were grotesque.

Patricia nodded, her stomach threatening to stain the white

tablecloth with its contents.

"Look, this is a lot for you to absorb, Patty Cake. I'm going to stay with a coworker for a few days and give you some space."

Patricia walked the short distance toward home from the hotel alone. The house was now quiet, Brian holed up in his room. Her obsession with Ray's cubbyhole kicked in. She had often checked the hiding place and found it untouched. She crawled into the closet and lifted the peg. Did it move more easily, or was she just imagining it after so many times? She no longer needed a flashlight and submerging her hand, the vacant space was like silk as she dipped her fingers. In a matter of moments, her whole arm disappeared into the hole as she sprawled in the closet, the floorboards pressed against her lungs.

Everything was gone.

✚✚✚

Olivia jolted awake the next morning. Did it have to do with Dank? Bits and pieces of the previous day percolated to the surface. The problem was Becca didn't come right out and say what she wanted, only that someone had squealed about what went on at the place.

Becca took her seat in English. "We have an assignment due today, right?" Olivia nodded. "Whatcha got?" She grabbed the paper from Olivia's hand. "Thanks." She copied the work, changing some things and making obvious grammatical mistakes.

And then the rest of the week, her friend became elusive, sometimes materializing in English or the lunchroom, and then melting away.

On Friday morning, Spider grabbed Olivia just before English and told her to meet him and Lauren at the corner by Tacos N' More after school. When she got there and saw no Dank, déjà vu crawled across her shoulders and plummeted to her tailbone. Spider directed the group to go. At Boise Avenue they turned onto Elm, stopping two houses from the intersecting streets.

They waited. Not long after, a figure came into view and started to cross the intersection. Dank. Olivia found herself running with them as they crossed the street and surrounded him. Lauren and Spider paired in back, making her the escort on Dank's right. The memory of what they had done to her made her want to cry out, but instead she swallowed hard as Spider began to taunt.

"Dank, ol' buddy, long time no see." He punched him hard in the arm.

Dank winced, losing his balance. He shoved Olivia, and when he tried to get past, Spider tackled him.

"You dick! Trying to hide behind a girl?" Hands grabbed Dank's hood, yanking him to his feet. "You know, when Becca said she thought it was you, I thought Dank? Dank wouldn't do that."

"I didn't do anything!" Dank covered his head as the first blows came.

"You calling Becca a liar? It hasta be you, asshole, squealing about the place." Lauren lifted her boot to stomp on his back, but he curled into a ball, and she missed. When Lauren and Spider were done with him, he cowered on the ground, his face bloody.

CHAPTER 23
SEASON'S GREETINGS

Gordon sat in the employee lounge, his back to the Christmas tree, the odd angle of the green branches surrounding his head like a disgruntled halo. Strange gaps occurred within the fake alpine fir as if shaped by a blind barber, many of the pre-assembled lights blackened. Employees in various phases of exhaustion waited for Hunter. In the mix was an assortment of college kids, the ones who volunteered to work Christmas and New Year's Eves. These bright lights perked up the moment Charlie entered the lounge.

The manager, wearing a Santa hat, jogged in, followed by Clerise dragging a sad, red sack that had endured way more Christmases than intended. She'd reported to Gordon that Hunter had sent her on a mission to find the crèche in storage. But the crèche was missing its star occupant. On her hands and knees, she had followed the musty trail of mouse droppings, prayed for no Hantavirus, and eventually found the baby.

Clerise's predecessor had taken it upon herself to station the crèche in the employee lounge, where she had tended it each day, moving three chipped wise men to various locations across the lunchroom. As inheritor of the manger project, Clerise reconnoitered the perilous journey the Three Wise Men made each year across the tops of vending machines, the fridge, and—one year—the microwave. This year, the crèche decorated the top of a file cabinet across from Charlie's desk.

Santa Hunter began handing out wrapped gifts.

Just what I need, Gordon thought, *another pocket wrench kit. Perhaps Michael would like it.* He saw Clerise open her gift—a bath set—take a deep breath and set her shoulders.

"Just a little thank you for rolling up your sleeves and getting us through a very successful season," Hunter began. "I thought you might want to know corporate sent out some preliminary results from Black Friday, and we're number one in the nation."

"Guess that means Gordon won the bet," a voice near the microwave called.

The whole store knew about the famous wager. He'd heard someone set up some action with a pool circulating the employee lounge. He moved his gaze to Hunter and noted the man's mouth curved in an approximation of a smile.

"You're right about the winner. Way to go, Gordo." Hunter spoke at him as if they were the only two in the room. "But I'm sad to report that corporate has a policy against betting." He rolled his eyes. "There are ethical problems with a supervisor making a bet with a subordinate. Best I can do is congratulate Gordon." Hunter began to clap, and like a flame on dry tinder, the room exploded in applause and cheers.

To Gordon, Christmas was usually a letdown, just one more day, even though the store was closed. Except this year, Clerise and Michael had invited him to celebrate Christmas and also the week of Kwanzaa. At Thanksgiving, Michael had searched the woods at Freelak for a thick branch, which Clerise said he had carved into a kinara to hold three red candles, three green ones, and one black for the celebrations. The holiday season had turned out to be one of the best, certainly since Maude had passed on.

That Christmas Eve night, he headed toward home, savoring the meal with Clerise and Michael. He glanced at the car flanking him.

The driver was Ray, who turned his head as if he hadn't seen him. Slumped against the passenger window was a female form, and from where Gordon sat, the person was not engaging with his neighbor.

That's strange, Gordon thought. *It doesn't look like her, except who else would it be but Patty? Hope she's okay.* Gordon felt an electric buzz running the length of his spine and to his feet as he recalled Brian's bizarre behavior the previous summer. No doubt about it, they were a weird family.

+++

As Olivia sat in the car, shivering and waiting for the heater to kick in, her mom maneuvered through the streets. The drive home from the midnight church service on Christmas Eve was eerie, quiet. New-fallen snow muffled the streets, a frozen haze of confetti engulfing the streetlamps. Houses blinded and comatose receded from the parkway, their walkways edged with legions of luminaries, now silenced. Carefully landscaped bushes strained in the white blanket.

Olivia rode numbly, wondering what would happen shortly. Compared to last spring, Becca was even more unpredictable. But her message was clear: Olivia better not wimp out.

+++

The frigid air burned Olivia's lungs as she jogged to the overpass, arriving just as Dank crept in, followed by Becca. No Lauren, so good. No competition that night. They huddled under the rail trestle, an arctic blast gusting through the tunnel, the sub-zero air smelling like the inside of a walk-in freezer.

Resembling a Gothic snowwoman with her pale face, coal eyes and mouth, black scarf, and hat, Becca reached into a garbage bag and handed each a golf club from the thrift shop heist.

"Where'd you get those?" Dank asked, his stitches a thin curved line ambling away from his mouth.

"Where do you think, dick wad? You think I made these plans this morning? I've been looking forward to celebrating the holiday season all year. First stop, the driving range. We'll do a little warm-up then get to the real game."

A few blocks along Boise Avenue, Becca turned north, the tree limbs joining across the street like webs created by hallucinating spiders. In the middle of the block was Olivia's old elementary school. To the rear was an array of playground equipment piled with cones of light drifts. Someone had built a snowman that was drowning in new snow.

Becca tossed golf balls from the garbage sack, made a tee of snow and placed one on top. She bent her knees, took a swing, and the ball fell flaccidly. The next try hit its mark, a window, now with a round, scream-shaped hole. Olivia prepared to run, certain the deafening noise would trigger an alarm. But nothing. She felt as frozen to the spot as the snowman.

"What's with you guys? This is the warm-up." Becca rummaged in the sack for another golf ball.

Dank teed up, bent, and swiveled his hips. "Saw this on TV one time." The ball plopped.

"See that on TV too?" Becca drove another, which landed on the roof.

"Same show you saw."

Olivia concentrated on packing a little hump to make a tee.

"Jesus, O, just hit the fucking thing."

Olivia swung, creating a divot down to the blacktop.

"Better try again." Becca leaned on her club.

Olivia squeezed her eyes shut, swung, and sent the ball flying through a second-floor window, the crack of shattering glass like the report of a pistol.

"Not bad." Becca beamed and waved her club for them to follow her.

Olivia had just crossed another line. She could rationalize pounding weenies into the lawn and pouring bleach on the grass as getting back at Brian. Dumping sugar in Ray's gas tank had felt pretty good. After all, Brian had ruined her boom box. Tagging Wrenowskis' house could be explained as a Halloween trick. Her eyes riveted on the scene before her: the school's broken windows, the playground, now a battlefield of trampled snow. She could rationalize all the other stuff, but not this.

Longing for her warm bed, Olivia followed, scooting in Becca's tracks. Cold had seeped into her bones, her nose had been running most of the evening, and her hat and hair were a frozen black mat. Dank's jeans were soaked, and he was jogging.

"Now for the real fun. We'll keep score. One with the most hits at the end gets —," Becca paused, considering, "— gets a baggie. Losers have to spring for it."

"How's that fair? It's your stuff." Dank banged the club on the street, dislodging snow.

"If I lose, I'll take the hit too. Are you in, girly boy?"

Olivia watched Dank swing the club as if warding off some invisible threat. They continued along the block. She weighed the risk of getting caught against the risk of Becca's wrath. She would be one of the losers. Not a problem. The problem was to make sure it appeared she'd lost fair and square.

"This is the one," Becca announced. On the front lawn was a Lane Realty sign with Patricia beaming out at them, her face pockmarked in snow.

A wail issued from Olivia's throat muffled by her scarf. "Becca, why are we here?"

"You questioning me?" Becca lunged toward Olivia, club arched over her head, her face vicious in the lamplight.

"No. No. Just curious." She followed the girl, Dank in her wake, the only sound the squeak and crunch of boots in snow.

Victorian scrollwork dripped from the eaves overtop a veranda that stretched the whole front of the house and around to the back. Olivia surveyed her surroundings, scouting a possible escape route. The lot was typical, about fifty feet wide and three times as deep. She scrutinized the neighbors' houses. Lights off in one house. Just a tree lit in the window of the other.

Becca motioned and they crept to the backyard, where a garage at the far end hid them from view. This was as safe as it was going to get. They teed up and took aim. Olivia rummaged in the bushes as if she'd lost her golf ball, while Dank's landed in the neighboring yard.

"This isn't as fun as I thought it would be," Becca said, studying the hole she'd just made in the house's backdoor window. She clambered onto the railing, reaching with the golf club to bat at the gingerbread, but failed to make contact. Holding onto a pillar for balance, she raised the iron and swung again, hitting the scrollwork. The trim cracked. She wedged the club into the spaces and with a grunt pried the wood. Gingerbread snapped dropping noiselessly.

"You fucker." Becca's voice, low, gravelly, the success giving her strength to dislodge more scrolls, where they splintered, broke, and lay cradled among the bushes and new snow.

"Becca, what the hell?" Dank pressed himself against the house, as if he pushed hard enough, the house would swallow him.

Olivia checked whether she could wiggle beneath the porch. She held her breath, on the alert for any motion from the flanking houses.

"Come on. I got an idea." Becca motioned toward the backdoor, cradling an armful of wooden trim. She reached in, unlocked the door, and snaked through the opening.

"Dank, get in here. O!"

Olivia shook her head. Both threw their clubs in the juniper bushes.

"Don't fuck with me, O." She yanked the girl inside.

Becca flicked on the light, scanned the kitchen, saw the spec sheets on the counter, and grabbed them. "Come on, we don't have much time." She disappeared through a swinging door. Dank switched off the light, but not before Olivia saw the terror on his face. From the other room came a loud thump. Olivia hoped Becca hadn't swung her club against a wall.

"I said, 'Come on!'" Becca reappeared. Beyond the swinging door, a chandelier glowed dimly. Olivia felt Dank's hands on her back and stumbled forward into the next room, Becca pulling her sleeve. In the middle of the carpet the specs covered the house trim. A broken smoke detector hung from the wall. Becca pulled out a potato chip bag from her pocket and topped the crumpled house specs.

"Hey, watch this. I heard potato chip bags make great lighter fuel. Perfect chance to try it." With her lighter, she touched the papers, creating small flames that consumed the edges and grew.

"Becca! Are you crazy? We gotta get out of here! What the hell are you doing?" Already Olivia's imagination saw a fire engine screaming down the street, followed by the paramedics and police.

"Crazy? So you think I'm crazy?" Becca raised her club. Olivia took a step back and cowered while Dank raised his arms to cover his head. The club came down with a dull thud, shooting a spray of sparks into the curtains. "You have no idea. Shit, yeah, I'm crazy." Down came the iron. "Mad." Sparks dove in random directions. "Mad, mad, mad!" She continued to beat the flames and then stopped, leaving a ragged, black circle with the burned oak floor exposed, bits of charred flyers scattered across the room.

"Let's go." Becca spun. "Got one more thing to do. Wait for me outside."

At the back entrance, Dank paced, scanning the neighboring yard and peering through the broken window.

"Jesus," Dank said. "We're screwed. She's gone psycho."

"No shit. We gotta get outta here before someone sees us." Olivia said. The smell of burned carpet had embedded itself in her nostrils. A moment later, a light in the second floor of the neighboring house flashed on, and as she lurched to dash across the porch, she felt an arm across her shoulders, jerking her back into the shadows.

"You move, they'll hear or see something." Dank's breath brushed across her cheek as he pulled her against him. She could feel his chest trembling as she stared at the light, willing it to turn off. She held her breath. The house went dark again, and she could feel Dank's hold relax.

"What the hell is she doing? God, I need a smoke," Dank murmured.

And then the backdoor opened, revealing an even darker interior.

"Okay, let's get outta here," Becca said, barging past them, the golf club slung across her shoulder. She tossed the garbage bag into the juniper bushes. "I didn't want the house to burn down, so I took a precaution." She giggled, twisting to face them. "Someone left the water running in the upstairs bathtub. It's fucking cold in there, so I turned on the towel warmer."

Dank bolted, followed by Olivia, neither stopping for several blocks. When Becca caught up with them, they neared the Forester museum. She lit a joint, inhaled, and passed it. Dank toked long and hard. Olivia took a big hit, hoping to calm. She thought of Gordon.

"What'd you say?" Becca asked.

"I just said, 'I wonder how Gordon is,'" Olivia said.

"Who?"

"He let me in his house and gave me breakfast when Patricia Wrenowski chased me in her van one morning. Nice old man."

"Hey, I gotta 'nother idea." Becca swallowed the roach.

"I gotta get home. I'm in a shitload of trouble if Mom wakes up and I'm not there."

"Me too." Dank's voice chattered.

"That's where we're headed. To drop you off at home, O. Don't you resent that little prick for calling you a lesbo? I resent that he trashed your locker with permanent marker. I told you, we have to be brutal."

They soon stood before the Wrenowski house. Becca surveyed the front yard, where a plywood Christmas card carrying the Lane Realty logo sat on the front lawn. She pointed to it, festooned with colored lights, burning one moment, a string of dark glass lying on the ground, the next. She danced down a trail of bulbs, a slight pop as they crushed underfoot.

Olivia peered at the second-floor window, shivering at the prospect of Patricia throwing up the sash like some perverted version of Clement Moore's *The Night Before Christmas.*

"Awesome, souvenirs!" Becca knelt under a blue spruce by a plastic Mary, Joseph, and Baby Jesus. Shepherds and ice-encrusted sheep gaped in disbelief.

Becca yanked the cords, and the lighted faces went dark. She kicked Joseph onto his back, then turned him on his head, jamming the club handle through the hole in the bottom. As if churning butter, she thrust, until Joseph split in half, collapsing in the snow. Becca flipped him over and smashed his face in.

"You know, I'm pooped. See ya later. By the way, you owe me a baggie." Becca lifted Mary, cradled the figure against her chest, and strode off, the club over her shoulder.

"Jesus." Dank scrambled to keep pace with Becca, leaving Olivia to retrace her tracks in the street and footprints left in the drive after midnight mass. As she reached the back of her house, out of the corner of her eye, she saw a light go on in the second story of the Wrenowskis'.

CHAPTER 24
NEW YEAR WISHES

Gordon had sat outside Charlie's office for quite some time. At first, he wondered if his supervisor was even there, but Clerise reassured him Hunter had arrived—as usual—shut the door, and there'd been no peep, not even a demand for coffee.

He rubbed his cracked fingers, wondering what Charlie had concluded from the sales report. Okay, so he'd thought Hunter's idea was ludicrous. And some events were particularly hokey. He'd had his doubts about the sugar plum party with Miss Junior College. But that had been the biggest hit. Lots of daddies came to ogle and buy outdoor recreational equipment, while their daughters, dressed in holiday best, partied in the home décor department. On the whole, the event turned out pretty well and the customers liked it. Gordon had to give him credit: Charlie worked hard, was the first to roll up his sleeves, and wasn't afraid to pitch in on the most mundane tasks, like stocking shelves.

Hunter emerged, nodded for Gordon to come in, rustled the report, and dragged his finger down the page, saying nothing, with an occasional nod, grunt, or frown.

"Well, old man, not bad for a first attempt. We did it. But then I knew we would." He flipped a page. "However … however, I noticed a couple of things."

Gordon decided to interrupt Charlie's thought process. "I think we did a remarkable job, considering this was a new concept that was late getting off the ground with some major snafus along the way."

"Gord, that's not what's bothering me. I'm reading staffing for the period. Way up, and I see you approved overtime."

"Not without a lot of thought about the impact. And it prevented catastrophes, like lack of inventory." Anger flashed through Gordon and settled behind his eyes.

"True. But you cut into our profit margin."

"And I kept you apprised."

"Gordon, that's not the reason why our staffing was over. You've been in this business a long time. A long time. While I appreciate your experience and wisdom, I wonder how useful you are in this technological age."

"Are you saying you think I'm too old?"

"Well, you're getting on in years. Workhorses like you pull the plow, but you've slowed down. I think you need to find that pasture."

"Pasture? What the hell're you talking about? Are you saying I can't do my job?"

"No, no, no, Gordon. I'm saying that you aren't as energetic as you once were. I won't dispute that you're a workhorse, but we need stallion blood, someone younger."

"This job is management. I don't see what stallions have to do with it. It requires experience and a steady hand, not trotting off in any direction without considering the corporation's vision and where the store should go."

"That's why I'm giving you lengthy notice, so you'll be able to go out in style and pass your knowledge and wisdom to your successor. You've earned that much."

"Lengthy notice? Hunter, my record is exceptional."

"Don't make this hard, Carlson. How old're you now? You deserve to enjoy your golden years."

"Golden years? Golden years! What's the reason?"

"Carlson, you're starting to make this difficult. Have you ever heard of a work-at-will state?" Hunter paused a beat. "Well, you're in one. I don't have to have a reason."

"Charlie, this is pure bullshit! I busted my ass to get that new department up and running. I know my way around this business. And if I hadn't, you would've been up a creek."

"Whoa, whoa, whoa, whoa there, fella. Try and get yourself back under control."

Gordon now saw what was going on. Hunter was goading him. If he pushed the right buttons, he could get Gordon to erupt and then have a solid reason for firing him. He took a breath and considered his next move.

"My point is that a young guy without the experience could not've made this happen. U Do It needs my ability to work the system, network colleagues, and draw on favors."

"Exactly!" Hunter's face took on the expression of having stumbled on a brilliant idea. "This is succession planning. You're passing on your depth of wisdom. A piece of you to carry on in the new manager. You'll be a teacher, a mentor. All those things you like to do and are so good at. Don't you want to end an exemplary career like that rather than being shoved out the door?"

"Well, yes, of course."

"See, Carlson, I'm not such a bad guy."

"I never said that."

"I thought that from you." Hunter pulled a frown.

"Fine, I'll prepare an orientation and training schedule. When will you advertise?"

"Don't need to. It's internal. I believe in giving folks a chance to work their way up."

"Good, he or she will have some background from this store. Who is the person?" he asked.

"Why, your assistant, Gordon."

"Rick? You're promoting Rick? Are you …?" He stopped. Charlie sure knew the right buttons. "Sure? I mean, he's a nice guy and all, but Charlie, he's not cut out for this."

"I see potential in him. He's got a ways to go, but that's what you're here to do."

"Hunter, I have to disagree. Because of Rick's inability to teach, the classes went down the tube. He was a loose cannon during the Winter Wonderland project. You know that's the main reason I had so much overtime to approve."

"Gordon, this is not about discussing an applicant. I've already made my decision. I've alerted corporate, and Rick's ready to come on board."

"You've offered the position to him, and he accepted?"

"Well, yes. Why do you think I assigned him to you?" Hunter froze, head elevated, waiting.

"So you've been planning this for quite some time," Gordon concluded.

"Didn't I just talk about succession planning? See, Gordon, that's why I think you're ready to call it quits. I think you're beginning to have trouble remembering things."

Gordon gripped the chair arms. "My memory's fine. Rick is an idiot. However, in a year's time when I retire, I can get him down the road quite a distance."

Hunter pulled a pile of papers from under Gordon's file. "I'm afraid we don't have the luxury. I suppose he could call you if something comes up after you've left, but that's up to you." He shoved forms across the desk. As Gordon scanned the documents, Hunter added, "Six weeks should work out. Corporate notified me the VP of Marketing plans a site visit then, a great opportunity to celebrate your years in the business. I'm giving you a chance to exit in a dignified manner. I'll have Clerise do the scheduling."

Gordon held the papers gingerly. His first impulse was to ball them up and throw them in Hunter's face. His second impulse was to lunge at him and smash his teeth down his throat. Except he sat, glued to the chair, unable to move.

"Gordon?" Hunter peered over his desk. "You still with us? I said you could go."

"You know, Charlie, I was just thinking. Bullies are usually junior high and high school fellas." He closed the door behind him and faced Clerise, her face a patchwork of anger, shock, and sadness, tears trickling down her cheeks.

"I can't believe it."

"Did you know?" he whispered.

She shook her head, the tears continuing to flow. She grabbed a tissue, and although he was stunned, he noted how beautiful her hands were, her long fingers, her almond-shaped nails. He nodded, took a breath and said, "Mark me as sick today, will you?"

+++

Patricia had a number of New Year's resolutions. The critical one was to find out who vandalized the Christmas decorations. Everything on her front yard had been destroyed, the Madonna had disappeared, and the smashed-in Joseph sickened her. What perverted person would do such a thing?

She had awakened on pre-dawn Christmas to noises on the front lawn and peered outside to behold the wreckage. Her Christmas card was in splinters, the spotlight crushed. The lawn was hillocked by numerous boot prints, broken shells of Christmas lights cupped in the divots. Now wide awake, she was taking in the scene when she sensed a movement on the street, but before she could get the window open, the person had disappeared.

Within minutes, red and blue blinking police cars crowded the curb in front of the house. Patricia found herself offering coffee and Christmas cookies to a troop of figures who milled in the foyer, dripping slush on the area rug. Ray handed out the steaming mugs while Brian sat on the stairs, lost in the melee.

Urps emanated from the police radio, which the officers ignored until something came over that made one stop and state into his shoulder that they were on their way. A quick conversation ensued, and two of them left. The crush was down to one man and three pajama-clad residents. The remaining officer seemed uninterested in the damage to the property. She watched as he munched another cookie and noted only a word or two on his notepad. She sighed. He obviously didn't consider this to be worth investigating.

After they left, Brian disappeared to his room. She followed Ray up the stairs, hissing, "I know somehow this is your fault and you're going to pay for it."

"Honey, I don't know what you're talking about." He rounded the corner to the guest bedroom.

As January progressed, all the police would say was they were working on some leads. That same Christmas Eve night, the elementary school's windows had been shattered by golf balls, along with one of her listings, the home almost totally lost to internal flooding.

Patricia sat in her office and fumed. She was positive that somehow this led back to Ray. Dear God, that she could free herself before someone else figured out he was the rapist. Once she found the evidence again, she should take it to the police. But if she did, Brian was too old now not to find out.

Bottom line, identifying who were in all the pictures was an issue of damage control. Get rid of Ray, protect her son, her business, and her standing in the community. But how?

✛✛✛

The old fridge grunted on and off, emitting an occasional stutter. In the neon of the overhead light, Gordon's back bowed over the retirement forms on the table. He finished studying the last one, tapped his fingertips and eyed the clock. He remembered it from as long as he had memories, so long that it was a part of the house, his youth, and the important events in his life. He had wanted to hold the clock's hands fast the day his father died from heart failure. He had wanted to be swallowed by it the day the Army chaplain arrived with the news about Lara. He had stared at it for hours the morning he found his mother in bed, cold in death, having gone sometime in the night. And he had ridden the minute hand around and around when the family's hardware store was lost. All those moments stuffed into that small clock on the wall. That it never burst surprised him, the lifetimes contained in the sweep of the second hand.

How had this happened? Gordon played back instances where Hunter had been made a fool: Gordon's well-earned respect from the other employees, his refusal to tolerate Hunter's prejudices. The final blow was the Winter Wonderland Department opening and losing the bet. Gordon had humiliated his boss in front of the store employees as well as the nubile Miss Junior College, whom Hunter had been trying to corner the week before. Charlie was after revenge.

Nauseated with anger, he hunched over the papers. He could train Rick for the next six weeks. Knowing the idiot would screw it up as soon as he left felt somewhat satisfying, but he took pride in his ability to train people. His co-workers would think he'd done a poor job. He could use up all his sick time and vacation days, minimizing his remaining time at the warehouse. Except he knew Hunter would refuse the requests.

Or he could quit tomorrow, giving two weeks' notice. He may not owe Charlie that much, but he owed it to himself and the store.

So that was the decision to be made. Sticking it out for the final six weeks or giving notice. He could picture what would happen if he stuck it out. He'd face humiliation every day, knowing that no one could give a damn. No one had given a damn since he lost his own store. Each time, he had taken the booby prize, been the fixture that went along with the sale. Each time, he'd been squeezed for his community ties. Until now, when no one remembered who he was.

Midnight.

The clock's second hand swept on. Gordon grabbed a blank piece of paper and wrote.

CHAPTER 25
UP IN SMOKE

The sub-zero cold took Gordon's breath away. Now that he was retired, he could not afford both medicine and gas heating, not with his puny pension. He chose medication for his asthma.

He'd heard about programs to help the destitute heat their houses. But he wasn't poor, and he'd be damned if he'd let anyone invade his privacy. His family had always been self-reliant. He'd freeze before he'd go begging. Besides, he had a heat source, a newspaper log roller that had belonged to his mother. She had collected newspapers, and then she would burn them along with other unneeded mail. After her death, Gordon had continued piling newspapers, magazines, and mail in the living and dining rooms, intending to burn them. Day to day, month by month, year after year, the stacks had become mountains. The log roller would come in handy until spring, when he could bring in a load of wood from the cabin.

The system worked pretty well. Each morning, he busied himself with preparing the day's fuel. Sometimes a human-interest story or some scientific finding would catch his attention. Before he knew it, an hour or so had passed, and he would be aware of cold pushing up through his feet and legs as he sat cross-legged before the fireplace.

Nights were more challenging, when he piled the fireplace with cut wood. The problem was the fire had to be tended and his bedroom on the second floor was never warm enough. The answer was to sleep in the living room, where he could rouse himself when the fire ran low. But he lacked the strength to lug his mattress down the stairs.

However, Gordon was a resourceful man. He made himself a comfortable pallet with a cedar dog bed he found at a garage sale. The circular shape was a little odd at first, but he discovered he could pretty much fit in the large, stuffed round by sleeping in a fetal position, and the cedar smell was actually quite nice.

The biggest problem was Gordon loved old newspapers. He loved the stiff feel as the newsprint aged, the yellow coloration. They took on a different smell, less of immediacy and more of a kind of wisdom. He began to chip away at the newspaper piles, wondering if he could make the supply last until spring. No, not enough, and he was not going to continue his newspaper subscription just so he could burn it.

Then he realized he could do what the landfill plants do. He could burn his garbage. A solitary man of simple needs didn't make much. However, he noted that his neighbors had it in abundance. The easiest access was the refuse bin at the apartment complex next door, where the big dumpsters were hidden behind the garage, out of sight, and he could help himself without discovery.

Another way Gordon supplemented the heat was to increase his volunteer time at the museum. He had let his research slide anyway, and this gave him the opportunity to benefit both himself and the historical society. The building had been plumbed with radiators, giving off an even, comfortable heat. And, in order to protect the museum pieces, the temperature was always no less than fifty-five degrees. Balmy, when the outside was in the minus teens with wind chill.

That day as he sat in the ballroom going through memorabilia, he wondered if the whole retirement thing had been too mean-spirited, conceding that his primary motive was anger. He grinned, although it was more of a grimace, still coming to grips with the last of his tenure at U Do It.

When he had announced he was leaving, the majority of employees were crestfallen and surprised he did not wait one more year. Two were neither surprised nor crestfallen: Charlie and Rick. Their surprise was his decision to give two weeks' notice.

Gordon was gratified to see the reaction on his boss's face as he read the resignation. Charlie shook his head. "Gordo, you're missing the opportunity of a lifetime. The VP of Marketing will hand you the retirement plaque and have his picture taken with you for the hallway outside the employee lounge."

"Call me Gordon or Carlson, your choice. I will no longer answer to anything else," he had replied. And he would be damned if he was going to let that slime bag exploit his retirement as a photo op for U Do It.

Hunter was forced to plan a last-minute party. The man made a tepid attempt, delegating the work to Clerise and giving her an insulting budget for the event. Then she brought up that the newspaper and local radio station, not to mention the dignitaries in Forester, should be invited. A shoddy celebration would embarrass the Forester store, not forgetting how headquarters would view it. Hunter relented. "I don't suppose you know much about budget," he quipped.

"A bit," she replied.

Just a couple of days after his resignation, Gordon and Clerise were leaning into each other at a table in the employee lounge, when Hunter came in. Both turned their gazes toward him, a laugh suppressed on their lips in seeing him red-faced, standing in the doorway.

"Clerise," he barked. "Just because Carlson is a short-timer doesn't mean you can screw off. I want you to provide me with a progress report in twenty minutes." He turned on his heel.

"Gotcha, you son of a bitch," said Gordon. With less than ten days remaining, he was enjoying his role as thorn in Hunter's side, so much that he almost wished he'd stayed around the full six weeks, just to torture him.

Now, in the museum's third-floor ballroom, he toyed with whether the recent newspaper story about his retirement with its hilarious picture should be included in the catalog of historical records. Putting it to one side, he picked up a document in faded ink, minutes from a village meeting. The order of business was a sanction against Rupert Sipe for illegally selling spirits to residents.

Intriguing. Little existed about Sipe, the town's reprobate and the husband of Minette Forestier, Jean-Luis' surviving daughter. How that must have stuck in Jean-Luis' craw.

The motion to sanction the bootlegger was passed. The discolored paper and the picture had an eerie distance, the black and white faded to gray, making features almost indistinguishable.

In contrast, the picture of Gordon's retirement fiasco had that sharp edge of recent history, the ink stark against the paper as if still containing the embarrassment of it all.

A few days after Gordon resigned, Clerise had reported overhearing Hunter on the phone, apparently trying to negotiate. The corporation wanted to make a big deal of Carlson's retirement, old-timer sort of thing. Hunter couldn't backpedal without making himself appear ludicrous, as well as revealing he had planned the whole thing in order to drive Gordon out. The vice president, camera crew, and all the details were already set for February.

The store manager began a campaign to coerce Carlson into agreeing to come to a deferred retirement party. Hunter first tried to appeal to Gordon's right to a proper send-off and claimed two weeks wasn't enough time. Carlson responded he had always been a modest man and did not like a whole lot of fuss.

Next, Hunter said Gordon owed it to his family and the community. The ceremony with the marketing vice president would make Gordon's father proud. Gordon replied that Hunter had never met his father, so how could he pretend to second-guess what Gus Carlson would want?

As a last resort, Hunter implied there would be bonus money, and he would receive a lifelong, employee discount of fifteen percent.

Gordon countered with thirty-three percent. Hunter responded that he couldn't do more than twenty percent. Gordon replied thirty percent or no deal. Hunter conceded as a special consideration. Carlson agreed, but he wanted it in writing.

Hunter wrote up the agreement, stating that in appreciation for the many years of service in the hardware business at U Do It and to his community, for his excellent and caring customer service, and in acknowledgement of his exemplary management, U Do It was pleased to award Gordon Carlson an honorary discount of thirty percent on any and all merchandise he cared to purchase in any U Do It for the remainder of his life.

Gordon had debated whether to show up for the hullabaloo. Even the day prior, he had been arguing with himself. Clerise was no help. She said to do what he wanted, he owed no one anything. He questioned whether any decision not to show was based on anger, he was better than that. Clerise said he deserved to be angry. Hunter had manipulated him into the whole ordeal. Gordon added that he didn't want to sink to Hunter's scummy level. Clerise concluded that perhaps Gordon did want to go, in which case, he should.

Indecision got the better of him. It used to be so easy, he just abdicated. Back and forth, back and forth he went, asking himself what a host of others might do if they were in his place. The more he thought about it, the more his thinking tangled.

The night before the event, Gordon found his inhalers weren't abating his troubled breathing. The next morning, he rose fighting for air, dialed a cab, and went to the emergency room with a severe asthma attack. Thus, as the proceedings at U Do It unfolded, he was strung to tubes and under close observation by the emergency room staff.

Clerise later reported that the morning of the ceremony, the vice president arrived in a flurry of snow and attention. A special area in the lumber department where Gordon had presided for so many years had been cleared. By 11:30, the high school band was in place, news and local TV coverage ready to go.

Noon came and no Gordon. The band had warmed up, then warmed up again, and was now playing tunes from football games. The noise was deafening, rattling the metal shelves. Hunter called Carlson's home. No answer. He made excuses to the vice president, who was eyeing his watch. He stormed over to Clerise, demanding, "Where is he?"

She shrugged and suggested, "Late?"

Subsequently, the newspaper ran a front-page story about a long-time member of the community who had devoted his career to helping his friends and neighbors. A picture showed the ceremonial scene with Gordon conspicuously absent. Rick gaped with his mouth half open. Hunter's head was at an odd angle as if shaking it at the visiting dignitary. So much for the photo op.

Below was an interview with Gordon, conducted at his hospital bed, where he thanked his friends and neighbors for the honor of serving them all those years.

After he was released from the hospital, Clerise invited him to her apartment, where she, Michael, and Gordon ate pizza and watched the videotape Michael had made of the proceedings. The high point was when, after a long delay, Clerise approached Hunter and whispered in his ear. She had to admit that she did time it for the most dramatic effect. Within five minutes, Rick was on the stage, where the disgruntled vice president shoved the retirement plaque into his hands, and the whole fiasco ended.

Clearing the plates, Clerise asked if she could cook dinner for him some evening at his home. Picturing its condition caused him to hesitate, so that by the time Gordon could begin a reply, she had covered over the offer and moved onto another topic.

Now in the museum's gigantic ballroom, he contemplated this and the fact that he hadn't heard from Clerise since then.

He folded the newspaper, returned it to a box, and prepared to lock up with one last tour. With windows secured, heavy curtains closed against the creeping cold, the heat reduced to fifty-five degrees, the sound of his footsteps echoed across the bare floors.

He stepped toward his fire of paper logs and recyclables, picturing Clerise's cozy apartment. At the bottom of his heart, he knew he had missed the opportunity to extend his hospitality, and the friendship had foundered.

CHAPTER 26
GHOSTS

"Did you see them?" Becca grabbed Olivia's hand and leaned in as they emerged from the school, her friend's voice so low she strained to catch the words.

"Who?"

"The cops. Didn't you see them?"

"What cops?"

"The ones dressed like security guards. They're watching. They know someone here smashed all those windows at the elementary school and trashed that house."

"Those aren't cops. They're just security guards here to protect us from the rapist. Besides, we would've heard something."

"No, I can sense it. They're closing in. They know. See how they're staring at us?" Becca ducked her head, scanned the campus, and began a brisk walk toward Boise Avenue.

"No one knows anything. I keep telling you if they did, we'd've been dead meat a long time ago."

"Think of the reward." Becca stopped.

"What reward?"

"Have you seen how trashed that house is? And the school? There's a big reward. Always is, for something like this. Spider or Lauren will rat me out. You gotta find out who's gonna turn me in."

"Becca, they wouldn't snitch." This was getting too weird.

"Whichever one, you gotta tell me and you gotta stop 'em." Becca squeezed Olivia's hand tighter. They stood at the stoplight. She jogged away, glancing over her shoulder with someplace else to be, thank God.

Over the past several weeks, Becca had glued herself to Olivia. At first, the attention was great. *Lauren is pissed, so cool.* But now Becca obsessed about Christmas Eve, more and more convinced someone was going to figure it out.

As Olivia trudged home, she walked along the line of elms, skins of snow clinging to the sides of their trunks, their branches a tangled mess overhead. She spotted the museum. Seeing Gordon's station wagon parked in the side lot, she turned toward the entrance to visit him.

+++

Gordon eyed Olivia standing before him in the museum's foyer. Even for her, the pallor was alarming. No mistaking she had lost weight since he saw her last. Not knowing what else to do, he made her some tea in the kitchen and waited for her to give some indication of why she had stopped by.

"So what's new, Olivia?"

"Nothing much." She blew across the cup and took a sip.

"Still friends with Becca?"

"Why's it matter?" Olivia said. The hardness he'd witnessed at Halloween lurked in the flicker of her eyes.

"Just making conversation, that's all." They sat in uncomfortable silence. Feeling the pull of work upstairs, his attention jumped to the third floor. He asked, "Have you ever seen the ballroom?"

Once settled in the ornate room, two incongruous occupants in a space the size of a basketball court, Gordon pointed to where the chamber orchestra would have been stationed, where the ladies would have stood in little groups, the light laughter floating behind their fans as they bent exquisitely dressed hair toward each other. Men in evening suits and stiff collars would have filled their dance cards and whirled them into the circle of couples rotating to grand waltzes. Carrying the conversation was exhausting, so he decided to get on with his work and donned his white cotton gloves.

"What're those for?" Olivia pointed at his hands.

"To protect the documents from dirt and oil." Comfortably folded in a rickety, old office chair, he lifted the reel-to-reel tape he was cataloging and chuckled.

"What's so funny?" she demanded.

"Well, when I was young, I worked in my father's store. One day I delivered an order here. Grand Lotty was quite a fixture in this town, and she had a maid, Harriet.

"This particular blustery day, Harriet left me standing in the back vestibule while she fetched her shawl. I peered in the kitchen, making out the servants' stairs, and in the gloom, I saw a large curl of smoke. When she returned, I stammered that the house was on fire. She seemed angry. What did I mean the house was on fire? What did I mean there's smoke in the stairwell? She couldn't see anything.

"'You're as white as a ghost.' She howled with laughter. Well, I couldn't see what was so funny. The house might be burning down. Shouldn't she ring the fire marshal?

"So Harriet sat me down on a stool by the kitchen stove, where she stood stirring and tasting, preparing the evening meal and told me about the Forestier's youngest daughter, Violet. For me, at eight years old, death, especially the morbid kind of a little girl, captured my imagination.

"She swore the child somehow knew she would die young.

"Because Harriet was a servant, she slept on the top floor in a room next to the attic storage. One night, she heard wild howls. She couldn't be sure if they were of the living or the dead, but she braved the cold, dark stairs with her candle and made her way to the children's wing where she found Violet sitting straight up in her bed. At first, Harriet thought the child was having a nightmare. But her terrified expression was alert, and she jumped into the woman's arms as soon as Harriet crossed the threshold.

"Under a tarp over a cage in the corner, three finches squawked and thrashed. Violet insisted a girl was standing there, a sickly girl. Harriet shushed and rocked her until she fell asleep.

"The next night was the same thing. This time the birds made such a ruckus that Harriet uncovered them to find them beating their wings against the cage's bars. The birds calmed, but Violet continued to whimper that a girl was standing by the cage. The maid held her and tried to convince her that it was a dream.

"Harriet explained to me that this kind of thing happened when she was a girl. Some folks could see the dead. That night, Harriet realized Violet was one such person.

"On the third night, Harriet decided to sit by Violet's bed. At first, the child slept peacefully, then she began to toss and turn and cry out. Just like the other nights, she sat straight up, wide awake, and pointed. This time, Harriet saw something. Not a frail girl, but a wisp of smoke, ever so slight, on the wallpaper. And then it vanished.

"In the winter morning's light, Violet lifted the tarp. One bird lay dead. This was a bad sign. It meant there would be a death in the household. Harriet was worried for the child.

"The holidays had approached, and the household made preparations for the festivities on Christmas night. In those days, the celebrations were simpler. Mr. Forestier had a tree delivered from the Christmas ship docked in Chicago. He placed the bare tree in the morning room and decorated it with ornaments, treats, and little tin candleholders. And on the tree, Mr. and Mrs. Forestier placed an ornament that had arrived from relatives in New York.

"Most people think Violet tripped that Christmas night as she crossed the room to show her mother the ornament. But that's not what happened.

"At the end of the evening, Harriet oversaw the rest of the kitchen staff before retiring. Soon the house was quiet, still. The candles on the tree had long since been blown out.

"Harriet said she would never—as long as she lived—forget that night. She had crossed into the morning room and was just passing the doorway to the grand hall when she saw a light float down the stairs. Then Violet stepped into the entrance and made her way to the Christmas tree.

"Harriet called after her, 'Child, what are you doing out of bed at this hour?'

"The maid came close. The little girl was sleepwalking. Harriet knew that if she woke her, Violet would die. The servant had seen it happen once: A man was sleepwalking, someone woke him, and he dropped over dead. So all she could do was guide her.

"Violet searched under the tree. She found her new book, *A Visit from St. Nicholas*, and placed it on her small chair. Then the child felt among the branches. Her hand settled on the gift from the New York relatives. She plucked it from the bough and walked toward the grand staircase.

"She awoke, saw Harriet, and smiled. Didn't she see the girl standing on the stairs? The sickly girl wanted the ornament and asked Violet to leave the book for her to read. Harriet feared the poor thing was possessed.

"Violet moved toward the staircase and urged Harriet to come too. She climbed a step and held out her hand with the ornament. Harriet saw nothing. How could the Lord of Hell be out on this most sacred night?

"Harriet said, 'Come, child. You must be so tired. Come to bed. We can put your pretty treasure back on the tree until tomorrow.'

"Violet refused. She frowned and said again that the girl wanted the ornament, and Violet meant to give it to her. The next instant, the girl lunged and tripped on a brass tread rail, fell on the ornament, and cut her hand. At that moment, a white cloud formed and floated through the ceiling.

"The rest is well known. Harriet tended Violet as she became weaker, and the blood poison spread. One afternoon, Violet told Harriet that the girl she saw on Christmas night now had the ornament and was happy. Violet died soon after."

Gordon watched for Olivia's reaction. She fiddled with the sleeve on her sweater then said, "You think that's true? That some ghost showed up, wanted the Christmas ornament, and Violet tripped giving it to her?"

"What do you think?"

Across from him, Olivia perched on a metal folding chair, like a crow that had inadvertently flown into the ballroom. He had work to do. He wished she'd fly away. Except he hadn't talked to anyone in a number of days. And it felt good.

"I think it's fake."

"Could be. But then again I can't see the dead."

"Harriet said you do."

"I've never seen the ghost. Just the occasional bit of fog."

"Yeah, right. Where do you see it?"

"Well, just a few days ago, a funny-shaped cloud was over there." Gordon pointed to the wall.

As she squinted at it, he wondered if he was disclosing too much. But for some reason he told her, maybe because he'd been cataloging the information and it brought back sweet memories. And something else. Just that he'd never told anyone but Harriet.

"So was the ghost, like, in the lamp? Did it float around? I've seen those TV shows where they go ghost hunting. They show a picture with something smudgy in the middle."

"Nope, just this trail, like a scarf, that unfurled and flowed through the wall."

They were both quiet, the lack of sound as heavy as one of the brocade curtains.

"Can I see Violet's bedroom?" In the silence, Olivia's voice blasted across the dance floor.

"Sure. We could go now. It's a bit chilly because we turn down the heat when folks aren't around. But there may be a little warmth left from this afternoon when the second graders were here."

+++

Olivia sat on the bed's hard, unforgiving mattress and tried to imagine sleeping under the old, thin quilt. Heavy curtains, drawn across one large window, were parted by a small streak down the center, edged by the smallest light from the end of the day. In the corner was a wardrobe, the door open to reveal black leather button shoes, a dark dress, and a starched, white pinafore.

"That where Violet saw the ghost?" Olivia asked.

"I believe so. And that's the actual bird cage where the finch died," Gordon said. An ornate frame balanced on a stand over which hung a faded, fringed tarp.

Olivia drifted over and peeked under the covering. *This was getting creepy.*

"Where do you keep *The Night Before Christmas* book?"

"In this locked trunk." Gordon fished a key from his pocket and opened the lid. He lifted the book. "If you put these on, you can hold it," he said and handed her a pair of gloves from his pocket. "The historical society has a policy that only the docents can handle the books and letters, and they must wear special gloves to protect the paper. I'll make an exception in your case."

Olivia donned the gloves and reached for the book. Her fingers caressed the frontispiece, which bore the inscription, "'To Dearest Violet, Dec. 25,—Father and Mother.'"

She handed the book back, reminded of her own recent night before Christmas. She knew she needed to tell someone. Perhaps she could tell Gordon, but what would she say? That she was in this predicament was bad enough, the less said the better. She just wanted to know what to do.

Having lost her nerve, she trudged back along Boise Avenue, the elm branches the same tangled mess. At least she'd stopped by and he seemed okay to see her.

+++

Pausing often to recall the last hour or so, Gordon put away the memorabilia and re-shelved the tape recording. Olivia wanted something. He had known her long enough to pick up the clues. But the only real example he had was himself at that age. The adults he had trusted were those who sat back and waited, not trying to force him to 'fess up. His mother was like that. Then there was a teacher in high school who did the same thing because the teacher genuinely cared about him.

Kids could smell phonies, so if he wanted to get rid of Olivia, he would just pretend to care. He recalled her pinched expression when she arrived that afternoon, the way she kept asking questions as if stalling for time. When he thought of her working in his garden and sitting on the back stoop eating sandwiches; when he thought of her the night so drunk; when he thought of the difference he could make in her life, he knew he wanted to be like that high school teacher. To be important to her. Gordon decided to sit back and wait.

+++

For the past week, Becca had been holding Olivia's hand. She careened from one topic to another, now ranting about the old lady. "The aunt kept yelling, 'You are so fucking full of shit. Do you realize what you're doing to her?' Jesus, I am so tired of this. Why doesn't Mom just get it over with and O.D.?" She squeezed Olivia's glove. "Like I said, life used to get a hell of a lot worse."

They got to her street. Olivia knew something was coming about Lauren and Spider, and as they approached her house, the lights in the hallway as well as the front porch were on. *Good. Mom's home.*

"What did you find out? Lauren or Spider?" Becca's eyes were half closed, and her face said she expected an answer.

Olivia grabbed the first excuse she could. "Mom and the damn shrink have been on my case. I'm grounded," she lied.

"Yeah? How come you didn't say nothin'?"

"Fuck, Becca. All you talk about is nailing Lauren or Spider. How many times I gotta say they didn't rat you out."

"You sure about that?"

Olivia nodded and grabbed the knob. *I just need to get inside.*

"Well, Dank's learned his lesson, so there's just one other person. Better think about that, O." Becca gave a quick jerk of her head. "These old houses. It's a shame what happened to Wrenowskis' or the one that's for sale." She pulled out her lighter and flicked it, the flame jumping. Then she turned and headed down the walk.

A few moments later, Patricia drove toward her house, planning dinner and her latest marketing campaign. Approaching on the other side of the street was a teenage girl, dressed all in black. As she caught a slight glimpse of the face, she swerved to avoid a parked car. Her sudden braking made the girl look over, her gaze quizzical, then sullen, then filled with hatred. That face, which had hovered in Polaroid and copier form, a spectral inhabitant of Patricia's brain, was floating past her, glued to black clothing and attached to a backpack.

The girl kept walking.

All Patricia wanted was to get in the house, but the key kept missing the lock. Finally, as her back leaned against the closed door, she violently shook her head as if trying to detach something clinging to her hair. The face belonged to a friend of Olivia's, except this person was older, meaning she was at least a junior or a student who had been held back. The implication sent her grabbing the bottle of bourbon and making a fresh pot of coffee. Once perked, she opened the lid to the pot and just poured the liquor directly in, so that by the time Brian walked in, she strained to hold things together.

"Hi, sweetie, how was school? By the way, your dad's going to be late." Her voice felt too bright as she rattled the racks in the oven and turned it on. "Say, Brian, who's that girl Olivia's hanging around with? I thought she and Ashley were best friends."

"Ashley can't stand her anymore. She calls herself 'O.'"

"Oh," Patricia giggled. "Well, her friend looks like a funeral director."

"That's about it."

"So do ya know her?"

"That lesbo, Becca Toole? Olivia started hanging with her last spring. They're a gang at school."

"You mean a gang, gang? Like Crips and Bloods?" Patricia clutched the oven door handle to balance. "And watch your language."

"There're lots of gangs at school." Brian rifled through the pantry, grabbed a box of cheese crackers, and disappeared.

Sleep was impossible that night, and Brian was hardly out the door the next morning before Patricia was up the stairs and into his room. She'd read that teenagers need their own space, so her rule was to stay out, with the proviso that he clean occasionally and vacuum. Finding the yearbook in the bookcase by his desk would have been too easy, as would locating it under or behind the bed. He'd brought it home, sequestered himself in his room, probably read all the entries—maybe even twice or more for those he liked—and then dumped the yearbook somewhere.

No surprise to find his closet jammed waist high with the stuff he would have strewn around on the floor. She began to dig down, being careful not to disturb anything, noting a certain organization to it, a logic that underscored his ability with computers.

First was a thick layer of clothes. Smelling them told her they had been worn and designated as not yet ready for the laundry. Shirts were on top, followed by jeans. To one side were socks, just a few since he was good about throwing them in the washer after each wear. On the other side were briefs—not so good. She would have to figure out a way to improve his hygiene.

The bottom was a jumble of things. A shoebox revealed notes and folded pages of binder paper in swirly, girly script in pink or lavender pen. These were most likely from Ashley, but she wouldn't distract herself despite her curiosity. She recognized the wood box where Brian kept all his swim meet medals. Tucked next to that were odds and ends of action figures, along with three or four Pinewood Derby cars, some missing wheels and axles. Then her fingers hit something flat and a bit hard—the surface of a book, the annuals, one from high school and a couple of soft-bound ones from middle school.

Something slick peeked out between the elementary yearbooks. A magazine cover displaying naked women with big, round breasts. Porno. How in the world did he get this?

These women could have been little older than Ashley. Patricia had mixed feelings about Brian's obvious attraction. Ashley was a lovely young lady who was dealing with her own burgeoning sexuality. She had heard the PTA moms groaning about the frustration of raising teenaged daughters, and she was always glad she had a son.

Back to the task. The yearbooks.

Careful not to disturb Brian's cataloguing system, she lifted them out and sat back with legs crossed. She flicked through to the section of freshmen by homeroom. The girl was not in his and Olivia's class— which she would expect judging by her appearance. Six other home- rooms to go.

At the fourth homeroom, she slowed down. Who were these kids? Their heads strained back, their tough expressions would be at home in a criminal photo album. Sprinkled among them were kids who seemed to have stumbled onto the photo shoot, not sure why they were there. And the ones that were so indistinct as to hardly contrast with the background. At the end were two rows of blanks—those not pictured. Becca Toole was one of them.

Maybe Becca was in a picture from the prior year, in middle school. She re-enacted the same procedure but sought out the special needs class first. Nothing. No one missing. She began scanning all the classes. No Becca Toole, pictured or not. As she closed the book, her cheeks puffed and deflated with relief and disbelief.

All afternoon, the extent of Ray's monstrosity gelled. Patricia spent the time in the kitchen canceling her appointments, claiming illness, and drinking enough Kahlua shots that by evening she was concerned about slurring on the phone. In the freezer were the makings for beef stew. Easy. She pulled everything out, dumped the ingredients in a pot, and got it going.

Until this point, she had convinced herself that although technically the girl would have been underage, Becca could have consented. She hadn't let herself question what a girl would find attractive about a middle-aged, middle-class computer nerd. Ray didn't even drive a cool car. Did he supply them with drugs and booze? Was that it? Sex for drugs and alcohol? The likelihood of that kind of transaction was slim, although by the looks of this Becca, it was possible.

She was chasing ghosts. Except one was very real and could retaliate. Patricia's thoughts slowed as the realization sank in. The house had been repeatedly vandalized over the past few months, her Christmas decorations destroyed. One of her listings was severely damaged. Her mind whirled in one direction while her stomach churned in the other. By the time her son jostled her shoulder, she had thrown up and was lying on her side in bed with a foot on the floor.

At dinner, Brian's opening salvo was how out of control she was, while Ray slipped into his chair and helped himself to stew.

"What you mean 'out of control'?" Patricia stabbed a piece of carrot.

"I come home and find you passed out on the bed, drunk."

"I'm not drunk." She belched. "If I was drunk, I'd be slurring. I'm not slurring." She wasn't slurring. She was talking very carefully. "Ya know. Ya know, I do all the talking aroun' here. Ya know, I'm the only one talking. You never have anything inneresting to say. And I work so hard to get you in polite conversation. An' you jus' sit there!" That was hard to get out, but she managed it.

"We do too have interesting things to say."

"Don't talk with your mouth full, Brian. That's 'nother thing. You eat like pigs. You know, Brian, if you can't carry on p'lite conversation, you'll hamper your career."

"What career? I'm just a sophomore in high school."

"Doesn' matter. I saw you two smirking at each other. I know you have secrets. I can tell. You with your li'l secrets and don' include me." She could feel tears in the corners of her eyes.

"What little secrets, Patricia?" Ray's face was innocent. *Too innocent*, she thought.

"I know you're hiding something from the way you keep not saying anything." She skewered a hunk of beef and stuffed it in her mouth, gulped some water, and then choked.

Ray rose, slapping her back. She nodded, spit out the half-masticated meat, and waved him back to his seat. Brian disappeared into the kitchen. She could hear the water running and cupboards drumming. He asked if she wanted tea or coffee as he returned with a basket of bread.

"Here, have some of this. I think you've got the flu, Mom."

She took a roll and beamed at her son. "You are a wonnerful young man, so thoughtful. Kids these days...." She paused mid-thought. Then she got a brilliant idea. "I saw Olivia's li'l friend this afternoon. Wha's her name again, Brian?" Brian opened his mouth to respond. "No, don' tell me, don' tell me. Is Becca. That's right. Becca." Ray speared a piece of tomato, ignored her, and turned to Brian, who stared at his mom wide eyed.

The dishes jumped as she slammed the table. "Have you seen her,

Ray? Olivia's new li'l friend? Quite an eyeful, wouldn't you say, Brian?" She reached for the bottle of wine and knocked over her water glass, its contents running across the tablecloth.

Next thing she knew, someone was pulling off her shoes. She was on her side on her bed. A hand with hairy knuckles held a garbage can, while an arm supported her head and shoulders as she dry-heaved. The bedside lamp was on. She felt a blanket pulled over her. The lamp went out, footsteps out the door. Sometime later, a voice floated in the dark, near her ear and whispered, "Did you really think I was going to let on? This isn't going to get you anywhere. Patty Cake."

CHAPTER 27
PAPERS

From his cedar-chip bed, Gordon poked at the fire. As soon as the weather broke, he would make a trip to the cabin for wood. He toyed for a moment with asking Clerise and Michael to come along, missing them, as he did most days. But he dropped the idea and decided to go alone. They would all make a trip in the spring and finish Michael's squirrel experiment.

His piles of old newspapers and mail were shrinking, and he needed to make it last. The previous evening, he had burned empty milk cartons and TV dinner containers. The fumes had been particularly hard on his lungs. Then he had an idea. He could use the free real estate ads from restaurants.

As he added another log, the phone rang. At the fifth ring, he answered and heard Clerise's voice.

"I've been fired. I don't know what I'm going to do. My family can't help. The job market is awful." Her words sounded strangled.

"Clerise, what happened? How could that bastard do that?" Gordon, though thrilled to hear her voice, was stunned.

"With two words. 'You're fired.' When I asked why," she paused for a moment, "he said for violating company policy."

"Violating company policy? Clerise, that makes no sense."

"Remember when you asked me for those monthly inventory

reports? Well, I continued to copy them onto a floppy disk. When I smuggled last month's out, he must've seen me."

Gordon couldn't digest this. "What are you going to do now?"

"Not sure. Temp until I can find something. Gordon, I am so pissed!" He could hear her mouth turn away from the receiver, "I know, Michael, honey, I shouldn't say that. Let me see, a better way would be to say, 'I am very hurt and angry.' How's that?"

Her voice came back to the phone.

"Where was I? Anyway, Hunter called me into his office just after lunch. Nothing special about that. He had my file open. You know, I think he uses those to intimidate people. He had a stack of inventory reports. He said he saw me copy something onto a disk, print it, and take it. That I've been there long enough to know company policy word for word."

"Oh, Clerise. I'm so sorry. I never meant for you to get caught."

"Not your fault. I wanted to know what was going on. Anyway, I told him I took it home to finish some work, which was true. He asked where the floppy was. I knew then he wasn't buying the story. His expression. I've never seen anything so ugly. I wanted to run. The way his eyes set and that awful smile he gets. I said I was sorry. I was just trying to make sure he looked good for corporate. I swore I wouldn't do it again.

"He said 'You won't have to worry about that. Pack up your things. I want you out of here now.' I felt so humiliated." Clerise's voice broke. In the background, "I'm okay, Michael. I'm just a little upset. Gordon's helping me, okay?"

While she reassured Michael, Gordon surveyed the state of his house. How could he have her over to this? How would he explain the dog bed in the living room and no heat?

"I have some of those reports here too. Clerise, why don't you and Michael come over for dinner and bring those papers. I've got a couple of things I need to take care of in the next few days, but I'm free on Friday. How's that?"

He could hear her making a valiant attempt to stop sniffling. He added, "It's going to be okay." *That was stupid. I should've said something more comforting*, he thought as he replaced the receiver.

+++

Patricia stared from her bedroom window at the dark figures under the eaves across the street. Every so often she saw a flare from a cigarette. She thought about giving Olivia a ride to school so she could feel out if the girl knew about Ray. She could hear Brian's reaction to riding in a car with his sworn enemy. She saw Becca descend the front steps and amble down the block, while Olivia disappeared into the house.

As she turned to get ready for the monthly village council meeting, the image of Ray arriving home some evening to see Becca implanted a sick curiosity as to what he'd do. But so what? They both knew. Meanwhile, the police continued hunting for leads. At least they hadn't reported any new activity. But then again, his latest victims may not have come forward.

Her muscles tightened at the thought of him whispering in her ear the previous night. She knew she should turn him in, even without the evidence. She'd be a hero and a martyr. For a moment, she sighed, and a warm sensation flowed up her chest as she imagined the community regard. Except, Brian would be humiliated, taunted at school, and he'd have the specter clawing at him for the rest of his life. She couldn't do that to him. The photos had to still be in the house. She had to manage this, find the evidence, and blackmail Ray.

+++

Gordon carted piles of papers to an empty bedroom as temporary storage until his guests had come and gone. He had been meaning to sort all this stuff and clean the house for quite some time anyway. All the years' accumulation brought to the surface his inability to decide what to keep and what to toss. After Lara died, he had sat for hours, picking up and putting down her life. He'd been unable to do more than that. Each time he lifted a scrap of their marriage, it cut into his heart and grief oozed. Maude had reminded him he needed to go at his own pace, but at some point he needed to encounter the memories. Grieve and go on.

Rather than decide, he'd gathered Lara's things, with the exception of their bedroom quilt, and hauled them all to the guest bedroom, where they still resided.

The first floor now lay bare and dull, the area rugs bleached with dust. No wonder his asthma was bad. Several vacuum cleaner bags later, Gordon nodded at the result. The carpets had a threadbare beauty, echoing their years in a home that receded to the late nineteenth century.

The effort left Gordon grabbing for his inhaler, his lungs raw. Cuts serrated the webs between his thumbs and forefingers. The arthritis in his joints complained, and his back hadn't ached like this in as long as he could remember.

As one area cleaned up, another clamored for his attention, leading him to the windows and then the brass hardware and the grease-splotched cupboards in the kitchen. His days were long, and he had taken a leave of absence from the museum, the irony of that very organized project compared to this mare's nest not escaping him.

Late Friday afternoon, the old doorbell ca-linged. He ushered Clerise and Michael into the foyer and, as they hung their coats on the hall tree, he jammed his hands in his pockets as if he could pull out a topic of conversation. Clerise exclaimed about the beautiful banister, the gorgeous chandelier, and the pocket doors, the brass now miraculously cleaned. Not so miraculously, the dining table's maple surface gleamed. And on it were his files.

Through her eyes, he saw the house as it was when his parents were alive and he was a boy. Such a grand house, and it still was.

He had been preparing dinner when they arrived, so he grabbed the excuse to finish, Clerise following him to the kitchen. As they stood at the '70s-era counter, Gordon kicked himself for not fixing the handle on the fridge or the oven doors, for not repairing the ragged linoleum, for not buying some dishes that matched and weren't chipped, and for not sharpening the knives, washing the curtains, painting the wainscoting, and replacing the burned-out fridge light. Everywhere he turned was something he should have done.

They sat around the dining table, Clerise and Michael's heads bent over hamburgers. The sound as he crunched potato chips was deafening.

"We should get started." Clerise dabbed her mouth with a napkin.

Gordon nodded, rose, and gathered dishes. When the swinging door pushed him back into the dining room, Michael wandered the perimeter while Clerise arranged a stack of inventory data for the past eight months. Internally, he groaned. More piles.

"Gordon, do you mind if Michael turns on the TV in the living room?" she asked.

"Of course not. But I don't have cable."

"Michael, you can watch something on PBS." For a moment she regarded her son as he disappeared into the other room and then continued, "I was trying to find any pattern or trends. Let's review the events." She leaned across the table and opened a file. "You noticed the difference last spring, when Hunter announced all those changes in vendors."

"Our inventory levels dropped. A lot of merchandise was sent back as damaged or substandard. And I was concerned about availability for customers." He fumbled with a sheaf of papers.

"So." Clerise tapped her cheek with a pencil. "Hunter gives your classes to Rick and makes you quality control manager. Then he gets these bizarre ideas to market to black people and gay people, puts me in charge of the kitchen and bath department, and seeks out Herb for home décor. Okay, Charlie's a terrible manager, a bigot, and an idiot,"

Clerise concluded.

"You're right on all counts."

"Although maybe not, Gordon." Clerise scooted back her chair. "I'm coming by you, so I can see your reports better." As she lined them up, Gordon felt the slight pressure of her shoulder against his. And then it was gone. "The comparison from month-to-month shows an increase in damaged merchandise, but in certain departments. Big-ticket items that had to be special-ordered, like fridges or countertops, appear immune." She pointed to a column of figures. Her eyes darted, landing on his as she processed the information.

He averted his gaze and spotted a cobweb he'd missed. "The returns decreased when I became quality control manager," Gordon said. He could still feel her touch on his shoulder, and he was drawn to her enthusiasm.

"I think Hunter thought the position would overwhelm you, but you were turning things around. See how returned inventory shoots up again when he assigns you to oversee the Winter Wonderland project? That was a humongous undertaking. I think he banked on it failing."

"Clerise, I'm not sure that makes sense. He'd get himself fired."

"Uh-uh! He could distract you from the inventory problem, and he could always blame you if you didn't pull it off. Also, by having Rick assist you, you'd be training your replacement," she said. "And he was planning to fire you all along anyway," she added.

"He knew we were on to him and catching you with the reports confirmed it. Here's another thing: Remember how Hunter was such a good guy helping to stock inventory? If that kid hadn't run the fork-lift into the shelves at Thanksgiving, no one would have known about all those empty boxes."

Their fingertips collided as Gordon traced his finger down the page, and the moment intensified under the smoothness of her finger-nail. He expected her to pull her hand away, but Clerise, oblivious, kept her finger planted on the paper.

"I was so busy learning the kitchen and bath department I didn't have time to monitor the reports. And let's not forget that office assistant Hunter hired was busy creating a catastrophe." She inserted a thumb under the edge of the pages and pulled the report away. "Sorry, Gordon, I didn't mean to grab that before you were done. Was there something else you saw? I was so focused."

The table felt cool under his index finger. He shook his head, moving his hand to his lap. "You mentioned you might have more reports on floppy disks. Any chance you didn't delete them?" He could look at her if he concentrated on her hair and did not dwell on the gold flecks in her eyes.

"I have to confess, I'm kind of a packrat." Clerise's face clouded, then brightened. "And thank you, Jesus!" She slapped the table. "I dumped the disks in a shoebox. I could always get more from the supply room at work. But you know, now that I think of it, the old drafts aren't like the final ones Hunter sent in.

"You see, I would save a backup working copy on one disk, along with a hard copy in case the system crashed. Hunter would review the draft and make any edits on a final disk. I think he was changing the numbers. And I've got the backup disks to prove it!"

Later, Michael and Clerise navigated the front stoop, while Gordon watched them to their car. The next meeting would be at her apartment, where she had a computer and the disks.

He had survived them coming over. The thermostat now turned back down, he gulped thinking about the gas bill. Normally, he would replenish logs on the fire and get ready for bed. But not tonight. He wanted to ponder U Do It, Charlie Hunter, and Clerise.

+++

"Gordon, where have you been?" He opened the door to his house wider while Olivia pushed past. "Why didn't you let me know? I went to the museum after school to help you, and you didn't even tell me you weren't going to be there." Olivia whined, "You could have left a note. See, I slipped and fell. I have a big bruise. I could have broken my arm."

So much for my peaceful morning, he thought. The plan had been to ease into the day, relishing the previous evening with Clerise and Michael. "That must have been a pretty bad fall," he said.

"It was, and you weren't there."

"Well, how about some tea?" He was already heating water. He gestured to her place at the banquette.

She said nothing for several minutes. Then, as if resuming a conversation, "And I don't know what to do. It's so creepy." She shivered. "And maybe Spider was lying. I thought I could trust him."

"Spider," Gordon stated.

"Yeah, Spider. You know, one of the guys I hang with. And if I don't come up with something, they're gonna kill me."

"Kill you?" Gordon was lost. "Who's going to kill you?"

"Gordon, the others! Cuz Becca thinks either Spider or Lauren squealed, and if she gets caught, I'll get caught too. Along with Dank."

"You're not afraid of getting caught?"

"Naw. Won't happen. They wouldn't rat. Besides, that night I saw the cops at Wrenowskis' from my bedroom window. If they were gonna get me, they would've already." Gordon shook his head at how matter-of-fact she sounded.

"You mean Christmas Eve night?"

"Yeah. But I don't think they ratted. Spider didn't know about it, and Lauren loves Becca. But now Becca's lost it, and she threatened to burn down my house if I don't find out who."

Gordon was working a verbal jigsaw puzzle. Olivia scattered pieces, and he had to find a place for them until the picture formed. He gave a low whistle. "You were at the Wrenowskis' the night the decorations were ruined?"

Olivia nodded, blotting her eyes with a napkin. "There was nothing I could do. If I didn't show, I'd get beat up, just like Becca's thinking about Spider and Lauren. And she's a really great friend. She's protecting me from Brian. She lets me be part of something."

Gordon waited. After a while, she quieted and said, "I better get going."

He regarded her for a long time. "Olivia, do you think there may be something more important here? A lot of damage was done on Christmas Eve. Think about how those people felt. And it sounds like the same thing could happen to you and your mom."

She sniffled while pulling on her camo jacket, her face swollen under her wool cap. As he opened the front door, Gordon said, "I know you'll do the right thing." At least he hoped so.

+++

Having scoured the first two floors and come up empty, Patricia sat back on her haunches, the attic a pink insulated igloo. The pictures could be anywhere. She'd emptied each storage container, one by one, and carefully re-packed them. At one point, going through Brian's baby things, she swore under her breath she'd slit Ray's throat if she found any of that stuff.

She scouted the room for other possibilities and spotted the camping equipment. Within a half hour, she had everything laid out as if all that was needed was a campfire and fresh trout for dinner. The remaining item was the sleeping bag. *He could have even taken the pictures from the shoebox and hidden them in different spots,* she thought, the bag unrolling like a black snake's tongue. She squatted, deciding to take advantage of the opportunity to throw out some of the mold-inoculated gear. The search was exhausting, and Patricia reflected this wasn't her strong suit. She had always lost the Easter egg hunts as a child.

Now all the camping paraphernalia had to be repacked. All that work with no reward made her lethargic. She gathered the tent stakes into a pile. In the movement of lifting a pole and pushing it into the bag, her eye caught a piece of paper sticking out of the insulation.

Someone had dropped a piece of trash, an old Christmas card envelope perhaps. She returned to her task.

Her head snapped back to the insulation. The paper was neatly folded, like a note a teacher would write and send home. She reached for it, and before she even had it unfolded, she could see Ray's heavy script.

Wondered when you were going to find this. No, they aren't here. But that doesn't mean they're not here.

CHAPTER 28
SOLE OCCUPANTS

Ray's note was a gauntlet thrown at Patricia's feet. With a clarity she hadn't experienced in months, she inspected the attic's insulation, its cotton-candy-like texture leaving her hands itching. Before her were storage boxes edged away from the wall, creating a trail that followed the contours of the room. Clutched in her fingers was the second note, which she'd found a few minutes earlier.

It's cold up here, isn't it, Patty Cake? But not as cold as you are.

Fury propelled her around the perimeter again. Ray counted on her to explode, to recklessly hurl herself into the search. He counted on her interpreting the note to mean the pictures were not in the insulation but here, in the attic storage boxes. He counted on her grabbing her bottle of bourbon and drunkenly creating enough chaos to prevent her from ever finding them.

What he didn't count on was the opposite. Her frantic pacing slowed as she strolled to an old ottoman she would someday reupholster for her office. She extracted the two notes from her jeans pocket. Neither note had been in the boxes, so she was probably right to surmise the pictures weren't either. Ray was goading her.

The first note said the pictures were not here, but it didn't mean they weren't here. She could take it literally to mean they weren't in that spot in the insulation but were somewhere in the attic. Or they were not here in the attic but here in the house.

What about the second note? Tricky bastard. He wasn't saying she was cold from being in the attic, but that she was cold as in a game of hide-and-seek. She felt around the attic walls. And found nothing.

That brought her back to the ottoman. She poured herself a cup of coffee from the thermos she'd prepared in the kitchen. As she tilted the cup to drain it, her eye caught something in the corner of the door-frame. A third note.

From the depths of my sole, I hate to see you shiver, Patty Cake. By now you must have cold feet. The tools you need aren't here. Come down below where it's warmer.

She checked her impulse to dash the thermos at the wall. She thought wryly about how he'd misspelled "soul." *Except he has no soul.* She wanted to punch or kick something and for a moment imagined the satisfaction of punching Ray. No, beating him with something, like a shovel.

Her thoughts came back to his word choice of "sole," "feet," and "cold." She groaned, cupping her forehead in her palms. Below her feet was the whole house. She was back to the notion the pictures could be anywhere. Now she wanted to slice him like a ham. With the lawn edger. Or maybe the chainsaw Ray used to cut away dead wood on the trees. He was certainly dead wood in her life. Her musings began to congeal, and by the time she got to the second floor, she had a good idea of where to find the pictures.

She checked her watch, noting she had an hour to find the stash, change her clothes, and meet her new client. She could do it. They were here.

She sat on the steps so she could scan the basement. These old houses were often referred to as "painted ladies." The head would be the attic and the feet would be the basement where Ray stored his tools, and she thought ironically that the garden tools she needed to carry out her imaginings were right in front of her, parked until spring as polished and clean as the day he bought them.

More taunting from Ray. He knew if she was smart enough to figure out the evidence was here, she'd be stymied by where. He'd also know if she got into his stuff, just like when she'd found the cache in the first place. She scratched her hands, her whole body beginning to itch from her confrontation with the insulation. Even her feet.

Her feet! Of course, her feet! Computer programmers are precise. Up the stairs she ran for the flashlight, betting herself she would have the booty in her hands within the next five minutes. She ransacked the utility room for a laundry bag and a pair of latex cleaning gloves. Patricia catapulted herself down the last few steps, landed on the cement, and dashed for the corner. The outlines of her running shoes smudged the dried silt. She was careful to note where any footprints marred the floor. On hooks sunk into the beam, Ray had arranged the ragged jackets and ripped jeans he wore while doing outside chores. He'd placed his boots against the limestone foundation. She parted the clothes on the hooks to reveal a pair of knee-length boots. She lifted the first. Empty.

"I hate you!" she screamed, refraining from pounding the floor with it.

Out came its olive mate, heavier. Inside was the Polaroid camera. "Well at least I found this much."

She rocked back on her haunches, toppling onto her butt. "You asshole," she mumbled, righting herself and spied something in the shadows. Tucked against the foundation was the familiar shoebox. As she eased it toward her, the lid began to gape, the contents threatening to escape all over the floor. Deftly, she moved her hands to prevent the catastrophe, clutching the box against her belly, while opening the bag and then dumping the contents in. What to put in their place? Something that jostled the same way when the box was shaken.

In moments, she was back, recipe cards now inhabiting the shoebox. She dumped the camera in the sack with the photos and replaced it with a square cannister from the kitchen. No need for the Polaroid since she'd gotten another one. And anyway, considering who had been looking through the view finder on this one, and what he was looking at made her want to vomit. She adjusted the boots and stood, the shoebox resting against the foundation once more. She smiled as she made the same bristle pattern with the shop broom removing her footprints and where she'd fallen.

Okay, so it took more than five minutes, but she would easily be able to arrive on time to show houses to her client.

Already dark when Patricia returned home, she leaned against the van's door, fingering the rough edges of the bank's safe deposit box key, a flush of triumph coursing through her body. Above her was Hale-Bopp, a white, raised eyebrow in the mid-horizon. Patricia regarded it for a moment and thought of macaroni. She'd make macaroni and cheese for dinner.

CHAPTER 29
HALE-BOPP

Olivia approached her house in the late afternoon to find Becca huddled on the stoop, dragging on a cigarette. She threw the butt on the snowy lawn. "Where you been?"

"What do you mean where I been? Where you been?"

"All over. Looking for you," Becca said. She lit a joint and inhaled.

Hiding out after school at the museum had worked for the past couple of days, and she'd been able to avoid Becca. Until now.

"My mom and shrink are making me do community stuff." Olivia sat on the step, the cement cold against her thighs. "By the way, Buchard assigned a paper. On Hale-Bopp. We're supposed to take a civilization that existed 4,200 years ago, the last time it was here. What it would have been like for them."

"Hale-Bopp?" Becca was not following the conversation.

"Yo, comet?" Olivia pointed to the horizon.

"Oh, yeah, that."

"So whaddaya think of it?" Olivia asked.

"It's like my old lady. Swoops in and does a bunch of shit to screw up my life and then swoops out again. Who gives a flying fuck?" Becca's voice fogged as she took a toke and held her breath.

"That where you were the last few days?"

"Yeah. She's fuckin' nuts. Why you want to know?" Becca took another toke.

"I don't. I was talking about Hale-Bopp."

"Yeah, right. What did you find out?" Becca passed the joint to Olivia.

"About what?" Olivia's body jerked as she pictured her house in flames. She filled her lungs, buying time to come up with something, to sound nonchalant. "Oh that. I talked to Spider. He was in jail that night. His folks kicked him out cuz they caught him watching slasher flicks. They're like way into some Jesus thing and get all righteous. The cops busted him for being out after curfew. They hauled him in, called his old man, and then put him in one of their cells."

"How do ya know he's telling the truth?" The acrid smell of weed floated into the late afternoon air.

"He was practically next to the dispatcher. He could hear everything when the call came in about the school."

"So?"

"So did you tell him we were going there to practice?" Olivia asked. Becca shook her head. "See, so it couldn't've been him."

"What about Lauren?" Becca scraped the sole of her boot on the steps.

"I'm working on it. But I don't think she'd do that. Shit, Becca, the call to the cops that night was random, not Lauren or Spider."

"Don't cross me, O. I know it was one of them." She flicked her lighter and jerked her head toward the house. "I'm outta here."

Olivia watched her friend traverse the street, a black shadow against the white snow. The museum had become the only place of refuge for her.

+++

The next afternoon, Olivia arrived at the museum and ran ahead to boot up the computer. Gordon followed, lagging behind and contemplating his new assistant. She arrived ghostlike and said little. This was not like her. He wondered if she had done anything about the vandalism at Christmas.

At the leather bench on the second floor, Gordon paused, somewhat winded. The grand foyer and great chandelier spread below, Victoriana in all its elaborateness. Today, the crystals hung as if asleep.

This was the view when he and his mother used to call on Grand Lotty. She was bedridden by then, and she had enthroned herself in the sitting room on a daybed, an elaborate ivory cane by her side, and she wore clothes that had originated a couple of decades earlier in the Roaring Twenties. Like her diaries and position in the community, she was organized and thrifty.

As Gordon continued his ascent, he thought of Minette. Odd. Seeing she had died before he was born and his mother never mentioned her, he had always thought of her as just one of the pantheon of historic figures rather than as his grandmother.

Minette had sacrificed a lot. The descent in living standards and social rank must have been agonizing when she realized the exact consequences of her rash decision to marry the charming scoundrel, Rupert Sipe.

He shuffled toward his chair in the ballroom and he puffed on his inhaler, the sound like a faint whistle, the medication easing his breathing. At the far end, Olivia sat hunched forward at the computer. Most of the time she helped Gordon by entering dictated data. She was a whiz at transcribing, and he marveled at her agility on the keyboard. She acted embarrassed but also pleased at any compliments he paid her.

Sometimes he let her handle the documents and tell him which entries to make. She was quick and had the system down in a few hours. Gordon was amazed when she proposed her idea to reference documents by subject as the next step in the project.

"How come you don't have a wife?" Olivia split the silence.

"I did. Her name was Lara."

"You guys get divorced or something?"

"Uh, no." He finished reading a news article. "She died."

"Oh. Didn't you have any kids?"

Gordon entered the data from the article before answering. "We didn't get a chance. She was a nurse during the Vietnam War. She died before we could."

"Wow. I didn't know." She reached in a box and extracted some minutes from a village council meeting. "I didn't know women went. Did she have to go?" Olivia asked.

"Who? Lara? No. She wanted to go."

"Where's Lara buried?"

"She was cremated. I took her ashes out to my cabin and put them there."

"How come you didn't get married again?" she asked.

"I would have if the right person had come along."

"So, what are you going to do?"

"Grow old, I guess," he said.

"You're already old!"

Gordon began to laugh and cough, tears streaming down his face, threatening to ruin the letter he was holding. He raised a finger to indicate he wanted her to take the document and felt in his pocket for his inhaler.

"This is so rad. For once, all that library stuff and class work on alphabetizing and indexing is useful," she said.

Gordon pushed the valve to release the medication and breathed in deeply. "Glad to hear that," he managed to say.

"Have you seen any ghost stuff lately?" she asked.

"Nope. Not lately."

"Wish I could see it."

"Not much to see," he croaked and took a ragged breath.

She laid the newspaper in its box and crossed the room to where a small tray sat with a pot and mugs.

"Until I started hanging out with you, I never liked tea." She ambled back with the tray and lifted Gordon's empty mug. "Could I go make us some more?" she asked.

"Good idea," he said. The warmth would help his lungs.

How long Olivia was gone, Gordon couldn't say, less tuned into his surroundings than what was going on in his chest. This business with his asthma was exhausting.

Olivia set down the tray, a green lake of tea surrounding the mugs. "What's that sound you're making?"

"Just catching my breath." Gordon sipped the tea. "It's probably from being such an old man." He winked at her as she opened her mouth to protest. He could feel the warmth of the tea on his chest as he swallowed and hoped this would help the medication. He focused on relaxing, keeping his concern about the severity of the attack at bay.

"Have you seen this?" Olivia held up the front page of a newspaper. "'New Volunteer Firemen Sworn In.'" One of them was Gus Carlson. Was that your dad?"

"Yep. Why don't you do the reading and entering by yourself this time?" He felt the space between his words lengthen. Olivia gave him a skeptical look and began the task.

One of his childhood memories was that cold December when his father was sworn in as a volunteer fireman at the Forester Village Hall. The heavy doors to the entrance had swung open, as men, in a single movement, palmed their fedoras and women tugged at their gloves upon stepping over the threshold. The entryway was full of voices, greetings, conversation, and hubbub punctuated by laughter as towns-folk surged into the auditorium.

His father had left them at the door to go backstage, so he and his mother took aisle seats about halfway down. But neither he nor his mother saw the swearing-in. While the town's folks settled and waited, Gordon's breathing became tighter and tighter. Within mo-ments, he was struggling for air. He remembered his mother's face, determined and calm, patting his back as she led him to the entry, where she asked for help to get him to the hospital.

"Gordon, you're sure wheezing a lot," Olivia declared. "And now you're gasping."

"You know," Gordon gulped, "let's call ... it quits."

He lumbered behind, turning off the lights.

"Are you okay?" Olivia waited on the stairs.

"Fine. I'm fine, just a little tired. You go along and I'll finish closing up." He waved her on and heard her rapid footsteps on the stairs, then the front door closing. The only sound now was the high-pitched whistle of his labored breathing. The mansion had never felt so deserted.

+++

The scent of dying winter floated into her nostrils as Olivia reached her street. Pasted in the horizon was Hale-Bopp, a comma fallen over by its own weight.

She still had hers and Becca's Hale-Bopp English assignments to write. This time she did not resent the extra work. Writing Becca's would be a no-brainer; researching the Egyptians had been fun. Now thoughts about her essay were sucking her along, as if riding the tail of that giant ice ball.

"How's it going, honey? How was the museum?" Donna asked, crossing the lawn and pausing beside her on the stoop.

"Fine. How was work?"

"Steady. How's Gordon?"

"Fine, I guess."

"Isn't it strange? We didn't even know about Hale-Bopp until a couple of years ago. I mean, we all know about Halley's Comet, so we were expecting it. Remember all that buildup? And what a disappointment." Donna tilted her face and gazed at the horizon. "Well, sweetie, I'll call you when dinner's ready." She patted Olivia's shoulder and went inside. Shortly, the living room and porch lights went off.

Olivia tucked the backpack under her bottom to ward off the cold, trying to get her mind around the splotch in the sky. All those ancient civilizations, whose people had observed it, were nothing more now than crumbling monuments surrounded by tourists on camels. And 4,200 years before that, shaggy men and women, holding children in their arms or by the hand, stared into the night, a fire behind them in a cave.

Hale-Bopp had just materialized one night those thousands of years ago, when people must have thought the light in the sky was some kind of omen. Did they worship it? When Hale-Bopp disappeared, did they long for it to come back?

Becca was like Hale-Bopp, her appearance changing Olivia's life. She had showed up and had seen her as more than smart and fat. Around her, Olivia was awed, excited, and scared. And empowered. For the first time her outside and inside felt like they matched. When Becca disappeared for days at a time, Olivia longed for her to come back. But as time went on, less and less. Maybe one of these days Becca would just disappear for good, solving everything.

She lowered her eyes to the Wrenowskis' house. Before her was evidence of Becca's power for horrible devastation. Like ghosts of Christmas past, she saw herself, Becca, and Dank in the front yard.

Dank. Maybe he could give her some answers. Then Gordon could tell her what to do. She rose, hoisted her backpack, and decided to go write the essays.

+++

A dull evening escorted Gordon as he made his way home. Mentally, he ran through his routine and tried to remember how much fuel he had for his fire.

As if he were trapped under a pile of lumber, the boards pressing on his ribs and lungs, he had been taking more asthma medication than he should to help his breathing. He wondered how long he could keep going like this. The time until he could draw Social Security felt like years rather than months away. He didn't like to dwell on it. Or the fact that he was reminded of Lara today. Fortunately, the events were long enough ago that the pain was polished flat and smooth. But thinking of her gave him pause to reflect on those years since her death—where he had been and where he was going. The thought goaded him: How different the past ten years may have been if he'd had the money to pay his store's loans.

He paused on his front lawn, where across from his house Hale-Bopp streaked across the horizon. In this global village of Earth, the comet had just one name and one meaning. The last time it sped past, each civilization would have called it something different, with some kind of meaning attached.

His name would have meant something at one time too. Now Gordon was name branding for gin, a product. He had been a product of sorts, part of a transaction from one hardware store to another.

He'd read a newspaper article proclaiming that bar codes with all a person's information on them were just around the corner. Certainly they were. After all, pets had them now. He remembered when folks bemoaned that soon everyone would become just a Social Security number. That sounded fairly benign compared to being a product branded with a bar code.

Was it any better that long ago a name meant you were a tailor? Perhaps railing against a summary was universal, whether a name or a bar code. Was that what all those boxes in the museum were? A community's railing? Evidence that Forester's citizens were greater than a summary?

Lara, branded in his life, was greater than her name. Her greatness was her wanting to make a difference even though it cost her life. And Maude was greater than Patricia's silly story. She was a life-shaper. All those children she taught. Even Patricia was more than her real estate sign. In the end, he could have been greater, more important than a nut—he made a small gasp at his own joke—or bolt, had he connected with others. Tears in the corners of his eyes were cold in the chilly air, his empty house behind him like a shroud.

His lungs began to seize, and he reached for his inhaler. Empty. A rasping sound issued from the back of Gordon's throat as he struggled to catch his breath, his heart now racing. He needed to get inside.

In the foyer, he opened his mouth as wide as he could, his lungs clawing at the air, panting, trying to decipher the directions his brain gave him. Call 9-1-1? No insurance, no money. No dignity. No, he couldn't do that.

What could he use? An old nebulizer. His mind scrambled to recall where he had stored it, and with a gulp of air, he tore up the stairs, coughing and wheezing as his shin hit the last step. The cupboard under the sink in the bathroom held a toilet plunger and spare rolls of toilet paper, which scattered under his panicked fingers. The medicine cabinet doors slammed against the wall, revealing deodorant, a can of shaving cream, a razor, and some aftershave. But no nebulizer.

Back down the stairs he staggered. He halted at the coat tree, pulling it over as he fell into a fit of coughs and gasps. On the floor, he scrabbled through the pockets of his old U Do It bib, clutching the slim hope that they contained a vial with a bit of medication. The pockets turned out ... empty. He arched back, as if his chest were tearing away from his insides. Maybe one was in the glove compartment of his station wagon. Gordon stumbled across the veranda toward the steps, drowning in the air that wouldn't enter his lungs. He gulped, swallowed, gasped once, twice, falling forward to lie on the grass, with a memory of a freshly caught trout, mouth opening closing, suffocating. He stared at the sky, at the distant crescent in the mid-horizon beckoning to him.

If he were Hale-Bopp, he'd study the blue marble below to see what mankind had stamped on Earth to change its surface, to brand it. As quickly as a slight intake of air, he was over Forester, then landing as a shadow, where around him were his family and all Forester's residents through time.

He felt a form against his, and his arms wrapped around Lara. She turned and smiled up at him.

"My sweet Gordon."

They wavered in and out, ethereal, followed by a Babel of noise and smells before, alone, all went black.

CHAPTER 30
ENCOUNTERS

The railroad underpass was a river of arctic air, while she waited as Dank pulled out a Camel. He cupped his hand, passed Olivia a cigarette, and wiped his nose with his glove.

"Why did Becca do that golfing thing?" Olivia concentrated on kicking at spray-painted cement.

"She wanted to, that's why."

"But why did she trash the Wrenowskis' so badly? Brian is such a little dick I couldn't give a shit about him anymore. We screwed him over last fall, and he can't do anything about it. But she practically demolished the Lane Realty house. We could be in a shitload of trouble."

"O, you are so lame. You think this is about Brian?"

"Then why choose that house? It was so not random."

"Shit, O, are you 'tarded? Brian's asshole dad did her. He pretended like he had some great shit. Took her to a vacant house and drugged her."

Olivia's body felt encrusted in ice. "What? Ray Wrenowski? You're messing with me."

"Fuck no. He did. Almost a year ago." Dank took a deep drag, cigarette between thumb and forefinger. "She's been out to get him ever since."

"You're full of shit."

"I swear. I saw the picture. The asshole took a picture and then put it in her pocket. Becca found it after she came to. She could remember his face and nothing else." He spit out a fleck of tobacco. "She was ballistic. Still gets that way, so don't even go near there with her."

Olivia frowned, the constant swish of cars on the distant parkway, in her mind a continuous line of dark green sedans like Ray's.

"Is something going down?" Dank threw the still burning butt.

"No, just needed to talk to you. Trying to figure out what to do." The wind, now bricks of ice, rushed through the underpass. "Becca's obsessed with Spider and Lauren. Thinks one of 'em ratted her out to the cops for Christmas Eve. She wants me to choose. And you know what that means if I don't."

"Yeah, she's getting more and more whacko. Jesus." Squatting in the frigid air, he held out two more Camels, both lit. Olivia relished the harsh burning in her throat and the way the tobacco calmed her.

Dank rose, tossed the butt, and walked off. "Sucks to be you, O."

+++

The message Patricia left on his work answering machine was cheery and vague. "Meet me at the Hobson Hotel. We can have dinner. I have something to tell you."

When Ray arrived at the dining room, Patricia was waiting for him, one cocktail in hand, a gin and tonic on the opposite side of the table, where he would sit. In her purse were copies of the pictures, the originals now tucked away in a safe deposit box along with the camera. Why hadn't she done this to begin with?

He perused the menu, and Patricia felt as if she was finally able to observe him objectively, rather than through some kind of emotional haze.

"I assume you closed the sale. Your phone message didn't say." Ray lifted a linen napkin and snapped it open.

"In fact I did, but it's more that we don't get to spend much time together these days. I've been so worried about you, Ray, and there just wasn't the chance to ask. How is that colleague you're trying to help?"

"Colleague?"

"You know. The one whose …," Patricia dipped her voice, "the one you've been trying to get into a program because of his problem."

"Problem?" Ray's eyes peered over the top of the menu. "What do you have a hankering for, Patty Cake?"

"I'm going to take a gamble on the catch of the day. Haven't had fish in a while. Been to the basement lately?"

Ray slightly dropped the menu, the only physical indication he'd heard her. "A few days ago, why?"

"Well, I was down there a couple of days ago myself. Funniest thing. You won't believe what I found."

Ray slapped the menu on the linen tablecloth. "I thought we had worked that out. They aren't mine."

"Odd that creep you're protecting didn't mend his evil ways. Know what? I think you're too kindhearted, Ray. There's more pictures."

Ray's countenance hardened, his eyes reptilian, and Patricia wondered if that was what his victims saw. "You have more to lose than I, Patty Cake. I'm not a hotshot in Forester. You want to trash that?"

She smiled. Predictable. He was predictable. "Ray, I'm not the molester. I'm the poor innocent wife who tragically stumbled onto these horrid pictures. Betrayed by the man she thought she knew, she risked it all to make sure he was brought to justice. I can come out of this a hero."

"If you're such a hero, Patricia, why haven't you taken them to the police?"

"I never thought you could be so selfish. What do you think this would do to Brian? That's why I haven't turned them in."

He was silent for a moment. "That what's going on with you? That why our marriage sucks so bad these days? I tell you, Patricia, I'm fed up with this, and I've lost patience with you."

"Lost patience? We're on the verge of ruin because of you, and you blame me?" Having this kind of argument while constraining her volume was becoming too difficult. Patricia paused, pressing her chest as if that would make her voice softer.

"Yeah, I've lost patience. I come home in the evening, and God knows what kind of shape you're gonna be in. Half the time you're passed out, dinner is still frozen or in a can or at the take-out."

"I'll take you to court, Ray, and you won't ever get custody of Brian. Way I see it, we can tell Brian the divorce is mutual. You can move out and get an apartment closer to work."

"You've got to be kidding. Or are you drunk as usual?"

"Neither." She rummaged in her bag. "Does this seem familiar?" She laid a picture on the tablecloth. The linen was so white, pure, and clean and the copy so dirty as to leave a slimy trail as she slid it across to him.

A waitperson approached, "Good evening, my name is James, and I'll be your waitperson this evening. Can I bring something else from the bar and an appetizer to get you started?" He tilted his head, folding his hands like a priest hearing confession.

Ray covered the picture with a napkin. "We'd like to order now. She'll have the tilapia, and I'll have steak," he said, glaring at James. As the waiter opened his mouth, he added, "We'll have the salad with house dressing, rice for her and baked potato for me, no toppings, just plain."

The waiter nodded and retreated.

"Ever see her before?" She slid another across. "Or her?" He shook his head. "You are a cocky bastard, Ray. I've got more. Wanna see them? I'm sure you'll recognize at least one."

"My word against yours, Patricia."

"Wanna bet she couldn't identify you?" She pushed the picture of Becca to him.

He stared at it a moment and scooped them all in his lap as James sidled over with salads. Ray ignored him and began to eat.

Now this is unpredictable, Patricia thought. She would've bet he'd be all over her with "Patty Cake" and "this can't be" or "I'm sorry, I won't do this again." Instead, he kept eating his salad. She picked at the lettuce. The entrée came, sat, and became cold. Over-solicitous James crept to them and asked if something was wrong with their meals, then scurried when Ray demanded the check and leftover containers.

Patricia rose, grabbed her purse and coat. "Don't even think about coming back tonight. When I get home tomorrow afternoon, I expect to see you've taken what you need for the next couple of weeks. If not, I turn the originals over to the police. They're not in the house any longer. I'll start the divorce proceedings." She pulled on her gloves.

+++

Olivia rang the bell at the museum, hopeful he would call down the stairs or be in the kitchen with the kettle on. Another docent opened the door. No, Gordon wasn't coming in this week.

Where was he? His house had been dark the past few days, and she needed to talk to him. Olivia strayed onto lawns and mashed in the icy covering over the late winter snow, leaving round holes like some winter gopher had been at work. Fuming and jittery, she decided she had to follow through. She never purposely sought out Lauren. However, Dank said Becca had also been hinting to him about Christmas Eve.

She was trapped. Either she'd get beat up by the gang or by Lauren. She chose the latter and made her way to Lauren's street, where huge old mansions squared off against each other in outrageous opulence. She found the girl striding toward her monstrous, white, broad-shouldered home.

"What do you want, you shit?" Lauren greeted her.

"Just wanted to talk, that's all." Olivia scrambled, straddling the pavement and grass. Lauren ignored her and kept walking. "Do you think Becca's okay?"

Lauren stopped and spun, "No, I don't think she's okay. She's hanging with you."

"Tough shit. I like her too. And if you really liked her, you'd help me figure it out." Olivia took a step back.

"I don't need to figure it out. I already know."

"Then you know why I'm here, don't you? She thinks you ratted her out for Christmas Eve," Olivia said.

Lauren raised her hand and struck. "You sneaky bitch."

Olivia deflected the blow, Lauren's fist slamming her elbow. "You really want to do that? You think she'd believe you over me? I just say the word."

Lauren raised her fist again, her face crinkled in rage. "You do that, you'll get worse."

Olivia could see Lauren assessing the information and grabbed the opportunity. "I think she's majorly losing it. She thinks it's either you or Spider ratted on her. Spider was in jail and didn't know she was going to wreck the school and that house. That leaves you."

"Do you think I'm fucking nuts? If I snitched, I'd be dead right now. Besides, if I did, how come the cops haven't grabbed her?" Lauren took a step back.

"So what's this all about?" Olivia had her spooked.

"Shit if I know." Lauren broke eye contact.

"You just said you did. Dank told me Brian's old man did her a year ago."

"Did her? Did her!" Lauren's voice rose, anguish contorting her face.

"Dank doesn't get it. He's a walking dickhead."

Lauren's face crumpled. "Wrenowski took her to this house that was for sale, so she could try some shit he'd bragged was real good and then deal it for him. I took care of her after it happened. She had this Polaroid. You could see cum smeared on her belly. He raped her and then musta jerked off when she passed out. I found her huddled at the place. She was pissed, beating the dirt."

Olivia moaned, and tears congealed in her throat. "Why didn't you take her to the ER? That asshole could've been caught."

"What planet are you from? Becca absolutely would not go. Said they'd take her away from her aunt and send her to another foster home. Said they wouldn't believe her."

"But what about the picture?"

"She crumpled it and threw it in a bush at the place. Wouldn't talk about it. Threatened us all if we did anything. Just said he'd get his. I can't believe she thinks I did that. I love her, and things were fine until you brought her all that crap back from New York. She's just using you, you bitch."

Olivia's shoulder sagged, her arm throbbing. "So now what?"

"Figure it out. You tell her I ratted, she won't protect you, and you are so dead." Lauren retreated, her middle finger raised.

+++

The last of the day would be gone soon. Olivia wasn't sure what she'd find at the place. Without much information, she began working her way around the enclosure. She brushed away a mantle of dead leaves covering the hard earth, searching for signs that something had been dropped. Nothing. Olivia moved on feeling for anything that might be a crumpled Polaroid.

She scooped away more debris. Her own scraping obscured another subtle noise, the swish of bushes parting. She rose in time to see Becca shove her way into sight.

"What're you doing here?" Becca's fierce eyes surveyed the tangled branches mounded with snow.

"Uh, waiting." Olivia rifled her jacket pockets to pull out a pack of cigs, scuffing the leaves over the cleared ground.

"Bullshit. You know you're not supposed to come unless there's a deal."

"I thought Dank said to meet here." Olivia offered the pack.

"Who's been here?" Becca demanded, pointing at a cleared spot.

"How the fuck should I know? Like Lauren said last time, a homeless dude." Olivia shuffled her boots spreading leaves. "Anyway, how you been?"

"Why you give a shit?" Becca grabbed a cig and snatched the lighter Olivia offered.

"Cuz I do. I care."

"You care," Becca exhaled.

"Duh. Why you think I do your English homework for you?"

"Cuz I'd beat the crap outta you if you didn't." Becca's eyes narrowed as she studied the leaves.

"Whatever. Paper's due day after tomorrow. So here it is, bitch." Olivia made a big show of opening her pack and extracting the essay.

"Tell Dank he's in major trouble if he ever does that again." Becca grabbed the notebook papers. "You all are such dipshits."

"Sure, I see him first, I tell him." Olivia hoisted her backpack, Becca on her heels.

+++

By the time she could get back to the place with a flashlight and a baggie, the undergrowth had melded with the day. On her hands and knees, Olivia resumed her search under the bushes. Something shiny glinted. Just a gum wrapper. Something white and soggy was an old ball of notebook paper. Cigarette butts lay like fly larvae. Cardboard packages, limp and disintegrating, decorated the bare limbs. When she reached the end of the enclosure, no Polaroid had surfaced. Her face was scratched, her jeans were wet, and her back hurt.

She began to work her way back with the hope she had missed it, this time scraping deeper where the ground was dry and hard, the soil covered by a dense canopy of twigs. More garbage. As she moved to make the next pile, her frozen fingers grasped a crumpled white square. The photo.

Gingerly, she picked up the edges, careful not to touch it, and slipped it into a baggie.

In her room that evening, Olivia pulled the evidence from her backpack and peered through the baggie. She was not prepared for how Becca looked, head to the side, eyes closed, the expression on her face inanimate. Naked.

Beneath the overhead light, the photo transformed from eerie to tragic. Hardly resembling Becca, it could have been any girl. She turned the baggie over. *Thanks for the great time.* Ray's heavy script. Her anguish ignited in rage. She contemplated her next move. She should take this to the police. Her rage turned back to anguish. She and Becca would get busted. If she didn't go to the police, she still had to deal with Becca's craziness. Getting beat up by the others was too real, so for the present she decided to hold on to the picture. Maybe it would protect her. If only she could find Gordon.

CHAPTER 31
CLERISE

You must be Olivia. I'm Clerise, and this is Michael."

Olivia regarded the woman sitting by his bedside and the boy with a math book open perched on a chair in the corner. "Gordon's talked about you. Is he okay?" she murmured.

"Doing better. Doesn't sleep as much."

Olivia edged into the hospital room and planted her back against the wall. Attached to all the equipment, he appeared so frail. Clear droplets formed in an IV bag and trickled down the line. Gordon turned his head toward her, settling further into slumber.

"This is too weird. I volunteered at the museum the day he, like, got sick. I mean, I musta been the last to see him."

"One of the neighbors, Patricia something, happened to be driving by and saw him lying on the parkway. Thank God she had a cell phone. Otherwise, he would have died."

"Wow," was all Olivia could muster. "So, you know him pretty good, right?"

"Yeah. He's helping me with a science project at his cabin," Michael said, punching numbers in a calculator.

"What's that yellow stuff?" Olivia pointed to a bag hanging by the side of the bed.

"Pee." Michael focused on the calculator's screen.

"Oh." Her stomach was queasy, as bad as when he talked about his wife dying.

Gordon began to stir and opened his eyes.

"Can I get you something to drink, Gordon dear? Water?" Clerise asked.

She called him 'dear', Olivia thought. *Does this mean they've hooked up or something? He's so old. Eeew, gross.*

He nodded as he raised his head, eyes recognizing Olivia.

"You weren't okay, huh?" Olivia said. It came out as an accusation. Should she have known this? His being in the hospital could be her fault. He wasn't supposed to be sick. And Clerise and Michael weren't supposed to be here. He was supposed to tell her what to do about Becca and the picture.

"Well, I guess it was more than I thought," Gordon said, taking a deep breath and adjusting the sleeve of his gown.

"This is, like, too scary, Gordon. What would I have done if you'd passed out in the ballroom?"

"Called 9-1-1." Michael glanced over.

"I wouldn't remember to do that. I would've freaked. Besides, the phone's way downstairs." Olivia pictured Gordon on a gurney jostled down the three flights of stairs by two grim men.

The curtain separating Gordon from his roommate rippled, and a man in blue scrubs came in carrying a food tray containing Jell-O and broth.

"That all you get?" Michael asked.

"For now, yep." Gordon dipped a spoon in the broth. "Want some?" When Michael raised a nostril, Gordon gave a weak laugh.

"Say, Olivia, would you be willing to babysit? Sometimes my temp work keeps me from being home when Michael gets out of school," Clerise said. "Also, can I give you a ride home when we leave?"

"Sure. Glad to." Olivia could relax a bit, relieved she had another way of avoiding Becca until Gordon could help her figure it out.

+++

"Olivia!" Patricia called from her driveway. She crossed over to the Dimatos' yard. "How's Gordon?"

"Okay I guess. I just got back from seeing him at the hospital." Olivia hoisted her backpack.

"Who was the woman dropping you off?"

"Friend of Gordon's. Patricia, I'm sorry but I need to get in. I still have homework to do." A jumble of images flooded her mind—Ray foremost—and she took a quick breath.

"Well, I just wanted you to know a girl was here this afternoon. She sat on your front steps for a while and then left. I think she's a friend of yours?"

Olivia began to turn toward her house. "Thanks."

"Short black hair. Wore a black jacket and jeans." Patricia reached her side.

"Thanks for letting me know." She mounted the steps her shoulders prickling with unease.

"Who was she? She looks very interesting." Patricia followed Olivia onto the veranda.

"Just a friend." Olivia backed toward the door.

"I notice you've been gone a lot lately. I'm usually around in the late afternoon. Anything you want me to tell your friend if I see her?"

"No. I see her at school. Patricia, I've got to go. I'll be in a shitload of trouble if I don't." Olivia twisted the doorknob.

Patricia's face froze for a moment and then she retreated. As the girl opened the door, her stomach seized. Patricia was renowned for being a snoop, but this was more than weird. She wondered if they knew, if Brian knew.

+++

Gordon dozed in his bedroom. The hospital had released him, and before he could say otherwise, Clerise had volunteered to fix dinner for him in the evenings as well as keep an eye on him.

Until the emergency, he had managed the parts of the house they saw and limited the amount of gas he used to when they were over. When Clerise and Michael brought him home, the house felt as cold as the outdoors. He was lucky that on top of everything, his pipes hadn't burst. He had not moved his burn piles out of their storage upstairs, so the only oddity was the cedar dog bed in front of the fire. But she didn't say anything.

His bedding carried the aroma of his water conservation plan—several weeks of unwashed sheets. His head poked from a checkerboard quilt he and Lara got as a wedding gift. The strong medication Gordon was on placed memories like objects across the room, just out of reach. These decades later, he had to think for a time before he could remember who had made the quilt for them. Some relative on her side. At the time they opened the gift, the relative watching for that first reaction, the quilt was fresh from the sewing machine and hours of knotting by arthritic hands.

A lovely and quaint gift, the quilt itself was less sentimental than the memories of lovemaking, where they would snuggle under it and giggle, afraid of making too much noise. Lara, for all her confidence, was shy about that. Leaning against the pillows, the quilt a wild skirt at their waists, they made plans. Lara wanted to become a nurse anesthetist, which meant a bank loan, followed by a tour in the Army. They hugged each other in post-orgasmic contentment, deciding that Lara would try that new pill for birth control until the time was right to have children.

After she died, her packet of pills remained in the medicine cabinet. He remembered reaching for his shaving cream, spotting the pills, and wanting to throw them as far as he could. At other times, he feared what would have happened had he had to raise a child without a mother. One afternoon, he became so enraged he grabbed the pills, threw them on the floor, and stomped them. And stomped them. And stomped them. At the thought, he could still feel the tattered plastic and powdered white residue beneath his foot. He had walked out of the bathroom and into their bedroom, pulled his and Lara's quilt around him, and sobbed.

During their small years of marriage, each had claimed a certain corner of the quilt, and Lara always made the bed with it arranged just that way. After her death, Gordon was just as picky, dirty sheets beneath and all.

Clerise knocked on his door, and Gordon fully awoke. On a tray, she had a bowl of stew and bread. She handed him his medications, stacked the pillows, and balanced the tray on his lap. Then she sat on the edge of the bed.

"Gordon," her tone alerted him to some topic that would invade their carefully arranged friendship, "one of the things I treasure about you is your generosity. You've been so good to Michael and me, taking us on vacations to your cabin and helping me try to recoup something from U Do It. Most of all, you are giving Michael a chance he won't understand until he's older. And I'm deeply grateful." The spoonful of stew mixed delicious flavors in his mouth. He chewed and waited. "This is hard and complex. I don't know how to start."

Gordon nodded. She was ending the friendship. He might as well get it over with. He swallowed, "Clerise, just start anywhere," and busied himself with a slice of bread.

"I'm struggling because I can't get much regular temp work, and anything I'm qualified for takes me away from Michael for too much time."

So that was it. Gordon's chest could relax. "I'm glad to have him come here when you have to work late."

"Gordon, that's so kind of you, and I would just jump at that offer." She fiddled with an edge of the quilt. "I know how important your privacy is. I need mine too. I think that's why we get along so well. We respect that in each other."

"And?" He was not used to Clerise dancing around an issue.

"I can't. I can't continue renting the apartment on the money I'm making. The work. It's not regular enough. I can't count on it, and Michael's father, he's ...." She stopped, picking her words. "I don't want to send Michael to live with him or anyone else. He needs me and the stability of me being there for him." Hearing the desperation in her voice was excruciating.

"Gordon ...." She stared at the quilt for a long time, and he began to drift. "Gordon...." Her voice trailed and he opened his eyes. "Gordon ... I'm ... I want you to know how fond I am of you." Her face wobbled in the lamplight, and he strained to focus. "I'm afraid for you. This last asthma attack was very serious. Your doctor's concerned about how often it's happened in the last couple of months." She took his hand. "I'm afraid about what could happen next time. Or that you wouldn't be able to take care of this house you love so much." She began to bounce his hand in time to her words.

"I'm afraid not only because of the asthma, but for how you're living and what that means for this happening again." Clerise's words were confusing. The sentences made sense, but he was straining for their meaning.

"Gordon, I know what getting fired did to you with Social Security still a few months away. I can see what you're doing to hang on. Your courage and creativity aren't surprising. Honey, you can't keep living like this, or the next attack could be fatal. I would be devastated. I don't know what Michael would do." She grabbed one of the napkins, blew her nose, tears darkening the quilt's threadbare patches.

"You don't have to heat the house with wood and old newspapers. I found the stacks of rental magazines from the restaurants. You are so clever. But you're risking your life.

"I've given it a lot of thought. You don't want to end up in a nursing home. I need to be there for Michael. You have limited income, and I could pay you rent and pitch in. The house has plenty of space. You could decide where we'd be. I noticed the basement has been lived in. Or maybe we could live in the attic."

Clerise studied his hand, which she had alternatively massaged, squeezed, and bounced. The sensation had been quite nice. Then with a pat, she placed his hand on the quilt. "Michael and I are gonna go back to our apartment now. I'll stop by tomorrow to see that you're okay and don't need anything." As she left with the tray she said, "I hope you'll think about my idea. No matter what, Gordon, you're important to Michael. And to me."

How soon they left, he could only guess. In the yellow lamplight his fingers rested on the quilt and the small, damp splotches, which remained.

CHAPTER 32
LARA

In the era of macramé plant hangers and wall pieces, they had been a birthday present from Lara's best friend. The wall hanging had hovered above the bed in pseudo-hippie style, and by the window, a spider plant slept in a twine and bead nest. While Lara was not a macramé kind of woman, the gifts inhabited their bedroom because of her love for the friend who had made them. Gordon didn't like them much either, but after her death, they continued their presence, a shard of Lara's sweet temperament. The plant was the first to go—the baby browning, followed by withered plant legs, and, finally, the mother.

The hanger dangled, a twiggy tangle, gathering dust, and Gordon was foggy about when it disappeared. What he remembered was that about six months after Lara died, Maude breached her policy of not intruding into the bedroom sanctuary.

She had habitually left his clean clothes outside the bedroom door in a plastic laundry basket. His job was to fill it with dirty underwear, shirts, and jeans. Theoretically, he was also supposed to strip the bed, but he didn't have the energy. Not that the linen had any sentimental value, he just plain did not have the energy.

One night he fell into bed, his face hitting sheets wrapped in the scent of detergent, and he noticed that the spider plant embraced in the twiney bag was gone along with the wall hanging.

Now he lay under the quilt and stared at the ceiling, trying to calculate when Maude would have removed the macramé artifacts. His mother would not have thrown them out. Instead, they would have accompanied other memorabilia to one of the storage boxes in the attic.

To concentrate, he stared at the twin humps of his feet, scheduling tasks for the day. Whether Clerise and Michael would come over or just phone was hard to say.

The inhaler's contents made him jittery and following a train of thought was labyrinthine. However, his breathing was doing a lot better, so he eased himself out of bed and before long was stepping downstairs to the basement.

The dimly illuminated place was temperate, compared to the deceptive weather outside. The conversation with Clerise the previous night returned, and he tried to imagine them here. A tenant had occupied the basement during World War II, as evidenced by a bent chrome circlet with empty shower hooks next to a York toilet and flaking paint on the limestone foundation. He could picture them crouched down here like refugees. The thought nauseated him. This was a solution reserved for the desperate times of war.

He made his way to his workbench that retained the time-honored oily smell of his family's store. Hanging on pegboard were pristinely maintained hammers, screwdrivers, and wrenches. On a shelf, he had arranged old canning jars containing nails by size. Now, he selected a jar, scuffed his way to an old folding chair, and sat, unscrewing the lid.

After Lara died, running the hardware store and nurturing the garden became his routine. The hardest part was the garden's paradox. Maude did not invade this space and Gordon craved the solitude. They relied on the harvests from the humidity-infused summers for the arctic winters. Nurturing the growing plants took energy that evaporated in the heat leaving him exhausted. He would find himself squatting in a row of vegetables, his aching haunches the notice he'd ceased to work. The smell of rotting vegetation was the most difficult, reminding him that Lara was not in some make-do operating room in Vietnam and that he still had her student loan to pay back.

Was there anything he could have done? Business had been okay, not great. He had customers. Just not enough. There must have been something he hadn't done that could have saved it. Over the years, he had dissected every detail over and over. There must have been something.

For a long time, he sat, his legs like two bent spider appendages, the chair creaking as he shifted his weight. Dipping his fingertips in the jar and extracting a small bunch of nails, he dropped them back in, one by one.

A thought attempted to form in his jumpy mind. He grabbed at it, forcing himself to concentrate, straining to keep it from dissipating. Nothing. He turned the concept around. Nothing. Lara's death, his acumen as a businessman, or anything he could or could not have done, had nothing to do with it. Nothing.

He eased himself up the stairs and crawled into bed, the room dark, and yet he could picture the quilt's colored patches as he pulled it around his chin. Her death had been needless and stupid. Lara, who had dreamed with him and cuddled and supported him, had died needlessly.

"You must come home immediately." Maude had phoned him at the store, her tone the calm authority she had when a tornado was about to strike.

He walked into the living room. An Army chaplain stood.

"Mr. Carlson," the chaplain began, his eyes the eyes of one who has to do this, has to struggle with so much meaningless tragedy. "I am so sorry. Your wife's been in a car accident."

Gordon should say something. Encourage him to go on? He regarded Maude, her face receding behind her large glasses.

"A group of nurses went out for a night on the town." The chaplain laced his fingers. "Lara was one of them. The driver failed to navigate a turn, plunging the car over the edge of a steep hill. It is my sad duty to inform you that Lara did not survive."

"Was Lara alive when the ambulance arrived?" Gordon had hoped for some last words that the chaplain could pass on to him, someone with whom he could connect, who had had contact with her.

"No. She died instantly."

As he had gone through her belongings, Gordon hugged a fantasy of his wife, in an operating-room mask, gown, and gloves in some battle zone makeshift hospital. She would have been the unsung hero to many soldiers. All those wounded she had no opportunity to save. That life, that education, that money, gone. How was he going to pay back that student loan when his business was suffering? Their plans had not included her death.

He now reached for his inhaler, his wheezing worse than it had been for days. He would not call anyone. He would just stay still and rest.

+++

Charlie Hunter stood behind his desk. He had Gordon's file open. In his hand he held a bill. "You must pay this, Gordo. You owe it. Your wife never paid."

Michael came in with a plate of peanuts. "I have a new game, Gordon. You have to move the inventory without being gobbled up by the squirrels."

Clerise, in business attire, marched through the door. "Here you are, sir." She produced a report. "Here, Gordon." She handed him a checkerboard tablecloth. Gordon wrapped the tablecloth around him like a blanket. "You'll also need these." She gave him a box of checker pieces.

"Gordy, you must pay," Charlie called out.

Maude, enthroned in her rocker, opened her address book. She ran her gnarled finger down the page and said, "Tell Charlie to go to hell. You don't owe a cent."

"But what about our store, Mom?"

"It's a casualty of war, dear."

"Then I'll protect the house."

"You have nothing to worry about, son. Patty can sell it for you as soon as she finishes her English essay. But don't let her snoop through the window." Maude faded into the chair's fabric.

Lara stood in the doorway wearing her operating room scrubs.

"You went and died. Lara, why did you do that?"

"Here, sweetheart, put this on. When you wake up, you will be all better." Lara offered him an anesthesia mask.

"I don't want to be better. You didn't have to die." His throat felt clogged by a log jam.

"Oh Gordon, why do you blame me? You think I did it on purpose?"

"You didn't have to go out that night. You didn't have to be in that car." He sobbed.

"But my love, we take a risk everyday just by getting out of bed. I promise you will feel better. Just put this on."

"Lara, what is this?" He strapped the mask to his face.

"It's time, sweetheart. But don't leave it on too long, or you'll be too late for Olivia."

His voice muffled as he inhaled behind the mask. "Lara, I meant to ask you about her. How will she manage the garden with all that rot?"

"You need to talk to her. After all, she rang the doorbell."

"But Lara, Clerise calls me 'dear.' She cried on our quilt."

"I know, honey. It's just an old quilt. She'll wear a beautiful caftan when she gets married."

"Lara, I'm sorry. I'm sorry about everything." Tears mingled in his hair, trickled down his neck.

"Oh, Gordon, all this time."

"Am I better yet? How long do I leave the mask on?"

"My sweet Gordon. You should have taken it off ages ago."

+++

The phone rang again then stopped. He eased into consciousness, feeling as if a crowd had just departed, the bedroom's clarity arriving as he watched the last of the dream's inhabitants fade. Lara's familiar psychic imprint lingered for a moment as he savored it. He was awake now, the pillow soggy.

He swung his heavy legs over the side and balanced his feet on the hooked rug. He faced the bed and made it, square corners, tucked in. Then he unfurled the quilt and noticed for the first time the gaping pieces of fabric, sad mouths that had worked their way loose over the years. He folded it to place in the storage box in the attic.

Finding the box was like searching for a book in a library, but this was Maude's system rather than Dewey's. These were not flimsy storage containers. They were meant to last for several decades or longer. Contents left nothing to ponder, a box labeled "Gordon/Lara Keepsakes 1968." Well, that solved the mystery of when the macramé pieces disappeared.

He wasn't surprised to find that under the box's lid Maude had reserved enough space for the quilt. He sat cross-legged, betting his memory about the condition of the wall hanging and plant hanger. His crooked smile emerged when he saw he'd lost the bet. He was right about the twine; he was wrong about the condition they were in. Someone's brave and muddled attempt to begin with, the hanging was more of a mess than he remembered, like a gnome's ravaged hammock. What he did remember was how he and Lara would hoot: Their joke was if things didn't work out, they could always pawn the hanging.

Resting on top of the macramé was a worn, black book with a note. Gordon lifted the exactly folded paper and read, "My dear Gordon, It's important to move on. Love, Mother." The flyleaf of the book read

"For brave, dear Maude. May this hold your courage. Best wishes, Your Grand Lotty. September 1930."

He knew his urge to sit and read the diary was his usual tactic to delay, but he would read it later. Placing the journal aside to take downstairs and setting his jaw, the way Maude used to, he lifted the quilt, laid it in the box, and closed the lid.

CHAPTER 33
MAUDE

To get the rooms ready for Clerise and Michael, Gordon moved the stacks of old magazines from the bedrooms followed by another day of meticulous cleaning. He stumbled through a request for Clerise's help to move Lara's things from the guest bedroom to the attic.

Gordon's gaze often returned to Clerise's slender fingers and hands forming a basket around an array of silk scarves to lay them in a storage box. He smiled as she folded blouses, skirts, and slacks as if they were bound for more than a journey upstairs.

Boxes packed and stacked, the last item perched on the bird's-eye maple dressing table was Lara's jewelry box, which Gordon opened, its mirror unreflective for decades. Tucked in velvet-lined cells was an assortment of earrings, barrettes, and necklaces. And a golden circle nesting in a corner: Lara's wedding band, which he squeezed in his palm then tucked in his shirt pocket to store in the attic later. At that moment, he recalled his dream, Lara in her scrubs and her promise that when he woke, he would be all better. Clerise's head was bent over the bed, the linen bundled for washing and the chenille bedspread folded over an old wool blanket belonging to Gordon's father. He caught the light on her hair and neck, and in that moment, when she raised her eyes, crinkles radiating from their corners, Gordon inhaled and knew he was finally awake.

"Ready to take the boxes to the attic?" Clerise pointed to the stack.

He took the jewelry box and found a space for it in the last storage container. "Nope, let's take them to the thrift store."

"Gordon, are you sure? You don't have to. There's plenty of room."

"Yes, I'm sure. I've got all I need." And he patted his shirt pocket.

He was surprised at how easy it was to absorb Clerise and Michael's belongings. Then came a debate about disposing all of the newspapers, whether to burn them in the fireplace or deposit them in the recycling bin. Michael came up with the answer: Haul them to the cabin on the next trip to check the squirrels and build a great fire for roasting hot dogs and marshmallows.

The next morning, Gordon made a cup of tea and settled into Maude's rocker, where he started to read his mother's diary. The gas heat was comforting, Clerise was at a temp job, and Michael was at school. Neither would be home until midafternoon. Gordon figured he would be finished by then.

Opening the diary, he scanned for entry dates but found none, as if she were recording her thoughts and experiences without regard for time. Maude began her journal with descriptions of life at teacher's college in Chicago. The initial entries were mundane, as if she were getting her bearings for journal writing. Then she began to reminisce:

From the safety of teacher's college, I can look back on my childhood as it really was. The fact is Papa was a drunk who was barely able to provide for us.

As I was growing up, Grand Lotty helped as much as she could. Because Papa hated my grandmother, the only places Mother and I could see her were at her home or in church. Grand Lotty sent a clear message to the town: Anyone who did not show her daughter, Minette, the respect she deserved would pay for it.

One Valentine's Day, Mother and I went to Grand Lotty's for tea. I had made her a Valentine at school on which I had composed a greeting. She received it with delight, praising my artistic skills, but more importantly my poetry.

Grand Lotty spent a lot of time questioning me. I remember feeling nervous, her eyes seeming to pierce my mouth and throat, as if watching for each word to roll out. Then she spoke to Mother. She said I was a beautiful and intelligent young lady and that my abilities needed to be nurtured.

Contrary to what most of the community thought, Papa was not constantly drunk. If he had been more predictable, Mother and I would have been better able to protect ourselves. Certain events would cause him to drink. If he suspected Grand Lotty was giving Mother money, he wound up like a chain on a winch the moment he thought we were going to visit her. After breakfast, he would disappear to the barn and drink throughout the day while working on his still and bottling his spirits to sell.

By evening, he would stumble to the dinner table, and I learned we could not anticipate what would catapult him from mean to violent. If we could distract him until he passed out, we would be safe.

Mother and I developed an array of skills. The most successful was to retreat to the hayloft. But that took timing. If Papa was not drunk enough, he would follow. The smell of straw often carries the memory of Mother crouched in a corner, the sound of Papa's belt slicing through the air as she pleaded for him to stop.

Once the alcohol attack had passed, he would shyly stand at the kitchen door, apologizing and extending a gift to Mother, something frivolous. He would have something for me too. As I grew older, I realized the meaning of the gifts was we would have that much less to spend on what we did need. Mother's anxious look would soon pass, and then forgiveness would flood her face.

Papa began to drink more and more, wearing her down. By the time I was in my last year of high school, her ability to think quickly had vanished.

Gordon closed the diary. He knew about Rupert Sipe's infamous still, but it never occurred to him what that could mean. Gordon tried to remember if he had seen any pictures of his grandfather—certainly none in the house. He recalled one at the museum in an old newspaper with a caption about his arrest on charges of bootlegging. The man's hair crept down his neck, his features saggy, and his expression stated that if he were not handcuffed, he would beat the photographer with his own camera. Indistinct in the photograph was his grandmother, Minette, in a coat, boots, and no hat. Whether she was hugging herself from cold or fear was impossible to tell.

Gordon opened the diary again. The entries changed.

Life at school is lonely. I think of Gus often. I wish I had paid more attention to our early encounters. I would have more to cherish now.

The day I became aware of him was the day he shambled toward the front of the class to read his English essay. Tall, mostly arms and legs, which moved in uncertain coordination down the aisle, he bumped my desk, kicking my shin. As he leaned to apologize, I noticed how his suspenders dug into his shoulder blades and how his shirt with its frayed collar was too small for his frame. That was the first time our eyes met as his low voice muttered his concern that I was hurt.

After that, I scanned the school hallway for him. Most boys did not go beyond the eighth grade, instead going to work on their family farm or getting a job, so it was unusual that his family had him complete high school.

The problem was how to get close enough to strike up a conversation without being too forward. Then I got an idea. I knew he worked in the Carlson Hardware Store after school, so I offered to purchase some harness bits for Papa. That began our friendship, and to my de-light, Gus was not that shy or tongue-tied.

Gordon grinned. Maude had won Gus's heart. He went to the attic to see if he could find her high school yearbooks. As a boy and young man, he had occasionally asked his mother if he could see them. Her reply had always been that someday, she would dig them out.

Maude's practice of not wasting anything and her obvious affection for Gus meant a box containing memorabilia would be in the attic. But the high school yearbooks weren't where Gordon thought they'd be. By sheer persistence, he located them, in a box hidden in such a dark corner that he would not have found it had he not been hunting for its contents.

He meandered through photos of young people in fashions he as-sociated with old silent movies. When he found her picture, Gordon was astonished. She was beautiful! She was slim, wearing a fashion-able dress, her black hair in a bob, her head held a little high. Gordon smiled, wondering if Maude was copying the movie star photos of the time.

The next year, his mother could have been someone else. She had become frumpy, peeking out of glasses, with a down-turned face. Then he became alarmed. Pages had been crudely ripped out, the edges near the spine jagged, like ugly cuts on the skin. He hurried back to the journal, hoping for an answer.

When I turned sixteen, Papa became stricter than ever. He would lecture me on how lecherous men were and then laugh, pointing at Mother and adding, "I ought to know, right, Minette?" I found it hard to believe that my mother, who was old and worn, her hair unkempt, was the same person as when she was young, when she was Minette, with everything at her feet.

Papa remembered Mother's power and how he had prevailed over stiff competition. He knew what that would mean for me.

As I became a young woman, Papa began to drink more and to grill me on which young men were paying attention to me. He would rouse me at night, calling from my bedroom doorway, his drunken face contorted into an ugly sneer as he maligned the young men's families. He warned me to keep away from them or I would have him to deal with. And often he took a belt to me. Did I think they were interested in me? They were only interested in him and what he had to sell.

Then one night he stumbled forward and landed at the foot of my bed.

After that, he became bolder and perched on the mattress. One night, he passed out across my legs, and I lay there until morning, afraid to wake him. Meanwhile Mother was moving down her own path.

How long had this been going on? Gordon rummaged through his memories for clues referencing this part of her life. Maude had never even hinted that her childhood had been anything but mundane, monotonous.

She then did not write about her mother and father for many pages, as if taking refuge in thoughts about Gus.

I received another letter from my darling Gus, the third this week. I can imagine him late at night at the dining table writing each sentence with such care. Like he promised, we are brought together by the mail.

In my senior book, he had tucked a note. It read "I will think of you in the coming months. We will see each other soon. Until then, the mail will keep us together. Yours Affectionately, Gus."

A box of Gus's letters would be somewhere in the attic. Part of Gordon felt like he would be intruding if he read them, so he decided he might not hunt that hard. He turned back to the journal, and his dread grew.

Papa found my senior book with the note from Gus. I had hidden the book well, but not well enough. His rough hand on my shoulder woke me. He was kneeling on the end of my bed. He showed me the book and ripped the pages out. He tore Gus's note and scattered it on the blanket.

I miss that note—Gus's first real declaration on paper that I was important to him. I had cherished it.

Gus's latest letters contain more and more declarations of love. I have tried to be careful about my responses. If I have to sacrifice my happiness, I do not want to mislead him. Gus can't leave his family's hardware store. If I take a teaching job away from Forester, it would mean the end of our relationship. If I take a teaching job near Forester, I would have to return to that nightmare. When Papa gets out of jail, he will come after Mother and me, and Gus will be in danger.

Gordon turned the page to find a piece of onionskin paper, a letter from Grand Lotty.

My Dear Maude,
A quite unusual event occurred, of which I think you should be aware. I received a note last week from a gentleman you know, asking for an audience. Quite perplexed, I replied with a time and date. I know his parents well, their credentials impeccable, but I know him only as their son.
You can imagine my surprise as Harriet escorted Gus Carlson into the parlor. He is the exact image of his father. This tall, young man had taken great pains in his attire. Throughout the interview, he would

discreetly tug at his stiff collar, and if I had ever seen him in clothes other than stained dungarees, it would have been at your high school commencement.

Although long periods of silence were scattered throughout our afternoon tea, he made a valiant effort to keep the conversation going. He may have read in my face the increasing confusion as to the reason for his visit. He set down his teacup and hunched his shoulders as if that would boost his courage. He asked for your hand in marriage.

How appropriate for him to regard me as the natural source of approval or denial. Should you choose to accept this young man as your future husband, we will discuss the particulars upon your return.
With Affection,
Grand Lotty

Gordon didn't need to guess why this letter was there. He could picture the resoluteness on his mother's face as she folded the letter. On the facing page, another entry began:

I decided I wanted to go to teachers' college when one of my teachers commented on how clever I was. Papa would never let me go, and anyway he did not have the money. I would not be able to attend without Grand Lotty's help. She was my hope. She knew what a risk Mother and I took when we called on her, so I tried to be as discreet as possible and hoped Papa was not watching me.

That afternoon, Grand Lotty listened intently, asking critical questions, frowning over my answers. Then she said she must consider the request. I was so afraid she would say no. When I met with her the following Thursday, she agreed to sponsor me with the condition that she would make the arrangements. From this perspective, I realize she had to take into account how Papa would react and treat Mother.

By this point, Mother had overcome her aversion to alcohol. The house was as unsightly as she was unkempt. I would arrive home from school to find the two of them in one of three states—passed out, euphoric, or battling. Mother had learned to fight back. The night after I met again with Grand Lotty, I tried to talk to Mother and ask her help. She was forgetful, and in a rage, told Papa I wanted to go to Chicago.

The writings swerved away to daily college life. And then Gordon's heart broke.

The smell of alcohol in the air is suffocating as the doorway to my bedroom frames his silhouette. He is in a drunken rage. He spits at me that I am a whore. Going to teachers' college is just a ruse. I am not good for anything and never will be. He leers, his face crazed. He acts slowly, moving toward me. I try to be strong and not let him read the fear. His rage hypnotizes me, and I cannot move. I scan the room for a possible escape.

He creeps onto the bed. And then he springs, hands spread to pin me down, knees apart to keep me down.

I roll onto the floor and under the bed. He lands on an empty mattress. I wedge myself between the bed and the wall. He shouts at me from above, grabbing at the sleeve of my nightgown and wrenching it to hoist me up. I pull back. The sleeve rips. He claws at my feet, but they are curled against my buttocks. Papa jumps and rants. I shrink further into the corner. Again and again he jumps on the mattress. And then the bed collapses. He hurls the bed away from the wall, and I crawl for the door. He grabs my feet. I turn over and try to wiggle out of his grip. I kick and kick. He bunches his fist, pulls back his arm, and I feel his knuckles collide with my nose, the taste of blood filling my mouth. I scream. Mother is hiding or passed out. She will not hear me. Papa's fingers dig into my shoulder blades. With both hands, he rips my nightgown apart.

I do not know how I make the long walk to Grand Lotty's. I ring the bell and pound and call. The lights go on. Harriet opens the door a crack. I find myself on the foyer floor, staring at the chandelier. Grand Lotty kneels at my side, her long, gray braid draped across her shoulder. She helps me to stand and directs Harriet to call Dr. Gibson.

The warm bath stings. How odd, hearing my own sobs echo in the bathroom. I have a gash under my eye. A slight move farther by Papa, and I would be blind. My nose is broken.

The policeman arrives, and Grand Lotty receives him in the parlor. She has wrapped me in blankets and propped me up with pillows. How cold I am even though it is summer!

I am watching myself in a play. A young woman sits on a couch in the parlor next to an older woman in a nightdress and robe. The young woman's face is puffy and bruised. The older woman frowns. A police officer with a notebook perches on a chair. A brief entrance and exit occur when the maid brings in a tray with sandwiches and tea. The police officer asks questions, scribbles in a notebook, his mouth a grim line beneath his stubby nose. The officer's exit line is, "I expect I will have a few more questions, Miss Sipe, but your father will be arrested within the hour."

In the days following, Grand Lotty instructed that I would live with her until I left for teachers' college. Mother was not to contact me.

Gordon raised his head and stared at the fireplace mantel. His parents didn't talk about Rupert and Minette. When pressed, Maude would answer that her mother had a hard life. When asked about her father, she would reply that he made his life hard for himself and many others. That would be the end of it. Maude wrote:

Grand Lotty writes regularly, and she has been kinder than I could have imagined. She often asks if I need anything or perhaps, I might like some little extra item.

This morning the school's matron entered the classroom, causing a rustle of excitement. She came directly to me and said that a gentle-man was in her office with an urgent message, and I must come im-mediately.

A summons from the headmistress is never a good sign. As I en-tered her office, my heart first jumped for joy at the sight of my beloved Gus and then fell when I saw how pale his face was. He must have come to inform me of Grand Lotty's passing. He appeared to reflect the same happiness and apprehension I felt. He sat on the sofa, and I took a seat on the far end. Suddenly, he moved to my side and grabbed my hand.

"Your mother has passed away. One of the neighbors found her in the barn."

The shock left me speechless. Over the past few months, Mother had written often, her letters full of regret. Once she lamented at hav-ing married Papa, that if I could have been born from a better match, how different life would have been. Her greatest hope was in my for-giveness and my return to Forester.

I never answered her letters and did not send word through Grand Lotty. I realize now that she protected me as much as she could. So that is the guilt I must bear. The headmistress has given me leave to attend Mother's funeral. Papa remains in prison. It is important for me to go on.

Gordon closed the diary and pressed it shut with both hands. For a long time, he sat stroking the cracked cover as he rocked back and forth, his mother's journal in his lap.

After a while, Clerise's face hovered before him. His inhaler ap-peared, which he mechanically took. She said he must eat something. She faded. Gordon continued to rock. She returned. Hands reached through the lamplight to place a plate and bowl by his side on the end table. She reappeared and took an armchair next to his. She called to Michael. The rocker moved him back and forth. Memories: ordinary days, Lara and Maude. Sunlight, his garden. His father. The hardware store. Gus's funeral, Lara's funeral, Maude's funeral. Grand Lotty in the Forestier mansion on Boise Avenue. The kitchen clock, hands sweeping around and around.

Gordon stopped rocking. Clerise stood and leaned toward him, her arms enveloping his shoulders. He rose, the diary falling to the floor, and they held each other, her head against his chest.

CHAPTER 34
RUPERT SIPE

Gordon sorted through the contents of the boxes in the ball-room, searching for a particular news article and found it, dated January 4, 1931.

Local Citizen Found Dead in Jail Cell: Former resident Rupert Sipe was found in his cell late Thursday evening by guard, Sgt. Joseph Duggan, the prisoner having hung himself. Sipe was serving a sentence for the assault of his daughter, Miss Maude Sipe. This was the first such conviction of a Forester resident in its history. Sipe, a known bootlegger residing on the outskirts of the village, had been arrested on several occasions on charges of selling alcohol.

In a much-publicized trial, Sipe was prosecuted for drunken assault of his daughter. Of Sipe's demise, Sgt. Duggan stated, "Generally, men convicted of this kind of crime do not survive long in prison. To other inmates, this kind of crime is the most heinous. Sipe's apparent suicide is not surprising. Sipe is survived by his daughter, Maude. Arrangements for Sipe's interment are pending."

Gordon paused for a moment, eyebrows meeting. He scrolled through the word processing program for an entry he'd written several months ago and nodded to himself at the error. Grand Lotty's journal entry about a visit from "M." was not Minette as he had originally thought. Rather, Maude had made the visit. These months later, the entry had a different quality, containing truths twining through Grand Lotty to Minette to Maude and now to him. The memories of the afternoon teas he'd endured with his mother and great-grandmother replayed, and he recalled the polite conversations, what was not said. Grand Lotty's contentment was more than an old matriarch in her dotage; she was proud of her granddaughter.

Maude was more than the woman who had assured their block survived. She had also survived. Her no-nonsense approach had irritated him at times. She lacked whimsy. And he tried to remember what made her laugh. Did she ever? A chuckle, perhaps, but he had never seen her in stitches, reveling in the kind of laughter that caused tears to run down her face or left her gasping, out of breath from hilarity.

His thoughts boiled: Maude's school yearbook. How beautiful she had been. The ragged torn pages. Imagining her terrified face, he couldn't inhale or exhale. He puffed at his inhaler as his lungs seized. Sipe grabbing Maude, cowered and frightened. Her nightgown, torn. And no one to protect her. His mother! His mother! The rage flew up his spine, roared down his arms, and gushed out his fingers as he hurled the contents of box after box, the sound exploding against the walls. He stood panting and wheezing before a lava flow of old letters, pictures, and newspapers.

Gordon kicked an empty box at the thought of Patty's contrived myth about Maude. It was a lie, just as Olivia had said. Stories were no less important now than thousands of years ago, when bands of men, women, and children sat before a campfire. Those stories meant survival. They were shared, talked about. Maude's story was a declaration of survival and courage.

Wasn't history lining up facts to get at the truth? But if you don't have all the facts, how do you have the truth? Gordon shook his head. He thought he had all the relevant facts about his mom, until he found her diary. But how do you determine which facts are relevant? With important people like Jean Luis everything was relevant.

But all those ordinary people whose lives were filled with facts could bring about change. Rape and incest occurred in the past, but they were not talked about, not acknowledged. No one had been there to prevent what happened to his mother. Absent Maude's diary, a piece of history that could bring about change was absent. His breathing settled and he gathered a batch of newspapers, returned them to the box, and considered putting Maude's diary in the museum. The truth is more than just facts. He had a room full of facts, but what good are they if they don't bring about change? If they don't encourage people to act?

He surveyed the mess spewed across the ballroom and knelt to retrieve a sheaf of papers. He thought about all those years volunteering there, that he had shut his own life up like the museum, his past like these boxes. Each time he had arrived at the museum, closed its heavy door, and leaned against it, his life had embraced stasis in this huge ballroom with its shabby wallpaper and dusty sconces.

The disgorged documents made a trail toward the door and Gordon reflected that his effort to catalog all those pieces of history was his meager attempt to get at the truth. The truth was that his life could have been more. Could be more.

Leaving the pool of memorabilia, Gordon strode toward the stairs, intent on getting home. To Clerise and Michael.

CHAPTER 35
CURSOR

Patricia leaned against the shopping cart as she consulted her grocery list. Another bonus she hadn't thought of. With Ray gone, she had to think about only herself and Brian. She must've really got to him with the threat to turn the pictures over to the police. Well good. The evidence was safely in the bank should she need it. She sighed noting the next item on the list. Problem was he had moved into an apartment only about a half-hour drive away. To be near Brian, he said. I it had been half a state away, she'd sleep better. But at least he was out. Breaking the news to Brian of the trial separation went as expected. Brian was angry and refused to speak to her, while Ray had been his usual wimpy self.

She glanced up in time to see the museum board president pass at the other end of the aisle and turn her cart toward Patricia, barreling forward as if bent on a head-on collision. The president stopped her cart inches from Patricia's.

"Patricia dear, how fortunate to run into you. I was just wondering what in the world you're up to these days. You just never seem to be accessible. Not good if you have any aspirations of being re-elected to the council." Her condescending tone left Patricia wanting to slap her silly, but the woman was a powerful force.

"Life has been hectic lately, but I always return my calls. And I would be especially prompt if I got one from you."

"I did phone and you didn't return it. Maybe you forgot. I know how busy you always seem to be. I would hate to think that you have overextended yourself and are unable to fulfill your obligations to the village." She smiled at Patricia from behind the shopping cart, leaning slightly on it as if about to ram it at her.

Patricia put on her concerned village councilwoman face. "Oh my. Are you sure you dialed the right number? I want to assure you I'm fully tapped into the vein of this community. In your generation, I realize women weren't capable of juggling a career on top of a family." *Take that you old bat.*

"Well I read in the minutes that you are leading a sub-committee to work with the police to catch the rapist tearing apart our community. Pity to see no one else volunteered." Her jowls wobbled as she shook her head.

"Yes, it is. But that won't stop the council from assuring the criminal is caught and brought to justice. The council is doing everything it can to get the word out."

"I also noticed nothing has been reported in the council minutes since then. Don't tell me you dropped the ball." Patricia felt like yanking the woman's perfectly coifed hair.

"Why no, dear," Patricia decided to try out the phony endearment. "I'm afraid there is nothing to report, other than the police continue to gather evidence and follow leads."

"Oh my. How discouraging. Since you ask, while it may seem a little extraordinary, I would be happy to volunteer for your committee as a concerned citizen."

I didn't ask anything, Patricia forced a smile. "Thank you so much for your kind offer. If I need some extra help, I will most definitely call you." She put the cart in motion and wheeled around the woman.

At her next meeting, the task force reported that the rapist had struck again. While the police thought this was the first rape in a number of months, she knew otherwise. The recent victim had come forward. The others had not.

The police detective working the case stated that the locations of the rapes were still unknown. His first thought was to check the neighboring motels. No one matching the girls' descriptions had been to any of them. They concluded the attacker must be taking them someplace else, an apartment or maybe motels in other communities. The investigation was stalled. None of the victims could remember anything other than the rapist wasn't very tall. Yes, she had the goods on Ray, and she had hoped it would make him stop. Apparently not. Was that sicko continuing to take pictures?

She inserted her key into the back door, the floodlight blinding her temporarily. For a moment, she was in total darkness, until she opened her office door. Her desk glowed from the screen of her computer. Odd. She was sure she'd shut it down that morning. On the black screen a white cursor blinked. Where was her WordPerfect program? Instead, just the black screen. She switched her computer off, her fingers tingling as if receiving a small electric shock. This DOS stuff was what Ray did all day.

Part of her said to leave the PC alone and turn it on later. The other part of her pushed the "on" button. The screen flared and went blank. She hit the Enter key. Nothing. She tapped keys, looking for movement on the screen, for the cursor, for anything. It remained impassive. She turned it off again and did a cold boot. Nothing. She did a hot boot. Nothing. Panic spread across her chest. This was her client list. Her ability to access the multiple listings. And it was gone. Taped to the side of the deck was a note. Ray's writing. "You take something of mine. I take something of yours. This is just the beginning. It's up to you how you want to end it."

CHAPTER 36
ONLY A HOUSE

Gordon was tickled that an attorney as famous as Petey Robb had agreed to see them. He must be at least seventy-five. The attorney asked, "So, Gordon, are you going to save your house and a block like your mother?" Maude's former star student touched an archive box, his gnarled fingers ancient tree roots across the top.

"Not exactly. But maybe we'll help the people in this community."

For a long moment, the lawyer surveyed Clerise. "I hope you are not offended when I say how beautiful you are. At my age, I beg to be entitled."

"My beauty is nothing compared to my brain." Clerise smiled and the attorney grinned. Gordon realized how important this meeting was on another level. He wanted Petey to like her.

The two clients pulled out their reports and notes about U Do It and Charlie Hunter. Petey's head tilted, as if listening for emanations from the pages themselves.

"No doubt it's suspicious," Petey said. "However, the financial statements aren't damaging to you, so for you, a case doesn't exist. I have some pals who will get the documents to the right person at the head office of U Do It. I suspect the corporation will conduct an investigation on whether Hunter was colluding and had some kind of kickback scheme going."

The lawyer raised a bony shoulder. "Both of you said something about Mr. Hunter's treatment of you. Tell me more about that."

The interview now veered in a different direction as they replayed the events, and Clerise began to nod. "Harassment and discrimination," she said.

"You are right about your brains far exceeding your beauty, Ms. Harper." Petey began to rise, "Both of you need to make an appointment as soon as possible. These days, I've limited my practice to those cases that catch my attention. But whatever the issue, Gordon, your concern would have interested me. I respected and admired your mother in so many ways."

That evening, Gordon brought one of the last jars of tomatoes into service for his spaghetti sauce.

"I want to run something by you, Clerise." Gordon speared a lettuce leaf. "I'm thinking about the next few months. The fact is my priorities are changing."

"Does it have anything to do with me?" Michael asked.

"Well, that's a good question." Gordon ruminated. "That's a good question. I'm not sure. It depends. Yes, it depends."

"On what?"

"Michael, sugar, this is a discussion with me and Gordon. This is a good time to go do the dishes."

As the dining room door swung shut, Gordon said, "I've been thinking about my retirement and all. Timing is everything. The market is slow right now, but I don't think I've got a lot of alternatives."

"And?"

"The thing is I've managed to get by so far, but for what?" As he talked, Gordon remembered the pet bed before the fire, the Spartan existence. He could survive, but …. "Being old and retirement and all."

"You're not that old. Look at this house."

"I'm old, and the house is older. I'm only going to get older, and so is the house. And pretty much all my life I've been taking care of it. I don't know that I can forever. Taxes and insurance. That's always been the big priority."

"Of course, Gordon. You don't want to lose your home."

"But I won't be able to afford to keep it, let alone maintain it. Someone could find me someday with the roof falling around my ears and me a dried-up tomato. I've decided there isn't very much here for me. It's only a house." His voice dropped. "It's only a house."

"So, what do you want to do?"

"Sell it. But that means you and Michael wouldn't be around anymore."

"Let's talk about your home first."

"If I sell the house, I could finish renovating the cabin and move there. I've been going to Freelak since I was a kid. Folks know me. I used to help 'em out. I could do handyman work or something."

"Sounds like you've been giving it some thought, Gordon. I could see you doing that." Clerise smiled, but her eyes didn't match it.

Gordon rubbed his thumb across the calluses on the pads of his hands. He noticed the fatigue around her mouth. *She seems tired*, he thought. "But what about you and Michael?"

"I haven't made any decisions, other than I know we'd have to move eventually anyway."

"Okay, so I guess I'll talk to Patty. I've heard it's taking quite a while to sell these days. That'll give me time to work on the cabin. But I don't want to leave you and Michael stranded."

"Gordon, it's a great plan. Things are going to work out just fine." He felt as if her eyes were lifting him up, holding him. "I promise. And in the meantime, I'll help you finish the cabin."

✦✦✦

The gesture of shaking hands with Patricia to seal the deal changed the landscape around Gordon as if he'd been asleep and dreaming of it. He paused at the foot of the Wrenowskis' driveway to see Patty standing in the window. He grinned and arced his arm as if hailing a cab. Then he proceeded to cross the street, ambling along the sidewalk. He stopped often on the short walk home. If he were to measure his life in footsteps along the block, here would be when his father died. Here was when he met and married Lara. Here was when Maude saved the block. By the time Gordon passed the path to Bubba's front door, Maude had died. At his property line, he had closed the doors to Carlson's Hardware for the last time. And the gravel driveway was his existence until he met Clerise.

The house before him had been built by his family, had been around for a hundred-plus years, and had been maintained in great condition, thanks to his careful tending. That feeling all the way from the Wrenowskis' coalesced. Maude had hosted the Forester Days picnic each year on the front porch and the lawn. Not him, but Maude. He had been the keeper all these years. With a confidence he hadn't experienced in a long time he was content to move on.

+++

Clerise decided not to accept a temp position for that Friday, and again they loaded the station wagon for Freelak. Michael carried on a monologue about the huge bonfire they were going to build and maybe the squirrels had come out of hibernation. Now, as he wheeled the station wagon onto the highway, Gordon inched his arm across the bench seat, and his fingers rested in the nape of Clerise's neck. She scooted closer, the warmth of her body touching his as they rambled toward Michigan.

+++

The house had been vacated for a couple of hours when Patricia climbed onto the veranda. Good. He would be gone for the weekend. Now was the time to try and get a glimpse inside. Gordon had been aggravatingly reclusive for so many years, but knowing him, he had maintained the interior. The Victorian would net quite a bundle, and she wondered if he was aware of it.

She stood at the front door, nose steaming the pane. Damn! The old rippled glass and defused light revealed just a scant bit of detail. At the living room window, she could make out the dim reflection of glass panes from the pocket doors. In the gloom, she could see nothing more definitive.

All the kitchen window revealed was the back vestibule. An unusually warm morning for the end of February, she sat on the cement steps and lit a cigarette. She considered buying it herself.

The question was where to put her office. She took a last drag and tossed the butt. She spied the garage, illuminated in the pale sunlight. Careful not to get her shoes dirty, she stepped toward the building and scouted the structure's potential. She lit another cigarette, then crouched to peer through the window, leaning forward and just catching her balance. The cigarette sent a spray of sparks as it fell, just missing her new coat.

A one-car garage was a small space but could be a darling little office in pristine white. Flagstones would lead the client to the side door, over which she would put a white wooden arch covered with sweet peas and dark blue morning glories.

And then it hit her. *I can hold the annual barbeque on the front lawn just as Maude used to,* she thought. She returned to the stoop, lit another cigarette, and smiled as she considered. *I can host a Christmas open house.*

Except for one small problem: Ray. Okay, not so small problem. Bottom line, she still had his original photos. No question, they could come to some kind of a deal. Maybe she could bribe him to move out of the state or into Chicago or anywhere but here and the neighboring villages. She tossed the unfinished smoke. What an idiot. Did he really think she wouldn't be able to rebuild her files?

The other small problem was Brian. Would he still be sore because of last summer's debacle with Gordon and the boom box? He was so hostile these days. Even engaging him in the décor of his new bedroom would flop. Well, he would just have to live with it.

Patricia checked her watch. She could now drop hints about this great property that just came on the market. The ethical issues could anger Gordon, so she should try to sell to a client for the present. Business had been slow. Her listings had been sitting like everyone else's. But that could be an advantage in buying Gordon's house. No buyers in sight except for her.

+++

Bubba was the first on the parkway. A late-night talk show fanatic, he was ensconced in his chaise lounge and engrossed in Letterman's opening monologue when something flickered through the lace curtains of the windows facing the side of Gordon's house. For a moment, he ignored it, and then, as if his brain caught up with his sight, he lurched out of the lounge and ran to the window. He grabbed the phone and dialed.

Black smoke and bright orange flames cavorted while firemen waved their hoses in graceful arches across the parkway, toward Gordon's house, Bubba's house, and the apartment behind as streams of sleepy occupants exited into the street and joined Bubba to take up a vigil.

CHAPTER 37
A RECTANGLE IN THE SOIL

Late morning found Patricia parked in her van, the engine idling as she tried to digest the difference between what she saw and what she'd seen the day before. The crude reality of an incinerated house intruded on her fantasy. Her dream office lay in rubble at the end of the drive as latent steam dissipated from the debris. In frustration, she cried out and banged the steering wheel, inadvertently honking the horn. The saving factor was she did not own the property.

+++

Even from her front lawn, Olivia could see the devastation, the eerie heat from the previous night a memory on her cheeks. She and Donna had remained at Bubba's side until the fire was out. She now made her way to the front of Gordon's house, which was a lake of freezing water dotted with chunks of charred wood. She barely recognized the interior, the inferno having blasted out all the windows, leaving the pocket doors skewed and clinging to the hardware. Miraculously, the fireplace mantel was unscathed. She could see into the dining room, where the chandelier threatened to crash to the floor, while the whole back wall where the buffet and swinging door had been was gone.

For a long while, she slid her boot along the icy surface. The devastation kept her gaping. Frozen, black rivulets trailed down the gravel driveway between Gordon and Bubba's houses, the backyard that had once been populated with vegetables, now a battlefield.

+++

Bubba appeared as Gordon, Clerise, and Michael crawled out of the station wagon. Gordon stared in wonder at the sawhorses sporting amber caution lights barricading the house, quite festive except for the wreckage they guarded. Within the perimeter, a couple of firemen used crowbars to pry open the walls, searching for any evidence that the fire still smoldered.

"Well, I guess I better get a phone at the cabin," Gordon said.

"Looks like yer house's pretty much gone, Gord," Bubba said. "We tried to find ya. Oh, and the fire marshal's on his way. He wanted to come by as soon as you got here."

Gordon stood in the street, peering between the flowering plum trees, felled as if some giant hands had parted them. His demolished home issued a cold, wet smell like a doused campfire.

The marshal photographed the scene, stating that the fire appeared to have started at the back and garage. An investigative team would come by first thing in the morning. Initial interviews of neighbors revealed nothing unusual; however, given the recent vandalism, arson was a possibility.

Uncertain what to do next, Gordon felt Clerise take him by the elbow. She clasped Michael to her other side, and Gordon allowed himself to be put in the passenger seat, his hands shaking violently as he tried to fasten the seatbelt. He'd never ridden while Clerise drove and was fascinated by her expertise as she pulled away from the curb and made their way down the street past the Dimato and Wrenowski houses, windows glowing yellow in the twilight.

Michael chose a pancake restaurant for dinner, and as the boy took a forkful of syrupy waffle, Gordon marveled at the meal's ordinariness. Clerise sat next to Michael in the booth, her attention focused on her son, as she leaned over, put her arm around him, and planted a kiss

282

on his head. Gordon could feel the corners of his mouth heading upward at the joyousness of it.

They could be any group having dinner, a family perhaps, and a thrill went through him at how nice a thought that was. Clerise raised her head as if sensing him. "How are you doing, Gordon?"

"I'm okay, considering I just lost my family home. Not quite how I envisioned parting from it." His voice trailed off, then picked up again. "I was just thinking about calling the insurance company tomorrow and about all the paperwork. Sell the house, burn the house. Either way, it's lots of paperwork." He knew his chuckle at his own joke was somehow connected to the shock. "But you know? Wasn't that why I was paying high premiums? For full replacement value? Wasn't that why I did it all these years? In case of something just like this?"

In the following days, Gordon focused on taking care of the immediate problem, relying on a frayed checklist in his head and accessing a safety deposit box containing detailed descriptions of the house's contents, pictures of the interior, and appraisal of their worth. He may have been only a keeper of the house all those years, but he was prepared for haggling with the insurance company over its contents and their value.

With a deep sigh, everything settled for him as he thought of his mother and her reaction to all this nonsense. As Maude would say, "Why make such a fuss over burnt up wood when the insurance money will allow you to complete your perfectly good home in Freelak?"

The fire marshal issued his report stating the fire had started at the garage and then jumped to the house. Because of the house's balloon construction, the conflagration shot through the side walls and engulfed the attic. Inspection uncovered no proof of arson or of any carelessness on Gordon's part.

Gordon salvaged any hardware he could for use in his cabin in

Freelak. He tucked the doorknob and banister with the ornately carved bird and animal heads into a crate. And, to his surprise, he also found the doorbell peeking from a heap of broken glass. He and Clerise stood holding hands as the fireplace mantel and tiles were loaded onto a truck and covered with a tarp for the travel to Michigan.

Its gears and engine noise spilling the length of the deserted street, a bulldozer began to dismantle the house's skeleton. As the pieces dispersed, Gordon pulled out an inhaler. He did not even know where his thoughts would begin. It was a funeral, a ceremony, a memorial, a shrine. And a celebration. For a moment, he thought of the macramé, the quilt, Maude's diary, Lara's wedding band. They had been in the attic. He remembered the kitchen clock, whose hands had swept so much tragedy in his life, now gone. He felt Clerise's shoulder on his and roped his arm around her waist. They gazed as a rectangle in the soil took shape, the crew deconstructing a hundred years.

CHAPTER 38
TACOS AND MORE

The museum volunteer had said Gordon was taking a break and made it clear she didn't want Olivia coming around. And now with his house burned down, she hadn't a clue where to find him or Clerise.

That left getting stoned at lunch and floating through classes. Olivia was flunking. Keeping track of a thought—let alone an instruction to do something—was beyond her. That lame counselor, Tony Baloney, was on her case, playing "What's Your Drug?" And he'd announced another meeting with the old lady. Becca said meet at Tacos N' More after school, that she had awesome news.

"Heard about the fire at that old man's place," Becca said giving her order to the counter clerk.

For a change, Olivia waited until Becca had extracted some balled-up bills from her coat before pulling out her wallet. "Don't tell me," she said.

"Right, like I burn houses for fun. You think I forgot, don't you, O? You don't tell me by tomorrow, Lauren or Spider, you know how creative I can be."

Olivia elbowed her way to the booth and sat across from Spider, Dank and Lauren. She gazed out the window, could feel Lauren's caustic stare, and imagined the boots and fists if she gave her up.

Spider didn't deserve it either. He'd done nothing. She closed her eyes and almost retched.

Becca's tray thumped on the table and she slid next to Olivia. "Listen up. I'm gonna get some great new shit and branch out."

"Branch out? Becca, we gotta great thing going here. Why you want to blow it?" Lauren's hand slammed the table.

Becca rose in her seat. "We? Lauren, since when do you get a say in this?"

"Since I don't want to end up at Cook County Juvey." Lauren also rose, and the two girls leaned across the table toward each other. Olivia pressed herself against the window as if that would take her out of Becca's line of vision and away from her spastically opening and closing fists.

"Fine." Lauren sat back down, and Becca began to outline the next deal.

The stuff Becca now sold was totally scary. Weed and 'shrooms were nothing compared to this. Olivia could feel this change like an awful green sky, frightening, signaling catastrophe. She stuffed fries into her mouth.

Spider froze as his hand reached for a taco. "Did you see them?" he whispered. "Don't look. There. There they are again." Lauren and Dank focused on their fries and nodded.

"Yeah, I saw them. Let's go." Becca stood.

Behind Tacos N' More, the group reconvened.

"Fuck," Becca said. "When'd they get here?"

"Who?" Olivia knew this was a dumbass question.

"Didn't you see them? You must be blind." Becca shook her head. "Okay. Let's get outta here. I gotta think about this."

They now dispersed, as if each was the point of a star shooting across the neighborhood.

Olivia wandered Boise Avenue, trying to piece together what just happened. She was at a crosswalk when Ray's sedan sped through the intersection, and she would have missed seeing the car altogether had she not glanced over her shoulder. Was that someone in the car with him? The thought chilled her and the picture in her backpack weighed like a bolder. She wanted to shuck it and run. She stared at the web of elm branches, trapped. Whatever was going down with Becca would add another reason not to go to the police, would continue to put her house at risk or maybe something worse. The crossing light turned green, the blinking white walker urging her to take a step. Shelter, she needed shelter. She reversed and ran toward the museum.

+++

Gordon roamed the old mansion, feeling disoriented at his first day back. The fire had severed a towline, a habitual way of moving through Forester. The museum had morphed, as if he were now just a visitor, a tourist taking in the sites and staying at a local motel. He put on the teakettle, hoping the little routine would make everything else regain its rhythm.

He was surprised when he entered the foyer and saw Olivia hanging up her coat and scarf. "Haven't seen you in a while," he said.

"You know that volunteer woman is mean. She wouldn't tell me anything. In fact, she told me not to come here, but I did anyway. You weren't even at home. And then with the fire, you had no home to even be at. And I couldn't find you, Gordon." Olivia stomped for emphasis, the echoes clattering against the marble floor.

Her anger was exactly what Gordon needed. Within a few minutes, the two of them ascended the stairs, donned cotton gloves and sat at the computer in the ballroom.

"What's up with you, Olivia? You sound out of sorts today." Gordon said.

He was about to ask the question again when she said, "Yeah, what of it?"

She was agitated, so all he had to do was be patient and she would talk.

Mid-thought, she began, "Becca didn't want to screw Ray. He took her to a vacant house and drugged her. That's what Lauren says. Dank doesn't get what really happened. Lauren took care of her. Becca was ballistic."

Olivia's language jolted Gordon and being involved in a conversation he hadn't heard from the beginning, he was doing another verbal jigsaw puzzle. "Is this about Christmas Eve?" That seemed like a good place to start.

"Christmas Eve? How could this be about Christmas Eve?" Olivia scowled.

Okay, this piece did not belong to the Christmas Eve picture, so it had to be another one. Olivia had said something about Ray, Becca, and rape, which both Dank and Lauren knew about. "Are you talking about Ray Wrenowski?"

"What other Ray would I be talking about? It's not too awful or anything! I'm gonna be sick."

Gordon wondered if he should move her away from the memorabilia and gently took the news article she was holding from her hands.

"Don't you think she should've gone to the police?" Gordon asked.

"Are you kidding? First of all, do you think they'd believe her? They'd take Becca away from her aunt and ship her off to some other foster home." Olivia shivered.

"If he's done that to her, he's done it to others, and he won't stop. Why doesn't Lauren go to the police? Have you asked her?"

"God, Gordon." She rolled her eyes, and Gordon saw she thought he was mentally deficient. "For sure Becca'd get back at her."

Gordon had a hard time believing his neighbor would be guilty of something this despicable. There had to be another explanation. His instincts to slow down and get the facts kicked in. "How do you know? They could just be making it up."

"You think I'm lying? Ray took a picture. Becca threw it in the bushes. And I found it." She gestured to her backpack, crumpled in the corner.

"Ray's in the picture?" Gordon asked.

"No, but his writing's on the other side. He drugged Becca, raped her, took a picture, and then wrote on the back."

"How do you know it's his writing?"

"Gordon, I live across the street. I've seen his handwriting millions of times."

"Olivia, you have to take it to the police," he said.

"I don't have to do anything. You have no idea how bad I'd get beat up. Or worse."

"It's your choice, Olivia. Do you think your friend is the only one this happened to? Do you want to know that you could have stopped other girls from being raped and didn't?"

Olivia blinked at him, setting her jaw.

"What about Becca? If you care about her and she can't defend herself, don't you want the rapist caught for her sake?" *Maybe that will get her to go to the police,* Gordon thought. He clawed through his brain for reasons that would convince her to get help. "It's just a matter of time before someone comes forward who can identify Ray or whoever did it. When that happens, they will find out about you."

"No, they won't." She glared at him. "Who can prove it?"

"You'd be surprised at what the police can dig up. Either you take the picture to them or they will find out about it. And when they do…"

"You are so out of touch! Cuz I hang with them and you think they're scum, you think I'm scum too." She flung off the cotton gloves, and before Gordon could respond, she'd grabbed her backpack and bolted down the stairs.

In the sudden silence Gordon removed his gloves, smoothing the fingers as if they might point to a solution, and tried to think what to do next.

+++

On the first-floor landing, Olivia stopped and sat on a step. *Shit, shit, shit. As if there wasn't enough shit going on. Now this stupid old man is threatening me. He didn't have to do this. He's ruining my life.*

She pulled out a joint. Who gave a fuck? He'd be up there for hours. She took a deep toke. A small spark flitted off. And what was that all about? Him and Clerise. She took another hit and felt the smoke fill her lungs until she had to exhale.

He was supposed to be on her side. Could he really be that stupid? And she'd been giving all this time to help him, and when she needed him, he did nothing. A couple of flakes speckled the carpet. Olivia ignored them.

She reached into her backpack for the plastic bag with the Polaroid. She had examined it so often, it no longer caused her breathing to twist. Now, this was just another girl who happened to resemble Becca. Olivia tucked the picture back in her pack and leaned against the stair.

She appraised the sconce in the hall leading to the back. The light flickered. She scrunched her eyes. It flickered again, like Tinkerbell had landed. Then the crystals on the chandelier glimmered and fogged over. This was creepy, yet kind of rad. Wow. Ghosts. She saw a transparent oval in the corner.

"Violet, you are such a wuss," she whispered. "At least you could show yourself. Ghost kids show up all the time in movies." An evanescent hourglass took shape, protruding from the wall.

That thing is larger than a five-year-old, but hey, this is good shit. The lump wobbled, undulated, meandered.

Olivia tugged the backpack, hauling it down the remaining steps. The shape was a dirty window distorting the wallpaper pattern and, like shadows creeping across the day, moved slowly, slowly toward the door until it rested, fluttering the white lace curtains in the window.

Olivia felt pulled, not forced, but compelled to move toward it.

When she reached the haze, it disappeared, her hand landing on the icy doorknob. Tilting her head to one side, her vision focused with intense clarity on the street outside. She yanked the door open and ran.

+++

Upstairs, Gordon argued with himself. He should stay out of it. This was something Olivia should handle. Problem was she didn't look like she was going to. She was just a girl still, who didn't understand how serious this was. He thought of going to the police himself. But what would he say when all he knew was that a possible picture existed of a possible rape?

Those other girls. The ones who had already been hurt and the ones who could be. On the way to the museum, he'd passed a green car parked in the driveway of a house sporting a *For Sale* sign. He now knew it must be Ray's sedan!

He propelled himself down the stairs, stumbling on the tread and catching his balance. Grabbing his jacket, he was out the door in a flash. It all made sense. Ray on Halloween, arriving home late at night with no costume on, Ray's sedan parked in odd locations, Christmas Eve at the stoplight, Ray with a passenger slumped against the window. He headed his station wagon toward the vacant house.

+++

Olivia rounded the corner to her street, Gordon's ruined house like a missing tooth in a perfect mouth. As she neared the Wrenowski house, she could see the porch light, but otherwise everything else was dark. No one home.

For a long time, she sat on the Wrenowskis' front steps, shivering in the night, glancing at the backpack by her side, picturing its contents. What would she say? Who would arrive first? Pieces of ideas tumbled out but refused to arrange themselves in any order she could use.

No wonder Brian was so creepy with an old man like that. She stared at her house across the street, its porch light anticipating her and her mom. She could just go home. She could tell Gordon she'd tried to do something but couldn't find anyone.

She glanced at her watch, thinking hours must be passing. And then someone appeared at the end of the block.

+++

Ray's sedan was parked in the driveway, the house dark, with the exception of a light in the back. Gordon edged his car against the curb and waited. As the minutes passed, the wagon's air chilled around him. No Ray.

Olivia had changed a lot. She was running with a tough crowd. But he had no reason to think she was lying. Then again, if this was true, how come no one had come forward before and identified him? They couldn't all be troubled teens like Becca.

Then he saw why. On a side path leading to the back Ray supported someone, exerting a lot of effort to make progress.

Gordon edged his door open, easing his feet onto the street. Ray, his back to Gordon, now hugged the body under her arms, dragging her toward his car. He propped the person against the sedan while he fumbled to get the door open.

Gordon stood before him.

CHAPTER 39
THE DEAL

Olivia rose as Brian approached. She observed him jerking his head in several directions and read something in his face she hadn't seen before. Fear.

"What're you doing here?" Brian continued to scan the perimeter.

Olivia sauntered toward him. "Good question, asshole." *He must think Becca and my friends are hiding someplace.*

"So whadda you want? You're trespassing."

"Yeah, right," Olivia barked.

"Get outta here, you fat cow." He moved to shove past her.

Olivia blocked his path and grabbed him by the arm feeling him flinch.

"I'm calling the police. You attacked me."

"Go ahead." She tightened her grip and swiped her leg behind his, causing him to land on his butt.

"You're in such deep shit, Olivia. My folks'll sue."

As she bent her head to meet his eyes, she thought, *He's afraid of me.* She lifted a boot with an urge to kick him so hard he'd remember it forever. But she let go of his arm, and Brian scooted back, stood, and dusted himself off.

"Gordon and I know about your dad." She slung her backpack over her shoulder, turned, and trotted diagonally toward the far street corner. She rounded the edge of the block, her eyes on the brightly lit shops, beyond which lay the police station.

Olivia jumped and turned at the voice emerging from the shadows.

"Yo, thought I'd come over and hang with you."

She felt a trickle of sweat gathering between her shoulder blades as she slowed her pace. "What the fuck, Becca? You gonna be my goddamn babysitter?"

"O, I've been thinking. They'll be tailing me tomorrow. They know who I am. Lauren too." Becca closed the distance.

"What'd ya mean 'they'?" Olivia stopped, backed a step and then another.

"My competition. You know how hard I work to get the best shit? Whatever anyone wants I'll deliver. And my competition wants to take away all my hard work. Where you going?"

"Nowhere, changed my mind. I'm freezing, that's all." Home was not that far away. Becca was hyped on something, so maybe Olivia could outrun her. Or maybe her mom would round the corner on her way from the train.

"Well, listen up. You were sitting next to the window, right?" Olivia nodded. "Good, that means Dank blocked their view. They won't know you. You're gonna have to do it." She sidled toward Olivia.

"The deal?" Olivia inhaled, choked on her saliva, and began coughing. Tears seared her cheeks as she grabbed her breath.

"Yeah, you gotta do it." Becca said slapping her back.

"Why doesn't Spider or Dank go?" Olivia wheezed before the coughing fit began again.

"Cuz they've seen 'em before. They'll never think it's you."

"Shit, Becca. I don't know how to do this! I'll fuck it up for sure." She strained to get the words out.

"No you won't. Wear one of your Daddy's little outfits. No way they'll tail you. You'll be perfect. Just be your old loser self."

Olivia gulped. "The old lady and I gotta see Baloney tomorrow afternoon, and then I gotta babysit tomorrow after school. I can't go." Her breathing became less jagged.

"You're gonna do this." Becca's face was stone. "See? We all don't like that you're wimping out. I chose you cuz you have what it takes. You cut at lunch. You'll be back before your next class, and you won't miss your little date with your old lady and Baloney. O, you don't want to blow me off." Under the streetlamp, Olivia could see the harsh eyes. "I'll tell you what you need to do tomorrow. Got it?" Becca put her arm around Olivia, her tone soft, tender. "I know you can do this for me. It's easy. You're my girl. I protected you when you needed it. Now you owe me." She put her other arm around her and leaned in, Olivia flinching, her body stiffening for oncoming pain. Instead, she felt the pressure of Becca's lips on hers, and then the girl pulled back and whispered, "You're my girl. Remember?" She grabbed Olivia's backpack and spun her around. "So as my girl, I'm gonna carry your books."

Swallowed by the darkness, the two walked back toward her house, Olivia feeling as if her resolve to go to the police had been left under the streetlamp.

"So who was it?"

She tightened her body, anticipating what would come next. "Becca, when're you gonna drop that? I know what happened. I know about Ray."

Becca twisted, hurling the backpack into the street. "Who told you?" She grabbed Olivia by the shoulders and flung her against a tree. The bark bit into Olivia's back, and her head knocked forward. "Who told you?"

Olivia raised her arm toward her face, expecting a punch. She whimpered and gathered courage. "What difference does it make? We all know. Lauren is totally destroyed. She loves you. Dank and Spider are dumbasses. They get only that it was bad. We all love you."

"We all love you," Becca mimicked.

"You don't think that's true?" Olivia quivered and met Becca's stare. "Why do you think they hang around? Why do you think no one's turned you in?" She didn't dare break eye contact. "They want to get Ray as much as you." She pushed her advantage. "And they wouldn't squeal."

Becca's shoulders drooped, and she stepped toward Olivia again. The girl cringed. Becca wrapped her arms around Olivia, hugged her, her face buried in Olivia's shoulder. Just as quickly, Becca let go, moved back onto the sidewalk, tilting her head back. "All right. Fuck it. It's forgotten."

Olivia remained against the elm tree, marking Becca's movement like she would a predatory animal. She took a tentative step, concentrating on her backpack in the street and what was in it. If Becca knew, if she suspected anyone outside the gang knew about it—let alone some old guy like Gordon.

"It's just … It's just I'm sorry, O. I didn't mean to scare you. Here," she reached into her jacket and pulled out a small film canister. "Here, I'm sorry. I mean it. I don't know what I'd do without you."

Olivia took the canister. This was something Becca didn't just give away. She retrieved her backpack, its weight like it had doubled since being tossed.

"I'll have more for you tomorrow, when you come back. I'll give you a cut. If this doesn't go down, if you bail, I'm in deep shit." Becca's eyes were desperate. "I need you, O."

Olivia nodded, turned, and walked back toward home.

"Just do it for me this one time," Becca called.

CHAPTER 40
TURN ABOUT

Ray startled, dropping his car keys. "Gordon! Am I glad to see you! Can you give me a hand here?"

"Hand? You need a hand?" Gordon blinked at the absurdity of it.

"Yeah, I was checking on this listing for Patricia and found this girl passed out in the house." With a groan, the slumped figure began to slide. He grunted as he righted her. "I need to get her to an emergency room."

"That where you dump them when you're done?"

"Dump them? Done? What are you talking about? She needs help. God knows what she's taken."

"So that's what you do. I read about that stuff. She won't remember a thing."

In the dim streetlight, Ray's face receded farther into the shadow of his hat. "Gordon, this is preposterous. I'm worried. Is your asthma acting up? Patricia said you almost died."

What was he hearing? "I am just fine. Never better. I know about the picture."

"What picture? You think I did something to this girl? Gordon, I'm your neighbor."

"Then you won't mind calling 9-1-1."

"Great idea, Gordon. Don't know what I was thinking." Ray shook his head, the girl threatening to topple over. "You go across the street and call. I'll stay here."

"No, Ray, I'll stay here with the girl, and you go call. You better hurry."

"Okay, we better lay her down. How about the back seat of your station wagon? It's got more room." The girl moaned.

In the dark, Gordon could feel a smile creep out. "We don't have time, Ray. Let's lay her in the back of your car. I'll stay here while you call."

She was lighter than she looked, bundled in a haphazardly buttoned coat, hat, and scarf, her legs hanging limply as the two men eased her onto the back seat.

"I'll go next door and call. You get in and make sure she's okay."

Gordon leaned against the sedan. "Better I stand out here, keep an eye on her, and flag down the ambulance."

Ray melted into the dark toward the neighboring house. Within minutes, sirens and lights announced the ambulance and police. Emergency medical technicians donned latex gloves, moved Gordon aside, and went to work. Simultaneously, two police officers flanked him.

"Mr. Carlson, you're under arrest."

CHAPTER 41
BUSTED

That evening Patricia's worst fear came to pass. As she took her seat in the precinct meeting room for the monthly task force on progress over catching the rapist, the officer leading the group said, "We have a lead. Members of CASS, Communities Are for Safe Streets, have been monitoring the schools for suspicious vehicles. One of the volunteers spotted a green sedan, parked opposite high schools in the area on several occasions, but the car took off before they could get a license plate number."

She'd known eventually Ray would slip up. The bastard thought he was invincible. Her business, her political ambitions, all fell out of focus. Yes, she had the evidence, but that wouldn't protect Brian from public condemnation, guilt by association because he was Ray's son. She scanned the maps on the walls of the room as if they might indicate a safe place to take her boy. Nowhere. Nowhere in this township would be safe.

+++

Olivia hadn't been in a police station since her grade school visited as part of drug prevention education. Her first thought as she crossed the threshold with her mom was that in her backpack was a baggie with a Polaroid picture of a girl who sold drugs, taken by a man who drugged girls. And that in her possession was a canister containing drugs the girl in the picture sold.

Police response had been immediate when she announced she had information that would lead to the capture of the rapist. She and her mom were ushered to a desk where an officer now sat preparing to take her statement and the evidence.

"Olivia, tell me again about this picture and this." He pointed to the canister.

She started to sob, shaking so violently that the officer had to repeat the questions often. As if they were well-shuffled playing cards, she flung answers randomly.

When she had calmed the officer said, "Tell me what you know about Gordon Carlson."

"Gordon?" The walls wavered. "What's he got to do with it?"

"It's okay, Olivia. Just take deep breaths." The officer handed her a glass of water.

"Gordon? No, no, no. You don't understand. I told you. It's Ray Wrenowski who raped Becca."

"And what can you tell me about Gordon Carlson? You said you've known him for a couple of years, that you have been to his house many times, and that you have helped him at the museum. Has he ever tried to touch you?"

Donna's face couldn't have been paler, and her palm was a cold and clammy compress around Olivia's. She squeezed her mom's hand and realized the kind of world she had been experiencing was way beyond anything her mom could have imagined.

+++

In a fog of despair and confusion over the past few hours, Gordon emerged late that night with his lawyer, Petey Robb. For a long time, Gordon had been kept in a room that officers were careful to lock each time they entered or left. A call to Clerise enabled him to assure her he was okay and to ask her to get Petey involved. While he waited, the officers continued to enter and exit the room, carrying a clipboard on which were forms they meticulously completed. They all asked the same questions, the whole time Gordon in shock that Ray could be so evil.

The rustle outside his door quieted, and he saw why when Petey entered the room. The lawyer was smooth, polite, and no doubt used to the respect and status afforded him by his many years in practice. Conversation focused on Gordon, whether he would be charged, what evidence they had to hold him. Petey nodded the way someone does when he knows he's won.

An officer entered and informed Gordon he could leave, that someone had corroborated his assertions. Gordon smiled: Olivia had done the right thing. When he asked about the girl at the vacant house, the officer said she was okay, adding, "There's a drug, Rohypnol, which most people know as the date rape drug. My guess is that's what the girls were given. It prevents people from remembering anything."

"How could Ray do that? How would he even know how to get a hold of it?" Gordon blinked as if trying to clear the memory of that evening out of his eyes.

"If someone wants to do something bad enough, he'll find a way," the officer commented.

CHAPTER 42
SCORE

After several tries, Olivia got her locker open the next morning, exhaustion making her eyes refuse to focus on the dial. She wished she could squish herself in, shut the door, and just disappear. She felt like a piece of neon bubble gum in the outfit, coat, and hat that she'd dug out of her closet. And she had to remind herself over and over that the police promised she'd be safe.

She had been forced into a box: either she cooperated, or she would be busted. If she complied, the police said they had more options about what happened to her and Becca. They just wanted to get Becca's supplier. If she didn't do her part, she would be arrested for dealing drugs.

Becca wouldn't see it that way. Olivia had ratted her out.

She had just slammed her locker shut, when she felt Becca grab her arm. She yelped.

"What? You promised." Becca's face was yellow in the fluorescent lighting.

"You scared me. I was just thinking about what I need to do was all."

"That better be all." Becca's jaw squared. "Here's the deal. Take Boise Avenue to the railroad bridge, go one block, and turn left. Double back and do the circuit again. Go under the bridge to the old limestone quarry factory. Wait at the dumpster." She shoved a padded pencil case into her hand. "You give him this, and he'll give you a backpack. Don't fuck this up."

"Who will I look for? Don't I say like a secret word or something?"

"Like it's gonna be crowded? I'll meet you outside the gym when you get back. And here. I got you something, O. I'm sorry I was such a bitch last night. It's just that you have more guts than you know. But I know it. And I know you're the best thing that's ever happened to me." Becca shoved a sack in Olivia's hand and dashed out the door.

The school's fluorescent lights were overbearing as she opened the small leather bag Becca had thrust at her. A silver bracelet. Whether Becca bought it or stole it didn't matter. She had betrayed the one person who cared about her.

The police had directed her to head home at lunch. She would tell a vice team where the deal was going to take place, and they'd take it from there. Instead of going to her first class, she left school and dragged herself along the sidewalk. She needed time to think.

The day was bitter. Trees, although still black and bare, hinted at eventual leaves, the twigs swelling slightly in the late winter. Drivers moved their cars with more confidence than the weather indicated.

She drifted toward the village shops, thinking about what had happened at Tacos N' More the day before. Some subterfuge was involved, or Becca would have told her to go directly to the old quarry and the dumpster.

More than just the fear of getting caught, Becca was afraid of something else. Afraid enough that she took the risk to send Olivia. Why would Becca have sent her unless the danger to Becca was so great that she was willing to risk the deal getting blown?

As she approached the stores, her neck hairs crawled, registering movement in her peripheral vision. She thought, *Oh my God, they're out there. I don't even know who they are or what they look like. But I can feel it. I can't go home! They'll know where I live.* She could imagine vague figures grabbing her and her mom someday as payback. No, she couldn't go home yet.

The shops became a possible refuge. And with two other customers on her heels, she ducked into a new espresso place, melding with the knots of customers jostling their way to the counter, blocking the sight of anyone loitering outside, and hopefully ditching whoever was following her. Olivia pretended to contemplate oddly named sizes and types of coffee, as if to order something in particular, and searched the walls for a pay phone. The sign to the restrooms caught her attention, so she elbowed her way to the hallway. Nothing. She could hide in the bathroom, and maybe it would all blow over. But the police were waiting for her, and she had to risk it.

She took deep breaths and stepped out of the store and changed course toward the local precinct. She cut through an alley and descended a slight hill where the side street was deserted. All she had to do was get around a corner, past one more cross street, and she'd be in the safety of the police station. She fingered Becca's gift, tucked in her pocket.

When she rounded the corner, a hulky figure shadowed behind a hoodie sprang toward her. She turned to run in the opposite direction, back to the shops, but another gigantic figure occupied the sidewalk. She darted into the street. He lunged, grabbed her shoulders, and she felt a hand clamped over her mouth. Before she knew it, she had been stuffed into a van followed by the guy in the hoodie. She scrambled to the other end of the bench seat, wrenched the door's handle. It was locked.

"Going someplace, bitch?" The guy shoved a gun in her face.

As if searching down her throat for her voice, Olivia came up empty and just stared at him.

The gigantic guy jumped in the front passenger's seat and the driver gunned the engine.

"What the fuck? That bitch, Becca, think we such dumb shits not to know who you are? Well, we goin' someplace and you gonna take us. Got us a little negotiatin' to do."

Olivia whimpered, "I … I … I was just going home."

"Bullshit! You tell us where it's goin' down." Gun Guy, next to her, circled the nose of the weapon around her face.

The old quarry factory was not a location she visited often—in fact, just about never. One of those relics that adults remembered nostalgically, dense brush now surrounded the abandoned grounds, any grooming having long ago vanished.

The van stopped, motor still running, the smell of exhaust coursing through the interior. Passenger Seat Dude jumped out, the driver remaining behind the wheel. Air as cold as her terror hit her when the door slid open. Arms grabbed her with her backpack, hauled her out, and dumped her on her feet. Gun Guy followed, barrel still focused on her face.

Before her, ice and weeds cracked the asphalt that had once been filled with the cars of factory workers. The derelict building's limestone walls were a sad advertisement for the product in back. Squares of rotting plywood covered windows long ago violated by rocks. She could see where someone had pushed a board back to gain access.

"Okay, where we meetin'?" Gun Guy asked.

"Dumpster" was all that came out of Olivia's mouth.

Something bit through the fabric of her jacket and notched her flesh. "You give any clue we're not together in this, and you're just one more bit a work I have to do. Got it?" Passenger Seat Dude said.

Gun Guy jammed the barrel into her hip, and they goose-stepped toward the factory. From the corner of her eyes, on either side of her boots, she saw a pair of large basketball shoes in colors that Forester High School deemed as gang related. A burning substance trickled down her leg. And they continued to march. Olivia stopped, bile filling her mouth. Her escorts kicked her forward, while vomit dribbled down her chin and onto her jacket. Moving in concert, they rounded the corner of the gutted, weather-stained building.

Before them, the dumpster huddled against a cyclone fence, closing off the quarry's gaping mouth, from which many of Forester's buildings had emerged.

They approached their destination, and Olivia's brain went blank. She was a pair of legs, a pain in her side, stinging in her back, and arms constrained at the elbows; she was a vomit-spattered jacket wrapping a pink striped sweater; she was a pair of jeans stained with urine on the inner legs, steaming in the cold.

Up close, the padlocked dumpster's dark blue, enameled surface was pockmarked with rust, supporting a decomposing mattress. Olivia would have collapsed onto the soggy surface had that been a choice.

The trio stopped. The old factory was deserted. They waited. She kept her gaze on her old Moon Boots. If someone later asked her how long they milled around, she would have said hours, all day. The panic began to settle, and she could glimpse over the top of it, finding the ability to think a bit. Olivia tried to sneak a glimpse of her companions. Hands in gloves gave no additional clues to their owners. No female voices. She took a gamble and raised her gaze.

"Keep your head down, bitch." Sparks flew across her vision as a hard object connected with the back of her head.

More time passed. The chill made her want to jog to keep warm. Not an option. Maybe someone would send out a search party when she didn't come home. But how would they know where?

Gravel crunch from the back of the factory meant the supplier had arrived. She stumbled as she was shoved forward.

"Yo, zup?" Passenger Seat Dude on her right began.

"Whoa. Who the fuck are you?" The dealer's hand dove in his pocket. Olivia knew he was expecting Becca.

"She got detention," Olivia stammered, "and sent me instead."

"Detention? You fuckin' with me?" The dealer nodded at her companions.

"No, bro, Becca sent me special, and my bitch brought it." The gun rammed into her side for emphasis.

The knife blade receded, so she could pull off her backpack. She yanked the zipper. It refused to budge. Cold as she was, sweat trickled down her back, more urine down her legs, and dry heaves pushed their way up her throat. The dealer's gun waggled under her nose while she tugged on the jammed zipper.

"Please, just wait a second," she begged. "I know it'll work. I promise." She yanked again, sobs breaking the surface like a swimmer too long under water. "Just give me a second." Olivia pulled off her gloves.

"You fuckin' with me!" The dealer now moved his gun in an arc as his other gang members materialized. Three of them in a line behind the dealer, jackets concealing hands and firearms as destructive as Gun Guy's. Passenger Seat Dude grabbed the bag, used the knife he'd had in her back to slice the canvas. Books, spiral notebooks, and papers spewed onto the ground. Along with the pencil case.

The dealer snatched the case, weighed it in his hand, and then opened it. Hidden by the hood of a Bulls jacket, he swiveled his head, his attention divided between the gun on the trio and fanning the money.

"Good doing business with you." He tossed over a backpack, an exact match to Becca's. Passenger Seat Guy grabbed it before Olivia could take possession.

"Yeah. See ya 'round." Her companions twisted her like some kind of military move marching back to the van the way they came, the ripped backpack abandoned on the tarmac. In that moment, Olivia got a glimpse of their faces. Her diaphragm compressed, forcing a small, strangled "ha" at the memory of her granny. She was about three, and she was angry about something. Granny had said, "You look like that and your face might freeze." Granny was right, at least for these two.

"Shut the fuck up!" Again sparks crossed her vision, and she slumped, feeling the lug on the toes of her boots as they dragged her.

As they squared the corner to the front parking lot, the spray of gravel and multiple cars greeted them. Lights trilled across the tops of patrol cars, and steel gun barrels reflected the dull day, while from a distance, sirens screamed, more police on the way. She must have hit the tarmac sometime during the next minutes, resulting in stitches on her chin. Then handcuffs chilled her wrists. Her neck hurt as a hand pushed her head down and into the squad car.

How she got to the police station, Olivia hadn't a clue. All she could recall was crying into her shoulder and worrying about getting pee all over the back. Gordon said later that it would be mild compared to the other stuff that was no doubt on the seat.

At the station, a woman police officer took over and led her to a room, where her clothes were exchanged for a jumpsuit and shower clogs.

"Girl, you've got yourself into some deep shit. You know you were being followed?" The woman, slim and older, had an attitude Olivia envied. "Well, you were. Those are bad ass dudes." The officer jerked her head. "Good thing we kept surveillance on you. We hadn't, we'd a been visiting you in the ER. If you were lucky. Your mom'll be in soon, and your dad is on his way."

Olivia waited, the LCD clock blinked and flicked hypnotically, each passing minute a reminder of where she should be and what would probably be going on. The biggest worry would have been homework and what to do on the weekend. How ordinary and comforting. If only.

CHAPTER 43
GNARLY

Patricia knew immediately why they were there, her shoulders quaking at the reality of it. He'd finally gotten caught. Under the porch light, four police officers huddled together, a lumpy mass on the threshold.

"Is Ray Wrenowski home?" the beefiest one asked.

"He doesn't live here anymore. He moved out about a month ago. What can I do for you, officers?" Patricia crossed her arms over her chest, not sure whether the shivering was the cold evening or her terror at whether she would be found out too.

"We have a warrant to search the house." They shouldered their way into the foyer.

"By all means. But you won't find any of his stuff here. He's taken it with him. We live separately now."

While two of the police departed for Ray's apartment, the other two began their search with less gusto than upon arriving, methodically emptying drawers, cupboards and closets. Their repeated inspection of the same contents indicated they were disappointed to find nothing. She figured they would leave as soon as the house was in satisfactory chaos. At least Brian was at chess club and wouldn't have to witness this.

In the meantime, she was pretty much limited to following them from room to room and watching them lay waste. She wondered if inane chatter could get them to leave sooner. She remembered being told she had the ability to sustain a monologue indefinitely on only the most mundane of topics. At the time the remark felt like an insult, but in this context it seemed like a noble skill.

Hoping she could drive them out with hospitality, she brought them a slice of homemade apple pie, which they declined although the rail thin officer hesitated. One headed toward the living room, and the other clutched the handrail to ease down the steep steps to the basement. Undecided whom to follow, Patricia mentally tossed a coin and landed on the lower level, continuing her monologue as if there had been no interruption.

At one point, the officer stopped, a garden boot in his hand, while the other felt the interior for anything suspicious. He frowned as he pulled out the square cannister Patricia had placed there. "Mrs. Wrenowski," he said, "I don't want any coffee or pie or cookies or dinner. Ma'am, I really need to concentrate. I'll call you if I want anything."

Dejectedly, she climbed the stairs to survey her office, now converted to a landslide of client files, the officer in the process of hoisting her computer.

"We'll need to take this as evidence," he said.

"Those are my client files. There's personal information in there," she said. "It has nothing to do with Ray."

"Then you shouldn't mind. We'll give it back to you when we're done."

The thought that she needed to play more of the innocent wife prompted her to ask, "Is there anything I can do to help you find what you're looking for? After all this is a pretty big house, but as I said Ray took everything with him." He grunted, and she took that as a no.

She had time to reflect as each room's contents were trashed, reminding her how glad she was that she'd exorcised those incriminating pictures and the camera. The police had nothing to link to her. She could be the wronged wife with a clear conscience.

The other thing she had time to contemplate was Brian and what to do next. The minute the police walked out the door, she'd be on the phone to her best friend, Tootie, in New Mexico.

The officers then departed, vocally dissatisfied with their apparent failure to find anything incriminating. All was quiet in the house.

Not twenty minutes later, she heard Brian cross the foyer to the kitchen.

"Mom, what happened?" He waded toward the fridge, whose contents were unloaded onto the tile floor, the granite countertops now camouflaged by pots, pans, cutlery, and dishes.

"Something bad. I don't know. It's your dad." She grabbed some dishtowels to sop up the broken eggs, a gelatinous goo that would be difficult to remove from the grouting.

"Dad?" He turned toward her, a mound of lettuce, carrots, and bean sprouts at his feet, and then his head swiveled around the room's contents. "You made this mess, didn't you? I thought you'd stopped drinking!"

"I did. I did stop drinking. Brian, just help me clean this up, and then we can talk about what happened."

"Clean it up yourself." Brian made his way back to the foyer and bounded up the stairs.

A few moments later her son's angst-soaked voice called down. "Mom! Why's my room trashed? I told you to stay outta here." She could hear him now at the head of the stairs. His footsteps made a dull thud on the carpet and grew louder as he made his way toward the kitchen. "Mom, what the hell is this?"

Patricia's head felt as scrambled as the house, and she realized she had no plan that wasn't grotesque for how to tell her son. "Brian, what have I told you about swearing in this house? I want you to pack a few things. We're on a flight that leaves Midway at midnight. We're going to stay with Tootie for a few days."

"Tootie? We're going to stay with Tootie? But we can't. I can't. I've got papers and tests."

"Sweetie, I'll call the school. I know they'll understand when I explain the situation."

"What situation?"

"And besides, spring break is next week. You'll be able to make up the exams."

"I don't want to make up the exams, and Tootie is an airhead."

"Don't talk about your godmother like that!" *Good*, she thought, *something to distract him until I can figure out what to do*.

"I'll try to explain as soon as we're on our way. Go pack your things. I'll finish cleaning up the kitchen. The rest I can deal with later." Patricia bent to load the perishables back into the fridge, ignoring Brian. She could feel him in the doorway, watching her and then backing away.

She was just placing the plates in the cupboard when the phone rang, sending the stack she was holding crashing to the floor. Ray, no doubt. What does the innocent, wronged wife do? After the sixth ring and just before the answering machine kicked on, she lifted the receiver, the trashed house reminding her how he'd trashed their lives.

"Patricia, I need your help."

She was silent, his wheedling voice grating her nerves. Then she took a long breath and said, "My goodness, Ray, what's wrong?"

"You know what's wrong. They were at the house too, they said."

She regarded the shattered plates and wondered if someone would be listening in. "Who are you talking about, honey? Are you all right?"

"I'm at the police station. You need to find a lawyer. You have a lot of contacts, so I'm going to need a good one. A really good one."

"Well, Ray," she said, her voice dropping an octave. "I'm sure they have a phone book you can use. You understand that my first priority is Brian. I'll get back to you in a couple of days." And before hanging up, she added, "Everything's going to work out."

+++

Traffic inched forward, and Patricia massaged her neck, one hand clenching the steering wheel. Brian sat next to her, and in the lights, she marveled at her son, how he had grown. Again. His shoulders had broadened, his face beginning to elongate. His profile in the headlights made her long to hug him, to become a human shield from what was about to happen, when the news hit the press about his dad's twisted behavior.

Thank God, he took after her family. When he looked in the mirror, the last thing she wanted him to see was any resemblance of his father.

The line of cars moved forward as the bottleneck freed. This was the moment to tell him, while they were both in the car and traffic was moving fast enough that he couldn't bolt, which was what she feared most. She regarded his wonderful profile, such deep sadness surfacing. After this moment, everything would change for Brian. Patricia could feel that moment in her hand. She was tempted to wait before telling him, to clasp that moment a while longer.

"Brian, I'm not the bad guy. In fact, I'm the good guy, and I hope you'll see that. I'm getting you out of here."

His contour widened as he glanced over. In the streetlights, she couldn't see his expression. Traffic thinned and picked up more speed. Patricia would be at the terminal parking lot in a few minutes. She couldn't delay any longer. "Your dad's been arrested."

"Arrested? He's too wimpy to be arrested. Must be someone else."

"I'm afraid not. He called just before we left. He's at the police station." She could hear him inhaling, preparing to speak. "Sweetie, let me finish. This is hard enough without you interrupting. You know the rapist that's been around Forester? Well …."

"Yeah, I know. I kinda thought."

"Thought what? Don't tell me you knew?"

"Yeah, I guess. I found this box of pictures in the basement. Pretty gnarly."

Too late, Patricia slammed the brakes to avoid hitting the car in front of them. She felt the whiplash from behind and heard the horrible sound of metal connecting. Instinctively, she thrust her right arm across Brian's chest to protect him from careening forward, only to feel the whole of his weight against her elbow as her arm shattered.

CHAPTER 44
THE MILKY WAY

The moment the eighteen-wheeler crushed their car would never be insignificant. Moments she thought were insignificant at the time were—in the end—very significant. Driving to the airport, where she thought about the timing of telling Brian about his father. And if she'd delayed a bit longer, as she'd been tempted to, maybe Brian's last words wouldn't have been "Pretty gnarly." Or there wouldn't have been last words. He'd still be alive.

Her arm stretched across him would've been what he felt last. Now pinned and bolted and still going through physical therapy, it was evidence that it had always been about Brian and protecting him. So she was okay with those days when it throbbed with deep pain.

Selling the business had been a bitch. Moving to Santa Fe had been a bitch and starting over was a bitch. Patricia's language startled her, but she had to admit it was the only way to describe it. Her contacts in Forester said the new owner had opened a real estate office at the other end of town. Lane Realty melted into oblivion.

Patricia figured she had invented herself before, why not now in Santa Fe? Answering an ad for an assistant in an art gallery, she discovered the job involved the same skills as selling houses. Selling was selling after all, and she was good at it. After two years, she fleshed out a business plan to marry the two: real estate and art. Her market was the wealthy, enchanted by Santa Fe and wanting someone to set up a retreat for them.

She went back to being Patty Lane. She adopted the Spanish Mexican dress, and she grew out her carrot hair, letting it turn gray. Tootie said Patty reminded her of Georgia O'Keefe, so she submerged herself into her new identity, just as she submerged herself into everything else.

In the evenings, the stars captivated her. Whole bands swathed the sky, and Patty could imagine Brian sliding along the Milky Way, like he had scooted down the slide into her arms as a little boy. Except now her arms fell to her sides. Empty.

CHAPTER 45
A SLICE OF PIE

By summer, two legal teams existed preparing two cases. One case was against U Do It Corporation and Mr. Charles Hunter for racial discrimination and harassment toward Clerise Harper. The other was against U Do It Corporation and Mr. Charles Hunter for harassment and age discrimination against Gordon Carlson. A team formed in Petey's ancient office, the participants anything but ancient. Women and men in custom-made suits arrived with legal assistants to take notes. At times, Gordon and Clerise sat in other grand offices in maroon leather chairs at inlaid wood conference tables, while lunch arrived and then was discreetly taken away. Despite Petey's dated and angled appearance, these hotshots attended his moves and insights like first-year law students.

In the fraud case, Clerise and Gordon became key witnesses. U Do It attorneys and accountants deposed them for hours. Clerise's role was pivotal: she was suing for racial discrimination. U Do It was countersuing for stealing company property. Taut cords appeared in her neck, accompanied by headaches and blue-black circles around her eyes. One night she broke down, sobbing, and Michael began to cry as his mother rocked and hugged her knees.

"I can't do this," Clerise wailed. Gordon gathered them on the couch in their rented apartment, an arm around each, handing out tissues and grateful for the wet patches on his flannel shirt.

He was thankful every day for his foresight to keep the house insurance his top priority. Sometimes he had wondered if he had been too cautious, wasting money over something he suspected would never happen. But, thank God.

+++

As he heard the first utterance on the phone, a sick feeling crept into his stomach. That familiar voice. Would it haunt him forever?

"Gordon, it's your old friend Charlie Hunter."

"This is unexpected. How did you find me?" Gordon motioned to Clerise and mouthed, "Charlie."

"Oh, I managed. But hey, I wanted to let you know I heard about your house. I am so sorry. House you grew up in and all."

"Charlie, I don't think it's wise for you to be calling me. Your lawyer should talk to my lawyer."

"My lawyer should talk to your lawyer about my concern over your wellbeing and sympathy about the loss of your house? Sounds a little strange to me."

"Charlie, I'm going to say goodbye before this goes any further."

"Okay, I can respect that. I can see how you would be more loyal to some legal suit than to our friendship. I just wanted to have a chance to apologize, that's all."

"I appreciate that, Charlie, but it's not a good idea. Maybe when this is all over." And Gordon hung up the phone.

Something didn't sit right about the conversation. Clerise agreed. Hunter was not the kind of person to do something out of regard for someone else. He always had an angle, so they were not surprised the next day to arrive back at the apartment and find a message on the answering machine.

"Gordon, we got disconnected before I could give you my phone number. I'd hate for us to lose touch. And maybe one of these days, we can grab a cup of coffee. Or tea. Of course, my man, I wouldn't forget you like tea. Remember our bet and you won? Give me a call. I am sorry about your house, and you know, Bud, I'm sorry about a lot of things. My number's in the book."

Gordon admitted he was curious. He and Clerise made a bet. Clerise said Charlie would be more interested in Gordon's discrimination suit, while Gordon said it would be Clerise's. "After all, you be black woman, Clerise. Yes suh!"

"And you are old and ancient and over forty," she mimed leaning on a cane.

+++

As Gordon entered the family restaurant, he noticed a woman sitting directly behind his former boss. Charlie folded the menu. "I hear they have good pie here," was his first comment.

"One of my favorite restaurants. As I said on the phone, I'm not so sure this was a good idea." Gordon slid into the facing seat.

"Hey, I buy you a cup of tea and a slice of pie. What's the harm in that? I'm trying to make amends here, Gordon. What are you hungry for?"

"Gooseberry, but let's have separate checks. That way …"

"Whatever you say, Gordon. I just want to make it right. I don't blame you. Corporate never said who, but I figured it had to be you. And Clerise, of course. I admit forcing you out the door like that was pretty rash. If I had it to do over again, I wouldn't have done that. I would've realized I could trust you." He nodded to the waitress as she placed the pie before him.

"Trust me?" To Gordon, the conversation wasn't tracking. What did this have to do with age and race discrimination?

"You can't have much in the way of savings or pension from all those years at that salary. Times must be tough right now. And Clerise, single mom with a young son. Frankly, being African American, she's going to be wasted. All that talent. As I said, I would've done things differently."

"I understand you wish you hadn't done what you did, but where are you going with this?"

"I'm saying I was stupid. You guys were on to me. That's all. Anyway, I'd like to make it up to you. And to Clerise too."

"Make it up to us? Charlie, I don't think that's possible."

"Sure it is. We can all make this go away. I can pull some strings and get Clerise plugged in where she won't be typing her buns off for the rest of her life. Or I can set up a college fund for Michael. Anyway, run it by her and let me know. We're taking a big risk meeting like this today, but I bet you agree we can all come out of this okay."

"Charlie, why would I want to get involved?"

"Oh, I get it, Carlson. What's in it for you? Besides that 30% lifetime discount you tricked me into." He winked. "You didn't think I wasn't aware of what you were doing, did you? You're a smart man, Carlson. You know a good deal when you see one. I should've figured that out. Instead, I was too busy arranging things with the vendors. That Winter Wonderland debacle was pretty funny."

"Well, I'm not laughing, Hunter. I busted my ass and then you fired me."

"Didn't fire you, you retired. But you're sharp, man. You might like folks to think you're old and senile. You're about as senile as me. Someday, Bud, we'll look back and have a great laugh. In the meantime, I want to get you set up. I've got a business idea I bet you won't be able to resist."

Gordon placed his fork on his plate, the pie nothing but a few crumbs. He signaled the waitress. "Could we have our checks? We're done here."

+++

"Well, who won the bet?" Clerise emerged from her bedroom as Gordon closed the apartment door.

"Neither. We were both wrong."

"Both wrong?"

"He was trying to bribe us about the embezzlement and fraud. The plant Petey arranged was a woman, and after Charlie left, I caught up with her in the parking lot. I think Petey will find what she heard useful."

CHAPTER 46
FAMILY

Gordon folded the *Chicago Tribune* and smoothed it, his thumb running along the crease. The day lay before him, and Clerise, hunched over a cup of tea and the local newspaper, smiled, "So? Did they get Hunter?"

"Yep." He patted the paper as if it were a boy who had done a particularly good job. "We're mentioned in the article as having uncovered the operation."

"Makes us sound like sleuths," she said.

"Well, we were in a way, detecting something wrong with those reports."

"I wish we'd done better with our suits, but at least we got something, and I didn't lose the countersuit. I don't know what we would've done if they'd won. I'm just glad it's over. What's on your list for today, Mr. Carlson?" Clerise rose.

"Well, I've got to see a couple of customers and to check on some orders at the store." Gordon glanced out the kitchen window at the lake, mounded with last night's snow. "Gotta clear off the ice for Michael. Isaac's coming home with him after school, and they're going to practice. Sky's clear. I think I'll do that before I head out this morning."

"By the way, the frame store called and Michael's picture from science camp is ready. I'll get it on the way home from work. I've been meaning to ask: How is Olivia these days? You haven't mentioned her in a while."

"She's fine, likes being a senior, says her new home is very modern. She got accepted into some prestigious summer computer program and wants to design a computerized catalog of the memorabilia at the Forester museum."

"That's fantastic! We should have her out here sometime. Anyway, I'm going to take a shower and then go into the office. Bring home your receipts, and I'll do the books tonight." She leaned over and kissed him, then padded down the hall.

Later that morning, Gordon hefted a shovel filled with snow, clumps flying onto a growing mound. From the middle of the lake, he could stand in front of the cabin. While completing the additions, Clerise had often said they must preserve its heart. From his spot on the lake, he could see they had.

Bubba asked him once if he liked his new life better. He had answered that it wasn't about one or the other. It was about the whole. And the ability to see it that way.

Having lived in the real thing, all these faux Victorian houses springing up around Freelak made him smile. But he didn't smile too broadly. They were the core of his business as well as Clerise's job at a new law firm in town, while she pursued a law degree.

Gordon swelled with pride at her accomplishment. And she was swelling too. If the baby was a girl, she would be Charlotte Maude. As far as male names, in the running was her father's name, Arthur. Gordon liked the sound of Art Harper-Carlson.

He lifted a broom, still new and shellacked, to sweep the ice of remaining snow. The boys would have a great surface for hockey.

CHAPTER 47
HIDDEN PICTURES

Olivia parked the car on a glaring sun-bleached street at the outskirts of the Forester Days parade. The knowledge that the museum was in the cooler shadows made hurrying all the more desirable.

She stood in the foyer of the mansion, eyes raised to the chandelier, hoping for the wispy form she'd seen that night. "Hey, Grand Lotty," she whispered.

A woman appeared, a docent dressed as Harriet. "Can I help you? I'd be delighted to show you Jean Luis Forestier's home."

Olivia scanned the staircase and shook her head. "Thanks anyway."

"Are you lost?" the woman asked. Her face fell in disappointment.

Olivia paused, smiled, and said, "Nope. I'm meeting Gordon Carlson. I'll be back in a while."

She turned and charged into the humid June morning. There was just enough time to go to her old block and be back.

On the front lawn of her former home was a small bike parked next to a wading pool. From the color, she guessed it belonged to a little boy. No doubt the lavender walls in her bedroom had had a makeover.

The Wrenowski house had transformed from barn red to discreet sage, taupe, and forest green. How ghostlike the front yard had become. If Patricia had been around, right now she would have been directing Ray and Brian in setting up the barbeque. But no one was home. When she looked at the yard, she saw the snakes of crushed Christmas lights and the plastic Joseph, face smashed in.

Thinking about Brian, she wasn't sure how she felt. Her memories of him floated past in random order. Walking away from him, choosing not to beat him up, was the last time she saw him. She couldn't quite grasp that he was dead. Seeing Ray's face plastered behind the TV news anchor during the trial had been surreal.

The distant sound of a band made her wonder whether Ashley was riding in the parade as a queen or princess. Drums and horns filtered through the trees and around houses, reaching her as if the band's music were coming from beneath a giant pillow.

She followed the sidewalk to the far end of the street so she could perhaps gain some new perspective. But all she saw was just a long row of upscale houses, deserted right now while their occupants attended the parade.

Her final destination was the weed patch marking Gordon's former residence. Moving in the clingy air, she felt looser, thanks to being on the track team at school. She'd never be a star athlete, but it helped with the anxiety.

Every once in a while, she felt creeped out. Concentrating was impossible, leaving her immobile. She was not stupid enough to refuse the medications to help her get through this. Thank God for drugs. And then a giggle bubbled on her lips. Things were getting better.

Bubba appeared on his front lawn where a battered wooden table sat at a haphazard angle.

"Need some help?" Olivia crossed toward him.

"So how's life, Olivia? Gotcher future figured out yet?" Bubba stood at the other end of a vinyl tablecloth, the two easing it onto the table's surface.

"Not quite, Bubba, but I'm going into computer programming at college in the fall. Remember that project Gordon worked on at the museum?"

Bubba paused, holding a fist full of plastic cutlery, and wrinkled his brow. "Oh, yeah, he was putting stuff in the museum on the computer."

"I helped him for a while, and now I'm going to develop a computer system."

Bubba nodded, and Olivia could tell he was thinking about something else. "Wonder if he's going to bring dandelion wine this year."

"You never know." Olivia opened the last of the folding chairs. "I'm gonna go by where Gordon's house used to be. Haven't been since Mom and I moved."

"Yer welcome to come to the barbeque. Yer mom and dad should come too."

"Thanks anyway, Bubba, but I've got a graduation party with my class at Our Lady of Redemption High School."

She crossed Gordon's driveway and paced the perimeter that had once been Gordon's home. Filled with topsoil, it resembled a raised bed, borders defined by the limestone foundation. Weeds competed for space, having had the run of the yard.

In the back, a few charred bricks were all that indicated the immolation. She'd wondered how the memories—like Brian stalking her— would feel, and she was glad for the sense of peace. Toward the far corner, where a couple of rose bushes struggled, Olivia spotted tomato plants, kind of leggy, but nevertheless on the way to bearing fruit. A quick trip next door and she returned with some napkins, paper cups, and cutlery to extract the tender plants.

The bugles and drum syncopation sounded closer, and Olivia knew the parade must be winding down. Now she would have to hurry to meet Gordon, so she scurried along the side streets.

Thank God no one at Our Lady of Redemption knew anyone from Forester. What could she say? Spider and Dank testified at the drug trial and were shuttled away to some juvenile detention facility. She was saddest for them, for the decency they handed her if only to let her bum a cig or pass her a joint.

Lauren was the real conundrum. Even before the story broke in the news, a *For Sale* sign sprouted in front of her house and she disappeared. Maybe her parents bribed her way out.

To be able to think about Becca and not dive into a major depression had been an ongoing struggle. Over and over again, her parents, Gordon, and her psychologist had told her she had had one choice, to cooperate with the police.

At times, she was furious at Becca pretending to like her, manipulating her just like she did everyone else. Her shrink said to keep the issues separate. One was the drug dealing, which Becca would have done anyway. The other was the rape, and no one deserved for that to happen. Olivia's truth was they were intertwined; otherwise, Becca would never have befriended her. Becca was a survivor, so she'd vanished. Did she even have a chance at anything better? At least, she hoped Becca didn't get taken from her aunt.

For the most part, Olivia had moved on. Still, once in a while ….

+++

Gordon rarely came to Forester anymore, just for the annual block party and to tell the story of Maude. The real story.

He contemplated his upcoming meeting with Olivia. He thought about the young people in her life. Kids like that girl, Becca, or Dank or Spider. They were like those pictures in that children's magazine, *Highlights*, where a drawing of a car or key was hidden in the picture challenging the reader to find it. Like the drawings in the picture, those kids disappeared into the walls of the school and didn't exist as far as most people were concerned. After he lost the store, he had become hidden too. Then Olivia knocked on his door.

By the time he pulled into the museum's parking lot, the Forester Days parade was almost over. He hoped he hadn't missed her. He climbed the museum steps and from habit jingled his key chain, his fingers landing upon the brass key. The door was still unlocked, so the docent must still be in the building. He entered the foyer and as he always did, marveled at its grandeur.

A woman came out of the morning room, startled at seeing him, and said, "I'm afraid we're closing."

"Yes, I know," said Gordon, and when she took a quick inhale, he added, "You must be new. I'm Gordon Carlson."

She brightened. "Oh, Mr. Carlson, I've heard so much about your great work for this museum. And to think you are the Forestiers' great grandson!"

"Well, I'm here to give my key to a friend of mine, Olivia Dimato, who will be developing the computer system for the museum this summer and finishing the project I started. I expect there wasn't much traffic today. Usually isn't."

"No, just that young woman. She came into the foyer, stood for a couple of moments, and mentioned she'd be back in a while. Otherwise, rather dull, actually."

"In that case, I won't keep you from your family festivities."

He stood under the chandelier, and Harriet crossed his mind, then Grand Lotty, Maude, and finally, Lara. Tucked under a wall sconce was a tendril, as ephemeral as a memory, and as it faded Gordon smiled. He didn't know when he'd be back again. That was it. Out the door to see Olivia moving through the trees and carrying tomato plants, her bright face dappled by the shade.

READERS' GUIDE

1. One of the themes of this novel is bullying. Do you think our attitude has changed since this novel took place in the late 1990s? If so, how? Were you ever bullied as a kid or as an adult? What about those who bully? Or is the parent of a bully?

2. In Chapter 7, At the Museum, Gordon muses about the role of nurturing in his life and in the community. How is nurturing portrayed? Why do people or a community nurture the past? How is nurturing portrayed in your life?

3. The difference between truth and lies is a thread throughout the novel. Are there instances that justify lies? What purpose do myths like George Washington and the cherry tree serve? In this story, how is the truth like hidden pictures? Gordon muses: "Wasn't history lining up facts to get at the truth? But if you don't have all the facts, how do you have the truth?" What are your thoughts about facts and history?

4. In Chapter 9, Lost Dog, Becca compares her life and future as a foster kid with Olivia's. Discuss. Do you think Becca got the same treatment as others? What does that mean with respect to the rape? What is the attitude toward foster kids in your community?

5. Guilt is a major theme in this story. Why does Gordon feel guilty? How does Maude's guilt affect Gordon? Would Gordon have been able to act if he had not found and read Maude's diary?

6. Invisibility is a theme in Hidden Pictures. How is this handled? Who is invisible in your community?

7. Patricia and Becca are complicated characters. Do you think they are antagonists? Does your opinion of them change as the story progresses?

8. Hidden Pictures asks the question: What does it take to create change in a community? What do you think it takes to create change in a community such as Forester? What do you think it takes to create change in your community? In Chapter 12, Between the Lines, Hunter says, "Be uncomfortable. That's where change happens." Where do you think change happens?

9. Olivia is awakening to her sexual orientation as a lesbian. Discuss how sexual orientation was regarded during the period of the story. Do these issues resonate with the gender identification and sexual orientation issues kids face today? Are they handled in the same way? Differently?

10. Hunter's behavior toward women, older adults, minorities and people of color and people of different sexual orientations is outrageous. Clerise comments in Chapter 21, Thanks, that "it's still there, just gone underground." Compare the period of this story to now.

11. This novel has elements of magical realism. What purpose do you think it serves in the story? Besides ghosts in the museum, what other incidents are haunting the characters? Is there an incident in your life that haunts you or haunted you? How did you handle it?

12. In Chapter 32, Lara, Gordon is told, "…we take a risk everyday just by getting out of bed." How does this relate to Gordon's response to the tragedies in his life?

13. Fat shaming of Olivia courses throughout this novel. Why do you think fat shaming is so ignored in our society?

14. The cycle of violence in relationships is a thread in Hidden Pictures. How does this compare to the community in which you live today?

ACKNOWLEDGMENTS

Hidden Pictures is about a village just outside Chicago. It took a village to bring this story to you, the reader. Foremost I want to thank Jim, my faithful reader, cheerleader, and guide, especially for providing input on employer issues. Seamus and Connor gave critical insight into adolescent psychology and navigating the turbulent waters of those teenage years.

Susan Taylor and Kathy Williams had patience to wade through very early beta reading. Lindsay Pierce and Mimi Nickerson were critical later readers, whose encouragement and suggestions helped shape the final product.

The novel would have imploded like an overbaked souffle if Irene Luvaul, hadn't provided that critical editor's eye. Thank you! Thank you! Connie Jasperson supplied support and input that significantly improved the novel.

To the Olympia Writers' Group—Alan Shue, Kiki Powers, Vanessa Torres Palensky, Tiffany Grassman, Chris Murray, Sid Doyle, Donnie Whetstone, Peter Dodds, and Marlee LaMontagne Riggin—I owe such a debt of gratitude for your encouragement, critique, and patience through the first draft.

Thank you, Teri Thunberg, Diane Bingaman and Kate Dixon for your friendship and good humor. We need to pop a cork on this one.

A novel like this is particularly susceptible to procedural and knowledge errors. Darlene Raffelson in Tumwater's Fire Department enlightened me on fire inspection protocols and procedures. Lara

Flynn was instrumental in my understanding of home insurance policies. I want to thank the staff at the Olympia police department for insights on gang behavior with apologies for taking many literary liberties for this period in time. Keith Schuster gave me a primer on fraud detection. Linda Barnhart provided review and advice about asthma, especially the historic perspective about the condition.

The Tuesday Morning Panera Writers' Group—Connie Jasperson, Lee French, Jane Martin, Melissa Carpenter, Heather Kitzman and Ellen King Rice—held my hand sharing valuable advice and resources on publishing. Additional publishing mentoring came from Liz Osborne, Diana Vincent, and Paul Sating.

Amy St. Onge's beautiful cover design wraps this up as a gift to my readers.

And finally, thanks go to Frank Brink, my dad, who regaled the family with the stories he always planned to write.

www.ingramcontent.com/pod-product-compliance
Lightning Source LLC
Chambersburg PA
CBHW030711190726
48286CB00001B/280